GW00493882

Leaning on the Wind

LEANING ON

THE WIND

A novel

Beverly Mills Publishing Co.
Auckland

Published by Beverly Mills Publishing
1996

Copyright © Bevan Haysom 1996

Beverly Mills Publishing Co.,
Box 310, Mairangi Bay
Shore City, Auckland, NZ
Fax 09 444 2571.

Graphics and Cover by K J Graphics
Box 56-381 Dominion Road
Auckland, New Zealand.

Pre-press Photolithography by
Prism Reproductions Ltd
29 Enfield Street, Mt Eden, Auckland, NZ.

Literary advisor and editor Jeanette Cook.

Legal Deposit at National Library of New Zealand
70 Molesworth Street, Wellington 1.

ISBN 0-473-03959-1

Printed and bound in Australia
by Griffin Paperbacks, Adelaide

ACKNOWLEDGEMENTS

To Bev for her forbearance and support, to my children David and Sally and to Lisa and Wendy for their willingness and enthusiasm on computer and printer.

Also to Jeanette Cook, literary adviser and editor who helped me so diligently with this, my first novel.

My thanks to the staff of the following museums and libraries:

The Public Record Office, Kew, London
National Army Museum, London
Greenwich Museum
National Archives, Wellington
General Assembly Library
Alexander Turnbull Library, Wellington
Auckland Public Library
Philson Library
Auckland War Memorial Museum Library

This is a story
of love and hate,
of war and peace.

It is a story of two races striving
to find a common heritage and
of the indomitable courage of
both in their struggle.

Only the words and actions of the main characters
are ficticious, the remainder being a true
account of the times.

INTRODUCTION

This is the story of a nation where a new method of colonisation was tried by the British, who in their treaty with the inhabitants acknowledged the right of the indigenous people to the ownership of the land. It is an account of the hopes and aspirations of the Maori and their struggle for survival and also of the aspirations of the new immigrants, with the same hopes, the same sense of adventure, the same doubts and a love of their new home that all New Zealanders, whatever their origin, have today.

Great Britain was in the middle of the Industrial Revolution that necessitated a change of direction. Men, women and children were crammed into the towns. John Kenneth Galbraith states, 'the Industrial Revolution was not a sudden, violent thing but it was the kind of revolution you could actually see. People everywhere were being drawn from the country villages to the towns and to jobs in the mills. In Scotland they were also being abruptly expelled from the countryside in consequence of the rising demand for the principal industrial material which was wool.

Between 1811 and 1820, by common estimate the landowners cleared 15,000 highlanders from their estates to make room for sheep. The operation assumed the definitive aspects of a final solution. In March the tenants had been given two months' notice to get out. But they were still around, for they had no place else to go. So the agents of the Laird moved in with fire and dogs. They were especially careful to burn the roof timber of the houses, for that meant, in this treeless land, that the houses could not be rebuilt, the people could not return. A few houses, it was later held, were burnt without taking the precaution of evacuating the more aged and enfeebled inhabitants.'

These then, were the people who were forced to the towns and with their sons and daughters looked for a new life in Canada, Australia and New Zealand.

J B Priestley tells us that...'In the later 1850's it was estimated 48,000 mixed British and Irish emigrated every year to Australia and New Zealand, most of them going to the goldfields of New South Wales. Some, such as the soldiers and sailors 'came one day for the day and never left, got off the bus and forgot to get on again'. Whatever the reason for arriving they found themselves in a land of open skies and clean fresh air where 'what a man could do was more important that who he was.'

On reaching New Zealand the immigrants cleared thousands of hectares of land, went to war, farmed, fished, prospected for gold, established courts and schools and above all sought a new way to live alongside the indigenous people, the Maori. They avoided the final solution of extermination that was attempted previously with the American Indians and acknowledged the Maori had, to quote the governor, Sir George Grey, 'in all respects, equal rights in their land possessions with those enjoyed by their European fellow subjects, the intention in this respect to show that the rights of peaceable citizens of whatever race, are carefully respected and to give the natives so valuable a stake in the country that they are not likely to hazard it lightly.'

Even Charles Dickens, who used the pseudonym of Boz in his contributions to the 'Morning Chronicle', at the end of 1846, after working on his story, 'The Battle of Life', which he completed in an hotel in Geneva, wrote, 'I see the good old 'Times' is again at issue with the inimitable B. Another touch of the blunt razor on B's nervous system...... dreamed of 'Timeses' all night. Disposed to go to New Zealand and start a Magazine'.

Today we have another revolution - the technological revolution that necessitates another change of direction. Computers, to a certain extent, are taking over the work of many people. Before, it was the industrial revolution which destroyed the old values and left many homeless and workless.

Compare these newspaper cuttings written one hundred and forty one years apart.

Pictorial Times London 1 July 1843:

Sgt Scotchmer of the G Division brought a little girl, named Mary Anne Swan before Mr Combe and made the following statement: 'About half past ten o'clock, Police Constable Conner 215G, being on duty on waste ground at the rear of Whartos Street, found the girl lying there.

The child burst into tears and said she had no money and could not get lodging anywhere. Connor took her to the workhouse. The officers of the workhouse refused to admit her, alleging that she had not slept in the parish on the previous night. On their way back to the station the girl said she was starving with hunger; the constable gave her his own supper and also threepence in order to provide a lodging for herself instead of being locked up in a cell.

She was fifteen years of age and utterly destitute. Mr Combe sent her to the Islington workhouse with a request that they would admit her into that establishment.

and

Auckland Star, N.Z. 23 February 1984

37 picked up in parks

Auckland police were today trying to find homes for 37 young people found living in city parks.

In the past 48 hours police youth aid officers picked up youngsters, aged 12 to 15, in the Auckland Domain and in a park near the Orakei Basin.

Senior Sergeant Des Hall, of the Auckland police, said the youngsters, both male and female, were found with a few possessions and little money, none of which appeared to have been stolen.

Mr Hall said officers regularly made such 'pick-ups' because 'everyone knows they are out there and someone has to do something about it.'

He said attempts are being made to find the youngsters' parents or to put them in Social Welfare care.

Lord Macaulay, born in 1800, who wrote 'The History of England' which was published in five volumes and who also contributed to the Edinburgh review, wrote, *'one day some traveller from New Zealand shall in the midst of a vast solitude, take his stand on a broken arch of London Bridge to sketch the ruins of St Pauls'*.

He said *'the true history of a country is to be found in its newspapers.'*

The main characters of this book are fictitious. However, many of the minor characters were real people and the events are a true account of the times, taken from the newspapers of the day and from the writings of those who were there in both peace and war.

1

Manor Farm
November 1856

JEREMY ST CLAIR brushed aside the rain-drenched hawthorn and stared up at the house. A white mist smothered the trees behind and spilled into the hollow where a dairy stood leaning drunkenly against a grey stone wall. Damn, he thought, nothing has changed. The last time he had seen Paula she had been distant and off-hand but the letter she had sent him in Devon had been light-hearted and full of affection. She had begged him to come back to Manor Farm. There was something about her he could not understand. He felt more at home on a battlefield than in her drawing room. At least those days were over. Soldiers lying shrivelled with cholera at Varna, the shortage of equipment, bodies dragged into the pits at Alma and the sound he would never forget, the whop of a shell landing in the mud and the crash as it exploded beside him. He knew all Paula's moods, her wantonness and that inexplicable coldness she sometimes showed and yet, inevitably he was always drawn back to her. His farm was in the hands of an agent in Totnes, and he had to make up his mind what he would do now that he was selling his commission. Much would depend on what she had to say.

'Good morning, Jeremy.'

Startled, he turned to see Paula smiling up at him from the path below. She ran up the steps and, brushing past him, opened the door. 'Come in,' she said.

He followed her into the sitting room. The curtains were half-drawn and an oil lamp cast a pool of yellow light on the table by the bookcase. A log fire was smouldering in the grate.

She turned and faced him. 'I have missed you,' she said.

Jeremy wondered about that. She rarely showed her feelings behind those big, dark eyes.

She lowered herself into a chair and motioned him to take the seat opposite. 'Have you sold your commission?' she asked.

'I am signing the papers next week.'

'And your wound. It does not bother you?'

'Not particularly.' He glanced at her quickly. 'Where is your brother?'

'In the music room.'

'Does he still play the piano all day?'

'And he composes a little.'

'Who looks after the farm?'

'I do, more or less, with some help from our farmhand. You remember Jos?' The ends of her mouth dropped. 'The farm brings in nothing these days.' She paused for a moment. 'I have really missed you.'

'Then why not come back to London with me?'

'I cannot.'

'And why not?'

'I have to look after Gerald.'

Jeremy's anger showed in his voice. 'Your brother is old enough to look after himself; he does nothing but play that damned

2

piano . . . . Paula, why did you invite me back here?'

She took a deep breath. 'For no particular reason.'

There it was again. Retreating into herself, keeping him at arm's length. A feeling of loneliness welled up inside. This was the Paula he could not understand. Jeremy gazed at her well-defined eyebrows, her white teeth.

'I have to make a decision soon. Decide what I am going to do,' he said.

'Are you going to live in Devon?'

'For a while perhaps.' He paused and leaned towards her. 'Paula, will you marry me?'

The sound of his voice seemed to float from somewhere near the ceiling. The words had come involuntarily, without thought. She sat in her winged chair framed by the red leather, a picture of white lace and jet black hair. Lines of worry creased her forehead as she twisted a plain gold ring on her middle finger.

'Haven't you thought I might ask you one day,' he asked.

'Yes, I have.'

'Well then?'

She looked at him quickly as though she was about to tell him about the love for her brother and for the moors that stretched behind the house. Her breasts showed firmly in the tight bodice she was wearing. Jeremy's thoughts went back to the days when they were children together. She still had that wild gypsy look.

'Well then?' he asked again.

'Jeremy, I cannot.'

'Why not.'

'Gerald needs me.'

'Your brother only thinks of himself and his music. You must find out what life is really about. I am going to Italy soon. Come with me.'

'I cannot leave him.'

I cannot leave him. That had always been her excuse. She was trapped in this broken-down house with a farm that did not pay its way. 'Paula,' he said, 'we could do so much together. Think about it carefully. Can we talk tomorrow?'

She watched the minuscule pieces of soot fly up the chimney. They glowed brightly for a moment and then vanished. She loved the house and the land around it. Jeremy did not seem to know

3

what he wanted with his life. She looked across at him.

'Yes,' she said, 'I will think about it.' She pushed herself out of the chair. 'I will get supper.'

Jeremy walked over to the mantelpiece, picked up an ornament, studied it for a moment and put it down. He realized he should have waited for a better opportunity to propose. Paula had always placed her brother first. He had some sort of hold over her. Their father had never shown any love for her. He heard a voice on the landing. Paula came into the room followed by the housekeeper, Mrs May, who set up a butler's tray at the side of the fireplace. They ate in silence.

Paula emptied her cup and sat back in the chair. 'Jeremy,' she said, 'I do like you.'

'I hope you do, otherwise what have I been doing all these years.'

'I love this place. What are you going to do with your property in Devon? Oh I know you are not destitute but you must do something.'

'I have been thinking about that. I cannot make up my mind.'

'I understand,' said Paula quietly, 'you have only known army life.'

'True. Firstly with my parents in India, then the boarding school here in Yorkshire and finally the military academy. Remember our days on the moors?'

'What has happened, Jeremy? We were to build our dream home up there?' She pointed to the clump of trees. 'It was to have a lake with swans on it and wild roses.'

For three years, at holiday time, they had been together wandering along the streams, listening to the songs of the larks and watching the summer clouds ballooning across the sky. 'You can still have all that,' he said. 'Think about it carefully my dear.'

She looked up and sighed. It would solve the money problems. 'I will give you an answer in the morning,' she said.

For Jeremy it was a long night of sleeping and waking. At last the blackness of the room turned to grey and the curtains at the windows ghosted into their folded shapes. He lay there making plans. If Paula said yes, they could go to Italy. There was the future. Where to live? He would let Paula decide. Perhaps half the year at Manor Farm and half in Devon. Go to London for the season and bring her out of her shell. Hearing the sound of someone on the stairs he pushed back the covers and went to the basin that stood on the washstand. He splashed his face with the ice-cold water. Picking up the ring he had bought for Paula, he slipped it into his pocket. Downstairs, her brother was already in the dining room.

'Good morning, Jeremy.' Gerald spoke without getting up from his chair. 'Paula tells me you are going to Italy.'

So he had been talking to her already. 'I hope to. I have always wanted to go there.'

Gerald looked sideways at Jeremy. 'You should take Paula with you.'

'It seems she does not want to go.' Had she told him about the proposal? They helped themselves to the kidney toast, coffee and hot rolls.

'You have not decided what you will do, Jeremy?'

'No, not really.'

'How about farming?'

'I would like that but I only know soldiering. I suppose I could keep the farm my aunt has left me. I need something outdoors.'

'There is nothing in it these days.'

'That is the trouble.'

Jeremy thought, where is Paula? She is usually first down in the morning. He sensed rather than heard her behind him. Gerald gave no sign that his sister was in the doorway, but his manner had changed. He became stiff and formal, staring blankly past Jeremy's shoulder. Jeremy stood up and turned around. Paula had obviously spent a long time in front of the mirror. Her hair was brushed sleekly back and tied in a bun. Her cheeks were flushed emphasizing the colour of her skin. She may have painted her lips, Jeremy was not sure.

'Can I get you something?' he asked.

'Thank you.'

He brought in the dish and waited while she put a hot roll and marmalade on her plate. Gerald had left the room. They talked trivialities. He searched her face for the answer he wanted and at last she raised her eyes and looked at him.

'Jeremy dear, I could never marry you. You do not know what you want with life. Oh I know you have some means, but you are so impractical. It is one thing to feel that war is useless but anyone who resigns his commission for such principles is an idiot. I love it here. I love this house. I cannot leave it.'

He sat there pale and still, building a wall inside. Gradually he isolated himself from Paula. He was withdrawn, detached, insulated from the hurt and pain. 'I understand,' he said. 'I do not blame you. It is very beautiful here.' He attempted a smile. 'I will get the train back to London.'

For a moment Paula's voice lost its confident note. 'There is no need to go away. Why not stay a while.'

'No, I will leave this afternoon.' He remembered the ring and putting his hand in his pocket took out the package and handed it to her. 'This is for you. Remember if you need help at any time you can always use me as a friend.'

She put the box on the table. 'Jeremy,' she said, 'where will you go?'

'To New Zealand.' The thought had been in his mind for a long time. It was a solution to the unrest he had felt. A new country, a new start.

'New Zealand! It is at the bottom of the world. Martin Gould, two farms from here, shipped out three years ago and lost everything in a bush fire. He had to pay ridiculous prices for cattle, twenty pounds a head. Pioneering does not pay, Jeremy.'

'Others have made a go of it.'

'Yes, by buying land from the Maori and selling it to someone like you. I know. Ask Martin Gould. Don't be a fool, Jeremy.'

He watched her as she spoke. She was magnificent when she was angry. He smiled at her, a quiet, amused smile. She began to collect the breakfast dishes.

'Well,' she said, 'I know you only too well. If you have made up your mind nothing will change it.'

The good-byes were easier than he had expected. Holding hands they walked past the barn. The sun was hidden by the clouds, the pigeons were in their loft and Jos was feeding the pigs. The ground was damp and cold and yet there was an air of timelessness in the buildings that defied the season, an aura that generations of country people had created. The stream at the bottom of the field was in full flood. Some autumn foliage still clung to the branches of the elm but the beech and the oak were bare, starkly silhouetted against the sky.

6

'I will take the short cut,' said Jeremy.

They stopped at the stile and faced each other.

'Good-bye,' whispered Paula. Her eyes were bigger and darker than ever. She kissed him on the cheek. For a moment Jeremy wanted to crush her to him but the sound of a whistle up the valley told him the train was not far away. 'Good-bye,' he said.

Paula called out as he reached the road. 'Write to me.'

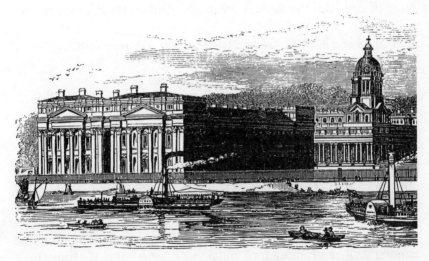

London

The fog hung low, turning the gas lamps into weak haloes of yellow light. Jeremy pulled up the collar of his astrakhan coat and paused briefly at a corner. A flower seller stood on the opposite side of the street, her cry lost to the growl of iron wheels on the cobblestones as a cart lumbered past. Not far away was Great George Street and Storey's Gate where Jeremy had his rooms, comfortable bachelor's quarters with trophies of war on the walls, his sword, his models, photos of the guns at Balaclava and the flask that belonged to his

7

friend Wilson, who had died on the heights of Alma. A cab loomed out of the fog. Jeremy held out his hand and stepped into the road as it crawled to a halt.

'The Barracks, St Johns Wood,' he called to the cabby.

Jeremy rubbed the inside of the window with his gloved hand. The river was somewhere below, a grey amorphous band. He would have to make some decisions, enquire about emigrating, go down to the farm for a while. He would always love Paula but he would have to get on with his life. In Regent Street the shop windows were glowing faintly in the half light. The cabby skirted the park, went out along Wellington Road towards the Eyre Arms Tavern and St Johns Wood.

Jeremy's gunnery friend sat waiting for him at the barracks. They talked with the familiarity of old friends who had fought together.

'Jeremy, it is not too late to keep your commission.'

'No, I have made up my mind, Tom.'

'There is a position available at headquarters.'

'Headquarters. Spare me!'

'What will you do?'

'I don't know. Perhaps emigrate. London is boring after the Crimea. I need a bit more excitement.'

'From what I have heard it was a little more than excitement you generated at Balaclava. It is a pity that will put an end to any active role for you.' Tom passed over some papers. 'Put your name on these.'

It took only minutes for Jeremy to sign away those years. The academy, the cramming for exams, his commission. He thought of that afternoon when they had spiked the guns at Balaclava and of his friend Wilson who followed him up the heights of Alma and who had died painfully in the pits. Tom shook Jeremy's hand, made some joke about a gentleman of leisure and it was all over. The cab took him back to his lodgings, this time past the Clergy Orphan's School and the cricket ground and finally along the edge of the river. He paid his fare and glancing up at the entrance to his rooms slowly climbed the stairs. 'Dammit,' he said aloud, 'I am getting out of here as soon as I can.

Devon
November 1857

Jeremy shaded his eyes and looked across the valley. His cattle were under a row of trees on a hill that climbed up to a cloud-laden sky. I will have to shift that lot, he thought. He walked up to the top of the ridge and faced the wind blowing in from the north. When he was a boy he had often stood on this spot on tip-toe, with the wind taking hold of him and suspending him on the edge of the cliff. He had felt free as he challenged the elements until he was forced to recover his balance again. Leaning on the wind, he called it. He shivered as a cold blast of air whirled around him sending the leaves of a nearby oak into the air. Every day he thought of Paula trapped at Manor Farm as he was trapped here in Devon. That unsettled feeling would not go away. In the summer time there was the tranquillity of the trees and the meadows but now there was only the cold and the rain with the clouds pressing down on him. There is only one solution, he thought, lease out the farm and get away to the colonies. He trudged back to the farmhouse, pulled off his boots and went inside. There was a letter on the hall table in Paula's handwriting.

'Dear Jeremy,' it said, 'I must see you.'

He left the next day taking the coach to London and boarding the train at the Vauxhall station. Paula met him in the drawing room. She appeared frail and subdued.

'Jeremy,' she said, 'I want to marry you.'

He went to clasp her and she backed away. 'No, no,' she cried, 'I must tell you, I am with child.'

He looked into her eyes. They were wide with despair. His heart pounded. 'With child,' he repeated.

She nodded and began to cry. 'I need someone, Jeremy. I need you.'

Jeremy took a step backwards. He remembered his promise to support her. He felt obliged to help and stared at her in dismay, angry that his love for her was still there. Perhaps it was her waywardness that attracted him, but now she looked so vulnerable. She needed him.

'Come to me,' he said and took her in his arms.

2

Liverpool
February 1858

Captain Graham watched the ship's carpenter put the finishing touches to the pig pen. He walked over to the rail and called to the first mate.

'Is everything on schedule, Harry?'

The mate looked up from the quay where he was supervising the loading of the last of the stores. 'Yes, sir!'

'Will we get away on time?'

'We should, sir!'

The captain grunted and returned to the wheel. A seaman

brought him a list and he signed it with a frown. More bloody paper work, he thought, the sooner we get away the better. The 'Winefred', built of steel, weighed one thousand three hundred and fifty-nine tons when fully loaded and two hundred and ten feet long, and was bound for Melbourne, Australia. There was the usual collection of emigrants on board, Liverpool Irish in steerage, the women in one hold, the men in another. It was impossible to keep the two sexes apart, but as long as they did not interfere with the running of the ship the captain would turn a blind eye. The cabin passengers could be just as difficult with their cliques and back-biting, but it should be no different from the other voyages. The fresh provisions would last until they were well down into the South Atlantic, then everybody would be on the hard tack — biscuits and bully beef and whatever the purser had up his sleeve. He looked over the side as a woman heavy with child struggled up the gangway. My God, he thought, we are going to have a Stepney parishioner before we reach Australia or I will eat my hat. He hated paper work. Birth certificates had to be sent to Stepney parish for all births on British ships, and there were the usual papers at the ports of call, for customs, the purchase of stores, and health clearances. He frowned as one of the crew detached himself from a group of stewards and approached the woman.

The purser glanced at the document that the pregnant woman's companion thrust at him and nodded. 'This way, Mr St Clair,' he said.

Jeremy took Paula's arm as she stepped on to the deck. Jos, her farmhand, followed with her dressing case. Picking a path through the maze of ropes and wrinkling her nose at the smells from the galley she followed Jeremy to the cabin.

It was even smaller than she had expected. There were two bunks against one of the walls and the main mast took up a great deal of space in the centre, where it disappeared through the deck above. The baggage had been taken aboard the day before — a large armchair, twelve bottles of fresh clean water, six petticoats and six shifts for Paula, a teapot, three pounds of soap, a saddle that Jeremy had bought from Peats in Bond Street and a box of books were among the belongings stowed in the cabin.

Paula put her jewellery box on the shelf attached to the mast and closed her eyes. 'Please God,' she whispered, 'I need your help.'

She stood motionless while the bitterness, the despair and the misery she felt washed over her. She swung around and faced Jeremy. 'You are to blame for this,' she cried. 'I did not want to leave England. Look at us! Crammed into this hole for an eternity and at the end of it, what is there? I hate you! I hate you!'

Jeremy closed the lid of the box that he was unpacking and rose to his feet. For a moment his anger flared. He recovered himself and looked into her eyes. 'You are here,' he said, ' because of your own doing. You are here because there was no other way out for you. You asked for my help, I have given it. You still have my love but you are wearing it thin. Do not destroy it completely.' He watched Paula slump into a chair. Immediately he was sorry for what he had said. She stared at the floor, sitting uncomfortably at an angle. This was not what he had promised. He caught sight of a water jug on the table and poured her a drink. She ignored it and continued to stare unseeingly at her feet.

'I am sorry,' he said, 'we are both tired. Why don't you lie down? I shall go up on deck while you undress.'

Jeremy watched the steam tug as it towed the *'Winefred'* from the wharf. A dark green sea crashed against the ship sending white spray over the deck. The outline of the coast gradually merged into the mist, and a gull riding on the wind dipped a wing in salute and glided back to land. Suddenly there was a sound like the crack of a pistol shot. The towline had snapped only a few feet from Jeremy. The ship plunged into a wave and lost way. He saw the tug steam out of a bank of fog as it turned back towards the *'Winefred'*. On the bridge Captain Graham shouted 'all hands on deck'. Sailors tumbled out of the fo'c'sle and manned the lines. The captain called to the mate above the noise of the wind. 'Break out the foresail, mister!' The big sail flapped and ballooned itself free. 'The inner jib!'

The *'Winefred'* steadied. Nineteen sails were unfurled. The sailors hauled in the braces and adjusted the angles of the yard-arms as she took up the challenge. Jeremy glanced at the sky and saw that the light was fading. He went back to the cabin, picked up a book and some papers that had fallen on the floor and looked down at Paula. She was asleep.

Paula had avoided any discussion about her child, as though she felt that silence would make her agony go away. They had been married in the parish church on the edge of the moor on a cold wind-bound day. He remembered looking through the altar window at the clump of trees on the ridge behind and making a vow that he would always protect and care for her and the child even though he did not know the father's identity. He felt he wanted to build a fence around Paula to shield her from her anguish, but she continued to hide behind a curtain that he could not penetrate. She would not let him close to her and drew back when he tried to touch her. He slipped into his bunk to dream of a child crying and a cold green sea pouring down upon it.

When Jeremy went up on the deck next morning a faint light showed in the eastern sky and a dull red glow hung behind some black storm clouds lying on the horizon. He thought of the past few months. He had cut his ties with England and there was no going back. Paula would need all the courage she could muster and would have to accept her situation. He heard a sound behind him. A man and a woman were sheltering behind a lifeboat on the leeward side. The woman smiled at him and murmured a polite good morning. Jeremy saw a pair of blue, wide-set eyes starred with grey and a wisp of fair hair poking out from under a bonnet. He introduced himself.

The man turned from the rail. 'Earle, John Earle,' he said, 'and this is my wife.'

There was something about the woman that intrigued Jeremy. The fair complexion? The eyes? An air of competence and self-possession? He was not sure what attracted him.

'Mr St Clair,' she said, 'are you travelling alone?'

'No,' said Jeremy. 'My wife is a trifle indisposed at the moment.'

'I am sorry to hear that.'

'I will look forward to introducing her,' he said.

The next day the wind had swung around to the north bringing cold, forbidding skies. Paula felt well enough to go to the saloon, and she and Jeremy found themselves seated next to the couple

13

that he had met the previous day. He introduced Paula and exchanged a few words with Earle. The man had an arrogant manner that Jeremy found rather odious. He glanced at the wedding ring on Mrs Earle's finger and wondered why she had married a man so obviously puffed up with his own importance. Breakfast was a polite affair. Jeremy left Paula exchanging pleasantries with Mrs Earle and went up on deck.

There was a high pitched whine in the rigging as the waves gathered astern, rose sharply and then curved down to disappear under the ship. A gale was brewing. The royal and topgallant yards were bare, the gaff topsail aft had been taken in and the upper staysails furled. Jeremy tightened the fastenings of his oilskin coat and watched the spray as it swept across the deck. Suddenly he stiffened. A dark shape stood out for a moment on the crest of a wave and disappeared as quickly as it had come. Imagination, he thought. He saw it again. A ship's boat was pitching madly in the trough of a wave.

Jeremy cupped his hands to his mouth and shouted. 'Boat to starboard!' He signalled to the first mate and ran towards the after deck. 'There is a lifeboat out there!' He pointed astern.

The captain was already at the wheel. 'Get two lookouts up top,' he ordered. 'All hands on deck. I want an extra man up here.' He clipped the words out and turned to the helmsman. 'Down helm starboard. Keep her going.' He looked for the mate. 'Where the hell are you, mister? Round up that foresail.' The men strained at the lines as the main and mizzen sails came around. 'Brace that main topsail.' He let the 'Winefred' fall away from the wind. 'Come on you beauty,' he said. The ship gained momentum. 'Helm hard over.' The upper and lower spankers were hauled to windward and the ship slowly turned.

The mainsail and the main lower topsails were braced further around. They shook, trembled, then filled. The 'Winefred' drove forward. The captain turned to the helmsman. 'Keep her full man, keep her full.' He glanced at the compass. 'Don't let her gripe.'

There was a call from the foremast. 'Boat, starboard, thirty degrees.'

The captain shouted into the helmsman's ear. 'Luff.' The ship gradually slowed. He turned to the mate. 'Useless to put anything in there, mister. Hang the safety nets over.' The 'Winefred' half sailed, half drifted down on the lifeboat. A lone man clung to a seat in the stern.

'Get up here,' the second mate bellowed. The man stood up for a moment and collapsed back into the bottom of the boat. It crashed heavily against the steel plates of the *'Winefred'*. Suddenly a scream came echoing from below. The shipwrecked sailor was in the sea, struggling around the stern. Jeremy grabbed a line and slid to the water. A wave hit him and sent him underneath the lifeboat. As he struggled he saw the legs of the sailor kicking wildly above him and a red stain spreading on the surface. He lifted and pushed the man back into the boat. Another wave slammed Jeremy against the side of the ship. There was a dull thud of flesh against steel and he lost consciousness.

The pain came from somewhere inside his head, a dull pulsating ache. In the half light Jeremy saw a bed, a lantern swinging from the ceiling and a curtain half open revealing a small desk littered with medical instruments. A hand pushed the curtain aside and the ship's doctor walked across and peered down at him. He put a lamp to Jeremy's eyes and grunted. 'You are lucky your skull is not fractured,' said Dr Nugent. 'Do you remember pulling that man out of the water?' He nodded towards the bed next to Jeremy. Dr Nugent took Jeremy's pulse and inspected a bloodied gash on his head. 'I may have to apply a leech to your temple to guard against inflammation of the brain.' He went to the table and mixed a concoction. 'In the meantime take this.' He watched Jeremy swallow the few drops of opium. 'That will sedate you for a few hours,' he said.

When Jeremy woke, Paula was standing by the bed. She bent over him and brushed the hair from his forehead. There was a feeling of intimacy between them that was lacking before. She told him of the rescue and explained that the man in the next bed was the only survivor from a crew of twenty whose ship capsized when the cargo shifted. The captain had thought to change course and put him ashore at Cork but had changed his mind and intended that he should work his passage until the *'Winefred'* returned to Liverpool.

'You have missed most of the storm,' said Paula. 'There have been two fights in steerage, a sailor fell from the mast and two pigs died when the pen was wrecked. Dr Nugent is useless. He tipples rum.'

'How do you know?' asked Jeremy.

'She-devil told me.'

'She-devil?'

Paula laughed. 'They all call her She-devil, her name is Caroline. She tipped a cup of coffee over a gentleman when they argued about the ownership of a deck chair. The captain threatened to put her in irons.'

'Is she cabin class?'

'Of course. She has money in her own right.' Paula stood up and put her hands low down on her back. 'I am going below to rest.'

Jeremy turned over and listened to the sounds of the ship, the creaking of the spars, the sea sliding along the hull and the occasional clang of the ship's bell as it sounded the half hour.

A whisper came from the other bed. 'You saved me from the water.' The voice had an Irish lilt to it.

A stubbly beard and a scarred nose was all that Jeremy could see. 'So they tell me,' said Jeremy. 'How long were you in the boat?'

'Three days. I managed to push off minutes before the old girl turned over. The others were trapped below. She went slowly poor thing. Leaning fifty degrees she was. Did not want to go. What is your name?'

'Jeremy St Clair.'

'Mine is Matt.' The sailor leaned over and held out his hand.

Jeremy grasped it and shook it firmly. 'You saved my life,' said the sailor.

Jeremy learnt Matt's life story. He had been born into a poor family and as a child had accompanied his mother in the fields where she slashed the weeds and hoed the crops. His sisters had been put to service as soon as they were old enough. He had been lucky to find a berth on a coaster and had been at sea for ten years.

One evening, when they were talking, Jeremy said, 'I shall need someone to help me when we get to New Zealand. Are you game to give it a try?'

For a moment Matt looked nonplussed, then he smiled. 'Sure,' he said, 'any time, anywhere.'

At sea
March 20th, 1858

Dear Gerald,

Well, here we are settling down at last. The ship has stopped rolling and we are past the Madeira Isles. But to start at the beginning. The very night we left a storm sprang up and tossed us about nicely so that nearly everyone was seasick. The ship shook fearfully and the sailors tumbled about so that old Dr. Nugent, the ship's doctor, had a busy time mending broken heads — that is, when he eventually plucked up enough courage to leave his cabin.

In the evening, 26 February, our lights were blown out. There was water all over the cabin floor and sleep was impossible. Most of the emigrants were down below and had the hatch fastened down upon them, poor things. Many of them are Irish and on St. Patrick's day they drank too freely, and in the end, as might be expected, there was a fight, but happily without any serious consequences. The last storm blew for thirty-three hours. Besides carrying away the top main yard it broke the upper part of the main mast. The sailors were up the whole night, the pig shed was shattered into fragments and squealing pigs were all over the deck. Two of them died.

Jeremy is well, although he was in the infirmary with a bad head acquired when he helped rescue a sailor we found in the Irish sea, but more of that later. Thank goodness we are now getting enough sun to dry everything out. The cabin windows are open, and the cocks which have been taken from their coop are exhibiting what some might call a respectable fight, to show, I think, that the storm has not quelled their courage. Why does the male have to show off the way he does?

I hope the village is looking after you. There is a large batch of preserves in the attic above your bedroom. If you let Mrs May know, she could get them down. I feel guilty about taking Jos away from you, and for leaving you for that matter, but no doubt you will find someone to look after you. Meanwhile, we are cooped up here in a cabin more like a den, and no better off than the ducks and hens that are quacking and cackling away behind me on the deck. I must go now to the cabin. Already it is so wearisome and every day the same, but I will write as often as I am able.

Your loving sister,
Paula

Paula closed her eyes and thought of the house tucked away in the valley. The trees would be budding up and soon bursting into green and the snowdrops and the daffodils would be bending with the spring showers. She felt the movement of the baby inside her and stood up, stretched herself and slowly climbed up the steps to the deck. Caroline was waiting for her. Paula sat down under the shade of the awning and they talked of the homes they had left and the uncertainties they both had to face.

'You will need help when your time comes,' said Caroline.

'The captain has found me a maid in steerage,' said Paula. 'Her name is Emily and she is very Irish.' She looked across the water. 'Oh, I wish my brother was here. I have been writing to him and I have asked him to follow us.'

'Is that wise?'

'I do not care. He can sell up the farm and use my share to pay his passage. That will leave him some capital to start again.'

'Does Jeremy approve?'

'He does not know,' Paula hesitated. 'I cannot love Jeremy. God knows I have tried. Perhaps if he was angry more often, I might want him but he is so even-tempered, so independent. He does not need me as Gerald needs me. I worry about my brother.'

'You love him, don't you?'

'He is the only person I have ever loved. Paula began to cry. She took a handkerchief from her pocket and dabbed at her eyes. 'Oh Caroline, what am I going to do?' The despair that she felt overwhelmed her.

Caroline reached out to find words to comfort her. 'Poor dear,' she said, 'I will help you all I can. I have always wanted a daughter but it has been willed that I cannot have one. You shall be both my daughter and my friend.'

At last Paula had found someone who would listen to her.

Someone in whom she could confide. She lowered her eyes, weeping. 'Jeremy is not the father of my child,' she whispered.

For a moment Caroline felt the shock of Paula's words then pity took hold of her. She patted the girl's hand. 'And Jeremy thinks it is his?'

'No. He knows it is not his.'

'And he still married you?'

'Yes.'

'You are a very fortunate girl.'

Paula flung herself up and faced Caroline. 'Fortunate!' she cried. 'Fortunate that my mother died when I was born! Fortunate that my father blamed me for her death! We never saw him. He was always away leaving us in a sterile world of servants. We had no love, Caroline. No love. Is it any wonder I loved my brother?'

'Paula, oh Paula,' Caroline whispered, 'what are we to do? How could this have happened to you?' She put an arm around her. Glancing along the deck she saw Jeremy approaching with the Earles. 'Here he is. Quickly,' she took Paula's arm and guided her below.

Rosalind Earle waited while her husband pulled up a chair. She took a book from under her arm. Jeremy recognized Captain Cooper's *Guide to New Zealand*. 'You intend to farm?' he asked.

'Possibly,' she said. 'It seems it is not easy. There are problems.'

'Such as?' asked Jeremy.

'That young men get used up before they go to the country. They spend their money at the hotels and frequently fall back on the refuge of the destitute — a government appointment. He says that officers of the army make good colonists.'

'Then there could be hope for me,' said Jeremy.

'You were an officer?'

'Yes, I was wounded at Sebastapol.'

'Rosalind!' Earle left the rail where he was standing and went over to Rosalind. He turned apologetically to Jeremy. 'I am afraid my wife is a trifle impertinent with her questions. She has definite convictions on a number of matters that should be left to men. She is a great admirer of Mrs Caroline Norton and moreover, reads her verse.'

'I think Mrs Norton has a great deal of courage,' replied Jeremy.

Earle frowned. 'I personally find her somewhat vulgar as are all the Sheridans.'

Mrs Norton was well known in London. The supposed mistress of the Prime Minister, Lord Melbourne, her marriage to Norton had not been a success from the start. He was uncouth, had refused her an allowance and had pushed her down the stairs when she was pregnant. When they separated the children were taken from her and she was forced to eke out a legacy from her mother by writing verse and novels.

'I think Mrs Norton has wit and a great sense of fun,' said Rosalind.

'If you can call kicking the Prime Minister's hat over his head at the French embassy particularly funny.' Earle's voice had an edge to it.

'I was in the courtroom,' said Rosalind, 'when George Norton was sued for the repairs to her carriage. He dragged his wife through the mire. He has taken her children. It is a cruel and legal fact that although mothers of illegitimate children are allowed access to their offspring, all others belong to the husband from the hour of birth. A woman has no legal existence away from him and even if he deserts her there is no redress. I joined in the applause in the courtroom when Caroline stood there and cried out that she had no rights, only wrongs. But at last a new bill is drafted in the House. A wife will remain in possession of her earnings and she will be able to inherit and bequeath her property as a single woman. It is the first trickle of success for women and will, I assure you, turn into a torrent one day.'

'Rosalind! That is enough!' Earle looked at his wife impatiently. 'I think it is time we went to our cabin,' he said.

'I have not finished,' said Rosalind. 'Tell me, Mr St Clair, why did you resign your commission?'

'I was wounded, but not too badly. I could have had a job at headquarters but I needed something more active. Besides, we achieved nothing in the Crimea and only made a series of bungles.'

Rosalind clapped her hands. 'I agree, I agree! And no-one was prepared to spend money on the hospitals until a woman spoke up.

Usually we are manipulated by politicians, but this time the newspapers put us in the war. Jingoism won the day.'

Earle bristled. 'Some people call it patriotism,' he said.

Jeremy watched Rosalind. She looked more in control than ever. 'Human nature rules the world,' he said. 'We get what we deserve.'

Rosalind's husband glared at Jeremy. 'The damned Russians asked for it in the Crimea the way they harassed the Turks.'

'That may have been so,' said Jeremy, 'but Gladstone had not planned for war, we British never do, we simply find ourselves in one from time to time.'

'Come, my dear!' Earle put his hand on Rosalind's shoulder and guided her to the door.

Jeremy wiped his brow. The ship was close to the equator and he felt he was being stewed in an iron pot. The sails were limp as the *Winefred* rolled from side to side. The sun hung suspended on the horizon and as he watched it slipped away. The stars appeared one by one and the tropical night closed over the ship.

According to Captain Graham's reckoning the *Winefred* would cross the line in less than twenty-four hours. He stood on deck making plans with the first officer. The Southern Cross sat low down in the sky pointing to the other side of the world. Another bunch of emigrants would soon be starting a new life. What made them leave Britain? Poverty? Ambition? Opportunity? A chance to have land of their own? He thought back on the voyage. The old doctor had been a problem. He had stayed in his cabin during the worst storm, refusing to go out and mend a lascar's broken hand. As they had approached the equator the men had climbed aloft a dozen times a day, working the sails, re-setting the spankers and squaring the yards to catch every movement of air. He saw some passengers lying on deck where they had dragged their bedding to escape the heat below.

'Shift that lot,' he shouted to the first mate. 'And send someone around to check that all the passageways are clear. I do not want the whole ship turned into a dormitory. We will start checking the new sails. Get out the nun's shift tomorrow.'

The first mate pulled in his breath sharply. The old man was in one of those moods again. The nun's shift would certainly be needed for the roaring forties they would encounter on the other side. The heavy stiff sails would be checked and re-sewn and new boltropes added. But there were more immediate problems. 'We will need rain soon,' he said, 'there is only one full tank left.'

'Then cut everyone down to a quart a day and there is to be no washing of clothes. What are the arrangements for crossing the line?'

'The passengers have passed the hat around. There is more than enough money for drink.'

'Damn them. I do not want any sore heads, and the ship will have to be properly manned.'

'Why not compromise? Those on watch can celebrate the day after.'

'Not a bad idea,' remarked the captain, 'but watch the steerage lot.'

'The cabin passengers have decided not to join in.'

'So be it.' The captain thrust his hands into his waistcoat pockets. 'Pass the word around. Any trouble, any fights and the culprits will be in irons. That goes for everybody. Cabin, Steerage, Crew.'

April 5th, 1858

My Dearest Gerald,

I sounded so miserable in my last letter. I have read it again and thought to tear it up but decided not to. One becomes horribly depressed, especially now the baby is getting nearer and I am worried. I do not feel anything, just this thing in front of me, getting bigger every day. Thank God I am not sick in the mornings any more. Dr Nugent said I am to rest all the time, and you know how I like walking, not that there's much room for it here, but Jeremy and some of the others pace the deck every day. The old doctor has been very drunk and disorderly and I have no confidence in him but I cannot manage without Caroline. She is a passenger who befriended me.

22

We have had more bad weather. One night there was a loud noise and when I opened the berth door all the lights were out and the cabin was awash. The steward was on the floor with one leg in a bucket and holding a broken jug handle. He was flat on his back. The chamber utensils were floating backwards and forwards as the water slopped from side to side. The seas had forced off the main hatch cover and washed it against the rails. We had cheese and biscuits wet with seawater for breakfast and then there were three days and three nights of that, but even the bad things must come to an end and all is well again. The captain has found me a maid from steerage. Her name is Emily and she is terribly Irish. She hurls her words out with such a superfluity of breath. I tell her it is please, not plaze, it is storm not storrum, but my efforts have little effect. I intend to teach her some etiquette.

We crossed the line with due ceremony, although the passengers were not initiated.

Poor Jeremy. He is so patient with me. All the gentlemen find him an excellent companion and the ladies swoon over him. I think I am beginning to be fond of him. The baby is close now. Yesterday I had the urge to tidy up my cubby hole and spent hours unpacking and repacking two of the boxes I keep there. Caroline says I have the nesting instinct.

There are dark clouds low down on the horizon and we are now well below the equator. It is getting cold again. I must finish this and get my wrap.

Love Paula

3

The Indian Ocean
12 April 1858

EMILY yawned and stretched her arms upwards. Life was boring, the same faces, the same talk, the same routine every day. She picked up a cloth to polish the seaman's chest as a shaft of sunlight blazed through the porthole highlighting the colours of the rug on the floor. She took a deep breath and savoured the fragrance of the polish as she rubbed around the whalebone inlays. She lifted up the finely plaited handles and turned the key in the lock. The sound of Jos's boots echoed along the passage. 'Better than a cowbell,' she thought.

Jos pushed the cabin door open and paused as he became accustomed to the light. He stood open-mouthed in front of her. Emily dabbed at an imaginary speck of dust. 'I am tired of you standing like a cow without anything to say,' she said, 'I am tired of this ship and what is more I am tired of her ladyship with all her lah-di-da. Let us do something for a change.' She went up to him and stood on tip-toe. 'Here, how about a kiss.' Her blouse was open and Jos could see the gentle swelling of her breasts. She stepped closer and tilted her face upwards. 'Come on, Jossy boy,' she whispered.

An unexpected feeling stirred in his belly. He looked down at her with her eyes closed, her long eyelashes resting on her cheeks. He could smell the perfume she had taken from Paula's chest. He pecked her on the cheek.

'Not like that, like this.' Emily slid her arms around him. 'I just might teach you a thing or two.' She smiled up at him. There was a noise in the corridor. She looked out to see Paula making her way towards the cabin, holding on to each door as she came, racked with pain. 'Emily', cried Paula, 'fetch the doctor and please find Caroline!'

Caroline was in the saloon when Emily burst in. 'The baby is on its way!' she cried.

Caroline picked up her shawl and called out to Jeremy. Dr Nugent was on his bunk with an empty bottle on the chair beside him when Jeremy leaned across the doorway and shook him by the arm. 'My wife needs you,' he said.

The doctor peered down at Paula. His strong hands probed and pressed Paula's abdomen as she stretched out on the chair. Another wave of pain came up from the depths. She gripped the doctor's hand until the agony passed away. They walked her slowly to the infirmary. The yellow lamplight flickered spasmodically and the dark shadows of the cabin posts swept across the bunk as the ship pitched into the waves. A coat hanging on a nail swayed to and fro and a beaker on the washstand clinked sharply against the marble top. Paula clenched her fists as the pain struck her again.

'Bear down!' Dr Nugent was a vague shape in the shadows. Paula felt another surge of pain. 'Bear down!' She gathered her strength and thrust her agony away. Why was she here? In a storm. A drunken doctor. The cold. The unbearable pain. 'Bear down.'

The cabin was in focus again. Paula stared at the air vent above her head. Sixty days out from Liverpool, sixty devils stabbing at her in the semi-darkness. Someone held her hand. A respite. Peace for a moment then it started again. A shadow fell across her as Dr Nugent took over. Paula closed her eyes and prayed.

Jeremy held on to the rail as the ship bucketed through the heavy seas. An albatross flying a few feet above the mast appeared motionless against the sky, gliding effortlessly as it poised above the main royal yardarm. Black clouds were crowding together on the horizon and sailors were battening down the hatches, coiling the ropes and folding up the chairs on deck. It seemed only a few years since he had been a boy in India with a father in the army who had brought him up with such unbending formality. There were the journeys from India to the boarding school in Yorkshire, the walks on the moor with Paula and the places they had searched where the marsh violets grew. There were the furloughs when his parents indulged him with a week in London then disappeared back to India, until one day a message came on the electric telegraph telling him that his mother and father had died of smallpox. His aunt had taken him in. Her land was in Devon on the River Tamar where sailing barges beat up the river to moor on the flats. She believed in the ancient rhymes and he had helped her place cakes soaked in cider on the branches of the apple trees as she sang.

> 'Here's to thee, old apple tree,
> Whence thou mayest bud and
> Where thou mayest blow
> And where thou mayest bear apples enow.
> Hats full, Caps full
> Bushel, bushel sacks full
> And my pockets full. Hurrah!'

Old Jonathon the herdsman had taught him a different tune.

> 'Apple tree, apple tree,
> Bear good fruit
> Or down with your top
> And out with your root.'

Jeremy tightened the fastenings of his sou'wester and glanced up at the rigging. A boom had broken away again and was battering against the side of the ship. A dozen seamen were struggling with the lines to prevent more damage. There was a lull in the storm and a strange silence. Suddenly there was a crash and a harsh scream in the rigging as the wind turned a full one hundred and eighty degrees.

The skipper rushed to the helmsman. 'Ease helm amidships!' The rudder was centred and the ship sailed through the water stern first, as the wind blew directly from the bow. The rigging groaned

26

and screeched as the masts bent dangerously.

'Now to port!' The captain put a hand on the wheel to help steady the ship as the helmsman gradually altered course. The 'Winefred' slowed, and turned gradually. For a short while she was in irons, her sails flapped wildly then filled again and she sailed free, bow first into the waves. A sailor looked up at the sky and shook his fist.

Jeremy turned to see Caroline edging slowly along the windward rail. The wind was tearing at her shawl as he went to meet her. He bent his head to catch her words.

'You have a son,' she said. 'The doctor wants to see you in his cabin.'

Dr Nugent motioned Jeremy to a chair and looked across at him. 'You know you have a son?' he asked.

'Yes,' said Jeremy with the beginning of a smile.

'I am afraid he is poorly.' There was a pause. 'Are you and your wife blood relations?'

Jeremy looked up sharply. 'Blood relations?' he repeated.

Doctor Nugent looked embarrassed. The child has a condition commonly occurring when the parents are related.' There was a pause. 'However, it can happen for no apparent reason. I do not expect him to survive.'

Jeremy looked hard at the doctor. Gerald. Could it be Gerald? It would account for much of Paula's moods, her manner, her distance from him. The anger showed in his voice. 'Does Paula know the child's condition?'

'Not yet. Would you like me to tell her when she has recovered in a little while?'

'Thank you, no.' Jeremy ducked his head to avoid the top of the doorway. 'I will talk to her myself.'

The big albatross flew overhead, sailing on the wind without a movement of its wings. It was motionless, effortless, a spirit watching and waiting. A group of people huddled at the side of the ship, sheltering from the sharpness of the cold air. Paula sat alone staring at the horizon, a pale shadow detached from the world. The sea was menacing and grey and the salt spray showered along the deck.

27

'I am the resurrection and the life sayeth the Lord.'

A line, loosely fastened, clacked, rat, rat, rat, against the mast.

'He that believeth in me, though he were dead, yet shall he live.'

Emily held Jos's arm for support. She was dressed in her best black skirt and jacket and was clutching a small white handkerchief. Caroline and her husband were there and Matt stood with his head bowed, whispering a *Nunc Dimittus* of his own, a hairy archangel guarding the pathetic bundle lying on the deck. The sailmaker had fashioned a shroud from the sail that had been torn in the storm and with infinite patience had cut and stitched the cloth and bound and sewn it, making a series of neat grommets laced together with a cord. The tiny body lay on a weighted plank.

'Man that believeth in me, though he were dead, yet shall he live.' Paula, dry eyed, sat motionless.

'And whosoever liveth and believeth in me shall never die.'

Jos shivered. The albatross hung in the sky like a shadowy conscience.

'Man that is born of woman hath but a short time to live and is full of misery. He cometh up and is cut down like a flower, he fleeth as it were a shadow, and never continueth in one stay.'

The passengers standing above moved closer together. Matt went down and gently rested the baby on a chute.

'We therefore commit his body to the deep to be turned into corruption.'

There was a splash and a long drawn out sigh that seemed to come from the sea. Jeremy looked up at the sky and put his arms around his wife. He looked for the albatross. The great white bird had gone.

April 19th, 1858

My dear Gerald,

I have had my baby and it has died. I do not want to discuss it again except to say that he had to be christened at once and was buried at sea. I have been thinking of you every day and when you receive this I want you to sell up everything and come out to New Zealand. You can use my share of the proceeds to pay for your passage and that will leave capital to start wherever we may be.

I worry you are not looking after yourself and not getting regular meals. I hope that you are writing and your letters will catch up with us somewhere. Jeremy has decided to stay in Melbourne for a while. Most of the passengers are disembarking there with the intention of settling and we have a number of introductions. I cannot wait for your news and will suffer Melbourne until we leave for Sydney. If you book a passage immediately we could be together in twelve months from now.

As I write the passengers are taking the opportunity of drying out their stock in trade. Every article from a slipper to a nightcap is floating in the breeze on lines attached to the rigging from fore to aft. On deck every rope and available space is covered. Everyone seems tolerably happy, the ducks are quacking, the cocks are crowing, the hens cackling, the pigs grunting, the sun is shining and the ship is sailing along at ten knots in the right direction, or so Jeremy tells me.

I have been making enquiries of the passengers. Before you make any more plans, write to Morrison's at 138 Leadenhall St or to Banes of Liverpool. They both ship to New Zealand. The Union Bank of Australia grants bills for monies without charging any percentage. I think this direct route is best but the overland one leaves from Southampton on the 12th of each month, via Marseilles, Malta, the Isthmus of Suez and Ceylon to Melbourne. They tell me a steamer runs once a month from Sydney to Auckland, the charge for which is first class passenger £15 and second class £8 or £10. Please come as soon as possible.

Your loving sister,
Paula

The first time Jeremy saw the whales they were on the port side between the ship and the islands of St Paul and Amsterdam, spouting in the distance where small bursts of moist air hung like miniature clouds. He went down and called out to Paula. Since the burial service she had been more aloof than ever, grieving for her child and taking no interest in the activities on board. As the *'Winefred'* sailed closer to the whales the black shapes were motionless but when they moved Jeremy saw a spark of interest in her eyes.

'They are beautiful,' she said. She leant over the rail to watch a calf follow its mother.

'Yes,' said Jeremy, 'a whaling ship might find them even more beautiful.'

Paula flung herself around and faced Jeremy. 'Men are cruel. Would they take the baby?'

'Probably. They are sperm whales. They have high quality oil in them.'

'What do they eat?'

'Squid.'

Paula made a face. 'Do they really suckle their young?'

'Yes.'

'It is hard to imagine.' A look of despair came over her face. The grief flooded upwards, engulfing her. She stood at the rail staring at the horizon. Her baby. Somewhere down there. The grey green sea. The cold. Oh God! There was no God. A loving God would not put her in the world so isolated. From the day she was born she had suffered in a sterile world of servants and a house that was always empty. 'Oh Gerald. Gerald. Gerald.' She spoke his name aloud.

Jeremy took hold of her by the shoulders and forced her to face him. 'Paula,' he said, 'listen, I married you because I loved you.'

She looked into the distance. 'And now you don't,' she whispered.

'Unfortunately I still love you.' Jeremy dropped his hands and turned his back on her. 'Gerald is the father of your child. Isn't he!'

Paula staggered to the rail and grasped it for support as Jeremy faced her and shouted. 'Answer me!'

She saw a pair of blue eyes boring into her. She thought, Jeremy really cares for me. He cares for me.

Jeremy repeated his cry. 'Answer me!'

'Yes', she whispered.

'What have you done? You have destroyed everything. What is left? When we get to New Zealand we will need to sort this out. In the meantime I want no more of you.' He turned on his heels and strode away as Paula collapsed in a heap on the deck.

She lay there until hours later, when Rosalind discovered her and called for two sailors to lift her and carry her below.

Scene at the gold diggings

4

Melbourne
June 1858

Matt high up on a yardarm felt the power of the ship as she strained forward, a powerful, lean, living thing slicing her way through the sea. The steady cadence of the bow wave and the rhythmical beat of the rollers were like a symphony. There was a force emanating from the ship that turned him into a superman as he battled with a sail, refusing to surrender to a forty knot wind that pinned him to the yardarm a hundred feet above the deck. He looked out to port. Low down on the horizon a long grey shape sprawled into the distance and as the dawn sky lightened he saw the Australian continent stretched out in front of him. There was a cry from the masthead. 'Land ho!' The rails were soon lined with people gazing at the country that was to be home for so many of them.

On the first day of June 1858, one hundred and two days out from Liverpool, they passed Cape Otway and rounded up into Port Philip Bay.

A feeling of excitement gripped Jeremy as he stood in a queue waiting with Paula and their three servants to be cleared by the customs men. As they went down the gangway Paula felt a stab of despair. If she could have turned around and gone back to Manor Farm she would have done so. She threaded her way through a jumble of boxes and coal dumps and paused as a group of men eyed the latest bunch of immigrants. Somewhere behind them a voice called out in an accent that might have come from Wapping Wall, full of confidence and tinged with cockney humour.

They climbed on to a low-back car and rolled along to Lyndhurst while the man driving the horses kept up a one-way conversation. 'Just arrived?' he asked and without waiting for a reply he said, 'Watch out for the government men.' He nodded and clamped his lips tightly together. 'You will see the government men. Convicts. Vandemoniums. Everyone is friendly and free with their drinks, but I warn you watch out for the government men.' Jeremy looked over to Emily who was sitting next to Jos, a little too closely, he thought.

They stopped at Lyndhurst for a meal and went on to Melbourne to take rooms in a public house in the centre of town. Jeremy did not expect to be in Melbourne for very long. They had introductions to two or three people, one from an army friend who had previously worked with the Governor and another to an official who had been in the colony for some time.

The streets of the city were well paved, telegraph wires ran along the principal roads and the land was planted with vines the size of raspberry bushes. There was a sense of freedom in the air.

They climbed the stairs to their room. At the door Paula paused, 'I should never have left England,' she said.

He waited for her to go inside. 'We have already discussed your situation.'

She sat down on the settee. 'The people here have no idea of rank.'

'It is a free and easy place,' said Jeremy.

'Barbaric is a better word.'

'I would not say that. I understand the entertainment here is like any drawing room at home. Are Wyndham and Caroline coming here?'

'Yes,' she paused. 'Jeremy, please be polite to Wyndham, Caroline is the only friend I have.'

There was a knock on the door and Paula darted over to open it. She ushered Caroline and Wyndham into the room. 'Will you have a drink?' she asked.

'Jolly kind of you,' said Wyndham.

Jeremy went over to the buffet. 'Rum and lime?'

'Thank you.' Wyndham took the glass and blew a smoke ring towards the ceiling. 'What are you going to do when you get to New Zealand? Buy land?'

'I have not decided,' said Jeremy.

Wyndham gulped at his drink. 'Neither have I. I had some bad luck at home and had to clear out really. I had an interest in a bank that failed and there were some personal debts as well. I was in the Horse Guards but they refused me the substantive rank of major and treated me with the most infamous injustice. I did not receive the majority I was promised. They told me to accept half pay as captain or sell out, which I did at a loss. The difference between a captain's and a major's commission was fourteen hundred pounds and my wife's family would not help me so here I am.' He paused, 'Mind if I have another drink?'

'No, help yourself.'

Paula glanced at Jeremy. 'Poor Wyndham,' she said. 'Perhaps we will be able to get you on your feet. You two should go out and have a look at the town while Caroline and I have a chat.'

Jeremy and Wyndham walked up Emerald Hill and admired a joss house standing on its own, separated from the other buildings by a piece of untidy waste land. In Little Bourke Street the shops were filled with carved sandalwood boxes, ivory chessmen, rice and dried shark fins. Wyndham poked his head through a curtained doorway. In the haze of a pot house some Chinese were smoking opium, blowing the smoke through their noses, passing little cups of resin

34

to each other. An old man was asleep on a mat, his feet drawn up together and his knees spreadeagled.

'That is something I have not tried,' said Wyndham, 'I understand it is cheap enough. They get completely drunk for a penny. I knew a chap once who went out east, he lived there alone, never married and had a boy to look after him who made up a pipe for him every evening. Just one a day. When Smithfield went home on leave he could not get back to China quickly enough. Mind you, he had slowed down a lot. Always had a dreamy look about him.' Wyndham stopped suddenly. 'Look,' he said, 'a pak-a-poo den. Ever played? You mark the Chinese characters and if they come up in the draw you can win a packet. Shall we have a go?'

'Not for me, thank you,' said Jeremy.

'I think I will.'

'Then I will see you back in the hotel.'

Jeremy returned to the hotel alone. Caroline and Wyndham were leaving for New Zealand in a day or two and, he thought, Paula would be without a friend to boost her confidence.

'Have you had a good day?' asked Paula.

'If you can call wandering around the pot houses and the dens a good day then I have,' said Jeremy. 'I do not know what to think of Wyndham.'

'You are not the only one. Caroline is not sure of him either.'

'Then why did she marry him?'

'You cannot tell how a man will behave until you actually live with him.'

'Does that go for me too?'

'You are different. After all we have known each other since we were children.'

'Does that make us more perceptive?'

They had lapsed into an uneasy silence when Caroline rushed into the room. 'Paula,' she cried, 'Wyndham has lost our passage money to the Chinese!' She threw herself on to a chair.

'Have you enough to get on board ship?' asked Jeremy.

'We have nothing,' said Caroline. 'My letters of credit have gone to New Zealand and all I have are a few miserable pounds in my purse.'

'I can lend you something,' said Jeremy.

Caroline jumped up from her chair.

'Can you? I will give you a draft from my bank. Oh Jeremy, I will never forget what you have done for me.'

Jeremy and Paula waved good-bye to Caroline and Wyndham from the wharf the next day. Wyndham had a hangdog look about him but showed no sign of remorse. As Jeremy and Paula sat in the cab waiting for the horses to start back to town, Jeremy turned to Paula. 'I do not like that man,' he said.

June 10th, 1858

Dear Gerald,

Australia is remarkably different from everything I have ever known and is truly upside down. The emu bird runs as swiftly as a horse, the kangaroo and some other animals carry their young in pouches, there are fish without scales, oysters on trees, black cockatoos with green tops and swans that are black. In the summer the rivers are fullest, horses and men wear veils and Wesleyan chapels have towers and steeples.

There are many ruffians in Melbourne and everyone needs to be on guard. There is indirect encouragement given to swindlers for when convicted of fraudulently receiving a cheque they are liberated on bail. Many attribute this sad state of affairs to universal suffrage.

We have been to the goldfields, about twenty miles from Melbourne on the Dandenong Ranges, and saw broken drays, carts, tents, dead bullocks and horses scattered about. Some 'diggers' have worked for months and have been compelled to give up while others have become wealthy in a few days. Last year, 1857, the gold shipped from the colony of Victoria was one hundred and one tons, valued at over £10,800,000.

Life is quite different here. A number of expressions in common use in Australia are similar to those used in England, like 'Well I never,' 'No fear,' 'No cocky,' but there are a great many slang words. The goldfields are called 'diggins,' a large glass of brandy is a 'spider,' a kettle is a 'billy,' and a companion is a 'chum'. As for the convicts they are variously called 'vandemoniums', 'v.d.s.', 'old lags', or government men. The word 'bloody' is used frequently and after a strange fashion. 'A bloody fine woman', 'a bloody sermon', 'a bloody set of swindlers', but for all that Australia is an exciting place and booming although prices are high.

We are going to Sydney where I hope your letters have been directed. I will die if I do not hear from you soon.

Your loving sister,
Paula

When Paula saw the brig that was to take them to Sydney she shuddered. She counted the pieces of baggage two or three times not so much to see if they were all there but to delay going on board. She looked down at the puddles of water scattered along the wharf and ignored a shower of rain as it swept across from the sea. 'Hurry,' said Jeremy and guided Paula towards the gangway. Each step along the way she had become more depressed.

'I met a man down here,' he said, 'who has three thousand sheep that he bought for a thousand pounds. He rents a run from a land-holder and gives half of the increase of the flock as payment for the rent. He will have an income of three thousand pounds in two years time.'

'Another bubble that will burst,' said Paula.

She went to bed as soon as she found her cabin. During the

night she dreamt she was back at Manor Farm, standing naked on the landing as invisible hands held her back. She cried out in her sleep and woke Jeremy. Her hair had fallen over her face. He looked down at her. How could anyone look so virginal and untouched? Was it her detachment from people? The way she isolated herself? She did not belong to this world unless it was to the house on the edge of the moor and the empty landscape behind. He lay on his bunk and listened to the wind and the rain as it lashed at the ship. They landed at Sydney in the evening as the sun was sinking over the Blue Mountains. In spite of the season, the weather was mild. A light haze hung low on the water, the land and the sky seemed as one with no beginning and no end.

Jeremy hired a horse and cart to take their baggage to an hotel. Later when they had settled in and explored the town he was surprised at what Sydney had to offer. There were museums, colleges, a mechanics institute, hot and cold public baths as well as police courts, hospitals and a railway. Inland, the country was a huge block of sandstone dotted with twisted, poverty stricken trees and with graceful ferns interspersed with wattles. Jeremy attended a sale of horses at Woollers in Pitt Street. He thought of buying a chestnut mare, a three year old that went for eleven pounds ten, but the shipping cost to New Zealand was too high.

Each morning, after breakfast Paula walked to the post office. There were no letters from home. They walked down to Port MacQuarrie and looked across to Sydney Cove. A barque lay at the wharf bound for New Zealand. Jeremy called out to the sailors coiling ropes on the foredeck. 'When are you leaving?'

A sailor hitched a coil on to a rail. 'Tomorrow,' he said.

'Are there any vacant berths?'

'Search me,' said the sailor, 'you will have to ask the captain.'

'Is he aboard?'

'I bloody hope so.'

The ship was a tenth of the size of 'Winefred' and the captain a different type of man from Graham. Short, less muscular, he carried a lot more weight than one would expect for a sea captain. 'Yes,' said the captain, 'there are two cabins available. They could be divided by screens if necessary. We sail at seven in the morning.'

At six o'clock the next day Emily bumped their boxes down

the stairs of the hotel for Matt to load on a cart. Arrangements had already been made for Paula's letters to be re-directed and they set off for Victoria Wharf. The barque was in the middle of the bay with her sails unfurled. The wind was fair. With mainsails and mizzens working they passed the flagstaff battery and at midday were off Sydney heads.

Emily stood on the deck with her bonnet fastened tightly under her chin and stared out across the waves. Twelve hundred miles away in the grey distance was New Zealand, with New Plymouth their final port of call. The Tasman Sea was living up to its reputation of a wild, unpredictable stretch of water in that degree of latitude called the 'roaring forties'. Emily watched Jos crawl up the steps and sidle over to her. 'This is the first time we have been alone since *'Winefred'*,' he shouted.

'We have not had much of a chance, have we?' said Emily.

'What has she been doing down below?'

'If you mean her ladyship, she is in a decline,' Emily mimicked her mistress. 'Her ladyship needs special care. Tincture of valerian and camphor mixture three times a day and twenty drops of laudanum at night. I have been plagued with lessons in etiquette.'

'Then she will not see us if we go to my cabin. How about that kiss you promised me?'

'Gentlemen do not say, "how about a kiss".'

'What do they say?'

'They do not ask for one. They are moderate, diffident and studious to please. Polite, their behaviour is pleasant and graceful. They are neither unkind, haughty nor overbearing.'

'Cor!'

'One does not say, "cor". One says "pon my soul". When they enter the dwelling of their inferior they endeavour to hide the difference between their ranks of life.' Emily gave a mock curtsy. 'And moreover, they avoid idleness. It is the parent of many evils.'

Jos put an arm around her. 'Come on,' he said. 'How about that promise you made?'

'What do you want me to do? Play Puss in the Corner like they did on *'Winefred'*. Turn the trencher? Hunt the slipper? Come on, I will make you some tea.'

In the cabin Emily picked up a kettle. She filled it with water from a jar and unscrewed the cap on the spout after lighting the small gimbal stove. Emily was in a kittenish mood. 'Her ladyship is trying to improve me. It is for my betterment, she says.' She curtsied. 'Sir, will you take tea? China or Ceylon?' She minced over to the teapot and poured the tea, reciting the verse that Paula had taught her. 'A wife, domestic, good and pure,' she said, 'like snail should keep within her door, but not like snail in silver track place all her wealth upon her back. Like town clock a wife should be, keep time and regularity, but not like clock harangue so clear that all the town her voice will hear. A wife should be like echo true, but not like echo still be heard contending for the final word.'

Jos stared at Emily. She reminded him of the painting of an angel that hung over his mother's bed. He could imagine her at the cottage gate welcoming him after a hard day's work in the fields. 'Do you want to get married?' he asked.

'Not bloody likely,' she said. 'Time to start the lessons, Jossy boy.' She brushed his hair back and searching for his mouth pressed against him. For a moment he felt bewildered then a sense of urgency took hold. She found a gap in his shirt and explored and caressed him with her hands. She stepped back and slowly undressed. He looked down on the firm round breasts and a waist that curved away to strong, warm thighs. She slipped into the bunk and smiled up at him. 'Come on, slow coach,' she whispered.

CAPE EGMONT
Missionary Station, Maori School, Sugar Loaves, Maori Graves.

5

New Plymouth
August 1858

MOUNT TARANAKI stood out against a pale blue sky, a snow-capped mountain thrusting up from the sea.

The captain changed course as dark clouds piled up behind, followed by a squall that tore at the ship. It passed as quickly as it had come, whipping up the sea ahead and bearing away towards the mountain. They passed the rocks called the Sugar Loaves and cast anchor two and a half miles from the beach. Emily stared in horror as a small boat arrived that pitched up and down alongside the ship. She clambered down the ship's side to fall into the bottom of the boat and was rowed to a buoy moored half a mile off shore. A line was connected to a post on the beach. They pitched up and down climbing the walls of surf until at last they grounded on the black sand. Some Maori and some sailors carried them ashore and dumped them above the high water mark. A horse and cart took them to town where they stopped at the Taranaki Hotel.

New Plymouth
August 20th, 1858

Dear Gerald,

*It is six months since we left Liverpool and here we are in New
Plymouth, New Zealand and settled at the Taranaki Hotel. The town
is a busy place, the barracks are full of soldiers, there is a mission
station and new houses are going up near the river Huatoki. Land
for settlement had previously been purchased from the Maori at a
place called Waitara, but there was some sort of a dispute which
ended, at least temporarily, when Governor Fitzroy restored the
lands to the Maori and moved the settlers to the river.*

*There are many Maori here. The word 'Maori' is also conve-
niently used to describe anything that is good, beautiful or superior. We often see the men shopping with their handsome young
wives, whose glossy black hair is beautifully arranged. Most of them,
male or female have graceful, well-rounded and finely formed figures carried cavalierly.*

*There are also a large number of soldiers here. No one is
allowed to sell, let or give the Maori the least drop of intoxicating
liquor under heavy penalties. Thus the laws of New Zealand com-
pel the Maori to keep sober by inflicting penalties and permit the
white man to get drunk by licence. On the other hand it is a bone of
contention with the settlers that the Maori own the major part of
the surrounding country but do not pay taxes for roads or bridges.
Merchants do well and auctioneers thrive, but the women are the
great guns of the province doing everything in buying and selling.
They have no servants, but feel no shame in doing the work. The
men frequently stay at home on Sunday to cook the dinner while
the merchant ladies with their white parasols and satin dresses attend divine services.*

*We have been told that eight months previously the Maori
had been fighting among themselves because one of them, called
Ihaia, wanted to sell his land to the Governor but another, Wiremu
Kingi, objected. The trouble had started when Ihaia's wife committed adultery. Rimene, her seducer was killed and buried in a Maori
fort but Ihaia wanted payment for the wrong. 'Utu,' they call it. When
this was not forthcoming he threatened to sell some land to the*

British. Ihaia and Kingi fought and Kingi was the victor. This oc-
curred only a few miles from a village called Heur in the Bell Block
where a public house and brewery now stands. We rode out there
yesterday. The village has all the ingredients of a civilized exist-
ence. We saw a Maori lass riding a horse. She carried a light
handwhip and was dressed in a bottle green habit with gloves and
hat, but alas she lacked shoes and stockings.

In a day or two we are visiting the Reverend Whitely, univer-
sally loved by both the natives and the immigrants, and deservedly
so as he is considered one of the most gentlemanly and best men in
the province. Do you remember him? He is a great friend of our
vicar. They were ordained together.

The people here get mail from England, Melbourne and
Sydney ten times a year and even from Africa once a year, yet I
have had nothing from you, Gerald. Please, please write.

Your loving but despairing sister,
Paula

Mrs Whitely put out her best white starched tablecloth and set the
bone china on the table. Her husband watched as she bustled about
the room. It was not often that they had visitors from England and
especially someone who knew his best friend. He saw the ox cart
driving through the stream at the front gate and called to his wife,
'They have arrived,' he said.

Tea was a polite affair, and afterwards they retired to the drawing room.

'Have you had any communications from our vicar?' asked
Paula.

The Reverend Whitely smiled 'As a matter of fact I had a letter last week describing your brother's wedding.

For a moment there was silence. Paula half rose from her
chair and slumped back again. She stared straight ahead, eyes wide,
her face ashen.

The missionary looked quickly at Jeremy. 'You did not know?'

Jeremy shook his head. Mrs Whitely ran to Paula and dropped
down on one knee. 'Poor dear, it has been a shock,' she ran into the

kitchen and returned with a glass of water and a few drops of laudanum. 'Take this.'

Paula closed her eyes. Mrs Whitely put a rug around her and turned to Jeremy. 'I think you should get her back to the hotel and to bed,' she said. 'Poor girl. The news has been too much.'

Jeremy drove back with Paula lying in the bottom of the cart. The sun was setting over the sea with long lines of red and black cloud stretching to the north. When they reached the hotel Paula climbed the stairs to her room and collapsed on the bed.

Jeremy sat on a chair beside her. 'Listen,' he said, 'it is time you came to your senses.' Paula began to sob. 'Your brother has made his decision and that is that.'

'I hate him,' she cried.

'What has happened was inevitable. I will send Emily to you.'

'I do not want Emily. I do not want anything. Leave me alone.'

Jeremy moved quietly to the door and closed it behind him. What next, he thought. What a mess!

New Plymouth
September 2nd, 1858

Gerald,

I know all. The Rev. Whitely is a gentleman much thought of here, so how much more cruel than to hear by a quirk of fate from this man that you are married and to that Elizabeth woman. John Whitely received a letter from our vicar only three days ago which mentioned your wedding.

You have used me Gerald for you own ends. Your promises and vows have meant nothing. The only thing that has sustained me these past six months has been the thought of your letters and that perhaps we could share our lives together again in New Zealand. Now that has all gone. I do not want to hear from you except of course to settle the estate. To commence you can ship out my bedroom furniture through Bowes of Liverpool or Morrisons at 138 Leadenhall Street, London. I do not want her to touch it. As for my share of the farm, you can get an advance from the money lenders and send it to me or, better still, everything can be done through Messrs Young, 61 Cornhill who arrange tonnage. They also give orders for money to be sent to any of the provinces on payment to them in London. We have to go north to Auckland soon. You can address any letters care of the Union Bank of Australia in that town.

Paula

The day began with the wind gusting in from the south, banging at the windows and ripping the green buds off the oaks, the elms and the peach trees that the newcomers had planted. A tornado appeared from the direction of the mountain, a black spiral of destruction that passed over the barracks, ripped up a fence and twisted out to sea. It disappeared into a rain cloud, as Jeremy leant over the verandah rail and watched two soldiers push open the bar-room door. Paula was lying on the bed behind him. She had not spoken since the night she had returned from the mission station except to ask Emily for ink and quill and paper.

'It's time we had another talk,' said Jeremy as he turned back inside. 'We will not discuss your brother.' He waited for a reply. 'We must work something out, I want you to understand that any money you get from home is yours, it will give you a little independence. If I were you I would write and clarify your position regarding the farm and the inheritance.'

'I have already done that,' whispered Paula. Jeremy nodded his approval. 'We must put the past behind us and start again Paula. We are on our own in a new country and need to help each other to make a go of it. I want children,' he said.

The shock of his words struck her like a blow. Children? After what had happened? Perhaps there was still hope.

'Rest now,' said Jeremy, 'and think of what I have said.'

Jeremy was at the newspaper office inquiring about a trial shipment of iron sand that had been sent to England for testing when a gun boomed over the town. The *'White Swan'* had arrived. He hurried back to the hotel. Emily and Jos were already packing the boxes and two hours later they were down at the beach. The steamer was hove-to beyond the line of surf, pitching in the heavy seas. The hawser attached to the buoy was tightening and slackening dangerously as they were pick-a-backed into the boat and the baggage loaded. A woman thrust a jug containing some baby food at Jeremy. With the other hand he untangled a child from some rope.

The wind was cold and wild and the crew made slow progress with the oars. Jeremy looked back towards the shore. The figures of the men who had launched the boat were almost lost against the banks of black sand. A wave broke over the boat. Another lifted them higher in the air. There was a roar of breaking water and the rope parted at the buoy. Jeremy turned to look for Paula. Another wave towered above them. Emily screamed as the boat rolled and the seventeen people on board pitched into the sea.

As Jeremy rose to the surface, with the child's jug still in his hand, another wave punched at him, pushing him further from the boat. Rising on a crest he saw Paula struggling to grasp the handle of a chest that was floating to leeward but he lost sight of her among the hills of water and the spray. He struck out towards her. A woman a short distance away cried out and he swam over to her. A large air bubble had formed in her shirt and held her upright as she floated like a balloon. Two Maori swimmers appeared from the direction of the beach pushing an oar ahead of them. They hung the woman over it and towed her towards the shore.

A wave picked Jeremy up. It broke on top of him and dragged him down. He fought his way back to the surface but another forced him down again. He pushed upwards as a fierce rip swirled him out and down into a hole scoured out by the current. Fighting for air, he felt a rock scrape along his back. The sea took possession of him. He could not fight any more. It was like the beginning of a beautiful sleep. Then someone took hold of his hair. The quick tug and the sudden pain brought him back to consciousness and he felt himself being carried up the beach and set down near an upturned boat above the high water market. He saw Emily and Jos struggling among the drifting debris. Matt was crawling up the beach. Maori soldiers and townspeople waded into the sea to drag out the exhausted passengers. Two children were taken up and put in the care of some women who were standing on the sand. There was no sign of Paula.

'Have you seen my wife?' he called to one of the men. 'She was on a sea chest.'

The man shook his head. Jeremy grabbed a piece of board that lay on the high water mark and dashed back into the surf. A tall Maori, bare to the waist, followed him through the first line of breakers and they began searching along the beach in the direction of the rocks. A wave twisted the board out of Jeremy's hands, it flipped in the air and struck him on the temple. Again he lost consciousness.

It was evening when he awoke. He was in his hotel bed. He recognized the painted flowers on the yellowing wallpaper. 'Paula!' he called. 'Where is Paula?'

A chair scraped across the floor. 'Jeremy boy. It is Matt. I am here.'

'Where is Paula?'

'It is all right, Jeremy. They are looking for her. They will find her.'

'Find her?' Jeremy struggled to get out of bed and fell back on his pillow.

'There are fifty people out there looking for her. There is nothing more you can do.'

'I cannot stay here while she is out there. I must find her.'

The sun had already dipped behind the clouds and the stars had appeared when they reached the beach. He strained his eyes and looked to the south. A group of people were moving towards him. Was it a stretcher they had between them? 'Matt!' he called, 'this way!' He ran to the group. The faces of the men were sombre and drawn. He knew it was Paula on the stretcher. He could not bring himself to ask about her. He stood staring at the shapeless form under the blanket. The men walked the last few yards and stopped in front of him.

'She is exhausted,' someone said, 'but she will live. We have pressed most of the water out of her.'

Jeremy bent down and took the blanket away from her face. Her eyelids flickered for a moment. He felt a burst of relief. It took just an hour to reach the hotel where Paula was rubbed down and turned into bed.

Jeremy woke the next morning to find the sun slanting through the window highlighting a picture on the wall. Through the lace curtain he could see the buildings on the other side of the street and the unpaved road. It was deserted except for a horse tethered to a hitching post. It must be mid-morning, he thought. He remembered Paula. He had an urge to go to her and then reconsidered, perhaps she should not be disturbed. But his feelings were too strong and he threw back the covers. She was in the room at the end of the corridor, lying on her back staring at the ceiling. A feeling he had not known for a long time welled up inside. He knew he still loved her. He knelt beside her bed and took her hand. 'I am sorry,' he said.

She turned her head to look at him. 'You are sorry,' she asked, 'and why?'

'For not understanding.'

'It is I who should be sorry.'

'I realize now, more than ever, how you have suffered,' he said. 'We must settle down and make a home together.'

She did not know what to say. She felt inadequate as she stumbled over her thoughts. He had said that they could have children and that he realized how she had suffered. 'I will try, I will try so hard,' she said.

6

Auckland
29 October 1858

A LIGHT WIND came from the direction of the mountain and a gentle swell rose and fell with a quiet regularity when Jeremy and his entourage returned to the beach to take a ship to Auckland. Black-backed gulls wheeled overhead. They waited while two bullocks were lashed to the small boat and slung aboard. Matt helped the women to climb up the ladder to the deck, and with a loud blast of the whistle the ship began steaming northward, punching her way to Auckland.

The ball was up at the signal station when they reached the Heads next morning and after the pilot was taken on board they moved carefully through the narrow channels to anchor in shallow water off the beach.

Jeremy found two shillings and sixpence for each of them to be taken ashore. Emily giggled as she was lifted onto a man's back, who waded through the shallow water to dump her on the sand. They were soon bowling along to Auckland town in a coach drawn by five, well conditioned horses.

Trees lined the fields, which were lush with English grasses, and climbing roses tangled with the hawthorn that stretched along the road.

Paula admired the gorse hedges. 'The fields are like those at home,' she told Jeremy.

They found a cottage to their liking on a road that ran down to the sea. It had stables at the back bordering a gully and from the verandah they could see the harbour and the islands in the distance.

Caroline and Wyndham were their first callers and Paula lost no time in returning the visit. Jeremy was at his desk when Paula called out, 'I am going to Caroline's for the afternoon.' She was wearing a new plaid shirt and a hat she had bought in London on one of her shopping sprees in Regent Street.

He thought, I have not seen her so relaxed for a long time. 'I shall see you at supper,' he said.

Caroline put Paula in the sitting room while she fussed over the teacups. 'What have you been doing?' she asked.

'Nothing exciting.' said Paula, 'We went to a concert at the Mechanics Institute. And there was a Wednesday meeting at St Matthews.'

'How are you settling in?'

'So, so. It was rather a come down for the first few days. There was no sensation at all. We have had a few introductions but they have meant nothing. People look at us as though we have two heads.'

'I can believe that,' said Caroline. 'Newcomers are immediately recognized in a town of only fifteen thousand people and are under scrutiny everywhere they go, an ordeal worse than being a member of parliament, but everyone is soon sorted out. Rank or family connections are nothing here unless supported by ability.' Caroline leant forward as she poured the tea. 'The main drawback is the difficulty of finding and keeping servants. If you do find one she will not remain single for long even if she swears to perpetual celibacy, which oath of course she will never keep. So there is a constant procession of young girls who call themselves housekeepers.'

Paula nodded, 'Emily does exasperate me at times but I suppose I should count my blessings. Sometimes I feel desperate and want to go straight back home on the first ship.'

'You are not alone,' Caroline sighed. 'Thank heaven I do not feel like that. We have nothing left back there. How is Jeremy?'

'Well enough.' Paula's voice had an air of resignation. 'I find it hard to do what people call my duty.'

'I know. I know.' Caroline patted Paula's hand. 'Has Jeremy made up his mind as to what he will do?'

'He has already bought a newspaper. His great uncle has one in Leicester but Jeremy has also leased a warehouse and put in tenders to supply the 'military'. It is quite bizarre really.'

'Then he is definitely going into trade?'

'Yes, isn't it disgusting? I shall not be able to lift my head at church.'

'I would not worry. Snobs are not abundant in the colony, practically every man and woman has to do something. More tea?'

'No thank you. I must be going.'

Jeremy was not at their cottage when Paula returned. He had gone to the boatbuilders at the bottom of the rise to look at the cutter which was to take him up the inlets and to the settlements dotted along the coast. Jeremy's boat was thirty feet long, fully decked and copper fastened with a sharp stern and a sheer fore and aft to make beaching easier. It was planked in the native kauri timber. He walked around the pit where men were sawing the logs that had been floated down from the hills in the west. Although he had been operating for only a month, business was good. Reluctantly he had bowed to Paula's wishes and put Wyndham in charge of the warehouse, and Matt had already made a journey south to buy up grain from the Waikato tribes.

Whaling ships called regularly to replenish their stores and to trade. The Americans brought churns from Boston, clocks from New York and tubs from Pennsylvania. Captain Clark, skipper of the 'Two Brothers', was one of Jeremy's customers.

Fashion decreed whalebone stays for the ladies, and oil was needed for the lamps. In one year, to satisfy demand, fourteen thousand right whales had been slaughtered in New Zealand waters. The mature right whale was fifty to sixty feet long with the head a quarter of a length of the body, its baleen plates suitable for ladies stays were finer and longer than any other. They mated in the spring and the calf was born nine or ten months later. 'They are almost human,' Captain Clark had told Jeremy. 'A whale calf plays with its mother like any child, pushing at her flukes and wriggling on her back. The mother suckles her young for at least a year and perhaps two.'

Three canoes were lying above the high water mark and the tide was creeping back over the sand when Jeremy started back to his cottage that sat on the hill near the public domain. A pohutukawa tree clung to the side of a cliff, its roots twisting down to the sea. Drifts of spent blossom stained the crevices a dark crimson, as though shedding the blood of the man-god whose birthday they had celebrated a few days before. Jeremy was about to step on to a plank across a muddy stream when he saw a woman approaching. Her head was bent as she picked her way through the pools of water. Something stirred in his mind. 'Good morning,' he said. He recognized the blue eyes. The fair hair.

'Mr St Clair, I do believe.' Rosalind Earle put down the bag she was carrying.

'Indeed. And you have settled here, madam?'

'Yes. Up on Constitution Hill. I have opened a school for Maori children.'

'So that is *your* school. Not only do you teach English and English manners but you have a choir as well. A very good one?'

'You seem well informed.'

He waited for her to say something more. Polite conversation. Anything.

'As you have already proved,' she said, ' nothing escapes one here. I have heard that you have commenced trading and bought one of the newspapers that have been struggling to survive. You must show me your list of goods. Well, we are sure to meet again. Good afternoon.'

He watched her as she walked along the shore. He knew there were a few schools for Maori children in the colony. The chiefs were eager to have their sons and daughters educated and taught to read and write, and half-castes also found a home there free from discrimination. Rosalind had started the school using an allowance she received from her people in Britain. That night Jeremy mentioned the meeting to Matt.

'Yes,' said Matt, 'her husband died a month ago.'

'Died!' said Jeremy. 'What happened?

'He and another were on the wharf. Somehow he fell on to the

52

deck of a schooner. Hit his head. Never recovered consciousness.

'She did not tell me,' said Jeremy.

'No,' said Matt, 'she would not be one to talk about it.'

7

JEREMY had finished writing up the weekly accounts when Paula walked into the study. She waited until he had put down his pen. 'Jeremy,' she said, 'I think I am with child.' She saw the delight in his eyes.

'Really?' he asked.

'Well, it is not the sort of thing one makes up.'

'Are you all right? We will need a nurse and a carriage for you.'

'Don't be ridiculous. Emily and I will manage quite well.'

'You must see Doctor Moore.'

'To make sure it is not dropsy? Be sensible, Jeremy.'

'You shall see Dr Moore and at once.'

The doctor called at eleven o'clock. Paula felt his hands under the bedclothes feeling for the baby, pressing on her abdomen and inspecting the raised umbilicus. 'I prefer to use my hands,' he explained. 'A stethoscope is all right for the lower classes — they are impressed by the appearance of additional attention, but really it is so much quackery and unnecessary. Everything is fine. Now you should endeavour to stay indoors in a quiet cool room to keep your sensibilities calm. We do not want the baby to be imprinted with harsh passions or disfigurements do we? Live tranquilly and take enough nourishment to gratify the appetite without loading the stomach. You can eat boiled beef, mutton or veal but no spices

54

or coarse vegetables, have fish but no sauce. Excessive use of wines, spirits, tea, coffee and chocolate is forbidden. You understand? I will examine you again at the seventh month. There is nothing to worry about. Do you want me to attend to you at the birth?'

Paula nodded.

'Of course,' said the doctor, 'you could have a woman if you wish, but I am an accoucheur and personally am against meddlesome midwifery.' The doctor bowed his way out the door.

Jeremy stood on the verandah thinking of their child. Parson birds with tufts of white at their throats hung upside down on the flax bushes, their long beaks thrust into the flowers. There was a regatta being sailed on the harbour. The watermen were rowing people from bay to bay as the great war canoes of the Maori, the Waka Taua matched each other in a race. These were the same canoes that a few years before had carried the warriors on raids along the coast. The Ngatiwhatua and the Paoa tribes situated between the Ngapuhi and the Waikato encouraged the white man to settle on the isthmus. Spring was the time of war when the Ngapuhi in the north invaded the Waikato and coming and going attacked the Ngatiwhatua and the Paoa tribes. When the Waikato went north they would also make a pass at the Ngatiwhatua and Paoa. So when the white man came, the isthmus was sparsely populated by Maori. Because of this the remaining inhabitants had been happy to sell land to the Europeans to gain their protection and to trade.

Jeremy weighed up the pros and cons of buying some property. Sections in town were expensive, while further out the Maori were reluctant to sell and it was difficult to obtain consent from all members of the tribe. In the Bay of Islands in 1845, where trade was carried on between the American whalers and the Maori and where sweet potatoes and fish were exchanged for blankets and guns, Governor Grey had called a meeting on the beach at Kororareka. He assured Maori that he had been sent by Her Majesty the Queen, not to set aside the Treaty of Waitangi that had been signed five years before this meeting, but to uphold it. He pledged that no portions of their lands would be taken from them, nor alienated in any way without their consent. They were at liberty to sell or withhold from sale any portion or the whole of it at their discretion, but, he had said, he would have them clearly understand that having once sold it was gone forever. Thirteen years had passed since that day.

Jeremy took a last look at the harbour and went inside to Paula. 'I have decided that Wyndham shall fully manage the warehouse and I will spend more time on the newspaper,' he said. 'I need more advertisements.'

Paula looked at him with a mixture of amusement and resignation. 'You have taken on more than you can handle.'

'No. I enjoy the challenge and the reporting . . . . Where is Emily?'

'In town. Probably at the Thistle Tavern.'

'The Thistle?'

'She has an admirer, a soldier in the 66th Regiment. She has also been making advances to Matt but not getting very far.'

'How is Jos taking it?'

'Badly.' Paula looked up from the cotton square she was edging. 'He simply mopes about on his own. He is in the stables.'

'Then he can come with me to Partington's.'

The mill stood on the ridge above the town. They loaded up bags of flour and bran and delivered them to the military. After leaving the barracks Jeremy drove the cart up to Rosalind's school. Rata, a half-caste girl brought refreshments to them in the parlour. She was the daughter of a princess from the land of the Waikato, the wild country to the south. Her hair reached down to her waist, her eyes were liquid brown and she was as supple as the lancewood. She was sixteen years of age and yet had a calm sense of authority that had been passed down through generations. She could recite her genealogy from the venerated chief who brought the tribe to the land of Aotearoa, the land of the long white cloud. She had learnt to sew and to cook European fashion, but preferred to weave mats and to sing the chants she had learnt at her grandmother's house.

'How long has Rata been with you?' Jeremy asked Rosalind.

'Almost a year,' she said.

'The children seem very happy.'

Rosalind smiled. 'I am glad you think so, some parents are suspicious of me. They are afraid that the boys will form liaisons with girls from other tribes who are considered inferior or deadly enemies.'

'What do you do about that?'

56

'I ignore it, but the Maori is proud of his culture as we are of ours, probably more so. In the Waikato they have built their own schools and have set up their own king. We have let them down, Jeremy. We promised to govern them in exchange for signing a treaty, to bring us together as one nation and perhaps they would stop fighting each other.'

'And is that not what has happened? In Australia and in America we declared the land to be ours, at least in New Zealand we declared the land not to be ours. When we buy it we give them the price they ask.'

Rosalind's eyes flashed. 'A few iron pots, a blanket, a plug of tobacco.'

'Those days have gone, Rosalind. If everyone thought as you do it means a contract could be re-negotiated every few years. Where would the commercial world be then?'

'We are not talking about the commercial world.'

Jeremy stood up. 'The Maori is intelligent, articulate and clever, but previously they did not know the value of their land compared with ours in England. They do now. That is why the Waikato are refusing to sell. That is why we have conflict in Taranaki. I agree that they have every right not to sell if they do not want to, but when they have sold the land, that is that. A contract is a contract, a person's word is his word, right or wrong.'

'At least we agree on their intelligence. I think I may be able to convert you.'

Jeremy smiled. 'I am willing to be converted. You are the paragon of all missionaries. I understand what you say in theory but it is the practicability of it all that is the problem.'

'And what does that mean?'

'We have only mouthed the words. We have said we will govern, that the law applies equally to Maori and European, and perhaps we do govern in the towns. But inland there is nothing to enforce it. The home government is reluctant to spend the money to appoint enough magistrates. It takes longer than six months to get a decision from England and that is why Governor Browne seems ineffectual. He spends his time writing despatches to England.'

'Then we agree in principle,' said Rosalind.

'Yes. Don't let us argue any more.'

'Where is Jos?'

They found him sitting on the steps with Rata. The afternoon sun was shining through the glass panels of the door making patches of colour on the porch. The tree ferns below were in the shadow of the hill and there was a certain sharpness in the evening air. Rata was plaiting a headband of flax and was teaching Jos the Maori language as she worked. She handed the headband to Jos. 'It is my gift to you,' she said.

Jeremy heard some of the children squabbling inside. A coach and four horses pulled up at the gate. The drag was tooled with embossed leather trappings and the horses well groomed and perfectly matched. Jeremy was admiring the plated lamps and the well preserved hickory shafts when an officer jumped out of the driver's seat and ran up to the steps. Rosalind ran to the doorway, somewhat flustered.

'Oh, Mr St Clair,' she said in a formal voice that Jeremy had not heard before. 'May I present Captain Newhaven, perhaps you have met.'

'No,' said Jeremy, 'I have not had the pleasure.'

'St Clair!' Newhaven's voice was pitched a trifle high and smacked of superiority. 'We have met, you know.'

'You have the better of me,' said Jeremy.

'The Crimea, I was an aide at headquarters.'

Jeremy frowned. 'Forgive me, that seems a long time ago.'

'Nine years or so. I am surprised to see you here. Of course, you sold your commission. Not surprising. It was pretty rugged.'

Jeremy coloured. 'I was wounded,' he said. 'I was offered a commissariat post but turned it down. It was too much like one of your soft headquarters sinecures.'

It was Newhaven's turn to bristle. 'Gad sir, what are you suggesting?'

Rosalind stepped quickly forward. 'Perhaps you would like some refreshment?' she said.

The two men stood off each other. 'If you would excuse me,' said Jeremy, 'I will call back later.' He nodded briefly and left the house.

When Jeremy returned Rosalind was alone in the kitchen. 'Your friend has gone?' he asked.

'Yes,' she said. There was a hint of steel in her voice. 'Perhaps you would come into the parlour. You men are worse than children.'

'Oh?' said Jeremy.

'Why can't you be civil to each other?'

'I have no quarrel with the man. It was he who let off the first shot.'

'He is the cousin of the Earl of Newhaven.'

'So? A second son of a second son. It is of supreme indifference to me what he is.'

'Jeremy, he was my guest. I would ask you to be civil to him, at least in my presence.'

Jeremy gave a mock bow. 'My apologies, but he is such an arrogant snob.'

'That is enough.' Rosalind walked to the door and opened it. 'I think you should go.'

He reached the path and turned around. 'My apologies again, Rosalind. I am afraid the man riles me.'

She flounced inside and slammed the door, Jeremy hummed a tune quietly to himself as he walked down the hill. So, he thought, interesting.

The recital by the 65th Regimental band to be held in the domain had been well advertised. Jeremy saw Newhaven standing by the rotunda and pointed him out to Paula. The entire military seemed to be there with the ladies dressed in their Sunday best, sporting parasols as they paraded along the shell paths. It was a clear summer's day with the sun warming the northern slopes that looked out to a sparkling sea. The band struck up a tune. Jeremy saw Paula's foot tapping in time to the music. For weeks she had been unwilling to face people, had not been to church and appeared to be unhappy and lifeless. He was surprised to see her enjoying herself at last. They listened to the band and watched the children playing among the trees until the sun dipped behind a hill. 'It is time we left,' said Jeremy.

Paula seemed reluctant to go home. She rose slowly and stood upright. Some acquaintances nodded and smiled at her. Newhaven appeared from behind a group of people and came towards them. He stopped, eyed Paula and bowed low in front of her. Jeremy made the introduction.

'Charmed,' said Newhaven.

'You must excuse me, we are about to leave,' said Jeremy.

'A pity,' said Newhaven, 'I wanted a word with you.'

'Oh,' said Jeremy.

'I believe you have the fastest cutter on the harbour or that is what I have been told.' Newhaven slapped his riding crop against his thigh. 'Thought you might be interested in a match. I have had a new boat built and would like to see how she measures up.'

'I really have not the time,' said Jeremy.

'Come on St Clair, have a go. You are not selling out again are you?'

Paula did not sense Jeremy's hostility. She saw this rather distinguished captain in a different way. 'Why don't you race, Jeremy?' she said.

Newhaven carefully altered the expression on his face for Paula's benefit. 'There you are, even your wife is for it,' he said.

Jeremy looked out at the water in the distance, glanced up and took Paula by the arm. 'Very well,' he said 'let me know the terms.'

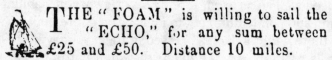

CHALLENGE!

THE " FOAM " is willing to sail the " ECHO," for any sum between £25 and £50.   Distance 10 miles.

N. B. The Challenge can be answered by another advertisement.   Money posted at A J. NICHOLAS, Victoria Hotel.

The advertisement was in Friday's edition of the opposition newspaper, and two days later they were racing. Sunday dawned fine and clear and there was little wind when Matt and Jeremy went down to the *Echo*. Matt baled a few cupfuls of rain water out of the bilge and wiped down the topsides while Jeremy rigged the *Echo* with a new set of sails. They left the anchor at the boatyard and pushed off early from the beach to the start. The wind had changed to a sou'wester blowing at a modest five knots. Jeremy eased the sheets and looked out for Newhaven.

The warning gun fired as Jeremy placed his watch on the stern locker. The tide had turned and was running strongly as Newhaven's boat came around from behind the jetty. Jeremy manoeuvred his cutter closer inshore as Newhaven tacked backwards and forwards in midstream.

'He does not know the harbour,' called Matt as he crouched up forward.

With thirty seconds before the start Jeremy threw the tiller hard over. Matt secured the jib sheets and looked across at Newhaven. The starting gun fired as they crossed the line together.

With the sound of the gun Jeremy's attitude changed. The easy, nonchalant facade disappeared and he became a machine, competitive, finely tuned and at one with the elements to marry the boat to the sea and the wind. He hugged the inside shore away from the tide as Newhaven set a more direct course to the buoy under the signal station. Jeremy looked up at the clouds. They were moving slowly from the west and the pennants on the side stays were motionless.

'He will get into trouble in the middle,' called Jeremy.

Matt who was stretched out on the deck raised his hand to signal his agreement. Twenty minutes later, Newhaven's boat the 'Echo' was level with them, but well out in the centre of the harbour. 'He is slowing down,' said Jeremy. The incoming tide was in full flood and Newhaven was almost stationery, battling against it.

'We have got him on this one,' said Jeremy.

They rounded the buoy well clear of Newhaven and although the wind had dropped again the 'Echo' took advantage of the tide against her keel and headed across the harbour. On the next leg 'Foam' gained on 'Echo', but she was still two minutes behind. Jeremy watched as a puff of wind ruffled across the surface. It caught the 'Echo', lifted her along for fifty yards and put her down again. A steady breeze came in and it was all over. The 'Foam', caught short of the mark, was forced to put about. As the 'Echo' crossed the finishing line Jeremy acknowledged the gun with a wave of his hand and went about to return to his moorings. They met 'Foam' on her way to the finish.

Newhaven was standing at the tiller. 'You were lucky, St Clair, you had the wind change,' he said. 'We will get you next time.'

Matt looked up as he coiled up a rope. 'Like hell he will,' he said.

In July Dr Moore visited Paula again. He gave her an opiate and rubbed her lower body with a fomentation of linseed oil to soften the surrounding areas. 'Could I have some lard?' he asked and, after dipping his hand into the jar that Caroline brought from the kitchen, he worked under the covers. The doctor felt for the enlargement of the uterus and for the weight of the head of the foetus as Paula lay on the red leather underlay that the doctor had brought. He grunted his approval. 'I can see no problems,' he said as Jeremy came into the bedroom. The doctor went over to the basin and washed his hands. 'I presume you will want a monthly nurse. I can recommend one. She is quite strong and free of encumbrances. I would say she is about thirty-five years old and not addicted to snuff or spirituous liquors, so she is ideal. She could assist me at the confinement and stay on to help with the baby.'

'I shall leave that to your judgement,' said Jeremy.

'Excellent. I would prefer to use chloroform if you have no objections. It is quite safe I assure you. I was a student with James Simpson in Edinburgh who discovered its wonderful effects in child-birth. In fact, he tried it one night for the first time at his home and inhaled the stuff before sitting down to supper. He was under the mahogany in a trice; his poor wife was frantic. The Queen has used it for confinements.'

'You will have to ask my wife,' said Jeremy. 'I think she may wish to be conscious at the birth.'

'Very well. If the pain is unusually bad I can always use cannibus indicus.'

Spring came early that year, then withdrew for a week or two as a cold wind blustered up from the Antarctic. Paula felt unsettled. She missed the nakedness of the trees and there was no real sense of seasons. The previous summer had seemed to struggle into autumn, then there were storms and a lashing of wind for a time, but the cold and the sleet she had known back home at Manor Farm did not touch this town by the sea. The baby was not far away and each Sunday, at church, she prayed for her child.

8

JEREMY was asleep when Paula woke him early in the morning. 'Send for Dr Moore,' she whispered.

The doctor arrived at seven o'clock. Paula was in slow labour and the pains were slight. He examined her, satisfied that the birth was not immediately imminent. 'I will come back later,' he said. 'Call me when the pains become more frequent. I will be at home, just up the road.'

As the doctor left the house Caroline arrived. She guessed that Paula was soon to have her child. 'Please God,' she whispered, 'let there be happiness in this house tonight and not sorrow.' Bustling into the bedroom she put on a brave face for Paula's sake. 'Good morning,' she said, 'you are causing a great deal of excitement today.' Paula tensed herself as the pain pierced her again.

Caroline took her hand. 'Are you taking chloroform?'

'No.'

'Why not? It was good enough for the Queen.'

'I want to be awake when my baby arrives,' said Paula. 'Besides, Dr Robert Lee says it is a sound principle of physiology and morality not to use it.'

'Poppycock.'

Paula smiled weakly. 'Dear Caroline,' she said, 'you are a trea-

63

sure.'

Dr Moore returned at three o'clock. After examining Paula he went into the parlour, where Jeremy was attempting to read a book.

'Tell me, Doctor,' said Jeremy, 'what do you think of anaesthesia?'

'I recommend it, but it is up to the individual. It stops the benign and salutary effect of pain on the emotions, although it also excites sexual passion. A friend of mine, Dr Tanner, recorded that it produced lascivious dreams when he operated on a prostitute.'

'Dreams, for whom? For the prostitute or the doctor?' asked Jeremy.

Moore looked down his nose. 'Women sometimes use obscene language under chloroform. It can be very distracting. As your wife does not want anaesthetic I will only use it as a last resort.'

The new nurse arrived and was shown to her room. There was a knock on the door and Caroline appeared. 'Doctor, I think you should come.' The pains had begun to assume a different pattern. Paula gripped the rails of the bed as the agony wound through her body. Caroline stroked her forehead. 'There, there dear,' she murmured.

The doctor re-examined Paula, moving his hands gently under the covers, exploring, pressing. He turned and nodded his satisfaction. An hour later Paula was needing help at more frequent intervals and the pain had increased. Jeremy paced up and down outside. Paula was suffering more pain in those few hours than he had endured in a lifetime. In sorrow shalt thou bring forth children, he thought. What a woman goes through for the sake of others. What fortitude! What a struggle for the beginnings of life! Jeremy motioned Emily away when she came with tea.

The hours went by. Then Jeremy heard Paula cry out. It seemed she had used up all her strength. A faint chirp and then a longer cry came from the bedroom. He knew at once that the baby had been born. A child's cry came through the wall again. He wanted to rush in and see his baby and to comfort Paula.

Dr Moore came out of the room and shut the door quietly behind him. 'Can we go into the sitting room?' he asked. The man's eyes were hiding something. 'Are you ready for a shock?' he said. Somewhere Jeremy heard a clock strike seven.

'You and your wife have been blessed with twins.'

Jeremy closed his eyes and sank back into the chair, hearing the doctor's words as though from a long way off. A distilled, quiet voice speaking in a low monotone. 'They are both very well, you have two sons.'

When Jeremy returned to Paula she was lying exhausted and half asleep, a crumpled heap in the middle of the bed. The nurse was enlarging a cap of fine cotton fabric which she placed on a baby's head. He knelt beside Paula and took her hand. 'They are beautiful,' he said.

'Say a prayer for them,' she whispered. Her voice was tired and weak. Turning her head on the pillow she looked a full minute at her babies and fell asleep.

When Paula awoke the monthly nurse was at the window drawing the curtains together. 'You are awake, Ma'am,' said the nurse. 'We will keep things rather dark for the first ten days. We must not expose your babies to strong light or too much air.' She bustled over to the bed. 'Now, until you can find some natural nourishment I am going to give them a tablespoon of fresh cow's milk mixed with two tablespoons of hot water and some loaf sugar. It will be very nourishing.'

Paula turned and faced the window. 'What time is it?'

'It is evening and you have had a good sleep. Your babies are well.'

Paula tried to recollect the events of the previous day, broken pictures of pain and relief, faces and voices and the first cries of her babies. 'Can I see them?' she asked.

'You will see them soon enough. Here is a tray with beef tea.'

Paula pulled herself up and rested her shoulders on the bolster at the head of the bed as the nurse re-arranged the pillows.

'Oh dear,' she said aloud, 'we will need another cradle.'

'You will need two of most things, but don't worry, we will see to that. Mr St Clair has arranged to borrow a bercaunette for the other babe. You must get your rest, remember you are the invalid mother.'

'Please nurse, let me see them. Do they look alike?'

The nurse paused. 'They are as different as chalk from cheese. When you have finished I will bring them in, just this once. It is extremely improper, remember. Infants cannot sleep too long.' She returned with the babies one by one and placed one on each side of Paula. 'There, keep them well covered. I'll take this pan to Emily.'

When the nurse had gone Paula turned her head to the baby on her left. She saw a well defined chin and two eyes looking at her. He's the image of Jeremy, she thought. Lifting the cap she brushed the tip of his head with her hand. She replaced the cap and sighed. There was a cry and a faint snuffle at her back. Turning quickly she saw a puckered face grimacing at her; dark furrowed eyebrows and long black hair poking out from under the cap. 'Gerald,' she whispered, 'you are Gerald.' She undid the cap revealing a mop of thin black hair. Untying the satin bows that fastened the woollen jacket she took it off revealing a full length cashmere gown that unfastened at the back. Soon the baby was lying naked on the sheet. 'I will call you Gerald,' she said.

As Paula replaced the clothes, the nurse came in the door. 'You must not uncover the child like that and never, never take off the headpiece,' she said. 'We must protect the eyes and ears from all currents of air. I will not be able to cope unless you follow my instructions. Properly speaking, there should be two nurses, one for the mother and one for the child.'

Paula's temper came to the surface. 'Emily will be able to help you,' she said.

The nurse looked down her nose and frowned. 'I shall leave the emptying of pans to the housemaid. I think we should understand what my duties are from the beginning.'

Paula held back the words she felt coming and sank back into the bed. She did not feel strong enough to argue. The nurse picked up the second baby and placed him in his make-shift cot alongside the cradle. There was a noise in the hallway and Jeremy came bounding up the stairs with a bundle of flowers in his hand.

'How is the patient this morning?' he boomed.

'Very naughty', said the nurse.

Jeremy raised his eyebrows and went over to the bed. 'Flowers,' he announced. 'Two bunches for two babies.'

The nurse took them from Jeremy. 'I am sorry, we cannot have them in here. They are pernicious and use up the night air. The rule is that all flowers and shrubs should be excluded from the bedchamber.'

Jeremy pulled a face and sat on the bed. When the nurse left he gave Paula a kiss on the forehead. 'The dragon has gone to its lair. Is she always like this?'

'So far, I'm afraid. She is a real stickler for the rules.'

'How do you feel?'

'Peculiar. Strong and yet weak. I just want to lie here.'

Jeremy grunted. 'Not surprising after what you have been through.'

Jeremy went to the window and pulled the curtains wide open. 'I want to have a good look at the twins,' he said.

'She will attack you.'

'Who?'

'The dragon.'

'Poppycock.' Jeremy took a child out of the cot and held it at arms length.

'Be careful,' said Paula, 'What do you think of them?'

Jeremy glanced down at the babies. 'They look like lumps of red meat.'

'Jeremy!' Paula pretended to be shocked. 'Whom do you think they are like?'

'This one looks a bit like the publican at the White Heart. Red faced, slightly sozzled.'

'Jeremy, be sensible. Have you thought of any names?'

'How about Castor and Pollux?'

'Look again. One of them is fair like you. Seriously.'

'Darling, you can choose whatever names you like. As long as the children are healthy I do not mind. I leave it to your good taste.'

'No. We will share it. I would like the dark one to be Gerald.'

Jeremy stiffened. 'Whatever you say, my dear.'

'Would you like the other to be named after your father?'

'Not really.' Jeremy paused. 'How about Jonathon?'

'Why Jonathon?'

"After Jon. Wilson. I'll never forget that day at the Alma.'

Paula cocked her head to one side. 'Gerald and Jonathon St Clair. That sounds elegant. We should have them christened as soon as possible. So many are lost in the first week. We will need godmothers and godfathers. How about Caroline and Wyndham?'

'We don't know anyone else, really.'

'Wyndham?'

'Be fair, Jeremy, you must admit he is not drinking as he used to.'

'Just as well. I am not happy about him.' Jeremy went over to the mirror and straightened his tie.

'It is settled then. Please fetch the nurse. You must have some supper.'

When Jeremy arrived at the warehouse the next morning, Jos was taking down the shutters. Wyndham who had walked over the hill from the west side of town was coming up the lane.

'Congratulations,' he called. Jeremy waited for him at the door. Wyndham was smiling. 'You will have to wet the babies' heads.'

'Tonight,' said Jeremy.

Jeremy's business had grown. In addition to the buying of grain and grass seed and other produce he had opened a section in his warehouse for the ironmongery and hardware and other equipment required by the settlers for taming the wild country that extended beyond the town. His connection with the whalers enabled him to bargain for items they brought from America. It was a wide assortment of goods. Butter churns, portable stoves, knife cleaners, clocks and even brass eyelets used for caps on the guns that the Maori and the settlers owned.

As well as the settlers, the Maori were enthusiastic buyers of implements and seed. They had been taught by the missionaries to cultivate and to sow in the English manner and had planted wheat crops in the middle of the Waikato district. Jeremy often rode down to the big river where Mr Selby had his hotel. From there he crossed the river by canoe to barter with the natives, who were becoming prosperous. He sometimes took an interpreter with him, a sub-chief of the Ngati-Tuwharatoa tribe whose lands edged the great Lake Taupo, in the south. Tukino came from the village of Pukawa and was acceptable to all native tribes. He was an intelligent, amiable companion and a useful addition to Jeremy's team, helping in the warehouse and acting as go-between with Maori customers.

At the end of the day, after Matt had closed the door and Jos had come back with the delivery cart, Tukino arrived at the warehouse. Jeremy took a stone jar of rum from the cupboard and put out pewter pots and measures. They sat around the office as Tukino talked.

'Have we not a better right to the true value of the land than the white people? Look what you gave us. A few blankets, half a dozen axes and some guns. Then you cut up the land and sold it for big money. That is why we chose a Maori King of our own. To make our own laws. And why should we not have one? Is not the Queen, the Tzar, Bonaparte and Pomare each for their own people? Then why not us? You have bought our land at sixpence three farthings an acre and are selling it for ten shillings to your own.'

'Tukino is right,' said Jeremy. 'Why can't we have a peaceful union of races and fair values for both of us.

'They will never be the equal to us.' Wyndham thumped his pot on the table.

Tukino ignored him. 'You know our King now. I was at my village at Pukawa two years ago when all the chiefs assembled and gave their word to Potatau te Wherewhero who was chosen to be King. I saw that tall flagstaff and the flag flown from it, with the same pattern as the one that King William of England gave to the northern tribes years before they signed the treaty. There were long ropes of plaited flax attached to the mast below the flag. The flagstaff stood for our sacred mountain, Tongariro. The ropes joined us all together. Te Heu Heu touched each in turn and spoke to the great chiefs sitting at the foot of the mast.'

'This is Ngongataha,' he said, 'The mountain near Rotorua lake. Where is the chief of Ngongataha? Who shall attach this mountain to Tongariro? The great chief of the Arawa tribe rose from his place and took the end of the rope and fastened it to a wooden peg, which he drove into the ground in front of his people. Next was the mountain you call Edgecombe, the sacred mountain of the Ngatiawa of the Bay of Plenty. Then came Tawhuau, the mountain in the wild Urewera country. Each tribe had its own rope representing the mountain dear to it. Hikurangi for the Ngatiporou, Maungapotutu, Tit-o-kura, Kapiti Island and Otauri for each of the others. The mountains of the middle island were there. Tapuae-Nuku, Kaikoura and the greatest of them all, Aorangi. They were for the Ngai-Tahu, and the chief Taiaroa drove those pegs. So each rope held a mountain. And in the middle stood the mighty Tongariro, supported by all the tribal cords which joined the soil of New Zealand to our King. The new flag floated above for all to see that Potatau te Wherowhero was our King.'

'And Governor Browne does not recognize him.' Wyndham glared at Tukino who sat with a composed expression on his face.

Jeremy left the men arguing. His horse was hitched to a rail at the back of the premises, and, taking off the nosebag, he mounted the bay gelding and took the road to Rosalind's school. Tying the reins to a trellis he opened the gate. A rose, released by the movement, nodded its head and was still. The entire fence was covered in trails of wisteria, pale blue racemes of colour contrasting with the green of the leaves, and an old perpetual rose, interlaced with vines, dabbed the fence here and there with its cabbage like blooms. As Jeremy went up the path he heard Rosalind in the music room playing the piano and singing softly to herself. The window was half open. Lifting up the brass catch he put his head inside. She looked up startled.

'Don't stop,' he said, 'That was delightful.'

'I am trying out a new song. Go around to the back. The children will let you in.'

Jeremy went up the steps two at a time. There were rows of shoes on shelves in the porch, high button-ups for the girls and lace-ups for the boys. Before he could knock Rata had opened the door, and he went into the kitchen. He walked through the hall door and along to the music room.

Rosalind turned and stopped playing. 'I believe you have twins,' she said.

'The word soon spreads.'

'Please sit down. And how are they?'

'Admirable.'

'And Mrs St Clair?'

'Splendid.'

'Good. I would like to call when I may. Please let me know when you are receiving.'

'I will.'

'How are you managing?'

'Reasonably well. The nurse is a necessity. I expect it will be different when she has left but I expect Emily will be able to look after them.'

'I saw Emily in town with a sergeant from the Commissariat,' said Rosalind.

'Another one? It was the 66th Foot last time.'

Rosalind stabbed a finger at the keyboard and played high 'c'.

'I think Matt is the one she would like to get hold of.'

'You are not serious.'

'Watch her next time they are together. She cannot keep her eyes off him.'

'I'm sure Matt is not interested,' said Jeremy.

'He likes them older.'

'Thank goodness for that.' Jeremy picked up a song book. 'What is this? "Vilikens and his daughter," "Reuben Wright and Phoebe Brown," "The Ratcatcher's Daughter".'

Rosalind jumped up and took the book from Jeremy. 'I know they are ineffably silly but I have been asked to help with a concert at the Mechanics Institute Hall.'

'It should be interesting,' Jeremy stood up. 'I have come to see if you need any supplies. We will be busy for the next few weeks. Everyone is sowing new pastures and there is a ship due in from England with a big consignment of seed.'

'You have not sent a bill for the last order yet.'

'It was only a small one. It is my contribution towards the children and the school.'

'Thank you but I have adequate resources of my own. I would rather pay.'

Jeremy coloured. 'If you insist. Do you need anything?'

'You will send the bill?'

'Yes.'

'Then we could do with the usual flour and sugar. The quality of your sugar is poor.'

'Loaf sugar is cleaner.'

'But too expensive.'

'Everything is rising in price, even rents. So many people arriving and nowhere to go, a desperate shortage of accommodation and wages skyrocketing, especially for bricklayers and the like.'

'I know. My casual gardener has left to better himself and I am at a loss to find someone else.'

'I will send Jos up. He can help.'

Rosalind frowned. 'You have just said you are going to be busy.'

'We will find time for that.

Jeremy left when Rata came to say that supper was ready. He dug his heels into the horse and cantered home. He strode into Paula's room and saw she had a baby at her breast. He moved towards the door.

'Jeremy,' Paula called, 'where are you going?'

'Nowhere.'

'Come back here.'

He walked slowly to the other side of the bed and looked down. 'I have not seen anyone feed a baby before.'

'Well, you are going to now, and often. The doctor came this morning and suggested a wet nurse, but he thinks he may have difficulty finding one that does not fill herself up on fried meats and cabbage and pickles. I do not want Gerald with colic all night, and so many nurses today drink gin. The doctor says it is the reason for the great number of criminals too. No thank you. I'll manage with cows milk and water if necessary. Your supper will be ready shortly. Emily has made a bed for you in the box room. You will be a little cramped for space but at least you won't be disturbed. Nurse will be here in a moment.'

'Then I'll go before she comes.' He found Emily in the kitchen basting a leg of lamb that was roasting above the fire.

'Ee,' she said, 'We could do with a bigger stove with all these newcomers in the house. I've had to put the meat on the spit.'

'I will help you,' said Jeremy.

'Thankee, sorr,' replied Emily. Her accent always became worse when she was flustered. She hurried over to a pot boiling on one of the rings.

Jeremy ladled the gravy from the dish onto the meat. 'I believe you have a new beau, Emily,' he said.

Emily blushed. 'Have I now?'

'From the Commissariat. What happened to your man from the 66th Foot?'

'Oh sir. You are teasing me. None of them are any good.'

'How about sailors?'

'They are the worst of the lot. Here today, gone tomorrow.'

'Go on Emily, you like them.'

'The man I like I cannot get, sir.'

'Who is that?'

'I cannot tell you, sir.'

Jeremy did not press the point. 'How are you managing with the new babies?'

'Well enough, sir. They are lovely. Can I be their nursemaid sir? Beg your pardon for being so forward.' Emily's eyes pleaded with Jeremy, 'I would be so good to them.'

Jeremy was touched by her sincerity and her intensity. 'We will see. It will depend on Mrs St Clair.'

With the arrival of the twins there had been a change of arrangements. Matt moved to a sleep-out in the stables, converting two of the stalls to a bedroom by knocking out a wall and partitioning the remainder. It suited his independent spirit and allowed him more freedom. Jos remained in his room at the back, off the kitchen, and Emily was upstairs in the attic bedroom, with a tiny window that looked out over the gully and the cemetery. She revelled in her new importance, walking the twins out in their carriage which had come from Sydney. In the evenings, before supper, she brought the babies into the parlour, where Jeremy and Paula rocked them in their cradles or held them for a short while. Jeremy still felt uncomfortable with them and handled them like pieces of delicate china. 'Half an hour with them is enough,' he confessed. 'When do they become intelligent beings?'

Everyone came to pay their respects to the new arrivals. Mr Jones the vicar, members of the St Matthews congregation and wives of the senior officers who lived further down the street. Rosalind visited early one morning and Caroline arrived with Wyndham sporting a new dogcart with cane sides and a smart two-year-old filly in the shafts.

'Have they come into a fortune?' Jeremy asked Paula when they had gone.

'She must have money from her family hidden away,' replied Paula.

Jeremy was not impressed. 'Wyndham tells me they have employed a maid.'

'Yes. I saw her in their carriage yesterday. I don't know where they found her, there is a real shortage of domestics.'

'And ploughmen and ditchers and spadesmen,' added Jeremy.

Paula busied herself folding some nursery squares. 'I cannot understand how people can live up to the hilt the way they do.'

'It is not uncommon in this town. The officers of the 66th are a good example, always in the gunshop, betting on drag races and boxing matches, dressing for balls, and yet everything is so expensive. Bread sevenpence a two-pound loaf and labourers on eight shillings a day. Talking of money, the monthly nurse finishes in two days. Have you definitely decided on Emily as nursemaid?'

'I suppose it is the best arrangement,' said Paula.

'Then for goodness sake let her know. She is up and down like the signals at Fort Britomart.'

The servant girl's eyes shone when Paula told her in the evening. She made three curtsies before running off to the nursery and Paula heard her telling the twins how she was going to look after them and they would go for lots of walks into town. The next day she took them to the domain, past the spring that supplied the households with water, and Emily saw an English blackbird. It was the first home bird she had seen except for a few pheasants in a cage.

The twins were christened with proper ceremony and Caroline and Wyndham were the Godparents. Emily's favourite walk with the baby carriage was into town where she spent her time looking in the windows of the shops that were spreading along the street as more ships arrived. The White Star line advertised regular sailings from London to Auckland for emigrants, with passages costing from sixteen pounds upwards, and so many had taken advantage of the offers that new arrivals without a trade were finding it hard to find work. For Paula and Jeremy there were receptions at Government House; Mr Varty was reading Mr Dicken's 'Christmas Carol' at the Auckland Mechanics Institute, and the Philharmonic Society held regular concerts in the hall.

Emily pushed the children up the hill and down the other side to the Greyhound Inn where she sat in her favourite seat inside the door. From there she could see the twins through the side window as she sipped a port wine and brandy. Her sergeant from the Commissariat usually came in at midday. He was in charge of the wagons that took supplies to the outposts to the south. A big man, much older than Emily, he had been in the colony for a number of years and had transferred from the 58th Regiment when they had left. He had fought in the Peninsular war and had come out with Headquarters Company. Emily felt important with a sergeant as a beau in tow, especially as he paid for her drinks. And there were often celebrations at the barracks, where she cut a graceful figure in her new crinoline dress dancing the 'Galopade'. At these events people tended to stick with their partners, in pairs, so she had him to herself instead of sharing as they did in so many of the other dances. Now and again there was a special celebration, with cricket matches on the barrack green and afterwards tables set up with beef and beer for the men. Only the parade ground was out of bounds, although the colonel's cows had free range there.

Ever since she had begun to look after the children Emily had felt unsettled. Whenever she saw Matt her heart jumped, and to avoid her embarrassment she took refuge in laughing at him and chiding him whenever she had the opportunity. He had become even more casual and devil-may-care and he had filled out with her cooking, but he still had that rolling gait of a sailor as he came across the yard for breakfast. Sometimes the babies were in the kitchen, and one day Matt picked one up and threw him into the air, catching him and laughing.

'Lawks,' said Emily, 'don't do that,' and she smacked Matt playfully as she took the child from him. As he put the baby in her arms it seemed to Emily that the whole world was spinning around. She held her breath. Her heart was beating so fast she was sure that Matt would hear it and she had to bend her head to let the blood come back to her brain. 'Get out of here,' she said.

Jos was easy to handle, and after a few months of moping he ignored her except for the normal passing of the time of day. He spent his spare time learning the Maori language from Rata. When he finished his work each Sunday he walked down the road and across the swamp to the beach at the bottom of the rise, past the Maori canoes dragged up at the foot of the hill. These dugouts came from the islands in the eastern part of the harbour and were laden with produce, sweet potatoes, corn, and peaches in season. One or two had the old original sails still set, triangular pieces of woven flax between poles. There were no carvings on these craft, but the great war canoes were still used to carry the tribes long distances. It was at this spot that, in 1851, Hori Ngahapu had landed with a fleet to protest against the wrongful arrest of chief Hoera.

The Ngati-Paoa with five large canoes and some smaller ones had swept into the harbour with three hundred men and, led by the great *'Maramarua'*, had come in on the high tide. Hori and his men had leapt ashore on the beach where Jos now stood. Performing a war dance they had demanded redress for the insult to their chief. Governor Grey had been warned and the 58th Regiment with four guns and a company of reserves of retired regulars had lined Constitution Hill and the Parnell Rise on the opposite side while Her Majesty's frigate, *'Fly'*, came down harbour and, dropping anchor off the bay, trained her guns on the fleet of canoes on the beach. Angrily the chiefs demanded satisfaction but the Governor refused to consider their request until they went away and made formal submissions to him. At last they obeyed the ultimatum, but the tide had receded on the mudflats and it was a long haul as they dragged the heavy canoes, foot by foot, back to the sea. For ever after this was known as the 'Long Hauling', 'Te Toangaroa'.

9

WHEN the children had learnt to walk, Jeremy took them down to the stream at the bottom of the gully where they searched for mountain trout and fished for small fresh-water crayfish. The creek was only three or four feet wide and had carved out a path deep into the yellow clay at the foot of the steep slopes. In the spring and in the winter it was a miniature torrent, but in summer it reduced to a trickle and stopped only to sulk in larger pools before disappearing into the swamp at the edge of the sea. The black-trunked tree ferns shaded the tracks that criss-crossed the whole area, their fronds blanketing the sky so that the sun and sound was shut completely out making a separate world, a green and brown tent made by nature for the children to play in.

Jeremy watched their characters develop as the days went by. Jonathon copied him in everything he did, although he was shy and tended to stand back. Gerald was aggressive and possessive, and Jeremy noticed that Paula appeared to favour the child who looked so much like her brother. When he challenged her, she was most indignant. All her old fire and determination returned. Clenching her fists and with eyes flashing she spat out the words, 'If your Jonathon is going to be like you, the complete gentleman, then that will be his concern. My Gerald happens to be a little quicker and sharper.'

Jeremy's jaw set firmly. 'I understand the twins are ours. Our Jonathon and our Gerald.'

Paula whirled around and picked up Gerald. 'Be that as it may, I am not going to let you take Gerald away from me.'

The realization that Paula was jealous of the children's regard for him came as a shock to Jeremy. He could not understand how she could feel that way. From the beginning he had treated the twins as comrades, patiently answering their questions and joining in their fantasies so that a bond had developed between them of which he was unaware until now. It was a sharing and caring that needed no explanation.

'I am not going to change my ways with the children,' he said in a quiet voice, 'I am going to treat them equally, and so should you.'

The war in the west of the northern island had ended over a year before, and although the tribes were still smarting from what they considered grave injustices there was an uneasy truce. Closer to home old Potatau had died and his son Tawhio had been elected King. He was still not recognized by Governor Gore Browne but that man had completed his stint and Governor Grey was expected on the *'Cossack'* any day from Capetown to take over the reins of government. As Jeremy walked past Fort Britomart he noticed a ship in the harbour and a crowd walking down the crescent towards the wharf. Jeremy crossed the road and stopped to allow the 65th Regiment to pass as it marched to the wharf to welcome Governor Grey. As the ship came alongside, a voice called from the shore, 'Is the Governor aboard?'

'He certainly is,' came the reply. A murmur rippled through the crowd.

The sun was shining brightly. Colonel Gore Browne was received with ringing cheers from the people as he stepped down from his carriage to welcome Sir George Grey. Business was suspended and shops were closed as more townsfolk walked down to the water and watched the band and the military parade that followed. When the crowd had dispersed Jeremy went back to the warehouse. His men were there, ready to close for the day.

'Well,' said Jeremy, 'I have seen the new Governor.'

'He is not exactly new,' replied Wyndham, 'When was he here before?'

'Forty-five to forty-nine', said Matt.

Wyndham reached for his hat. 'I hope he can clean up the mess that Browne has made. What does the new man look like?'

'Grey? Quite distinguished. At ease with everyone. He and Colonel Browne met very affably. When does Gore Browne go to Western Australia?'

'There is nothing official yet.'

'I hope he makes a better fist of it there than he has here.'

Jeremy poured Wyndham a nobbler of brandy. 'You must admit he had an almost impossible job to do. The trouble is that he is too honest and fair and presumes that everyone else is the same. He expected the regular army commanders in the war to be competent and they weren't, he relied on their judgement, and the settlers were harassing him. They were hungry for land while the missionaries had the ear of the colonial office at home. There were the politicians to cope with. He hated working with Mr Fox's lot, "snobs and men who would sacrifice the colony and themselves, if they could ruin me," I heard him say.'

'Do you think Grey will sort out this mess with the natives and get the land question settled?'

Jeremy thought for a moment. 'He was pretty successful last time. They respect him. He is quiet, very decisive, but not above asking for information before making up his mind. If anyone can do it he can.'

'I hope so. Certainly his performance in South Africa belies his appearance.' Wyndham took a sip of brandy, rolled it around his mouth and swallowed it. 'I think he has stacked up trouble there for future generations.'

'Why?'

'Transporting all those Kaffirs into the Cape Colony. I was there when General Cathcart destroyed the Kaffir power but after Grey arrived the natives were leaguing together to invade the colony at various points. Some old witch persuaded the chiefs to destroy their crops and cattle before starting so that they had either to take the land or starve. There were two hundred thousand of them. Grey very cleverly captured all the principal chiefs by out-manoeuvring them with secret marches and then waited for them to starve. There was death everywhere. Fifty thousand Kaffirs were dying before he went in with food. The villages stank with unburnt corpses. He brought thirty four thousand to the Cape and distributed them among the colonists as servants. For the remainder, after providing them with food and implements and seeds he settled them in British Kaffraria. That is how he solved that one.'

Jeremy looked thoughtful. 'We don't get better, morally, do we?'

Wyndham put down his pot and thrust his legs out. 'We can't deny our roots or human nature. I am from London. The Romans subjugated us nearly two thousand years ago then retreated back to Rome. Look at the Caribbean, China, India. We've won and lost America. Now it is the South Pacific. As long as there are nations, the stronger tribe will always be supreme and he who holds the purse strings holds government.'

'True,' said Jeremy, 'nothing changes. This century the spinning Jenny and the steam engine have taken the people's livelihood.' He waved a hand in the direction of the town. 'We have come here to make a new life. What contraptions will displace our great grandchildren in the years ahead?'

'Do you think the Maori will disappear?'

'Not in our time. Not the way the soldiers are inter-marrying.'

'Do you expect Grey to work a miracle?'

'No. But he will do his best.'

'Is there a Lady Grey?' asked Wyndham.

'Yes, somewhere. He was married to a Miss Stanley but on a trip to England from the Cape they quarrelled and have lived apart ever since.' Jeremy stood up and took the glasses to the bench. 'We should go home, I suppose.'

Back at the house Emily had already settled the twins in bed, so Jeremy had missed the children's hour in the parlour. They were no longer babies. Tired and crotchety, they were a little unwell. Emily was still keeping company with the sergeant, who was expecting a transfer any day, but her heart was elsewhere.

If only Matt cared for me a little instead of his beer, she kept thinking. It would be cosy in the stables. She tidied his room each morning, folded his clothes and made his bed, smoothing out the sheets and carefully tucking the corners in, but Matt did not seem to notice and took all things for granted. Every day she sat on the stool by the bed and breathed in the smell of the man's bedroom. Her heart cried for sympathy and genuine love, and for babies of her own.

It was February and very hot in the attic where Emily slept. She pushed at the covers and scuffed them down to the bottom of the bed as she lay in the dark staring at the ceiling. There was a full moon, its light slanting through the window, illuminating the room with a ghostly light. She rolled off the bed and stood up and yawned, scraping her hands on the low ceiling. Walking to the landing she was careful to avoid the gap in the floor that was the stairs and went to the other window overlooking the yard. The world seemed bathed in moonlight. Every article could be seen as though it was day. The foot scraper, the wooden pail, some harness hanging haphazardly on the stable door.

She heard the sound of a latch and saw Matt coming in the gate. He must have walked through the domain and crossed the bush covered valley to come in the back way from the Windsor Castle hotel. She watched him go to his room and saw the flicker of a match as he lit a candle. She waited. He would be getting undressed now, letting his jacket fall to the floor. She had an urge to run across the yard to burst into the bedroom and hang it up for him. She kept peering at the light as though mesmerized. An owl hooted from the clump of trees over-hanging the stable. The candle went out.

Emily stood looking through the window and shivered in spite of the warm night. Going to her room she threw a shawl over her shoulders and felt her way down the stairs. Quietly she pushed open the stable door. Matt heard the creak of the hinges.

'Who is there?' he called.

'Me. Emily.' The girl stood in the doorway.

'What do you want?'

'You.'

There was silence. Emily could hear Matt breathing.

'Come here, you little slut.'

She slipped into the bed and curled up facing him. He did not move. She wriggled across and put her arm around him, feeling the warmth of his body.

'Oh Matt,' she whispered, 'You are so big and beautiful.'

She had never felt like this with anyone before. This is what she had been searching for, the fulfilment of her dreams. For the first time she felt complete, as though at last this was as it should be. She was wrapped in a surging feeling of happiness, and Matt, handsome, strong, happy-go-lucky Matt, was within her, giving her this boundless measure of joyousness. She surrendered to her emotions and gasped and cried out in her rapture.

The storm had passed. With Matt against her, every fibre of her being was relaxed. She waited for him to speak but he turned without a word and tangled her hair with his hand at the back of her neck.

'Matt,' she said.

He grunted.

'Are you happy?'

'Uh huh.'

'I feel good. So good.'

'You had better not be here when Jos wakes up.'

'Can I stay a little longer?'

'Yes, but don't go to sleep.'

She closed her eyes, and dreamily stroked the finger on her left hand. One day she might have Matt's ring there and babies of her own. 'I will have to go to the twins,' she whispered and then giggled. 'It is like being married don't you think?'

There was no reply. Matt was asleep.

Jeremy rode back from the south not sure whether his journey had been successful. There was a strong undercurrent of native distrust and suspicion of the new Governor, in spite of the overtures that had been made and the efforts to gain their confidence by a new policy of dividing the land into districts and appointing magistrates and native policemen to administer justice. Gorst had been sent into the interior to watch and report the feelings of the Maori and to help in the establishment of the European type institutions, but the King people could not be bribed as easily as those further south, who were happy to accept the pay from the Crown. Jeremy wondered how loyal they would be in any conflict. At the moment they were happy to take the money and were eager to better themselves with their own schools and to plant crops with ploughs supplied by the government. It was called the Governor's flour and sugar policy. The military had commenced constructing a road to the river Waikato, a move which the King party treated with great alarm, 'lest,' they said, 'that cart of terror, the gun carriage should travel on it.'

Back in England the colonial office had confidence in Grey but read his despatches with a certain cynicism. They knew from experience that he was orchestrating something, but he was there to settle things one way or another, preferably without spending too much of their money. In particular they would consider favourably any arrangements the Governor and the colonists could agree on that would solve the problem of governing the Maori amicably. The colonial office was used to his methods. His despatches always started with a preamble, then came the dire warnings and finally the meat in the sandwich. In his office, thousands of miles away, Newcastle received one of the despatches and wrote on it. 'The overture to the grand opera that Sir G.G. is composing.'

Jeremy's thoughts went back to 1861. A few months after Grey had arrived he had talked to a spokesman of the King party at a large meeting. Grey had said he had come as an impartial friend with a very large force at his disposal to put an end to war and discord.

The chief, Tepene, had answered him saying that the King was important to Maori and to proceed carefully in working out any plans.

10

WHILE JEREMY was building up his business with the help of Tukino, by April 1862, the new institutions were rapidly extended by Grey until all native territory except that occupied by the Maori King and two other areas had been proclaimed twelve districts. The road of the 'cart of terror' was pushed forward but with winter approaching the soldiers would be forced back to their barracks.

Jeremy spent more time at home and enjoyed the opportunity to take the twins for rambles and to fish in the streams and waters of the harbour. He took them out on the cutter, using makeshift harnesses tied to the mast to keep them from falling overboard. Emily went with them on these excursions in fear for herself and the twins. Jeremy noticed that she was very quiet and that the zest had gone from her. 'Probably missing her sergeant,' he said when he and Paula discussed the day over supper.

'I caught her crying in her room,' said Paula.

Emily was lying on her bed while they were talking down below. She was worried. It had all been so wonderful and dizzying, with the whole world spinning around and the night sky bursting apart. She had stayed with him as long as she dared and had kissed him ever so gently, but he did not wake when she had slipped out from under the covers and rolled on to the floor. She would have to tell him tomorrow, she could not stand the uncertainty, with no-one to confide in. She was on her own, chained to the house and the twins, and for the first time in a long time prayed to Mary for help and forgiveness because she had been so bad for so long. She fell asleep and woke cold and shivering. It was still dark. She felt her stomach. There did not seem to be any difference, perhaps it was all a bad dream and she would wake up in the morning to find that her sergeant was still in town and Matt laughing and joking as usual.

Matt seemed to be in a good mood when she went to his room to share her dilemma. Fine, she thought. He will marry me and it will be wonderful to bear his child, to have her own to care for and to love, instead of someone else's.

When Emily ducked under the stable door she saw the twins helping Matt fill a bag of oats. They were arguing as to who should have the shovel and Matt solved the problem by giving them one each. Then he groomed and watered the horse. She found it difficult to begin the conversation.

'Matt!' Her voice was strained and low.

He saw the serious look on her face and waited.

'We are going to have a baby.'

His expression did not change but she saw his eyelid flicker. 'How do you know?'

'I know.'

'How do you know it is mine?'

Her heart sunk and a feeling of terror rose from the floor and invaded her. Her anguished cry echoed up into the roof. She put a hand to her mouth and stared at him. A fly landed on his forehead and he brushed it away without moving his head.

'What do you mean?' she asked.

'You know what I mean. It could be your sergeant's.'

She felt her heart pounding. 'You bastard, you bastard!' Throwing herself at him, she clawed and scratched at his face as the weight of her body pushed him onto the bed. He felt the blood ooze from the marks on his cheeks. She screamed out a string of unintelligible sounds.

'You little bitch,' He forced himself from the bed and threw her on to the floor. She lay there sobbing and unbelieving.

Matt picked up his hat, 'You had better go to your sergeant, you bloody whore.'

Emily heard the gate slam. She fainted and woke feeling cold and stiff. For a moment she wondered where she was and then the memory flooded back. With a cry she rose and staggered to her room.

When Jeremy came home Emily was upstairs. Paula found her sitting on a chair by the window staring at the sky with a wooden expression on her face. She spoke to her twice, her voice rising sharply, 'Emily. Emily!' The girl turned and looked at her. 'What is this nonsense? It is time you forgot about that sergeant. Get down those stairs immediately.'

'Yes, ma'am,' said Emily, and taking a deep breath made her way to the kitchen.

That night Paula spoke to Jeremy. 'I want to talk,' she said. He waited for her to continue. 'Emily has been useless this last month. I want you to deal with her.'

'She is moping for a beau,' said Jeremy. 'You must make allowances.'

'I have already made enough allowances. It is time she came to her senses.'

'What do you want me to do?'

'Tell her unless she changes her ways she will have to go.'

'I will talk to her, but we won't dispense with her as easily as that, she has been too loyal. There is something else worrying her. I will try and find out what it is.'

'What makes you say that?'

'She has changed men before and always bounced back.'

By the time Jeremy went to breakfast next morning Emily had already fed the twins. He poked his head in the kitchen door to let her know he was there. She was pale but appeared to be normal. Taking up his napkin he picked up a newspaper and read the opposition's news. The *'Dolphin'* had put her bowsprit through the customhouse office as she worked her way up to Queen St. wharf. There were specimens of gold from the Coromandel in Mr Keven's shop in the Crescent, some of it was pure and some had a solid shoddy look about it. The paper said it was only a matter of time before a reef would be discovered in that area. The nuggets had been washed from the bed of a stream called Wairau.

Jeremy put the paper down as Emily brought in the porridge and toast. As she went towards the door he called her back, 'Oh, Emily, I want to talk to you.' He waited while she returned to the table. She looked tired and ill. 'We have been worried about you. Is there anything the matter?'

'No, sir.'

'Are you sure?'

'Yes, sir.'

'We would like to help you if we can. You are part of our family you know.'

Emily looked as though she was about to cry, then recovered herself. 'I am all right, sir.'

'Very well then. Remember any time you need help you have only to ask me.'

Emily blushed. 'Yes, sir. Thank you, sir.'

'You may go.' Jeremy watched her walk out the door.

What can one do? he thought. He would make some inquiries. Caroline may be able to help, he would ask her at first opportunity. He went to the window. It was a clear and sunny day with a touch of summer still in the air. He would be able to do his accounts on the verandah. Going up the stairs he told Paula what he had said to Emily.

'I'll talk to her myself,' she said, 'after I have been to town.'

When she had gone Jeremy settled to his figures. Emily passed in and out but Jeremy pretended to ignore her. He heard the crash of a broken dish and a cry from one of the twins. It was eleven o'clock when he stopped and looked at his watch. His ink bottle was empty and he knew there was no more in the house. He walked up the hill to a neighbour. They talked about the discovery of gold and of the Act just passed by the council to protect imported birds. 'In a few years we may find we are surrounded with our own favourite songsters and with a good supply of game,' he said.

It was an hour before Jeremy could get away. As he opened his front door he was surprised that the house was quiet. The twins were usually having their dinner with Emily clattering around in the kitchen but there was no sound. He looked outside and called out. He saw a slate on the table. Picking it up he read Emily's childish scrawl: *Mr St Clair, I have to go away for ever. I am sorry. The children are locked in their bedroom. Emily.*

Jeremy put down the slate and went to the nursery. The door was ajar but there was no sign of the twins. He looked under the beds. A chair, dragged up to the door showed how they had lifted the latch and escaped. He went to the side verandah, to the back-yard and to the stables but they had gone. He called out their names, 'Jonathon! Gerald! I see you, stop hiding.' He opened the front gate and looked up and down the road that ran down to the bottom of the gully. Seeing a touch of red on the ground he stooped and picked up Jonathon's golliwog. Slithering down the muddy slope he came to the creek. He called out again, 'Gerald! Jonathon!' The only reply was the sound of the stream and the cry of a bird.

There were only two pools that were deep enough to hold the mountain trout where he and the children had fished and both were further down the gully towards the sea. Jeremy took the right hand track pushing aside the fern fronds as he ran. He came to the first opening where the stream tumbled into a dark hole half filled with water. The bottom was obscured by the shadows of the overhanging ferns and, lying on his stomach, he searched with his hand. There was nothing there. There was another pool only twenty paces further on and when he peered down he saw the reflections of the clouds overhead and the movement of a small trout as it flashed under the bank. Jumping into the water up to his armpits he began searching again. He felt the soft mud and the root of a tree twisting out from the bank. Then as he moved into the centre of the pool a small patch of colour caught his eye. Bending down he felt the fabric of a shirt and his heart missed a beat as he plunged down with both hands and dragged the small form up and threw him on to the bank. A yard away was the other twin. Jeremy pushed the child alongside his brother. He loosened their clothes and laying each of them on their stomachs, pressed down on their backs. Desperately he turned from one to the other as he forced the water from their lungs. For what seemed an eternity he continued to work on them.

In despair, he rolled their bodies over the trunk of a tree and breathed into their mouths, watching as their small chests inflated. As he put Jonathon down for the third time he fell with the boy on to the soft ground. Jeremy recovered his balance and turned to Gerald. There was a gurgling half cry from behind. Quickly glancing down Jeremy saw that Jonathon had moved. There was an almost imperceptible rise and fall of his chest as Jeremy breathed life into him. Gradually the motion became stronger until it became a regular rhythm. Jeremy stopped and called out, hoping that someone would hear. There was no reply except for the sound of the stream as it tumbled down to the sea. He turned to Gerald and firmly and gently, worked on him pausing now and again briefly to glance at Jonathon. In spite of the cold the perspiration ran down Jeremy's brow stinging his eyes. Jonathon remained unconscious but Jeremy could see the steady rise and fall of his chest. After half an hour of intense effort, Jeremy stopped and stood up, staring down at Gerald. There was no sign of life. Wrapping his jacket around them he picked the boys up and scrambled up the track. He ran to the doctor's house and rang the bell. The door opened and the doctor stood there, looking at them in amazement.

'Thank God you are home,' said Jeremy.

He shouldered his way inside. 'Jonathon is breathing,' he said.

'Put them down here.' The doctor indicated two beds on each side of the surgery. 'You look after Jonathon. Put him face down. Cover him with a blanket.'

As he was speaking the doctor was feeling for Gerald's pulse. He mopped away the froth and the mucus from his nose.

'How long were they under the water?'

'I don't know.' said Jeremy.

'There are some bellows in the parlour. Fetch them.'

Jeremy found them standing against the fireplace and returned to the room. The doctor closed one of Gerald's nostrils with a thumb and forefinger and held his mouth shut. 'Now,' he said to Jeremy, 'put the pipe of the bellows up the nostril.'

The doctor pressed the child's head gently backwards, freeing the upper part of the windpipe. 'Blow the bellows. Gently. Gently.'

Jeremy slowly closed the two handles together. The child's breast rose slightly. The doctor let the mouth free, and pressed on the chest. 'Again,' he said.

They repeated the movements time and time again, only pausing to see that Jonathon was still alive. They worked for an hour. Jeremy warmed bricks on the stove and placed them in the beds. At last the doctor stopped and gazed at the pathetic bundle on the bed. Jeremy could see the look of dejection on the man's face.

'I am sorry,' he said.

Jeremy's hands fell to his side and he looked at Gerald. Paula's favourite child.

The doctor went to Jonathon and felt his pulse. He was breathing normally and the colour had come back into his cheeks. 'I will give him some brandy and warm water,' he said, and went into his study to return with a medicine glass. The child spluttered and choked as he poured the liquid into him.

'You can leave him here.' The doctor put down the glass. 'It will be better not to move him.'

Jeremy wrapped Gerald in a blanket and carried him the short distance down the road to rest him gently on his bed. He uncovered the boy's head and brushed back the damp hair. Gerald appeared to be asleep, with his eyes closed and his long lashes falling over his pallid cheeks. At that instant the full realization of what had happened overtook Jeremy. He went on to the verandah and sank into the cane chair. The sun was still shining and the clouds were racing across the sky from the southwest as though nothing had happened. The windmill on the ridge was still turning. The harbour was sparkling as usual and a bee hovered over one of the last roses before climbing into its heart. He waited, dreading the next few hours.

At last he saw Paula. Jos was driving the carriage up the steepest part of the hill calling to the horses as he encouraged it up the incline. They stopped at the gate and Paula jumped down with a hat box in her hand. She laughed as she swung the box to and fro.

'You won't mind the money when you see this.' She waved to Jeremy and skipped up the steps. 'I have bought the most elegant hat,' she said. Paula stopped on the edge of the verandah. She could see Jeremy's face in the shadows. 'What is wrong?'

'Gerald.'

'Is he sick?'

Jeremy shook his head

'Tell me!'

He took a step towards Paula and put his hand on her shoulder. She shook herself free.

'What is it?'

'Come and sit down.'

'No. Tell me.' Paula's voice rose higher. 'Tell me.'

'Gerald has drowned in the creek.'

Her eyes were the first to change. They widened until the pupils were two enormous voids and Jeremy saw the glazed look of someone in despair staring at him in bewilderment.

90

'You have killed my baby.' she cried. 'You have killed my baby.'

Her anguish burst on Jeremy and filled the house with its sound. 'Paula, it was not I who left the children alone. I did all I could to save Gerald.' He put out his hand.

'Don't touch me.' she cried. 'Don't touch me ever again.' Flinging the hat away she rushed instinctively into the bedroom where her child lay and gathering him up in her arms rocked him to and fro, weeping in desolation.

Jeremy ordered Jos back into the carriage. 'Fetch the vicar,' he said, 'and Caroline.'

Jos held the horse's head and backed it onto the narrow road. The carriage raced down the hill with brakes grinding on the iron rims. Matt was the first to arrive. He took Jeremy's hand in a firm grip before going to the cupboard by the fire and taking down a bottle of whiskey from the shelf. He poured out two large tots of the neat liquor.

'Where is Paula?' Matt asked.

'In the bedroom with Gerald.'

'And Jonathon?'

'Up the road with the doctor.'

Matt looked at the clock on the mantelpiece. 'Wyndham is shutting up the shop,' he said. 'Is there anything I can do?'

Jeremy shook his head. They sat together finding comfort in each other's comradeship. The gate opened and Jeremy recognized Caroline's footsteps. He went to the door and opened it, leaving it ajar as he ushered her inside. She pressed his hand and murmured her sorrow. A mixture of caring and condolence. Jeremy pointed to the bedroom door. As Caroline pushed it open Paula burst into another bout of crying. People began to arrive. The vicar, followed by two women neighbours who made tea and searched in the cupboards to find a few cakes and biscuits. Jeremy and Matt brought chairs from upstairs and soon there were a dozen people in the house. A woman took a cup of tea into the bedroom. Paula was sitting on a chair, weeping silently and rubbing the child's cold hands as though she could bring him back. The vicar was attempting to comfort her. He said a short prayer. 'Be thine also the peace that passeth all understanding which the world could not give thee here, nor take away from thee now. Thou hast been spared all the pain and bitterness of this life.'

Paula broke into another burst of sobbing.

'Holy Mary,' muttered Matt.

Jeremy lifted Paula to her feet and walked her into the parlour across the passage. People came and went as she sat unaware of words and faces and sound. Rosalind came in with Rata and spoke to her.

'Where is Jonathon?' Rosalind asked.

'In bed at the doctor's,' said Jeremy.

'Is there anyone else there?'

'No.'

'I will go and look after him.' She let herself out the back door and Jeremy watched her pass the window and disappear around the side of the house. He went back to the parlour and drew up a chair alongside Paula.

It was evening when the undertaker arrived. The shadows were beginning to fall across the verandah and the visitors had gone, leaving only Caroline. Rosalind had returned and left again, taking Jonathon with her. The doctor had given Paula a potion, a confection of opium mixed with Peruvian bark and she was asleep in the spare room.

Jeremy threw a look at Caroline. 'I will be in the kitchen.' He went to the back of the house where Matt and Jos were sitting at the kitchen table.

'What has happened to Emily?' asked Matt.

The black carriage with plumed horses rolled slowly down the hill and up past the barracks. The children from the school walked alongside the coffin holding their posies, with Jeremy following them. Paula was too distraught to walk and was in a closed carriage decorated with black crepe. Rosalind was at the church. She had marshalled the remainder of her children into the choir seats. Paula stood in the front pew with Jeremy, oblivious of those around her. She went through the motions of kneeling and praying without hearing the sermon or the pure, clear singing of the young voices that soared to the rafters. At last the service dragged to a close and she found herself in the open air again. Jeremy took her by the arm and guided her to the casket. A flower fell to the ground and she stooped to pick it up, crushing it against her breast. As she stood outside, the people streamed past, a small group of the military, church friends, a few tradespeople. Some took her hand, and all spoke a few words. They came in twos and threes, face after face, a woman's bonnet, a shawl, a beard. 'Yes.' 'No.' 'Thank you.' 'Yes, you are too kind.'

There was a pause, and then the tide flowed again, until eventually it ebbed away and she and Jeremy stood alone. Scraps of conversation floated across the path. 'What a tragedy.' 'Beastly weather.' 'The Panmure punt's laid up again.' 'The concert at the Oddfellow's Hall.' 'Donations for the new stone church.' 'New Zealand fleece, sixteen pence a pound in Sydney,' and a voice saying, 'This way, madam.'

When next they stopped Gerald was carried along the narrow track, past wooden crosses and iron railings to put him to rest by a newly planted oak tree that overlooked the pool and the stream where he had played and died. They gathered around the graveside. Twenty or thirty people, a few children, the vicar.

'Ashes to ashes, dust to dust.'

Matt looked down at the newly turned mound and at the yellow, puggy clay. He turned to Jos. 'The sea is cleaner,' he said.

Jos remained beside the grave as the funeral party filed back along the track. He beckoned to Rata and waited as the mourners disappeared between the trees. She was standing lower than he was and her eyes were level with his own. He could see the soft melting sadness of them, reflecting her sorrow.

'Come with me to move the boat,' he said. As they skirted a newly dug grave Rata slipped and grasped Jos as she fell. For a moment he held her, reluctant to let her go, but she broke away and took the lead following a path to the bay where the 'Echo' was beached. They slid down a bank taking a short cut to the water. Rata waited for Jos to catch up to her.

'You English are so different.' she said. 'You are so cold. We Maori people weep when we are sad and laugh when we are happy, but you English.' She stopped for the want of words.

'It is not always good to show your feelings.' replied Jos.

'Why?'

'It is how we are brought up, we British.'

'You British! We are taught to be honest in our feelings. To weep when someone dies, to feast and laugh when someone marries, but you . . . . You are the same at funerals and weddings as though they were one.'

'But your father was English. Do you feel Maori or Pakeha?'

'At times like these I have a deep sense of oneness with my mother's people. This morning I wanted to sing a tangi waïata for Gerald. But sometimes I am neither one nor the other. Then I have a terrible feeling of loneliness, of not being wanted.'

Jos swung around and faced her. 'I want you, Rata. I love you.'

She looked down at the ground. 'I know. And I love you. But what of tomorrow? My father has forsaken my mother. She is a princess and I have been promised to a young chief of the Ngati-Maniopoto.'

'Let us get married now. We will ask Rosalind.'

Rata shook her head. 'She cannot say that I can marry. Only a meeting of my tribe, a runanga, can decide because my mother's father is a chief and even he must listen to his people.'

'A runanga? Have you been to one?'

'Once only. The whole tribe gathered. The old men spoke first, in the evening, and then after a meal the young people and the parents had their say. They were followed by the young girls who were to take husbands. Lastly the men who were proposed as husbands spoke and only then was agreement reached.'

'We can run away.'

'Look what happened when Emily ran away. The gods were angry and showed their displeasure. I have composed a song, a waiata for Gerald, as my mother would have done. We weep when someone dies and goes to his ancestors, when they make the journey to the farthest point of our land, Cape Reinga, the jumping off place of the spirits. There the dead slide down the pohutukawa roots into the sea to descend into the spirit world and take their place with their fathers. We do not bury our dead but place the body in a tree or cave until the priest tells us it is time to scrape the flesh clean from the bones and put them in the burial ground.'

'Sing me your song.'

The sun came from behind a cloud and the shadows dappled the opening as Rata plucked a piece of green vine from a tree and twisted it in her hair. For a moment there was silence as they stood opposite each other. Then Jos saw a change come over her as her face showed all the grief that was pent up inside. Rata sat herself cross-legged on the ground and rocked to and fro, letting out a high pitched wail from deep within her. It rose above the trees, a prime-val sound of mourning, and as her voice rose and fell the tears rolled down her cheeks. Trance-like, she sang a dirge in her native tongue for the child that had gone. Jos stood transfixed. He waited until the last sound had faded away. Rata, sitting motionless in the shadows, looked up at him with her tear-stained face.

'What did you sing?' he asked.

'A song of lamentation.'

'Tell it to me, in English.'

She faltered as she groped for the words.

Oh, how the new green shoot of the mighty totara has been torn from its branch.

See the tears dropping from the wound.

Staining the earth.

Alas my grief. Haere ra e Gerald. Farewell, O Gerald.

The sea is dark and sparkles no more.

I heard the distant thunder and saw the lightning's downward flash on Rangitoto's mountain peak.

Ka riro Gerald. Thou art gone Gerald.

Te kino, e-e-i.

Alas the evil of it.

He took her hands and lifted her to her feet. 'Rata, will you marry me?'

She looked at him with big brown eyes. 'Yes, my Jossy, no matter what my people say. But we must keep it a secret until I have finished my schooling, otherwise my grandfather will take me away. We must keep it very secret.'

He held her close, feeling the velvet softness of her skin. He kissed her.

'No, like this' she whispered, and pressing her nose gently to his they sealed the promise. Jos felt an overwhelming sense of con-tentment. They bathed in each other's presence on the edge of the fern glade, while the long green fronds laced the sky and the sun cast a patchwork of dancing shadows over them.

Suddenly Rata dropped her arms and started down the track. 'Quickly,' she said, 'we will miss the tide.'

* * *

A week after the funeral Jos and Rata were back at the boat. The sea was already retreating across the wide tidal flat when they reached the *'Echo'*. They took off their shoes, and Rata hitched up her skirt as Jos picked up the anchor and began pulling the boat towards Nicholl's boatyard at the bottom of the hill. Walking backwards, Jos watched the swing of Rata's long legs and the erect, graceful movement of her body as she followed behind with her long black, wavy hair tumbling over her shoulders. She was wearing European clothes, a blouse and a large skirt that came to her ankles but they could not hide her willowy figure. The hem of her skirt fell down into the water and she hung onto Jos's arm to tuck it up again. A flatfish darted from under their feet, making a whirling track of brown silt as it fled and a seagull hovered for a moment before settling on the end of the boom, tucking its wings away and watching with head to one side.

At the shipyard there was a trading vessel on the stocks, its skeleton ribs outlined against the sea. The workmen had already started on the planking, fixing the kauri boards with copper nails, while a short distance away two men were sawing timber to the widths required. Jos anchored the *'Echo'* at the low water mark and together they walked up Constitution Hill towards the school. Half way up the steep slope Jos said good-bye to Rata and watched her until she was out of sight before turning back to the house.

When he arrived Jonathon ran out to meet him. He saw Rosalind's carriage at the gate.

'Jossie, look what Aunt Rosie gave me,' Jonathon called excitedly. He was holding a small music box with an enamelled picture of a bonneted girl on the top and as he turned the handle, a pretty French tune tinkled out.

'See.' said Jonathon, 'I wanted to show Gerald but he can't see it. He has gone to Jesus.' The boy took Jos's hand and they climbed the steps together.

'Aunt Rosie said I can stay with her whenever I like. Rata gives me rides on her back and we play all the time. I can do a war dance. Watch.'

Jos smiled as Jonathon's little face contorted into a grimace and his feet thumped out the rhythm of the haka on the wooden verandah. He carried Jonathon inside, nodding a message to Jeremy that the boat was at the yard. Jonathon climbed onto Jeremy's knee.

'We could go for a sail next Sunday.' said Jeremy, looking at Paula. 'Try out the new tiller.' He was thinking of his wife and the need to combat the grief she was showing. He turned to Rosalind.

'Will you come for a picnic next Sunday?'

Rosalind ruffled Jonathon's hair. 'That will be delightful. After morning prayers?'

'Yes,' said Jeremy. 'Jonathon, say good-bye to Aunt Rose.'

The boy jumped down from Jeremy's knee and ran across to Rosalind. 'Can I come with you?' he asked.

'No, little man, you must stay here.' Rosalind went to the door. Paula interrupted her. 'Let him go if he wants to.'

Jeremy shot a look at his wife. There was an awkward pause. Rosalind stood at the doorway looking from one to the other as Jonathon tugged at her hand.

'All right,' said Jeremy as he turned to Paula, 'say good-bye to your mother.' The child went back and kissed his mother and ran down the steps to the carriage.

'Perhaps I should leave him here,' said Rosalind as she climbed on to the seat.

'He wants to go,' said Jeremy, 'and Paula and I need to be alone.'

As he settled by the fireplace the events of the last few days crowded in upon him. Emily. The drowning. Paula's reaction. The funeral. The grief he felt flooded back and he felt desolate. Marriage, he thought should double the joys and halve the worries. Paula seemed to find fault even with happiness and increased the worries by lashing out in her self-imposed isolation. He watched her as she sat with her eyes closed. 'Paula,' he said, 'I have said this before. Isn't it time we forgot our differences?' It was as though she had not heard. 'We must not let Gerald's death destroy everything.'

He was not prepared for the outburst. She leapt out of the chair and put her face inches away from his. 'Destroy,' she cried. 'You! You talk of destruction. Who destroyed my baby? Who brought me to this wild country? Who made sure I would never see my brother again? Who went into trade and dragged me down to that level? You! You did! And you talk of destruction. I would go home tomorrow but I can never lift my head again in England.'

She stormed to the fireplace and turned around, her face distorted with loathing. He realized for the first time what had held him to her. He pitied her. He now knew that it was no substitute for love. 'Paula', he said quietly. 'I am very, very sorry.'

He climbed the stairs pausing at the box room door. Should he go back to her? She would probably fly at him again, there was nothing more he could say to help her. As he closed the door he heard her sobbing in the darkness.

11

THE DAY of the picnic dawned fine and clear. There was little wind in the valley and the few clouds that Jeremy could see were moving slowly from the south. Jos and Matt left early with gear for the boat; a stern anchor, oars and a new mainsail. They were to pick up Rosalind in the dog cart. Paula had not spoken to Jeremy since the night of the funeral but she had prepared a hamper and was putting the finishing touches to it as he climbed down the stairs. He was surprised to see she was still wearing her house shift. 'You will have to hurry and dress,' he said.

Paula remained with her back to him. 'I am not coming.'

'It will be good for you, some fresh air,' said Jeremy. She fastened the leather straps on the basket. 'I am staying home. The food is ready.'

'You must come.'

'And why must I?'

'To get away. Breathe the sea air.'

'I am not coming and that is that!'

He picked up the hamper. 'Very well it is your decision, we may be late back depending on the wind.'

Arriving at the beach Jeremy found that Matt had the boat in the water and that Jos had gone to collect Rosalind. When she arrived Rosalind was surprised to hear that Paula was not coming.

Matt pick-a-backed her out to the *'Echo'* and they were soon sailing down the harbour in the freshening breeze, with Jeremy at the helm. He eased the boat along to avoid stretching the new sail and took full advantage of the tide. Heading the *'Echo'* towards the middle of the harbour he changed course to pass the extinct volcano that dominated the harbour on the port side. The sea was as blue as the sky and no-one spoke as they enjoyed the tranquillity. Rosalind was in the stern as they watched two blue penguins diving for a meal, while a hundred yards ahead a flock of terns fluttered over a shoal of herring. A school of dolphins broached alongside and disappeared to return in front of the bow, as though leading them through the passage between two islands. Rosalind watched them play. They seemed to delight in their antics, turning over to look up at her and changing direction with flicks of their tails, their sleek bodies quivering with power. Rosalind was fascinated as they swept up to the surface then dived to come up on the other side of the boat before veering away to the north.

The boat continued skirting the island until they changed course and pointed towards land. Rosalind strained her eyes to find an opening. It was only when Matt and Jos put out the oars that she spied a break in the rocks. 'A secret cove,' she cried. The water was crystal clear and she could see the sandy bottom below, dotted with small rocks and ribbons of sea-kelp that undulated gently with the swell that came in from the Pacific Ocean. 'It is like an underworld garden,' she cried, 'seashells, cockleshells. Look! Starfish! Pretty maidens all in a row.'

The tide was at its lowest when they dropped anchor and paid out the warp. Jos carried the picnic basket to the beach and put it above the high water mark where some long grass met the sand.

'Lunch time.' called Matt. He walked along the edge of the water and collected small pieces of driftwood that dotted the cove. Soon there was a fire crackling in a hollow and they undid the parcels of food that Paula had wrapped in linen napkins. The men lolled back on the sand as Rosalind undid the lid of the tea caddy and waited for the billy to boil. The sun was beating down and the sea in the cove was calm and clear. Jeremy looked out to the *'Echo'*. She was riding on the incoming tide, hanging limply on her anchors, and as he watched he saw the tail of a stingray cutting across the bay. I should have insisted that Paula come with us, he thought, and then he wondered if it would have been the same if she had. Rosalind brought him a mug of tea and a plate of food.

They had just finished eating when there was a sound of earth falling from the clay bank behind them. Jeremy turned to see a white man dressed in a pea jacket with cord trousers and wearing a hat with a fly-away ribbon at the back. A Maori woman was behind him carrying a flax basket. The man's face was lined by many summers in the sun.

'Let me introduce myself,' he said. 'Tonguer, Tonguer Brown. And er, my wife, Hokepera.'

Jeremy hid his surprise, 'Good afternoon.' He tried to guess who the man was. Perhaps a sailor who had deserted ship or someone who had left home under a cloud. He introduced Rosalind and the two men.

'I wonder if you could convey me to town if you are returning there?' asked Tonguer.

'You are welcome,' said Jeremy. 'Perhaps you would share our picnic?'

They watched as Tonguer Brown carved a piece of lamb from the joint and passed the knife to his wife. There were a number of white men who were living Maori fashion in New Zealand and each tribe vied for their services. The ruling chief often presented the renegade with a woman and there were a number of offspring from the unions.

'Have you been here a long time?' asked Jeremy.

'Yes. In New Zealand since 1833.'

Jeremy showed his surprise. 'On this island?'

Tonguer shook his head. 'No, but everywhere else. In the north and as far south as Piraki in the middle island. My wife was a slave of the Ngapuhi at the Hokianga but she returned to her own tribe here at Waiheke when she was freed at the request of the missionaries.'

Jeremy passed Tonguer a mug of beer. 'Then Christianity has made a difference?'

'Yes and no. It has helped stop the tribal wars but it will take a nation many years to change its nature.' The man spoke with an educated voice. 'I was the guest of the tribe, in theory, but was not allowed to leave them.'

'How did you get away?'

'I escaped on an American whaler, the *'Atlantic'*. Howden was her captain, from Warren, USA. We were wrecked off Akaroa and went ashore in a southerly blow so I went back to the Bay of Islands on a Frenchie, *'La France'*, from Havre.

'What was the Bay of Islands like?' asked Jeremy.

'The Bay was a pretty wild place. There is a gap in the whaling season when the ships come in to re-provision. They come from all over — Fairhaven, New Bedford, St Johns, Warren and other ports on the eastern seaboard. There would be a dozen ships anchored off the beach with blue whaleboats alongside painted the colour of the sea. There were usually one or two fetching water from the spring in the north cove, towing a string of water casks roped together. I remember one mate from New England always stood at his steer-oar, chewing on his tobacco, swearing at the crew as they stretched back on the ash oars. None of your quick jerky navy movements, but long, even powerful strokes. On shore were the girls, barefooted and bareheaded flaunting their bodies, swinging up and down the beach in their new print dresses and wearing earrings bought with a sailor's dollar. Ask yourself. Some of the men had not seen a woman for a year or more. The American captain, William Mayhew, had a store there. He sold gunpowder in casks, flour, butter, cheese, shot, even French bedsteads and silk hats, everything. Flintlock guns, blankets, slops and sarsaparilla. Bill Robertson was another. He repaired timekeepers and rated the chronometers by transit observations and kept Greenwich mean time with an astronomical clock. Someone else sold butter moulds, rum, lanceheads, pistols and knuckledusters.'

'So it could get pretty busy then? It certainly sounds rather wild!'

'I tell you, it was some place. You'd find the captains in the saloon parlour drinking whiskey or cognac, exchanging experiences with each other, hard men from Nantucket or Martha's Vineyard who were dictators on their own ships. Sometimes they cruised for over a year before the holds were full of oil and whalebone. And the crews! In their blue monkey jackets and duck trousers or dungarees and fo'c'sle caps of canvas. Men from the New England states. Jamaicans, Portuguese, Irish lads and perhaps a young man from Devon who had run away from a man-o-war or a flogging captain.'

'How did you get the name Tonguer?' asked Matt.

'From my whaling days. Down south at Piraki when a whaling ship arrived I would go aboard to act as interpreter and helped to tow in the dead whales. For that I got the carcass and the tongue.'

'What did you do with them?'

'Render them down. I got about six or eight barrels of oil from each whale. The French called us *carcassiers*. In those days Akaroa was practically deserted except for visiting whalers. A European, Jimmy Robertson, lived with the Maori. Jimmy collected stray carcasses and intestines from any fish that came ashore. He melted them down to a poor class of oil which he sold to the whalers. Then the Green family came.

'Who were the Greens?'

'They arrived November '39 to look after some cattle for a Mr Rhodes. I can remember the Greens arriving on the beach with all they owned, most of their belongings had been bought on credit from Rhodes against their wages. Green had a case of gin that he guarded pretty carefully. Mrs Green was busy keeping her two year old son out of the water. It was a wild place in those days with the forest right down to the foreshore. For the first few months the Greens lived in a tent.

'Barny Rhodes had heard that the French were arriving and realizing the middle island had never been formally possessed by the British was worried about his land purchases and that the French might take possession so he arranged for Bill Green to put up a flagstaff and if the French arrived he was to hoist the flag and drive the cattle under it. They were beautiful beasts, pure bred Durhams, descended from those sent out from England to Australia by Potter McQueen. Old Bill Green was a hard case. Of course there was no hotel and Bill used to buy any grog he could from the whalers and sell it to us. I have often had a drink of his unusual brand of milk from the casks hidden in the bush.'

'And you worked for Hemplemann?'

'The German? Yes. He had this station around past the Heads. Peraki.'

'You towed the whales?'

'That's right. Tail first, after we had cut off the flukes. I've pulled one for fourteen hours with five men rowing, often against the wind and tide. Killing whales is easy compared with towing. We could have done with one of those London tugs. You know, the jackals on the Thames. The shore whaling season is May to October. You can imagine what it was like. Freezing, wet, stormy. Sometimes we had to let a fish go and hope to pick it up later.'

'I'm expecting some oil from the '*Elizabeth Swift*' tomorrow,' said Jeremy. 'I might get you to look at it.'

'The *'Elizabeth Swift'*, I know her.'

'She is in the stream,' said Jeremy, 'with *'Rainbow'* and '*Mount Wollaston.'* Yankees. In from the whaling grounds.'

'I will go out to her tomorrow,' replied Tonguer.

They gathered up the picnic basket and Tonguer's wife pressed her nose with her husband to say good-bye. Jos waded out to pick up the stern anchor and pull the boat ashore. It was dark when Jos took Rosalind home.

Jeremy let himself into his house through the front door. A lamp was burning in the parlour when he went up the hall expecting that Paula had gone to bed. He was surprised when he saw her in a chair, asleep. As he entered the room she woke. 'What time is it?' she asked. She was in that half world of sleeping and waking.

'Nine o'clock. Matt and Jos are at Rosalind's.' He could see she had been crying. 'What is wrong?' he asked. She did not appear to have heard him. He repeated the question.

'Jeremy.' she said. 'I want us to have separate rooms.'

He walked over to the fireplace. 'Why?' he asked.

'I cannot cope anymore.'

He stood looking down at her. 'You must. Everyone else has to.'

'I cannot cope.'

'Why not?'

Again the silence. 'Answer me.' His voice sounded more abrupt than he had meant it to be.

'I do not love you any more.'

He tried to see behind those eyes. They were expressionless, black-brown barriers to her mind. He felt the emptiness again, the tug in the pit of his stomach.

'Paula, you are ill.'

'I am well enough to know what I feel.'

'Have you ever loved me?' He flung the words out. They echoed in his mind, inflicting a kind of self torture on himself.

'I did once,' she said.

104

'When?'

'On the ship, in the southern Indian Ocean. We were watching the whales. I felt you cared.'

'Paula, I do care. I have always cared.'

'You let Gerald die. We talk about different things, want different things. I am ashamed when someone asks me what you do and I have to tell them you are a merchant.'

Jeremy found his voice. 'Rubbish. In this country everybody works and it carries no shame. And what is wrong with being a merchant, I want to know.'

'We are socially unacceptable. We are never invited to the Governor's levees.'

'But we are. I just do not bother about them. Every Tom Dick and Harry can get an invitation.'

Paula's voice pitched higher. 'You did not tell me. You don't care about my position.'

'My dear, here it doesn't matter who you are. It is what you do that counts. A boatman can look you in the eye and is his own master.'

'And a servant can answer you back.'

'What do you mean?'

'Matt says what he likes to you.'

'He is a friend.'

'Poof!' She stood up and flounced to the door. 'Don't come into my room tonight.'

He threw some coal on the fire, and watched the sparks dance up the chimney. Placing the guard around the fireplace he took his coat from the hall stand and walked up the hill to the doctor.

'I am sorry to call so late on a Sunday,' said Jeremy.

'Come in. It is not often I get social calls.' The doctor stepped aside to let him pass.

'This is not exactly a social call.'

'What is the problem?'

'It is my wife. She is grieving for Gerald.'

'That is natural enough.'

'Yes. But she does not want to have anything to do with Jonathon or me.'

'What makes you say that?'

'She is very distant. Quiet. I grant you she has always been that way but she is silent for hours and will then suddenly turn on people with her tongue.'

'And on you in particular?'

'Yes. She wants a separate bedroom.'

The doctor put the tips of his fingers on his chin. 'Grief can show itself in many ways. It is not unusual under the circumstances. She probably has inflammation of the brain, I will need to cup her. I will call tomorrow. In the meantime see that she applies a cold cloth to her forehead. I will give you an aperient for her. Two pills to be taken every twenty-four hours until they act thoroughly on the bowels.' The doctor went to a cabinet and brought out some jars. Jeremy read the labels. Powdered aloes, calomel, sulphate of soda, senna. He handed Jeremy a dozen pills in a paper cone. 'Remember,' he said, 'two every twenty four hours.'

Jeremy hurried back to the house and tried the handle on Paula's door. It was locked.

'Paula.' he called. 'Paula. Let me in. I have something for you.' There was no reply. 'Paula. I have some pills for you. Let me in.' He tested the lock. Standing back he put his shoulder to the door. It burst open knocking a picture off the wall. There was a sound of splintering glass.

'Don't lock the doors in this house in future.' He tried to control his anger. 'Here are some pills.' He poured out a beaker of water from the jug on the washstand. 'Take two now. The doctor is coming to see you in the morning. You have chosen your own course Paula. So be it.' He walked out leaving the door open and went to the spare bed in the boxroom.

At breakfast next morning Jeremy gave Jos and Matt their instructions for the day while Paula remained in bed. 'I will be late,' he told the men. He groomed Sergeant and put on the fancy tooled saddle before riding slowly up to Rosalind's house.

'Is everything all right?' she asked.

He shrugged his shoulders. 'Middling', he said.

'What do you mean by that?'

'Paula does not seem to want Jonathon. She is not well.' Jeremy followed Rosalind into the kitchen. 'I don't know what to do.'

'Let time take it course.'

'The doctor thinks she has inflammation of the brain.'

'My God.' said Rosalind. 'She needs rest and care.'

'She does not want me.'

Rosalind turned sharply. 'Then she must be very sick. I will go and see her.'

'I would not if I were you.'

Rosalind looked quickly at Jeremy. 'Why not?'

'She does not seem to approve of you. Nothing that I can explain. Whenever I mention your name she becomes very quiet.'

'Why?'

'I don't know.'

'Do you think I can be of some help to Paula?'

'I really do not know.'

'Why not ask Caroline to spend a day with her.'

'That is a good idea, she seems to relate to her. Perhaps if I went away for a while things will be better. What shall I do about Jonathon?'

Rosalind sat down on the chair opposite. 'Talk to the doctor. If Paula does not want him he is welcome here. Would you like a cup of tea?'

'No thank you.' Jeremy picked up his riding crop.

When Jeremy went to the warehouse one of his regular customers, Mr Trust, was buying oats. A stocky, hardworking man, Trust often stopped for a chat with Jeremy when he came into town to get supplies. His three boys were examining a gum digging spear hanging on a post. Jeremy looked across at the boys. 'Ambrose is growing up,' he said.

'Fourteen in November,' said Trust.

As Ambrose drove their wagon out of the yard, Trust called out, 'Come and see us when you are passing our way.'

Jeremy was re-arranging the stack of sugar in the back room when the bell rang and Tonguer Brown walked up to the counter. 'That oil,' he said 'is first grade.'

'Thank you for your help,' said Jeremy, 'is there anything here I can do for you?'

Tonguer grinned showing a row of crooked brown teeth. 'What I would like is a game of billiards, I have not had one for years. There is a new saloon around in Shortland Crescent.'

'Sorry, Matt is not here, he is the expert, said Jeremy, 'but I could join you.'

'How about the boy?' asked Tonguer jerking his head in the

direction of Jos who was about to close the door.'

'He does not play.'

'Then it is about time he learnt. I will teach him.' The saloon was above a wine and spirit shop in a two storied building a few yards off the main street. Upstairs was a new billiard table. Jeremy took a half crown piece from his pocket and spun the coin.

'Heads,' said Tonguer.

'You lead,' said Jeremy.

Tonguer selected a cue and handed it to Jos. Jos stabbed at the ball and saw it trickle to one side. Tonguer winced.

'Tonguer,' said Jeremy as he played a draw shot, 'do you think the Maori King will cause trouble? There are rumours everywhere.'

Tonguer stooped low over the table and potted the black. He straightened up. 'There is trouble coming. They do not trust Governor Grey any more.'

'Why not?'

'He said he would dig around their King until he fell and there is the road you are making that can carry your carts of war. How many soldiers working on it at Christmas time? Two thousand. They feel that war is inevitable.'

'The Governor has stopped building the road.'

'Only because they are bogged down. Come the spring the soldiers will return. Besides, your Premier, Fox, is a fool. He thinks he has the Maori under control because they were courteous and feasted him. Of course he received their hospitality. That is the Maori way. But his words were firmly rejected by the King Party. Do you know what I think of Fox? He may have been a good leader in opposition; he's pugnacious, witty, even venomous. But he is ineffectual as a premier. His arguments are seldom sincere.'

'Did Gore Browne do any better when he was Governor?'

'He was too honest in his politics. Browne's conduct was selfless, especially in native affairs. The town people liked him. And as for the Maori, at least they were fair with him, but the Maori are always courteous in their own fashion, even in war. Look what happened with the 65th regiment. They were fighting at Te Arei. They would call out 'Lie down 65th', before they let off a volley. At one place, as a sap drew near the pa, the Maori called out 'Homai te Tupeha' and a soldier threw a packet of tobacco to them. Back came a basket of peaches. Later the Maori white flag went up and that was the end of that battle. Another time they helped the troops make a sap and a bridge to approach their own pa. You may think I am joking, but it is true. Listen. The British wanted green brushwood in large quantities for constructing the sap. The soldiers asked some friendly natives to get it for them and told them they would be well paid. The friendlies could not take the brushwood without the permission of the Maori fighters. Well, some fighters slipped out from their fort, cut the brushwood, bundled it in the sizes that General Pratt wanted and tied it up with vines. The friendly natives came and fetched it away, paying the fighters with the money they got from the commissariat. The Maori fighters in the fort used some of the money to buy blankets and shirts and gun powder. They watched the general's sap approaching shorn up by their own wood and when it was too close for comfort they left their fort and built another one a short distance away.'

Jeremy laughed. 'Thank you for that. Tonguer, you must call again. Do you think there will be war? Here?'

Tonguer was silent for a moment as he picked up his hat. 'It is inevitable,' he said.

Rosalind was at the house when Jeremy returned home. Jonathon was in the kitchen and the Wyndhams were there taking tea. Paula seemed nervous, and trembled as she passed the plates around the table. As the boy ran to him, Jeremy picked him up and swung him around the room. 'Come with me,' he said, and taking the lamp from the table went to the back door. 'I have something to show you.'

They crossed the yard to the stables. Jonathon walked in and peered into a stall. 'A pony!' he cried.

'It is yours,' said Jeremy. The newly imported shetland was still unsure of itself after the voyage across from Australia. He lifted Jonathon on to its back. The boy clutched its mane, a little unsure of himself. Jeremy lifted him down. 'Would you like to stay the night and feed him in the morning?'

'Yes please.' Jonathon's eyes shone.

'We will see what your mother says,' said Jeremy.

He closed the doors and putting Jonathon on his shoulders

galloped back to the house.

When Jeremy returned to the parlour he noticed Wyndham had helped himself from the decanter of port. Caroline looked embarrassed. Damn them, thought Jeremy.

'How were the billiards?' asked Wyndham.

'Fine,' replied Jeremy.

'You were a long time.'

'We talked about the Taranaki war and the king movement.'

Wyndham's face was flushed with the port. 'Nobody wants war but we don't want a miserable patched up peace either, bursting out again into fighting every year, ruining hundreds, injuring thousands, preventing the proper settlement of the country. We could finish it in no time if it was not for a few natives and the miserable pandering of the Governor. We do not want war, we want peace but there is only one way to get it. Defeat them once and for all. Confiscate their land. That is the only logic they understand.'

Jeremy ignored the outburst. 'Isn't it time you left,' he said.

Caroline glanced at Jeremy and took away Wyndham's glass. 'I want to go home,' she said.

Rosalind glanced at Jeremy and guided Jonathon to his toys in the corner. The child smiled up at her. 'Father said I can stay the night here with my pony.'

Paula swung around from the window where she had been watching them cross the yard. 'No you are not!'

There was an instant quiet. Paula turned to Jeremy. She was shaking as though she had an ague. 'You said I was to have a month without him!'

'The month is only a few days away. You can't feel like that about Jonathon.'

'I don't want him. He is too much like you. He probably pushed Gerald into the water.'

Jeremy stooped down and whispered to Jonathon. 'Go and play in the parlour.' He watched the boy walk slowly up the hall with his head bowed. A lamp spluttering from the ceiling cast an uneven shadow on the walls and on to the pathetic frame of the boy as he turned the door knob and disappeared. Jeremy about-faced and looked at Paula. It seemed that some obscene agency had entered him. The emptiness that had been hers.

Rosalind standing in the shadows was horrified to witness his

110

transformation. She gasped and clutched the kitchen table. She cried out, 'Jeremy!'

His head came around as though he had heard but could not see. He shook himself like a bear. The cry brought him back to sanity. He heard Rosalind say, 'I will take Jonathon. Now!' Opening the parlour door he went down the hall as she gathered the boy in her arms. Jonathon sobbed wildly as she held him close. An anxious Jos, hearing the crying, put his head in the door.

'Harness Sergeant up to the trap,' said Jeremy. 'Jonathon is going back to the school.'

Christmas crept upon them and burst into a flurry of activity to collapse on the day in an anticlimax. There was no laughter, no games, no songs. Only Matt was at the table with Paula and Jeremy and Jonathon, who had come home for Christmas. Jos had been invited to share dinner with Rata while Wyndham and Caroline had made other arrangements. It was a small, subdued party that sat down to the meal. Jeremy had bought a collection of small luxuries as presents for Paula, a cake of Pears soap, a tin of sweetmeats, a chocolate cup, a teacup with a saucer gaily painted with pink and mauve butterflies and a brooch carved in ivory with angels framed in twists of gold. Jonathon had a new saddle for his pony and a box of lead soldiers.

Jeremy had closed the warehouse for a week and Matt had spent his spare time around the ships at the main wharf. Someone hooked a shark and brought it ashore to hang it up outside the Victoria Hotel for everybody to see. Matt wandered up and down the main street peering in the shop windows. Prices were high. Milk 6d a quart, butter 1/6 a lb., eggs 2/6 a dozen and wages only seven shillings a day, but then the demands of the military accounted for the high costs.

After the holiday Jeremy called Wyndham into the office. 'Sit down,' he said, indicating the chair on the other side of the desk. The man's hands were shaking. Drink or worry? Jeremy asked himself. 'Wyndham, I am going to make a few changes.'

Wyndham jerked upright in his chair. 'What sort of changes?'

'It won't effect you so very much.'

Wyndham sank back and crossed his legs.

'I want you to have the title of secretary and take the running of the office out of my hands,' said Jeremy. 'You will sign the promissory notes with me.'

'Do you want me to do the banking?'

'Yes, you will handle the bills and the purchases. Just give me a summary of them at the end of each month.'

'What are you going to do?'

'Spend more time at home, I hope, with Paula and Jonathon.'

'Then Jonathon is staying with you?'

'Yes.'

'Paula is better?'

'I think so. She offered no objection when I told her.'

'You mentioned a few changes. What else?'

'Matt will be general manager.'

'And Jos?'

'He will get an extra sixpence a day.'

'That is very generous.'

'He deserves it. He is very loyal and willing.'

'I suppose he is.'

Jeremy stretched up his arms and put them behind his head. 'And I am making Tukino warehouse manager.'

Wyndham showed his surprise. 'Is that wise?'

'Why do you say that?'

'What will our customers think of being served by a Maori? Can you trust him? He could be here today and gone tomorrow.'

Jeremy frowned. 'I trust him implicitly.'

Wyndham forced a laugh and flicked an imaginary piece of dust from his lapel. 'The wagon needs new rims and the horse some shoes,' he said. 'Can we take them to Hardington's Bazaar?'

'Certainly. Jonathon's *Oliver* needs shoeing. Tell them we'll bring a pony in on Friday night. By the way Trust is coming in to town with his children. Ambrose, Nicholas and Richard will be staying with us.'

'I am surprised you encourage Trust.'

'Why is that.'

'He is a strange man. He won't let anyone on the farm to fish for eels and the Maori resent that.'

'He is only managing the farm for Kennedy. I suppose he feels

112

some sort of extra responsibility for it. After all he was a game-keeper in England.' Jeremy paused. 'Is there anything else?'

'No, that is all for now.'

Nicholas and Richard Trust laughed and chattered as they led Oliver into town with Jonathon running beside them. There was great activity at Hardington's when they went around the back to the stables. The omnibus was parked there and the horses had been put away for the night to enjoy some well earned bags of chaff. New carriages and traps were on display in the front, and saddlery and leather goods decorated the walls. At the back the children stood warming themselves beside the kiln that heated the iron hoops before they were sweated on to the wooden wheels. Jonathon plugged his ears and watched as the steam rose from the wheel platform while the smithy poured water over the red hot metal to shrink it tightly on to the rims. The children wrestled on the bales of hay until it was time to take Sergeant and the cart back and Oliver was left in a stall for shoeing in the morning. Four sleepy children tumbled into bed that night, talking animatedly until Jeremy growled them into a reluctant silence.

12

Jeremy woke with a start. He could hear the sound of fire bells ringing followed by the military alarm. He fumbled for the mother of pearl watch-stand on the table by his bed and lit a candle. It was a half after two. Glancing out of the window he saw a narrow trail of smoke blotting out the stars in the west. Something's gone up, he thought. He turned over and tried to sleep. A pink, flickering reflection on the wall of the room finally forced him awake. Looking out the window he saw the sky had changed to red. The glow had spread towards the south. Hardington's Bazaar! He ran down the hill and jumped across the creek. It was three o'clock when he reached the top of the hill. A group of people was standing on the barrack wall watching the blaze. The fire was completely out of control. Captain Daldy was directing the fire brigade with little effect. The intense heat was blistering the paint on houses on the opposite side of the street. Steady flames shot high above the roofs as the men pumped water on the sides of the buildings, but the water was reduced to a trickle as the well in the yard quickly dried up. The fire spread unchecked up the eastern side.

Jeremy ran down Victoria Street to the Greyhound Inn and to Hardington's nearby.

'Thank God.' He said the words aloud as he saw soldiers pushing out the carriages and traps from the front door while others had already released the horses and were driving them down the street.

114

A man was standing on top of the building, attaching some ropes to the cornices and the main studs of the timbered stables. They tied the ends to a horse and cart and pulled the main part of the building down. There was a splintering of wood and glass as it collapsed leaving a clutter of timber and bags of burning chaff.

Engines No. 2 and 4 were in the yard playing water over the roofs and sides of houses adjoining the horse bazaar. A brigade was outside the Thistle Hotel trying to save Mr Darley's house alongside. Showers of falling sparks were igniting the shingles on the roofs as men climbed up with buckets of water and wet blankets to contain the blaze.

Jeremy was forced by the heat to retreat up Barrack Hill with the rest of the spectators. They watched the fire advance steadily up the street as it spread from shop to shop and consumed everything in its path. It leapt across the space by the Greyhound Inn, feeding on the living branches of the trees in the garden. A roof caught fire and a building exploded outwards. Through a window, he saw an iron bedstead, strangely twisted, crash downwards. A liquid stream of fire poured on the pavement as barrels of rum and gin burst open. The fire swept up towards them destroying the old theatre. Rubbish and straw on the other side of the street burst into flames and bags of grain outside began to smoulder.

Jeremy saw small flickerings on the roof of the Blue Post boarding house. He called out to some soldiers who had come down from the barracks with blankets. The men ran to an engine and poured water over themselves. A whirling eddy of air carried the sparks towards Jeremy and tore off his hat. He ran inside the building and found a way on to the roof. Somebody set a ladder against the wall and together they covered the front of the roof with wet army blankets. They lay on the shingles and stretched out over the edge of the building where large patches of paint were peeling off. Jeremy stayed there, extinguishing the flames as the sparks ignited the dry timber. He looked across the street. The block was a mass of black timbers, flickering flame and debris. The cornerstones of a brick building across the way were bulging outwards and the wall leaned drunkenly where the iron stays had given way. A heap of earthenware and pottery lay broken in the rubble.

By four o'clock the worst was over. Jeremy clambered down from the roof and joined a subdued crowd of people gazing at the

115

ruins. He saw Hardington.

'The horses.' he called out. 'Where are they?'

Hardington turned and faced him as though in a daze. A groom standing within earshot called out. 'They are over the other side of the hill by the water in St George's Bay.'

Jeremy found his coat and walked back over the hill. His hair was singed and the smell of smoke clung around him. He found Oliver with the other horses. The pony shied when he approached, showing the whites of its eyes. Jeremy quietly held out his hand for the halter that was still attached to the beast and led him back home.

The Trust children walked the horse to Newmarket, down Khyber Pass Road which was built by the military, to the blacksmith's shop.

Jeremy watched Ambrose and Nicholas Trust shoe the pony for Jonathon. Ambrose was a mature lad and was capable of any farm work. He was his father's right hand man and a good shot with a rifle. Strong and upright, he had benefited from the discipline that his father had enforced but it was a hard life for the boy, up early each morning, milking the cows, then into the fields with the men. Jeremy could see the young muscles rippling under his shirt. Nicholas was working the bellows as Ambrose beat the shoes into their final shapes and plunged them into a pail of water to cool them. The steam curled up to the ceiling and the glow of the fire cast an eerie light on the heads and shoulders of the children making them look like little men. Which they are, thought Jeremy. Ambrose pared Oliver's hooves and holding the pony's foot firmly between his knees, he hammered the nails home into the hoof, securing the shoe.

Jonathon rode Oliver home while the boys walked behind.

'Father does not like Maori,' said Richard. He was finding it hard to keep up with the bigger boys.

'Yes he does,' replied Nicholas, 'but there are a few wild ones around that are strangers to the district, and some cattle have disappeared.'

Ambrose turned and walked backwards along the Macadamized road. 'He hates that Hau Hau tohunga.'

'What is a Hau Hau tohunga?' asked Jonathon.

116

Richard put an arm on Jonathon's saddle. 'He is a priest and believes that if he goes into battle shouting "Hau Hau" the bullets will not touch him. He came to our creek fishing for eels and father sent him away, just as he did with the poachers in England . . . . Mr St. Clair, can we have a sail in your boat?'

Jeremy looked down at the boy. 'If your father agrees I will take you in the cutter when I bring your supplies.'

'Will you?' Richard skipped up to Jeremy. 'Right up Turanga Creek?'

'Yes.'

'Where we load the firewood?'

'Yes,' promised Jeremy.

On the day, there was a cold wind and a choppy sea, but it did not deter the Trust children. They sailed down the harbour past the Howick village and the stockade and rowed up the creek to the landing. It was a good walk to Kennedy's farmhouse but with the flour bags on their backs they soon had everything stowed away. When Jeremy left to return on his own, they stood at the door and waved good-bye. Richard Trust, a happy eight-year-old scampered with his pet dog to the fence and climbed on it to wave good-bye.

Back in town Jeremy was surprised to find Jos on the beach when he sailed the *'Echo'* into the bay. The boy took the forestay and held it while Jeremy unloaded some pots of butter and a leg of pork that Mrs Trust had given him. He could see that Jos had something on his mind.

'Mr St Clair?'

'Yes, Jos,'

'That extra money you gave me.'

'Yes?'

'That sixpence a day. Would you save it for me?'

Jeremy smiled to himself. 'Certainly Jos. Why not put it in the Auckland Savings Bank?'

'I suppose I could, but I thought you might be able to get more interest for me, like you get for the money you let out.'

'Mm. But there is a bigger risk. You can guarantee that if someone is prepared to pay a high interest, he has not the same collateral.'

'What is collateral?'

'The land, stock, anything of value that can be sold if he defaults.'

'Land. That's what I want it for. To save up to buy some land. I already have ten pounds in the bank. Mr St Clair!'

'Yes.'

'If I tell you something, will you keep it a secret.'

'Yes.'

'Rata and I are going to be married one day.'

'Oh. When?'

'When I can buy a farm. Maori land where the soil is good. They always have their plantations in the places where the soil is best. You don't think we are silly wanting to get married?'

'No, Jos. Of course not. She is a fine girl. When you have saved up some money, I will help you with the rest.'

'Thank you. Thank you, Mr St Clair.' Jos put the box he was carrying on to his shoulder and ran up the hill.

13

By early February, Jeremy had put the changes to his business into effect and began to concentrate on the newspaper.

On Monday 10 February, word came through that the *'Orpheus',* a British warship of twenty-one guns and the pride of the Australian station, had been wrecked on the bar at Onehunga and many lives lost. In town, the churches were full. The preachers prayed for the souls of the men who had gone, and in the evening the flag at the fort flew at half mast and a gun fired every minute in melancholy farewell.

Tuesday was a day of mourning. As soon as he was dressed, Jeremy knocked on Paula's door. Usually she lay there pretending to be asleep, then would open her eyes and demand to know what he wanted. When he went in she was lying on her back, staring at the curtains.

'Are you coming to church today?' he asked.

Only her eyes moved to focus on a gown laid over a chair. He saw a prayer book on the dressing table.

'I presume that means you are.'

He stood looking down at her. The thought had come to his mind that the catastrophe that had made such an impression on the whole town may have made her realize that life was precious. That it would be worthwhile to have some sort of quality in it, a quality that had nothing to do with money or position, and there was so much to live for, if she wished.

'All business is suspended today,' he said. 'We will leave for the church together at ten-thirty.'

St Matthews was full with sailors, soldiers and townspeople. Jeremy and Paula took their seats. In the pulpit the vicar preached of life and death and the hereafter.

Subscriptions had already been raised for the survivors. They needed clothes, tea, sugar and tobacco. 'It is usual,' the committee had said, 'to differentiate between the officers and the men, but we aim to find ten pounds for each individual, irrespective of rank'. The survivors had already sailed on the '*H.M.S. Miranda*' the night before on their way to Sydney.

Rosalind was standing at the side of the churchyard when they went out into the sunlight, and Jeremy was surprised when Paula asked her to tea. When Rosalind arrived at the house Jonathon was waiting on the steps and he held her horse while she dismounted. Taking Rosalind's hand he led her into the drawing room.

'You can fire my cannon,' he said.

She laughed. 'I am not dressed for war.'

Jeremy watched the dimples dance on her cheeks. She walked over to the mantelpiece and studied the painting of a whaling ship that hung above it.

'And who are you fighting?'

'The rebels,' said Jonathon.

'What rebels?'

'Those that defy the Queen's laws.'

Rosalind threw a look of despair at Jeremy and shook her head. She took the chair he offered her.

'How is business?' she asked.

'Not good.'

'Oh?'

'The navy and the military keep me going but supplies are not easy. The Waikato Maori have almost stopped sending in produce.'

'Why?'

'They have turned to politics instead of farming. I have had no wheat and they have only brought in a few tons of cleaned flax. Christmas has always been a dull season with native trade but this year it was worse.'

120

Rosalind unpinned the brooch holding her neck-scarf. 'I can understand that. They buy the newspapers just as we do. What do they read? Someone calling them rebels because they are holding on to their own land. Correspondence saying that war is the only way to settle the impasse. You can't blame them for being suspicious. Gifts of flour and sugar won't solve the problem. Then there is the military road. And Gorst. They believe the Governor sent him to spy on them while setting up schools. The King people aren't fools. We have done nothing to uphold the law we promised with the Treaty of Waitangi, so they have set up their own courts to punish any such acts as murder and adultery. Ever since the Governor's arrival the Waikato tribe has been suspicious of him.'

Jeremy reluctantly agreed.

In the evening, Rosalind settled Jonathon into bed while Jeremy and Paula watched from the doorway. The child lay under the blankets with his chin on the sheet as he smiled up at them. Even Paula appeared to be relaxed. She pressed their guest to stay for a late supper, but Rosalind was anxious to return to the school.

'Rata can manage, but I prefer to be there at bedtime,' she said.

'Wait,' Jeremy glanced at Paula. 'I will ride with you.

The sun was setting as they put their horses into a walk. Rosalind turned towards Jeremy. 'You are going to tell me that Paula is better,' she said.

'The change tonight was extraordinary, I cannot understand it.'

'More like her better self?'

'I have never seen her like this.'

They continued down the hill until Rosalind broke the silence. 'She seemed to enjoy the Governor's levees while you were down in the Waikato.'

Jeremy looked up. 'What levees.'

'Oh dear,' said Rosalind.

'Tell me more. I don't mind her going as long as I am not dragged along.'

'Jeremy you must take her to more entertainments. After all it is a lively little town.'

'I have asked her to come out with me. She always refuses.'

'Perhaps it is the way you say it. Have you asked her to a levee

121

before?'

'No. They are silly social things.'

'Women enjoy them and so do some men,' said Rosalind.

'Who was there?'

Rosalind gave a short burst of laughter. 'Everybody. The military, officers from the 65th, the 40th, a band . . . I enjoyed it.'

'Newhaven was there?'

'Of course.'

'With his superior smile and riding crop.'

'No. He left that at the barracks. The riding crop I mean. Come Jeremy, perhaps that is why Paula seemed so different tonight. She needs to go out more.'

'She would hardly speak to me this morning.'

'So? Promise you will take her out more. Encourage her.'

'I will see.'

'Promise?'

'All right.'

They let the horses have their heads as they climbed Constitution Hill. Rosalind glanced at Jeremy. 'Is business as bad as you say?'

'Worse.'

'Can you manage?'

'Yes.'

'Regarding money, I mean.'

'I would rather not discuss money with you.'

'Jeremy, be realistic. We are friends.'

'It is not a woman's subject.'

She burst into peals of laughter. 'Jeremy. I know all about money. My father taught me how to handle his investments as well as his property. Everybody thought it was somewhat unusual but then he wanted me to be a boy.'

'I'm glad that you're not.' They both laughed.

'That's better,' she said. 'Have you enough money?'

'In terms of stock and debtors, yes, but no one is paying, and with little trading going on it is all tied up in slow moving goods. I am a bit strapped for cash. I don't quite know why.'

'I'll lend you some.'

He stopped his horse. 'No thank you.'

'Why not? Because I'm a woman?'

122

'Because you are a friend.'

'Imagine I'm a man. What then?'

'That's very hard to do.'

'Well?'

The sun had gone down. The sky had changed to a luminous twilight making the trees stand out like ghosts. The sense of distance had disappeared and the lights on the harbour were larger than life. Rosalind's eyes were hidden by the shadows.

'I could not accept,' he said. 'I want to keep you as a friend.'

She was not sure whether to be pleased or sorry. 'If you need help, ask me,' she said.

The next time Jeremy saw Rosalind was at an indoor picnic. There was a clatter of plates as he and Paula went up the steps. He heard a voice call above the conversation of a company of officers.

'Anyone for port?'

'No thank you.'

'Madeira?'

'No thank you. Porter please.'

There was a burst of laughter from inside. The doors of the living room were open and the chatter from the ladies spilled out on to the verandah.

'I want to make a speech,' said somebody.

A voice on the lawn called out, 'Wait until later.'

Rosalind put her head out from the doorway. She had a plate of food in each hand. 'We are lucky with the weather,' she said to nobody in particular.

The table had been wound out to it fullest extent and the crocheted cloth was almost hidden by the array of food, a cold collation, with all the meats imaginable. Two wood-pigeon pies, four lobsters, a quarter of lamb with a jug of mint sauce, three boiled chickens and two raised veal pies. A cold goose with green gooseberry sauce. And, of course, the desserts. Meringues, maraschino jelly, greengage tarts and cream.

'I do enjoy inside picnics,' said Caroline as she rearranged the settings for the twentieth time. She began distributing cushions at intervals on the carpet. 'No more champagne for me, I won't be able to get up again. That's if I can get down at all.'

The hostess came out with a gong. 'Gentlemen, the picnic is served.'

The men filed into the room, some reluctantly, others with the zest of appetite.

'Before we start, "The Queen".' A captain in a red coat and with a face to match bustled into the centre of the room. There was a flurry of bottles and the tinkle of crystal. 'The Queen, God Bless 'er.'

Peals of laughter echoed across the room as they sat cross-legged on the floor or stretched out their legs, cradling the plates in varying degrees of discomfort.

'This is better than being bitten by sandflies.'

'Or being covered in sand.'

'Odd's teeth. We may as well be in the field.'

'What? With this bevy of beauties. Not likely!'

'Paula, put a cushion behind my back would you please?' Newhaven was speaking. 'That is better.'

Jeremy walked over to Paula. 'I say,' said Newhaven, 'you missed a jolly do while you were away. Paula was the life of the party.'

Jeremy was quick to reply. 'No show without Punch.' He looked at Paula. Her eyes were on the carpet.

They went up to the table for returns. A lieutenant kicked over a glass of wine. 'No matter,' called the hostess as she helped someone to the pie. 'It has happened three times this week.'

After everybody had eaten more than they should they lay back on their elbows or rested against the walls, sipping drinks.

The captain took centre stage again.

'Silence, everybody. May I say a few words.'

Paula went into the hall and shut the kitchen door. The captain put his glass down on top of the piano. 'As you know we have been told off for Taranaki and have been turned into light cavalry. Half the squadron sailed yesterday. They swam the horses out and got them on board without injury, thank God. The rest of us leave on the 23rd, one hundred sabres in all. You can be sure we'll give a good account of ourselves. Settle the rebels once and for all. Probably Tataramaika is already in our possession, so matters will soon be settled one way or another and we know which way it will be.

Dear ladies, we will miss you, but it won't be long before we are back. Gentlemen, charge your glasses and drink to the ladies.'

'To the ladies.'

After the toast Jeremy walked over to Rosalind. The women began to pass around more plates. Rosalind went to the piano and fingered the keys.

'Play us a tune,' called Newhaven. 'The music sheets. Where are the music sheets?'

They found some in the piano seat. Rosalind ruffled through and selected a dozen pieces.

'Let's have "The Ratcatcher's Daughter".'

'And "My Johnnie was a Shoemaker".'

The men gathered around the piano as the women went to and fro with empty dishes. A subaltern came from the direction of the back door with a shotgun in his hands.

'Who's for target practice?'

They went into the fields behind the house and threw an old cap into the air, while each took a turn at shooting it down. Jeremy did tolerably well and so did Newhaven. Two teams were selected. They put a bottle on the fence and had shots at it with pistols. No one could say who had won so the men had a tug-of-war contest to decide.

It was almost midnight when Jeremy and Paula left, letting Sergeant make his own pace home. Paula tucked a sheepskin rug over her knees as they clattered up the hill. In the last few weeks she had been thinking of the situation they were in. She did not want to deceive Jeremy and had no intention to do so but there had not been an opportunity for a *tête-a-tête*. She drew a deep breath and gripped the side of the cart.

'Jeremy.' Her voice was unsteady. 'I want to say something.'

He took up the reins. 'Say on.'

Paula felt her heart sink.

'Come on, what is it?'

She closed her eyes. 'I have been going out while you have been away.'

He kept looking ahead, bolt upright on the seat. 'That is all right, my dear, as long as you are enjoying yourself.'

'You don't mind?'

'Of course not. I know I am a bit stuffy when it comes to that sort of thing. Besides I knew you had been to the Governor's levee. Did you enjoy it?'

'Who told you?'

'Never mind. You can't get away with much in this town. I'm glad you enjoyed it. As a matter of fact I saw the Governor myself a while ago.'

'How was that?'

'They knew I'd been into the King Country. Wanted to know what I thought of the situation. I was quite flattered really.'

'What did you tell them?'

'That it was a tinderbox, ready to burst into flames. The Governor showed me his aviary, the birds he brought from South Africa. They were fascinating. It was just before he left for Taranaki.'

'What is going to happen Jeremy?'

'I don't know, but he went off to sort things out. I would not mind betting he wants to tidy up down there and so leave the troops free to attack the Waikato. One front at a time. General Cameron's with him. Bishop Selwyn went to see Cameron you know. Asked him to go easy on the Maori. Do you know what Cameron said?'

'No.'

'Bishop, you do your job and I'll do mine.'

'You don't mind me going to parties?'

'Not if it makes you happy.'

Paula felt a tinge of regret. 'I do behave myself.'

'I expect you would.'

'And if I didn't?'

Jeremy turned and looked down on the top of her bonnet. She stared straight in front, waiting for an answer.

'I don't think you'd do anything else.'

She bowed her head. 'You have great trust in me considering.'

'Considering what?'

'Considering the way we've been behaving.'

'We've been behaving?'

'Well then, the way I have been.'

'One has to trust someone. Otherwise, what is the use of it all?'

She waited until the horse had turned into the gateway before replying.

'I'll try my best, Jeremy.'

126

14

It seemed to Jeremy the whole situation was ready to explode. Rumours were flying that Maori were assembling to attack and destroy the town. The Maori chief, Rewi Maniopoto stole a printing press and ordered Mr Gorst to leave the territory. Rewi wrote a letter to the Governor.

25 March 1863
Te Awamutu

Friend Governor Grey
Greetings. This is my word to you. Mr Gorst has been silenced by me. The press has been taken by me. They are my men who took it, eighty, armed with guns. The reason is to drive away Mr Gorst, that he may return to town. It is on account of the great darkness caused by his being sent to live here and tempt us and also on account of your saying that you would dig around our King until he fell. Friend take Mr Gorst back to town, do not leave him to live with me at Te Awamutu. If you say he is to stay, he will die. Let your letter be speedy to fetch him away within three weeks.
From your friend

Rewi Maniopoto
To Governor Grey at Taranaki

Winter came at last with the rain and cold. Now, more than ever, Jeremy relied heavily on the military contracts. As payments from the government were extremely slow, he planned his finances very carefully.

Once more he began to call on Rosalind each day. She was his sounding board, someone he could talk to in a relaxed way. She had a sharp brain and made no attempt to influence him, but at the same time her advice was sound.

'Why don't you ask the bank for a loan?' she suggested. 'I'm sure you would get one.'

He was wary of the idea. 'I've always tried to pay my way.'

'There is a limit to what you can do. You have plenty of assets. Why not use their money. After all, it is what banks are for.'

'I would rather not.'

'Go and see them, then make up your mind.'

When Jeremy next passed the bank, her words came back to him. He paused a few feet past the heavy doors and nodded to an acquaintance as they swung open to allow a customer into the street. He about faced and went into the bank.

The manager ushered him into the office. Jeremy St Clair didn't often come to see him. Something must be up, he thought.

'I would like to talk to you,' said Jeremy.

'Yes . . . cigar?'

'No thank you.'

'What can I do for you?'

Jeremy hesitated. 'I feel I am running close to the wind for cash. I usually have a reserve for bills payable, but if someone does not pay next month I could be in trouble.'

'Who do you think may default?'

'No one in particular, but I am not usually so short of cash.'

The banker nodded. 'We will help you. You have plenty of assets I presume. Are they encumbered?'

'No.'

'Well then, there is no problem. How much do you need?'

'I don't know precisely. As I said, I may not need a penny.'

'Well, if you can give me an idea and supply a list of assets and liabilities I can accommodate you tomorrow. You will need to take stock. There is a board meeting tomorrow night. Of course we will have to take a charge over your assets.'

128

'I have never done that before.'

'Don't worry. It's only a formality to give us a little protection.'

The manager stood up and held out his hand. 'We will see you tomorrow then.'

Jeremy went back to the warehouse and called Wyndham and Tukino into his office. 'We will be taking stock this afternoon. Does that interfere with any of your plans, Wyndham?'

'Er . . . no. No, I am sure.'

Tukino looked puzzled. 'Taking stock?'

'A list of all the goods in the warehouse and any that are paid for and not in store yet.'

'Ah.' Tukino smiled, 'You Pakeha.'

'For the bank.' Jeremy glanced at Wyndham. 'And I will need details of all the bills.'

Wyndham frowned.

'What is wrong?' asked Jeremy. 'Is it too much to do?'

'No, no.' Wyndham stood up. 'I will start right away.'

Tukino waited for Wyndham to go out. 'Mr Jeremy,' he said. 'I have something to tell you.'

'What is it?'

'Tonight, I must go back to my people.'

'Of course. We won't be late. You should finish at the usual time.'

'You do not understand, I am going to visit my sister in Rotorua and return to my people at Taupo.'

Jeremy showed his surprise. 'Why?'

Tukino was slow to reply. 'I feel I should be with my people. It is difficult for us in town now and the Mangere people where I sleep are unsettled. They are bringing all their pigs and fowls to Onehunga and selling them for what they can get.'

Jeremy considered for a moment. There wasn't much going on, especially with Maori trade. It would save a wage. He turned to Wyndham, who had walked in with the ledger. 'Very well,' he paused. 'Wyndham, Tukino wants to finish up. Can you make up his pay?'

'When?'

'This afternoon.'

'I can give it to him this evening.'

Jeremy nodded. 'I will leave it to you.' He held out his hand. 'Thank you for all you have done. There is a position here whenever you want it.'

Tukino was silent. Jeremy understood. The Maori could be shy as well as warlike. 'Good luck,' he said. 'I must go down to the wharf.'

The kerosene lamp was the only light in the office when Tukino knocked on the warehouse door and was admitted by Wyndham that evening. There was a thick envelope on the desk which Wyndham handed to him.

'Count it,' he said.

Tukino pulled out some banknotes and picked them up one by one.

'You are very generous.'

'No matter.' Wyndham looked him in the eye. 'Where are you going?'

'To Lake Taupo.'

'How long will you take to get there?'

'Ten days, thirty days, who knows?'

'I am coming with you.'

'Why?'

'To see Rotorua. The geysers. The mud pools. I will be safe with you, won't I?'

'As safe as you could be. I have to go a long way around. Some tribes are still our enemies and I must steer clear of them. Why don't you go to Tauranga like other Pakeha and walk from there.'

'I have searched for a boat to take me. There are none in the harbour.' Wyndham picked up a pack standing in the corner and put it over his shoulders. 'That's settled then,' he said. 'I'll pay you for it.'

'Mr Jeremy, does he know?'

'I will take care of that. You go on. I will catch you up at the corner.'

When Tukino was out of sight Wyndham walked slowly around the perimeter of the warehouse. He picked up a knife and put it in his pocket. Holding the lantern up to a calendar on the wall he read the date. Eighth of June, 1863. Feeling his way to the back door he tried the bolts. They were securely fastened. He took some

130

blankets and nailed them to the windows, and tipped over a basket of waste paper into the middle of the floor. Opening the side door a fraction, he threw the lamp onto the heap. There was a shattering of glass as he watched the flames lick hungrily at the paper. Quickly running outside he slammed the door behind him and walked briskly up the street. Tukino was waiting for him. Without a word they strode towards the Great South Road.

At the top of the Khyber Pass Road, Tukino stopped.

'Are you sure you want to come?'

'Yes.'

'It is a very bad walk. Across rivers, swamps, sleeping in the open.'

'I am used to that. I was in the army for ten years.'

'But you are soft now.'

'One of your soft Pakeha?'

'I do not joke.'

'Tukino, don't worry. You look after me and I will make it worth your while. I wish I had both my guns.'

'One is enough. We have a saying, 'Wishing never filled a game bag.' He looked back. There was a dull red glow reflected in the clouds to the north. 'See, another fire. You Pakeha have so much money you burn buildings to keep warm.'

When Jeremy arrived at the fire the roof of the warehouse was ablaze and the wooden shingles were twisting in the heat. A body of flame shot from the windows and the inside was already gutted. He ran to the back and tried to open the double doors to the yard but was beaten back by the flames. A military engine belonging to the 65th Regiment was pouring water onto the front of the building. The fire had spread to the Osprey Inn, licking at the walls and along the wooden guttering.

'Keep back!' The commander of the engine shouted above the roof of the flames.

'There's whale oil in there,' called Jeremy.

As he spoke a flash of smoke and fire erupted through the roof and there was an explosion. The men putting wet blankets on the face of the building ran back from the blaze.

'It is no good. We will concentrate on the other buildings.' The engine commander switched hoses to the front of the Duke of Marlborough Hotel.

Jeremy ran to the pump handle. A long hose had been placed in the custom-house well that supplied water to a large tank. From there it was pumped along the street to the other buildings. Another hose was laid down Vulcan Lane to the canal. He could hear the custom-house fire bell still ringing and the faint sound of the alarms in other parts of town. Water poured onto the roofs, gutters and verandahs of the adjoining buildings. A wall of the Duke of Marlborough crashed down. Mr Quigley's cooperage collapsed in a tangle of iron hoops and ashes. Jeremy wiped the perspiration from his face. A bandsman of the 65th took his place at the pump.

Walking slowly back to the warehouse, Jeremy saw it had burnt to the ground. Piles of glowing embers and black ashes. An iron brace that had held up one of the roof beams was leaning drunkenly at an angle on the floor of the shop. There was a pile of shattered glass in a corner and the remains of the stove lay on its side among the debris. He stared, unseeing, at the desolation.

'Jeremy!'

The voice came from somewhere behind.

'Oh, Jeremy!'

He turned. Rosalind was standing there. Tears were streaming down her face and she made no attempt to stem them. He walked over to her. For a brief moment he put an arm around her shoulders and searched for a handkerchief.

'Here,' he said. 'Don't cry.'

'Oh Jeremy.' His hair was wet with the spray from the leaking hose and there were smudges of ash on his face. The vile stench of smoke and destruction clung to his clothes.

'All your work gone.'

'I will build again.' His jaw set firmly. 'I won't let this beat me. Thank heavens I am insured.'

He looked down the High Street. Matt and Jos were walking slowly towards them with disbelief and shock in their eyes. They stood staring at the wisps of smoke curling up from the ruins. The darkness of the night accentuated the glow from the piles of embers. A brick wall crashed down.

'Keep away!' called Jeremy. They backed into the middle of

the street. 'Jos, go and find Wyndham and tell him what has happened. Bring the dray into town.'

Rosalind interrupted. 'You can't do anything tonight. Come up to my place. Have something to eat.'

They sat down to breakfast as the first sign of light appeared in the sky. Jos arrived with the dray. "Wyndham isn't home,' he said. 'His missus don't know where he is.'

Jeremy and Rosalind looked at each other.

'Perhaps he has another woman,' said Matt.

Jeremy suddenly became businesslike. 'Jos have some breakfast and then fetch the dray. Bring shovels. We'll start clearing up right away.'

All the lamps were burning at the New Zealand Insurance Company when Jeremy was ushered in to the manager's office. He proffered Jeremy a chair. 'Good morning. It has been quite a night.'

'It certainly has,' Jeremy sat down. 'You must have had some big losses.'

'Over seven thousand pounds. We'll have about ten claims.'

'Mine is probably the biggest.'

'I beg your pardon?'

'Mine. Apart from possibly Powley and Johnsons, mine must be the biggest.'

The manager raised himself slowly from the chair and walked to the door. He turned and faced Jeremy, peering over his spectacles.

'Jeremy, your insurance is not with us.'

'Oh yes it is!'

'I assure you, it isn't.'

'I had Wyndham change to your office two years ago.'

'Not this office.' The manager opened the door and called out to his chief clerk.'

'Edwards! Edwards, have we Mr St Clair's insurances?'

A face appeared around the door. 'Pardon sir?'

'Edwards. Have we Mr St Clair's insurances at this office?'

'No sir.'

Jeremy brought a small ledger from his pocket. 'Look! Entries for premiums. Fortunately I carry this with me.'

The clerk shook his head. 'Mr St Clair, I am certain we haven't your insurances. It is over a year ago since I talked to Wyndham. He told me you were insured elsewhere and to cancel them.'

Jeremy listened in disbelief. 'But I've been paying them regularly. Look!' He pointed to the entries. 'There! And there! Paid. Paid. Paid.'

The manager went back to his desk. 'Where is Wyndham?'

'We can't find him. I don't know where he is. The bank. My bank will have the details.'

The manager walked to the door again and returned a few minutes later. 'I have sent for Shepherd. I presume you still bank with him?'

'Yes.'

Shepherd saw two anxious faces looking at him when he walked in.

'Do you remember my insurance payments?' asked Jeremy.

'I wouldn't recall all your transactions, but if Wyndham gives me the details I'll look them up.'

'We can't find him.'

'But he came in yesterday afternoon. Drew money out for that cash purchase. Practically all you had.'

'What purchase?' Jeremy felt the hairs prickle on the back of his neck. His mind began to race. The new carriage. The drinking. Always money in his pocket. 'How much is left in the account?

'Fifty pounds.'

The insurance manager smashed his fist to the desk.

'He's done you, Jeremy. My God. He can't be far away. Have you any other cash?'

'No. A little I suppose. There'll be something in London. Four or five hundred pounds.

'That's a help. There's your house.' The insurance manager began pacing up and down the office. 'We'll have to keep you going until this is sorted out. I'll help you all I can. It's a little unusual but it has been done before. An *ex gratia* payment to show our good faith. Not much mind you. Say four hundred pounds. That's about a fifth of your loss. I'll put it to the board. Mind you, they'll want all your future business.' He looked across at the bank manager.

Shepherd cleared his throat. 'We can give you some sort of

loan Jeremy, with your house as security. Money's tight but you do own the land. Your military contracts are worth something and you at least know you are going to be paid eventually, although the government departments are damned slow. Come and see me tomorrow at ten.'

They rose and shook hands. The manager escorted them towards the door. Putting his hand on Jeremy's shoulder he guided him through the chamber. 'It will work out,' he said. 'You have what it takes.'

Rosalind was on the verandah rocking to and fro on her favourite chair when Jeremy called on his way home.

'Tea or whiskey?' she asked.

'I could do with a whiskey but it's a bit early. Make it tea.'

'I have just opened a tin of Earl Grey.' Rosalind brought out a tray. 'Don't tell me. No milk. One lump.' She took the tongs and dropped the sugar into his cup. 'Well?'

'Wyndham has disappeared.'

'Disappeared?'

'Absconded with all my cash.'

He watched her face. A look of disbelief. Bewilderment. Worry lines creasing her brow.

'Poor Caroline.'

Thinking about it later he realized it was just the thing she would say. 'It has almost broken me.'

'Oh you poor thing. Please Jeremy. Let me help you.'

'Thank you Rosalind, but I will manage. The bank has offered me a loan and the insurance company has come up with something as well.'

'Thank God.'

'They have been damned decent.'

'So they should.'

'I am seeing the bank manager at ten tomorrow.'

'Have you talked to Caroline?'

'No.'

"I must go to her. I never did trust that Wyndham. Call it women's intuition. She will be frantic.'

While Rosalind changed her dress, Jeremy saddled her mare. 'Good luck,' she called as she turned the horse's head for town.

* * *

135

When Jeremy let himself in the front door he heard Paula call from her room. He pushed the door open and sat on the edge of the bed.

'Something's happened,' she said. 'I can tell.'

He tried to be matter of fact, not to be theatrical, but the words sounded odd. 'We have had a fire. Wyndham has disappeared with the cash and I'm about bankrupt.' He watched the colour mounting in her cheeks. Her breasts rose and fell under the bedclothes. He waited.

At last she spoke in a low, venomous whisper. 'You! You sit there as though you were telling me we have been invited somewhere to dinner. And you're bankrupt. Ruined. Jeremy St Clair, I rue the day I married you. There has been nothing but trouble since. You are never here when I need you. Always away. This is the end as far as I am concerned. You can do what you like. I'm going my way and you can go yours.'

Jeremy waited for her anger to subside. "I said almost bankrupt. There is still hope.'

'Hope! Hope! You sound like the vicar. I want peace. Money.'

Jeremy felt his anger rise. 'Then you should have stayed at home. You won't get any of that here while we are colonizing this country.'

'Then what are we here for?'

'To make a place for future generations.'

Paula's voice rose higher. 'Get out. Go. Take your ideas somewhere else. Go and pander to that missionary woman. Go on. Get out. Get out!'

He stood up and looked down at her. 'Perhaps if your life had been as exemplary as hers you would not be in the position you are today.'

It was as though he had struck her with a lash. She recoiled and put her hand up to protect herself. From his words? From his anger? There was a long silence as any respect they had for each other was ravaged away. He felt empty. Sick.

Groping for something to say he was at a loss for words but he knew it was too late. 'I'm very sorry,' he said.

Downstairs the fire door on the stove shut with a clang. The daily help was stoking the fire. He climbed down and made his way to the stables. Strapping some tools on Sergeant's saddle bag he returned to town. Matt and Jos were already filling the dray with rubble. Jeremy took off his coat, rolled up his sleeves and joined them.

The banking chamber was empty when Rosalind went through the door at exactly nine o'clock the following day. The manager ushered her into his office. 'This is a pleasant surprise,' he said. 'You are early this month. The mail has not arrived.'

She put her gloves on the desk. 'It is not the remittance I am concerned about. Not exactly. I understand Mr St Clair will be coming in for a loan this morning.'

The banker looked up sharply. 'I'm afraid we can't divulge information about our clients.'

'No matter,' she said. 'I know the situation. I want to help. If you need a guarantor I will oblige, but he must not know of it.'

'That is highly irregular.'

'So? I can't see what harm it is. You will, I presume take a debenture over his assets.'

'Yes.'

'Then I will give you added security.'

'I suppose we can stretch a point. Keep it confidential. A private contract between the bank and yourself. It could help.'

'Good. Now I want you to double the amount of the loan you propose.'

'I beg your pardon madam?'

'I want to double the amount of your loan.'

'But that is highly improper. I can't do that.'

'Is my word worth nothing?'

'Of course not.'

'Then I want it done. Otherwise I may have to transfer my funds to a bank that will accommodate me, and then, of course, there is my father's money in London. Your head office may not want that moved.'

Shepherd gulped. 'You drive a hard bargain. I'll do what I can.'

Rosalind stood up and put on her gloves. 'Remember, give him what he needs and not a word to anyone. Send the papers around and I'll sign them when they are ready. Just let me know what the limits are.'

'For a woman you seem well versed in banking procedure.'

'For a woman, I am well versed in most things, Mr Shepherd. Does it surprise you? Let me tell you. As a woman, this is only the beginning.'

Before Shepherd could rise from his chair she walked to the door. 'Remember, we don't want to upset head office, do we?'

Jeremy was at the counter as she went out. 'Mr St Clair, I do declare. Good morning.' She gave him an exaggerated curtsy. 'So pleased to see you.'

15

The river was wide and deep where Tukino and Wyndham camped on the third night. They had skirted the Great South Road to avoid the military picquets and the occasional despatch riders that were the only signs of activity. The road itself was a quagmire, impassable for carts. The winter rain had come with a vengeance, but the king ferns and the giant trees gave them shelter and only in a few cultivated openings did they need extra protection. Sleeping under the fallen trunks of trees they made beds of moss and fern where the rain had not penetrated. Now the sun was shining and steam was rising from the leaves of the lacebark trees clumped together on the edge of the river. The ground was marshy, with sedges dotting the swamps, and from somewhere amongst the flax came the call of a swamp-hen.

Wyndham threw his pack onto a stump half submerged in the water. The rains had swollen the river and branches of trees and debris glided swiftly past, although where they stood was a backwater of brown weeds. A huge eel prowled along the bottom and disappeared under a log. Wyndham pulled off his wet boots and took a clay pipe from his pocket.

'Tukino, how do we get over this?'

His companion glanced across to the opposite bank.

'There is a canoe on the other side. It will come and fetch us.'

'When?'

'When there is someone there to paddle it.'

'That could be next week.'

'You must be patient. You Pakeha are always in too much of a hurry.'

'What do we do in the meantime?'

'Sit and wait. Perhaps I will be able to teach you some of the Maori ways. To be patient.'

'It might be more appropriate if I teach you our ways. Get things done.'

'Such as destroying our King?'

'Well, you can't have your King and our Queen as well.'

'Why not? I see no reason why any nation should not have a King if they wish for one. The gospel you taught us does not say we are not to have a King. It says, 'Honour the King, love the brotherhood.' Why should the Queen be angry? We could be in alliance with her and friendship would be preserved. The Governor does not stop murders and fights amongst us. The King does. Let us have order, so that we may grow as you Pakeha grow. Why should we disappear from the country. New Zealand is ours. It is our heritage.'

'If we do what the Governor says you can be rich, have money, pigs and carts.'

'The Governor does nothing unless a Pakeha is killed.'

'We white men have the money, the knowledge, everything.'

'All we ask is that the dignity which now rests on your Queen should rest on our King so that this land may be in peace and be honoured. But you Pakeha are like the white heron. It sits upon a stump and eats the small fish; when it sees one it stoops down and catches it, lifts up its head and swallows it.'

'A white heron? I have never seen one.'

'It is rare in this island. We have a saying. 'He kotuku rerenga tahi.' The kotuku, once in a lifetime.'

'Your women don't mind the Pakeha. God knows there are enough half-castes running around the villages. Perhaps we can beat you that way.'

'Never. Fresh water is lost when it mingles with the salt.'

'You bloody Maori are all the same.'

Tukino leapt to his feet. He raised his hand as though to strike Wyndham and then let it drop. 'You will never learn. That is the cause of all the troubles. You allow us no dignity. The lowest of you call our chiefs 'bloody Maori'. You debauch our women, make our men drunk. I am sorry for you.' He turned and walked down the river.

Wyndham followed him. 'Don't leave me.'

Tukino stopped and turned around. 'I gave my word to protect you. Will you never understand?'

Early the following morning there was a shout from the river. Wyndham looked out through the overhanging branches to see a canoe approaching paddled by four Maori. The short wooden dugout was different from the war canoes he had seen racing on the Waitemata. It was roughly hewn and narrow with seats tied together with unbleached flax and without decoration. He listened to Tukino haggling over the price to ferry them across.

There was little freeboard when they started up through the shallows out of the current. When they had gone a quarter of a mile upstream they turned the canoe and paddled strongly. The flood carried them rapidly down stream. By the time they had crossed the river they were a hundred yards past the landing place. They rested and paddled quietly back to a muddy landing cut into the left bank.

Wyndham watched as the Maori talked animatedly in their own language. Finally, Tukino turned to him.

'These,' he said, pointing to the two nearest him, 'are coming some of the way with us.'

Wyndham eyed the two men. They wore moleskin trousers rolled up to the knees, were barefooted and carried bandoliers over their blue shirts. Each had an old 'Tower' muzzle-loading rifle. The larger of the men wore a shark's tooth in one ear and carried a greenstone club in his belt. It was a foot long and made from a single piece of hard, green, polished stone. He was heavily tattooed about the face and had a savage handsome appearance. Picking up Wyndham's pack he strode down the path, with the others struggling behind. They trekked for two days avoiding the villages and lighting small fires using the fallen branches of the totara tree, which were smokeless. In the evenings, when they camped, the two newcomers went off to snare wood-pigeons.

'Why can't we buy food from the pa?' asked Wyndham, thinking of the fortified villages they had skirted.

'The tribes here are not friendly to me,' replied Tukino. 'My grandfather was eaten by them.'

'That was long ago.'

'We are still enemies. The Maori has a long memory. I do not trust them.'

'And our two friends. Who are they?'

'One is from Taranaki. The other from the Bay of Plenty.'

'I don't like the look of them.'

'The Bay of Plenty man is good. The other . . . .'
Tukino put out a hand with his palm down.

'Not to be trusted?'

'He is bad, and when you have one bad fish in a basket you have two bad fish.'

'Then why did you let them come?'

'This is dangerous country. We might need them.'

Without a pack to carry Wyndham was able to walk faster, and they began to make good time. Leaving the river they entered the forest again. The path took them further inland. The sky was completely obscured by the trees overhead and trails of vines tangled with their guns. Underfoot was a mat of mould from rotted leaves that had been dropping for centuries, so they made no noise as they marched in single file. Wyndham was fascinated with the birds that lived in the forest. The notes of the bellbird floated over them and fantails followed them continually, fearless of their own safety, picking up insects in flight that were disturbed by the travellers. That night they heard the call of an owl.

'The ruru,' said Tukino. 'It is the sound of doom.'

Wyndham had never seen so many tuis. They fluttered overhead, imitating the sounds of the bellbird. Their feathers were bluish or greenish black with a metallic iridescence and their throats were ornamented with two tufts of white feathers. Tukino pointed out a pair to Wyndham and laughed. 'Your parson bird. My father had four in a cage. He taught one to bark like a dog and to talk. See that man?' He jerked a thumb at the smaller of his companions. 'He is my tui. Wait and see.'

The next day they climbed a high promontory that gave a

142

grand view of the surrounding countryside. The Maori talked animatedly with each other. Tukino translated for Wyndham. 'There is a pa not far away. Sometimes they are our friends, sometimes enemies, depending whether they are ready for war or not. I am sending my tui to spy out the land. We will camp here until he returns.'

They waited a whole day after the small Maori had set out in the morning. When he returned Tukino listened carefully as his 'tui' spoke. The Maori with the greenstone club asked some questions. Tukino replied. He grunted. 'My tui talked to them,' he said. 'They will welcome us tomorrow. The ovens will be lit and there will be a feast of honour.'

That night they lit a fire in the open. Before he went to sleep, Wyndham questioned Tukino. 'Are they friendlies?'

'To you pakeha, no! To me? Sometimes. But winter is not the time for war. Sometimes they welcome travellers, share their food. It is the custom.'

'Are they cannibals?'

'Yes. When their priests decree it.'

It was a long time before Wyndham fell asleep. At about noon on the following day they descended to the river again. Wyndham could see a pa on the cliff face where the river turned to the west. Tukino halted and turned, signalling for silence. 'I am sending my "tui" to fly swiftly and quietly, and to return before we enter the pa.'

The small man slipped into the undergrowth avoiding the well-worn path to the pa. Half an hour later he returned and spoke in short, rapid sentences. Tukino stiffened. He clasped his gun tightly. 'The ovens are alight,' he said, 'but they are empty. He saw no food. We must make our escape. Quickly. Carry your gun downwards, ram it and cap it but don't cock it. We don't want it to catch in the vines and fire itself.'

Sliding down the bank they ran to where some canoes were tied to trees on the edge of the river. There was a cry from above. A party from the pa was racing towards them. Jumping into the nearest canoe and picking up the paddles lying in the bottom they pushed into the middle of the river. Seven of the enemy dragged their biggest canoe down the bank and gave chase.

Tukino thrust a paddle at Wyndham. 'Paddle, you bloody pakeha, paddle or you will be in a Maori oven before sunset.'

Wyndham drove his paddle deeply into the water. With four men working in unison they went quickly downstream. Looking back Tukino saw the enemy were on the river and slicing their way down towards them. There were six Maori with paddles and another standing in the stern with a gun, urging the men on. Wyndham felt the strain as he tried desperately to keep in time with his companions. They were experts, had used canoes on rivers and sea since they were children and were strong and fit. The sinews stood out on their arms as, with muscles braced, they plied swiftly along with the current. Wyndham was too afraid to look up. Panic-stricken he knelt on the rough stakes on the bottom of the canoe.

'Paddle, you bastard, paddle.' Tukino struck him on the back with his blade.

Slowly the big canoe closed on them. They went a mile further down the river.

Tukino shouted in Maori, 'Whaka paretai.' Make for the bank.

The bow swung around and headed for the shore. A chant echoed across the river as their pursuers changed course to cut them off. Fifty yards from the shore they were at equal distances from the bank with the big canoe upstream. Wyndham saw the native in the stern raise his gun. There was a puff of smoke and a report as a ball lodged in the side of the canoe. A cry rang out. The recoil from the gun had knocked the marksman into the river. His canoe rocked sideways. Another Maori stood up and the big canoe overturned, tipping its occupants into the swift current. As the enemy were swept down, two of them grasped the sides of the small canoe.

Tukino spoke quietly to them as the paddlers made their way to the shore. The canoe stopped on the edge of the current, where the eddies swung into a backwater, with the two enemy warriors still holding on to the gunwale. The big Maori stood up. Quickly snatching an axe from the bottom of the canoe he struck them savagely on their heads. Half stunned, they held on grimly. He turned the blade and struck again, once, twice, four times, severing their hands. The bodies floated slowly away, half submerged and gathering speed, disappeared.

144

Wyndham climbed up the bank and collapsed on the ground. The big Maori leapt ashore and, brandishing the axe, advanced within a foot of Wyndham. He made a move as though to strike him. Wyndham froze, paralysed. The Maori laughed, then put the axe in his belt beside his club.

Nobody spoke to Wyndham again that day. They had lost ground in their flight down the river and marched until dark without another word being spoken. He lay wrapped in his blanket that night, sweating in spite of the cold.

Tukino woke him with a kick from his boot. 'Breakfast,' he said and thrust a piece of half-cooked pigeon at him. 'We are in dangerous country, move silently and quickly.'

The path lay for the first few miles over a grassy plain, then, after halting for a drink of water, they ascended into the hills. Tukino stopped and pointed to a thin curl of smoke twisting slowly upwards from a valley. 'Enemy,' he said. Retracing their steps they found a new track hidden by freshly cut branches and halted overlooking a small lake cradled between the hills.

For the third time that day Tukino spoke to Wyndham. 'We stop here the night. No fires. Are you cold?'

'Yes.'

Tukino unwrapped a cloak from his bundle. 'Here, use this.'

Wyndham examined it carefully. It was woven of fine flax strips and liberally tufted with kiwi feathers. A design was worked around the edge, and it easily wrapped around a man. 'It is the most beautiful I have seen,' he said.

'It was my grandfather's, and his father's also. He was a mighty warrior.'

Wyndham slept well that night in spite of the money belt he wore hidden around his waist. Crawling out fully dressed from under the cloak, he stretched himself and taking his rifle went down to the lake edge to wash. The early morning mist was clearing. He crept along the bank between the flax bushes where the sedges and bulrushes met the lake. Thousands of ducks were floating on the surface. There was a big paradise duck which resembled a muscovy, its amber breast and white head reflected in the waters. The teal and the bright-plumaged widgeon were chasing each other in defence of their territory and long-legged plover strutted on the shore. In the distance he heard the boom of a bittern. Then he saw the white heron moving silently and gracefully among the reeds, neck arched, yellow beak pointing, one black leg stepping quietly after the other, its snow white plumage contrasting against the grey of the water.

He took his gun, poured in the charge, rammed it and dropped in a ball. Taking his box of caps, he selected one and drew back the hammer. The bird was making its way towards him. He took aim and waited as it approached. Suddenly a duck flew from the water with a raucous cry and immediately the air was full of birds. He fired. The white heron spread it wings and moved slowly and gracefully in ever-widening circles. Its head was drawn back onto its shoulders. Legs trailing, it winged its way, slowly across the lake and disappeared.

Wyndham let out an oath. He picked up his pipe that had fallen to the ground, replaced the cap in the gun and turned to walk back to camp.

Before he could move there was a splash of footsteps in the swamp. The big Maori came running from behind the flax bush, with his greenstone club raised and screaming out a war chant as he advanced. Quickly Wyndham loaded his gun with powder, put in a ball and slammed the butt down on a tussock. He had no time to ram. The Maori leapt at him with club raised. As Wyndham put his rifle to his shoulder there was a loud crash. The big Maori spun around and lay in a heap at his feet. Wyndham stood there, stunned.

Tukino appeared from the swamp with a smoking gun in his hand. They stood there, looking at each other. Wyndham spoke first.

'Why did he attack me?'

'You are a pakeha.'

'You saved me.'

'Yes.'

'Why?'

'You slept under my cloak last night. From that moment I became your protector. It is the custom.'

'He was a Maori.'

'A bad one. Not to be trusted. Come!'

146

'What about the body?'

'Leave it.' Tukino turned abruptly and walked back up the track.

Wyndham hesitated. He took the carved club from the man's fist. Balancing it carefully in his hand he felt its weight. He was tempted to take it and then changed his mind. Stooping down he snatched the shark's tooth from the man's ear and hurried after Tukino.

Tukino was rolling up the cloak when Wyndham arrived back at the camp. The small Maori was already waiting with his bundle. He glowered at Wyndham but said nothing. They struck out through the forest again, using a small axe to cut a path as they climbed further into the hills.

For another three days they travelled through the twilight of the bush until they reached an open plain of fern and scrub. Tukino sent his 'tui' ahead again.

'There are more enemy pas here?' asked Wyndham.

'No. It is friendly country now. He has gone to announce that we are here.'

After a long day with only one halt for a smoke, Tukino pointed to some dense bush below a hillside. Wyndham could see a stockade at the top. A puff of white smoke rose high in the air.

'Good,' said Tukino. 'They have opened the ovens. We feast tonight.'

They entered the bush through an arch of evergreens and Wyndham found himself in a space cleared of undergrowth with some bark huts at the far end. The Maori were lined up in front of them. As they approached no-one moved or offered to greet them. The three travellers formed a line and advanced. At once there was an uproar, with cries of 'Haere-mai! Haere-mai!' Welcome! Welcome! The old women were sitting on the ground with knees level with their chins chanting and crying. The men formed a bass accompaniment, filling the night with a crescendo of sound.

The karanga finished as suddenly as it had begun. Tukino pressed nose with everybody and Wyndham followed suit. The chief, dressed in a dogskin mat, made a speech. Tukino replied, congratulating them on the prosperity of the tribe and informed them he was taking a white man to see the land. 'Perhaps the pakeha will stay and buy some land so that you may keep warm in your old age,' he said.

Wyndham was introduced to the chief's wife, a plump good-natured motherly woman wrapped in a mat. She presented Wyndham with a small pig. The chief led them to a clearing and they sat down surrounded by the whole tribe. Some Maori maidens gave Wyndham some sprigs of an orchid.

Tukino leaned towards him. 'Now you shall see a real feast.'

The contents of the ovens were piled up in a pyramid in front of the main hut. First, there were eels and potatoes and wild New Zealand spinach in flax baskets, then two tubs of pork floating in melted fat. All eyes were on the food as their host came forward and, striking one of the baskets, called out the names of his guests. The givers of the feast stood back and watched their guests eating. Some of the pa dogs attacked the pile and were kicked away by the Maori.

When their guests had finished their meal the Maori helped themselves to what was left. As more ovens were opened there were yelps from the dogs and squeals from the pigs. The chief's daughter, a girl of about sixteen years, offered Wyndham a flax basket full of steaming pork topped with sweet potatoes. She had a pleasant expression. In one ear lobe was a shark's tooth and in the other a half crown piece. Her black hair was smoothed down and bound with a strip of flax, neatly woven, making a diadem across the forehead. She wore a woven mat with a girdle at her waist. The women's heads were decorated with wreaths of fern and flowering creepers and some wore earrings of polished greenstone. The chief's wife had her hair tied up with loops formed from the transparent filament of a leaf brought for that purpose from the South Island.

The celebrations went on well into the night. Wyndham saw the chief's daughter cooking a large rat over the fire. Her young brother went behind her and with a sudden jerk pitched it into the fire. The girl picked it up, brushed off the embers and began roasting it again. Again the boy seized it and ran into the bush. The girl caught him, but as they fought and scratched a dog took the rat and disappeared.

More wild pigs were taken from the ovens and it was midnight before the Maori fell asleep around the fire, one by one, until only the chief and Tukino remained awake. Wyndham took up his blanket and made a bed on the edge of the clearing.

It was daylight when the people began to stir. There was much argument as their hosts insisted that they stay but Tukino was adamant. Struggling through the undergrowth once again they left the pa and climbed upwards. At the top of a small waterfall Wyndham pulled his pipe from his pocket and sat down. As he did so the shark's tooth he had taken fell to the ground.

Tukino leapt to his feet. 'Where did you get that?'

Wyndham put it back in his pocket. 'From the Maori you killed.'

Tukino glared at him. 'You must give it away.'

'Why?'

'You are inviting an aitua. Misfortune. Even death. You must never keep the first spoils of war from the man you helped to kill. The first fish should not be touched. Throw it away.'

'No. That is stupid superstition. I am keeping it.'

'Then I can no longer be responsible for you. I tell you misfortune will strike us.'

'Don't be silly, Tukino. You are an educated Christian. You should know it is a lot of rot.'

Tukino put his face within six inches of Wyndham's eyes. 'You are a fool. I am a toa. A warrior. A chief. Where is your respect.'

'I answer to the Governor and the Queen.'

'You are a slave. Afraid of the Governor. You are all cowards hiding behind guns. You want to rob our country.'

'We only want the right to buy land.'

'And if we won't sell.'

Wyndham was silent.

Tukino paced rapidly up and down. 'Beware when war comes. You do not know the Maori. Nobody is safe. Make sure the settlers go back to the towns. Every one. Man, woman and child. I warn you. We believe he who strikes the first blow will be the victor. Take care.'

Tukino started down the track.

'Tukino!' Wyndham shouted. 'Come back. I have no quarrel with you. You can't leave me here.' He forced himself to smile. 'I am paying you well enough. Stay.'

The Maori walked slowly back. 'Very well. From now on you must do everything I say. Pick up your pack.'

The sulphurous smell of volcanic activity wafted upwards on the wind. They came in sight of the lake from high up in the mountains. It lay before them, glittering in the sunlight, a long stretch of water with an island standing alone.

'Mokoia!' Tukino pointed. 'The island where E Hine Moa swam. And Ohinemutu, the village where we will stop.'

Wyndham shaded his eyes against the glare of the sun.

'Who is E Hine Moa?'

'I will tell you the story. Sit down.

Rangiuru was the mother of a chief called Tutanekai; she was properly the wife of Whakaue Kaipapa, but she ran away with a chief named Tuwharetoa. From this affair sprang Tutanekai who was illegitimate but finally Rangiuru and Whakaue were reunited and indeed, Whakaue treated Tutanekai as his own son.

Now there was a maiden of rare beauty and high rank called Hinemoa who lived at a village called Owhata and had met Tutanekai on those occasions when all the Rotorua people came together. They often glanced at each other and in their breast there grew a secret passion between them, so that when Tutanekai sent a messenger to tell Hinemoa of his love she replied, 'Ehhu! have we then each loved alike?'

Always at night Tutanekai played on his horn and his friend Tiki on the pipe and on calm nights the sound of their music wafted across to Hinemoa so that she vastly desired to go to Tutanekai, but her family suspected something and each night pulled the canoes up on shore. She then thought to use six large gourds as floats and taking off her clothes plunged herself into the water guided by the music. At last she landed on the island and found Tutanekai who cast a garment over her and took her to his house. In the morning when a warrior drew back the sliding wooden window of Tutanekai's house he was amazed to see four feet peeping from a mat. The elder brothers were very jealous when they saw Hinemoa.

The descendants of Hinemoa and Tutanekai are, to this very day, dwelling on the lake of Rotorua and never yet have the lips of the offspring of Hinemoa forgotten to repeat tales of the great beauty of their ancestress and of her swimming over there.'

Tukino stood up. 'But I talk too much. Come. We still have an afternoon's walk ahead of us.

Wyndham followed the two men down the slopes to a scrub covered flat. As they approached the lake, the sulphurous smell became stronger and steam from the hot-springs on its edge rose in the air. A boiling pool flopped mud and slime up and down. 'Exactly like a porridge pot,' thought Wyndham. The scrub came to an end and ahead of them was a barren finger of land stretching into the lake. Tukino saluted a Maori who was squatting on some hot flat stones and passed on. Springs were puffing up steam on all sides and the natives were chatting, some bathing and some smoking, around the warm pools. A woman was cooking some potatoes in a flax basket, in a cavity that was bubbling furiously. The whole place was a perpetual vapour bath. Wyndham stared in wonder, forgetting the hazards of the last week. The Maori seemed civil and obliging.

Elaborate carvings in various degrees of decay lay scattered on the ground. The outer palisade of the pa had fallen down and lay on the hard white clay. Steam rose from the holes made by the decayed posts. Some of the huts thatched with reeds were deserted and beyond repair. Wyndham admired a magnificently carved figure standing alone, a three-fingered man with tongue protruding, painted in red ochre and black and white. A geyser commenced to throw up a jet of water, twenty feet high, played for a few minutes and subsided.

Tukino walked past the pools and jets of steam to a group of huts on a bank. A woman sat at the front door of one of them. She jumped up on seeing Tukino and ran to him. 'Haere mai,' she said 'Haere mai.' They pressed noses.

'My sister,' Tukino said, and introduced her to Wyndham. Her husband worked at a mill a European had built a few miles away. His face was fully tattooed. Tukino went down to the shore to meet a canoe laden with fresh water mussels, and brought back a basketful for the evening meal. They talked far into the night.

Wyndham was impatient to get away next morning. There were too many Europeans in the area, some settlers and some tourists who had come to see the amazing sights of hot boiling pools and geysers. They borrowed horses from the natives and rode to the foot of the hills in the south-west moorland where the ground was broken and rocky. There were stones covered with pure sul-

151

phur crystals, and hot mud and water springs in all directions. Steam poured out of the crevices and there was a constant sound of bubbling and hissing. They left their horses and continued on foot, skirting a green lake with distant views of another mountain. Tukino was now anxious to reach his home. They came to a lake called Tarawera and took a sail boat to its far end. Every headland was crowded with pas. Some were deserted.

'Each tribe has been at war with the other for six months,' explained Tukino. 'See that one, a heap of ruins. It was destroyed in a night attack.'

They passed along a stream that flowed through a swamp. There were wild duck on all sides.

Tukino made a wide arc with his arm. 'All these are tapu. Sacred. They cannot be killed.'

'Who said so?'

'The priests, the tohunga. At the proper time of the year, the 'tapu' will be lifted by incantations and prayer enabling the tribe to fill their storehouses once more. Tomorrow,' said Tukino, 'I will show you a most beautiful sight.'

'The terraces?'

'Yes.'

It was almost sunset when they reached Te Tarata, a succession of steps the colour of alabaster with water flowing from basin to basin until it reached a boiling crater at the bottom. Wyndham walked to the top, admiring the pools of pure blue water enclosed in the delicate shell-like basins. Trying several, he bathed, soaking up the warmth. He left his dirty clothes in a pool to boil clean and returned to camp to sleep.

The lake, Rotomahana, was small, not a mile across in any direction with wild fowl everywhere. There were white-winged teal and swamp hens strutting through the reeds. The three men followed an overgrown path of soft moss, then took a canoe to the opposite shore where rose coloured terraces climbed upwards. Wyndham looked down on the fathomless depths of the lake where it shelved and faded into exquisite shades of blue and green. It was the closest he ever came to God.

Here the small Maori said good-bye. Leaving the lake, Wyndham and Tukino followed a track and camped each night in the wild uncultivated country. At the fringe of a forest, Tukino halted.

'Listen!'

Wyndham strained his ears.

'The falls. I will soon be home.'

In the silence, Wyndham could hear the distant roar of a torrent, the continuous sound of thunder in the distance.

'Come.' Tukino began to run. They broke into the opening in brilliant sunshine. Below, the white water of the big river swept over a bed of boulders and crashed into a shallow pool of turquoise and green below.

'We can't cross this. I can't swim.' Wyndham turned his back shutting out the scene below.

Tukino ignored him and continued walking up the river. They climbed higher. The noise was deafening. A broad wall of water swept down from above, foaming towards the rapids they had left. Wyndham followed Tukino up a narrow zigzag track reaching the top a quarter of a mile further upstream. Here, the river descended in a series of steps. On the bank was a canoe.

'We cross here. Help me.' Tukino lifted the bow of the dugout and pulled it towards the river. 'Don't try to paddle. Keep still. I will guide you. We land there.' He pointed to some rocks further down on the opposite bank. 'The current will take you over.'

Wyndham climbed into the dugout. Tukino sat in the stern with a paddle poised. A quick push of the blade and they swept into midstream. They spun towards the top of the falls. Tukino jabbed a paddle into the water and swung the canoe into a hole where three black rocks rose above the river. Wyndham lunged at them with a cry.

Tukino shouted. 'Stop!'

The canoe tilted, righted itself then heeled over as the water poured in. Wyndham was swept out and wedged between two rocks. As he felt the current dragging them into the centre, Tukino reached out and encircling Wyndham with his arms held him against a jagged rock jutting out above the river. The water forced them both against the smooth stone surface.

'Tukino, for God's sake, help me.' Wyndham began to struggle.

'Keep still.' The Maori used all his force to stay against the ledge.

'I can't swim.'

'Shut up!'

'I can't swim, I tell you.'

Tukino shouted above the roar of the water. 'If you can slide towards the bank, even an inch at a time, the river will take you in.'

Wyndham made a half-hearted attempt to move. 'I can't.'

'Try.'

'It's no good, I can't.'

'You Pakeha bastard. If you can't then start praying to your God.'

'Help me Tukino. Take hold of my shirt!'

'If I let go now we will both go over the falls.'

Wyndham screamed. 'Don't let go! I've five hundred pounds in my money belt. You can have it all. Just save me.'

'Five hundred pounds. Where did it come from?'

Wyndham whimpered.

'Where did it come from? Did you steal it from Jeremy St Clair? Is that why you came with me?'

'It doesn't matter where it came from. It can all be yours. It will buy land. Anything. Keep you warm in your old age like you said.'

'You bastard.'

'You and I. We will start a business. A flax or a flour mill.'

Tukino's eyes narrowed. 'Yes, you can start a business almost at once.'

'I knew you would understand, Tukino. We can work together. You can find me a wife. Perhaps one of your sisters. We will be rich.'

'No, you won't have time for that.'

'What sort of business do you think, Tukino?'

'An eel business.'

'Eels? Is there much in eels? What will I do?'

'You'll feed them, Pakeha.'

Slowly the realization of what Tukino had said penetrated Wyndham's brain. His eyes dilated with fear.

'Tukino!' he screamed, "Tukino!'

The current swept him away from the rocks in a wide arc, picked him up again, held him for a moment in a whirlpool close to the other bank then swung him into midstream. The middle of the

154

river was silent and deep. It dragged him down and spewed him up again on the edge of the falls. His cries were drowned in the thunder as he plunged below.

16

'I am tired of men and military balls, I'd rather go to bed with a tin of chocolates.' Paula slumped on a kitchen chair and laughed. 'Isn't the *'Elizabeth Ann Bright'* disembarking the 18th Irish tomorrow? Imagine all those lovely soldiers.'

Caroline stopped pouring a pan of water into the sink and shivered.

Paula looked up. 'What is wrong?'

'I don't know. I felt as though someone was walking over my grave.'

'Perhaps you are missing Wyndham.'

'No. It has been a blessed relief not to have him around. For years I have felt as though I have been living on the edge of a volcano never knowing how he was going to act when he walked in the door. He could be the most loving when he was sober and at other times, when he had been drinking, the most violent, jealous and unpredictable.'

'Do you worry about him? Where he is?'

'Of course.'

'But if he walked in the door now.'

'I don't want him back, Paula.' Caroline shivered again. 'What is wrong with me? I feel prickly.'

'Nerves. Take confection of opium. How will you manage for

money?'

'Adequately. There's a trust my mother holds. She had no time for Wyndham and would not let me have too much at a time. I have written to her. I should get a reply in six months. In the meantime I will cope. How is Jeremy managing after the fire?'

'I must admit he is working hard. They were lucky it did not spread further. The engines made a good save. If it wasn't for the New Zealand Insurance Co., it would have been much worse.'

'Why is that?'

'Luckily they employ a permanent engine keeper and pay twelve volunteers to stand by their engines at all times.

'Everything has happened at once,' said Caroline. The first draft of the militia has been called up. There won't be any single men left soon between the ages of sixteen and forty. It isn't safe to walk the streets. The Maori are kidnapping the half castes and taking them away in broad daylight but no-one lifts a finger to stop them. Poor Mrs Kent worries about her son.' 'I'd sooner see my boy carried to the grave,' she told me, 'rather than be placed in the ranks. It will lead to the certain destruction of his morals.'

'I do think sixteen is a bit young. Jeremy says that war isn't far off.'

'Oh dear,' Caroline undid her apron. 'Are we going to watch the 18th Irish disembark tomorrow?'

'We certainly are. Let's dress up.'

'In our best?'

'Why not? You might land a captain and I might find a lover, tra-la.'

'Paula St Clair, you are impossible.'

The steamboat 'Sandfly' had already ferried six hundred bayonets ashore when Paula and Caroline arrived at the Queen St wharf. The Black Ball liner had anchored under the North Head two days before, after a passage of ninety days. It had been an average voyage, two soldiers and four children had died but five new-born took their place. The second battalion of the Blue Cuffs were lined up for inspection. As their commanding officer walked around the ranks the civilians stood on the edge of the wharf, admiring them.

'That one,' whispered Paula, 'The lieutenant up front. I like him.' She walked to the other side and back.

Caroline giggled. 'Don't be ridiculous, Paula. How can you

tell what a man is like until you have met him?'

'By his eyes. I look at the eyes and then at the *derrière*. He has a beautiful one.'

'Paula!' Caroline burst into suppressed laugher. 'You will be the death of me.'

They watched the inspection come to an end. The command 'fours' rang out. There was a ripple in the ranks as the band of the 65th Regiment struck up and the crowd ran forward to watch the Royal Irish start their ten mile march to camp. Paula and Caroline followed them up Queen Street until they were obscured by the children and the young folk marching behind.

Sergeant was glad to see them when they arrived at the dogcart. He flicked his head in recognition and stamped impatiently as they prepared to mount. 'Come home with me,' said Paula. 'Please. Jeremy will be there.'

Jeremy, Matt and Jos were sitting in the kitchen. There was a hint of excitement in the air. A gallon keg of ale was resting on the bench, it had been spigotted and a jug was half full on the table.

Paula frowned. Here he was, acting low again. Drinking with the men at her table and with Caroline to see it and prattle to all and sundry. She showed her displeasure by emptying a full glass of ale down the sink.

Jeremy raised his eyebrows, 'Did you see the 18th Irish?'

'Yes, we did.' Paula bent down to put some kindling in the stove.

'They are not a bad bunch,' said Jeremy. 'I saw something of them in the Crimea. They did a good job at the Cemetery. Won it for us.'

'They certainly look smarter than you lot.'

'We have some news for you. Matt and Jos have been drawn for the militia.'

Paula swung around. Jos was grinning and Matt was leaning back on his chair with a self-satisfied look on his face. 'My goodness. What does that mean?'

'It means they will be in the barracks when the Imperial troops go to the front.'

'Are you volunteering for active service?'

Matt laughed. 'At a shilling a day extra to end up under the sod? For 3/6 a day? Not me! I make it a rule. Never volunteer for anything. I will stick to patrol duty around town. The Imperials can earn their keep for a change.' He emptied his glass. 'Who's for town and a spot of billiards?'

Jos stood up. 'I must go and tell Rata.'

'That can wait Jos. I am going to have to take you in hand,' said Matt.

'But she is expecting me.'

'Always keep them waiting boy. Take advice from an old hand.'

Jeremy patted Jos on the shoulder. 'We will call there on the way home.'

'Where's it all going to end?' Paula asked Caroline. 'So much for our dinner.'

'Rumours are everywhere.' said Caroline. She led the way to the kitchen.

'What rumours?' asked Paula.

'They say that at last Grey has agreed to bring the native question to a head. The old troops are to be marched to the front and the 18th Irish will remain in camp while the 65th move to the front. The militia will mount guard on us.'

'The front? What front?'

'They are going to make one. Soon. To settle the land question once and for all. General Cameron's going to march south and if there's any opposition from the Maori he will force his way through. They are going to make conditions under which land will be granted to militia volunteers for settlement. Here, as well as in Taranaki.'

'What land?'

'They are going to confiscate some big blocks.'

'At last it is coming. Jeremy has been talking about it for over a year.'

'Will he join up?'

'I don't know. I don't think so. He says the Treaty of Waitangi was not signed by all the Maori. That there was no head of state who could have signed for all of them. He says you can't blame the Maori for wanting to keep his land.'

'He is in the minority.'

'Yes. He and the missionaries.'

'Wyndham calls them the religious fanatics at Exeter Hall and that may be so, for the Maori seem to have acquired a sort of morbid civilization from the missionaries. They can sing all the hymns but the fact is they use their knowledge to no good purpose. Don't you think their wisdom is decidedly serpentine? Earthy. Sensual. Devilish. If education has taught them to prefer boiled pork to fricasseed Anglo-Saxon it has also taught them to substitute the rifle for the tomahawk.'

Paula nodded. 'If it means prices will be sensible again, I am for settling it once and for all. Something has to be done. Here we are paying tenpence a pound for meat and look at Australia. There's no native problem there, not any more, and everything is reasonable. The same meat is tuppence and threepence a pound.' She sighed. 'It's all too much. Let's talk about something else. Sarah should be back soon with Jonathon. She can get us something to eat. We will have a sherry.'

'At this hour?'

'Why not? The men are at the billiard parlour right now, getting drunk.'

The three men had driven straight to the billiard rooms. Jeremy was watching Jos carefully. The boy was caught up in Matt's enthusiasm and was matching him drink for drink. His features were flushed and he shouted as he made a particularly good shot. Refusing Matt's advice and full of confidence, he began to play very well.

'You'll be the best billiard player in the militia,' remarked Matt. 'What are you going to do with all the money you get from the army?'

Jos had been thinking about that. As a soldier he would be earning equal pay with the men. 'Save it for a farm. Put it in the bank. I'm meeting Rata this afternoon and opening an account at the Auckland Savings Bank in Princes Street.' He looked at the clock. 'I'm late! She'll be waiting. I'll have to go!'

'Finish the game. First things first.'

Five minutes later Jos put his cue in the rack. There was a noise in the street and the sound of footsteps running up the stairs. One of the older boys from the school burst into the room. 'Rata!

Rata!' he cried. 'She's been taken. Taken by her tribe. We can't find her.'

Jos stared in disbelief at the messenger. Jeremy put his hand on the young Maori's shoulder. 'What happened? Quickly.'

'She left early to meet Jos. She was going to do some shopping. Two hours ago. They took her at the top of Shortland Crescent. Put her on a horse. She was crying.'

Jos leapt to the door. 'Which way did they go?'

'Toward Onehunga where they beach their canoes.'

Jos ran down the stairs and onto the street. Jeremy and Matt followed. When they reached the bottom, Jos was already half-way up the crescent. They jumped into the dogcart and caught the boy at the corner. 'Get in,' ordered Jeremy.

Jos was sobbing as he climbed alongside Jeremy and they continued towards the school.

'Jos,' said Jeremy. 'They've had two hours start. They'll be on the water by now. There's nothing you can do. Come with us.'

At Rosalind's school Jeremy pieced together what had happened. To the European it was impossible to distinguish between the Maori who frequented the town as to who were friendlies and who were so-called 'rebels'. Jeremy did not like the term rebel. He questioned how a man could be a rebel when his chief had not signed the treaty, but he was flying against public opinion. If the tribe had sold the land, then fair enough. They had accepted the treaty obligations, but the majority of the Waikato Maori had not done so. And Rata belonged to the strongest, most warlike tribe in the south, the Maniapoto.

She had waited outside the bank and recognized a group of her countrymen walking towards her. She had run back towards the school but a boy had seen her, overtaken her and after a fierce argument forced her past the barracks and placed her on a horse. Jeremy was not surprised that although a number of soldiers had witnessed the scene none had gone to her rescue. The situation had been tense for weeks, no-one wanted to provoke the Maori.

To begin with Jos was angry and churlish, blaming Matt for keeping him at the billiard saloon. Then, after a week of restlessness his mood changed to one of tense silence. He ignored Jeremy and kept to his room, where he brooded deeply. He took the headband that Rata had given him and pinned it to the wall above his bed.

The following Monday he and Matt received notice to report to the barracks for training. Dressed before dawn, they paraded for roll call and drill, formed fours, marched, ran at the double and performed bayonet practice. Bayonets at the ready. On guard. Up to a hanging sack filled with straw. In. Out. On guard.

They watched a soldier from the 18th Irish receive his hundred lashes for using abusive language to his pay-sergeant. The man was tied to a gun carriage and had to wait while the men were lined up on three sides. A doctor pronounced the man fit to receive the punishment. Jos stared with morbid fascination at the black-handled whip with the long narrow strip of rawhide dangling down. There was silence as the lash whistled down on the man's back. A bright red weal ripped and remained across his shoulders. Jos closed his eyes and began counting the strokes.

At fifty there was a pause. Jos saw the man's back, a mess of purple and red. There was a small rivulet of blood dripping onto the gun carriage. A doctor stepped up, wiped away the blood and examined the prisoner. A nod, a stir in the ranks of the soldiers, and the punishment continued. Jos could see the muscles in the soldier's neck tighten, his legs strained against the bindings. The lash continued to sing through the air and land with a dull crack. The man administering the punishment was tired. Perspiration stood out in beads on his forehead. The victim fainted and then recovered consciousness as the doctor re-examined him. There was a consultation and the order was given to continue. Then it was all over. The soldier lay motionless. A drummer beat out a tattoo. Jos heard a command and turned in line following the man in front as they marched out of the Ball Court to the rattling beat of a drum.

Matt and Jos did picket duty around the town. Even the bishop did his share one night, unarmed. Matt was cynical. 'What he expects to do without a gun if a Maori appears I do not know.' The town was jittery. A guard at one of the bays fired at a stake. Townsmen ran in all directions in their night attire and the alarm sounded at the barracks.

In spite of it all there were still the social occasions. Jeremy and Paula attended a ball where the army band played. There was laughter and dancing until after midnight. Newhaven was there.

'He has not gone to the front yet,' remarked Jeremy as he

guided Paula to a chair, 'and probably won't.'

Newhaven saw them, and in his usual manner went up to Jeremy.

'I thought you would have volunteered by now, St Clair.'

In spite of himself, Jeremy bristled. 'It is no concern of yours, Newhaven.'

'No, true. But I've noticed that any man worth his salt has joined one of the battalions. I saw the 2nd Battalion drilling this morning. Thought you might have been there.'

'I'll join when I think I need to, not before.'

Jeremy clenched his fist, forcing himself to remain calm. 'It would be appreciated if you would kindly retire from here. My wife has a crushing headache, and frankly I find you a bore.'

Newhaven laughed, turned on his heels and left.

'Jeremy!' said Paula. She was nervous and flustered. 'You should not have spoken to him like that. He has quite a lot of influence.'

'Influence be damned. He is not going to talk like that to me, or look at you the way he did, for that matter.'

'I want to go home.'

'No. Certainly not. He is not going to spoil our evening. Come, let's dance.'

Paula confided in Caroline the next day. 'Jeremy was so annoyed he actually danced with me. Quite well too.'

Caroline had a glint in her eye. 'Perhaps you two need a Newhaven in your lives.'

The following Thursday Jeremy came home with the news. 'The army is marching south. Grey is issuing a notice to the Maori on the Manukau and on the Waikato frontier to take the oath of allegiance and give up their arms.'

Paula stopped pruning a rose. 'And if they don't?'

'They have to leave the district or take the consequences.'

'And those are?'

'They will forfeit the right to their lands guaranteed to them by the Treaty of Waitangi. It means confiscation. Some of the troops have already moved, and occupied the stockades.'

'Oh dear. What about the settlers. The Trusts?'

'The Trusts should be safe. Too close to town. Most have already moved in to safety. At almost every settlement the Maori have elected to leave. They have been selling their pigs for what they can get. A penny half-penny, a pound. Princess Sophia has unearthed the bones of her ancestors and taken them to a place of security. The day before the Maori left there were speeches, war dances, guns firing and rum drinking. A fire was lit and everything they were not able to take away was burnt. At night, the Princess, with her large escort, carried away long heavy boxes in their canoes. John Featon was in a cutter which was lying anchored waiting for the ebb-tide, when they passed. Some of the boxes look too heavy to be the bones of their ancestors he thought, more likely to be guns.'

Jeremy glanced up at the verandah. 'But that is enough,' he said. 'Come inside. I am starving.'

On July 31 1863, Grey gazetted a proclamation. The die was cast. The town and its environs were at war.

Sergeant William Brown of the 65th was with his regiment at the village of Drury when Jeremy arrived with the stores. The camp was seething with rumours. It was four days since the Governor had issued his proclamation. The artillery had gone to the front and the 2nd Battalion of the 14th, The Prince of Wales' Own, had crossed the swamp-fringed stream that marked the boundary laid down by Grey. They were taking the fight to Maori territory.

Jeremy stood by as soldiers unloaded his cart. The escort from the 18th Irish had gone to the cookhouse for a meal and a sergeant was checking off the bags of flour and the barrels of salt beef against the documents. He was an old hand. His words came from somewhere deep in his beard. 'You were lucky to get through. They're swarming everywhere.'

Jeremy folded his list and put it in his pocket. 'Who are?'

'The rebels. Did you see any?'

'No. Are there some around?'

'Are there Maori around?' Brown gave Jeremy a look of contempt reserved for civilians. 'I'd say so. They won't be tame ones either. The sooner you get out of the way the better.'

'I thought all the settlers were in. You can't move for them in the village. No accommodation. Anyway, I didn't see a Maori on the road.'

Brown wiped his nose on his sleeve. 'You won't either. They are not going to stick their heads up out of the bush and say come and get me. They will shoot first.'

'It is certainly different from the Crimea.'

'You were there?'

Jeremy nodded. He watched Brown's manner change.

The sergeant cocked his head to one side. 'Then you'll know something about it. You don't look as though you were in the ranks.' He jumped down from the cart. 'Time for tea. Do you mind coming to the sergeant's mess, sir?'

Jeremy grinned. 'Anything for a mug of army tea.'

They sat at a table by the stove. 'Are there still some settlers out there?' asked Jeremy.

'Sure to be. They're a bloody nuisance. And fools. Because they've been friendly with the Maori they think they won't be touched. Believe me. I've been in this country a long time and I know the Maori. When he goes to war, he goes to war. No-one is safe!'

'Bishop Selwyn still travels around unarmed.'

'He's up here now. Even he is warning the settlers, fool that he is. Do you know what he told me? He didn't blame the Maori. There is no difference, he said, between them and the Scots at Culloden or the United Irishmen. They are fighting for their nationality, he says, and who can blame them. Blame them! Something had to be done or there would have been bloody chaos. The settlers have put their life savings into their land and more. Not that I've got any time for them, we spend half our days protecting them instead of getting on with it.'

Jeremy took a sip of the scalding tea. He frowned. 'Things have gone too far. I don't know the answer any more.'

'Anyway,' said the sergeant, 'when are you going back?'

'With tomorrow's escort.'

'Well then. You can handle a gun. I'm duty sergeant. Why not come with us? Nothing too dangerous. Just patrol. See what it is like yourself in this flaming forest. There's a man and a boy supposed to be lost in the bush. Do you want to come with us and find them?'

Jeremy did not hesitate. 'I will get my rifle from the cart.' He joined the sergeant, two soldiers and a bugler at the guard tent. They moved southwards down the military road.

'Who are we looking for?' asked Jeremy.

'A man called Meredith, a settler, and his young son. They went out fencing and did not turn up last night. The neighbours searched the village and the hotel last and we said we'd go out to-day if they did not turn up.'

Mrs. Meredith was waiting at the gate as they approached. She was pale and anxious. 'They usually come home at dusk,' she said. 'Robert Bateman and Jos Jones went looking for them last night with a lantern but could see neither hide nor hair of them. I know something terrible has happened.'

Her younger son, Joseph, was standing alongside his mother. 'I know where they were working,' he said. 'I was there with my father on Monday.'

The sergeant looked down at the boy. 'Will you take us there?'

'Yes. Last night we found a maul they were using and five wedges, but there was no sign of them.'

'Lead the way, lad.'

The house was in an open space close to the forest. They moved back amongst the trees. Brown turned to the bugler. 'Sound a call every two minutes. If they have lost their direction they will hear it.'

For twenty minutes the small party wound its way through the trees. 'How does your father get on with the Maori neighbours, boy?' asked Jeremy.

'Good. Really good,' said the boy. 'Except for the pig.'

'What pig?'

'It was last week. Our pig got lost and Dad and Fred found it at the Maori's place. They brought it home and old Simons the chief came and went really mad, he wanted five pounds for the pig because it ate his potatoes. Father refused.'

'What happened?'

166

'A couple of Maori came and took the pig when Dad wasn't home.'

'What is Simons like?'

'He's old. Walks all bent up.' The boy stopped. 'Here is the clearing and over there the wedges.'

They walked over to where the twelve-year-old was pointing. On the ground were the wedges but there were no signs of an axe or tomahawk. Some newly-split posts and rails were nearby.

'Is this Maori land, boy?' asked the sergeant.

'No. It's half a mile from Maori land.'

The soldier put the bugle to his lips once again. As the notes rang out Jeremy caught sight of two bodies on the edge of the forest.

'There they are!' He pointed down to where they lay between two trees. The man was in his late fifties and the boy not more than fourteen years old. The lad was half-covered by a fern.

'It's Dad!' cried the boy, 'and Fred!' He ducked away and ran over to the edge of the clearing, staring down at the bodies. His father was on his back and his brother turned partly on his left side.

Jeremy knelt down. There were six deep tomahawk wounds altogether on the man. Two to the body. Any of the head wounds would have caused instant death. The boy had a wound to the back of the head, another on the forehead above the right eye and another extended down the face. There was a gash across his throat cutting the carotid artery. Both bodies were partially stripped. The man had on a pair of drawers and a shirt and his moleskin trousers and boots were gone. The boy was almost naked.

Brown quickly took command. 'Crimmins, sound that bugle. Keep sounding it. If there's any of the bastards around they'll think we are a large party.'

Moving quickly they returned to the house. As they approached, Mrs Meredith came running out towards them. The boy gave a cry and dashed into her arms. She needed no other explanation. As Jeremy closed the parlour door he heard the boy crying. 'Father and Fred are dead. Dead, mother. Dead.'

An escort brought the bodies into the camp that afternoon.

'We would like you to stay for the inquest.' The adjutant spoke to Jeremy as though it was a request not a command. 'The day after tomorrow.'

* * *

167

It was raining when Jeremy ran between the tent lines to the store-hut where the inquest was held. A newspaper correspondent from another paper sat with him. William Morgan was a lay preacher, a baptist who farmed nearby and a part-time newsman. He had been in the country since 1853.

'Terrible business,' he whispered, leaning over towards Jeremy. 'There's only one thing to do. Arm the settlers properly and send them into the bush. If the Government supplies guns to so-called friendly natives I won't answer for the consequences. There's no excuse for it but for the Governor's infatuation for the Maori, and for his heeding the self-interested advice of a few gentlemen who get high salaries and only half-heal native sores because they would lose their jobs if they entirely healed them. Mark my words. It only needs a few interfering busy-bodies to stop us from putting an end to this nonsense. I hear the Catholics are to blame, stirring up trouble and actually encouraging the Maori to revolt. Sympathizing with them in order to get their confidence and to convert them to the Popish faith. You're not Catholic, are you?'

Jeremy shook his head.

'Didn't think so. As for the Maori prisoners, they live in tents behind the church under the wing of the bishop. I would not insult that very reverend and learned gentleman by saying he has become a jailer, but I do know they are enjoying the best of rations and the good things of life. Even hot joints while the soldiers fight on ordinary rations. There are to be no more prisoners, that's what the soldiers say. Their blood's up. It is all very well to say "If thine enemy hunger, feed him", but this sort of thing is going too far.'

As they finished talking the proceedings came to an end. Jeremy was not called. The verdict. Wilful murder by person or persons unknown.

As Jeremy came into the daylight troops were assembling on the high ground of the infantry camp. Morgan stopped an orderly who was walking past.

'What's up?' he asked.

'They've heard firing on the South Road. Didn't you hear the alarm?'

'No, which direction?'

'Shepherd's Bush.'

'Let's go,' said Morgan.

They followed a company of the 18th Irish and a detachment of the 65th. A troop of about thirty sabres led the way out on to the road and moved south. An ambulance cart brought up the rear and Jeremy recognized Dr White of the 65th. They caught up to the column a mile or two further on with mounted men in skirmishing order on each side of the road. The infantry were searching the edge of the bush. There had been an attack on an escort. After fifteen minutes riding, a cart came into view on a bend. The doctor was treating three wounded men in the shelter of the bush. Jeremy's thoughts went back to the Crimea as the doctor bound the wounds and gave directions about their treatment to the driver of the cart. 'Where is the escort?' he asked.

'Along there.' The doctor pointed down the road.

Jeremy and Morgan continued south. There were trails of blood where the wounded had dragged themselves from the open into the bush. A man from the 18th Irish was lying dead on the track and further on two more were among some felled trees on the right, about thirty paces from the road. A private had been axed and lay bathed in blood with his tongue plucked out. The ambulance cart arrived and carried away the bodies. Further along the road a pair of horses lay dead and the household goods of a settler were strewn on the road littered with broken boxes and books.

There was a store depot not far away where a deep gully plunged to the valley below. Looking down, Jeremy saw a team of horses struggling in the undergrowth. One was already dead. It was here that the main attack had been made. Eighteen carts in convoy and some stores had been proceeding down the South Road when the rearguard had been attacked from both sides. Under cover of the bush the Maori had opened fire on the advance guard. Outnumbered, the soldiers had retreated as about sixty Maori had closed in on them. Captain Ring had given the order to fix bayonets. The ten men charged at their opponents who fled into cover.

Jeremy was familiar with sudden death and the stoicism of the wounded. In the Crimea it was the Britisher and Frenchman against the Russian, with a few Turks thrown in, but here was a nation, albeit a small one, fighting for its own land and what it considered was its rights. Nonetheless he could not condone the mutilation of the wounded. Just as in the Crimea when the Russian lancers went in and destroyed the helpless men on the ground, so too, here, his sympathy with the Maori was badly shaken. As for killing children in cold blood, it was unforgivable. Certainly the Maori attitude was different. Steeped in the fighting tradition, war had been their main occupation. With customs handed down from generation to generation fighting had been part of their religion, administered by the priests. 'See,' their priests had said, 'How red the stars are. It means war.'

And war it was. In newspapers bad news flies on swift wings. Good news stumbles along and is often lost on the way. That evening, despatch riders thundered into town on lathered mounts. At the front, outposts of the 14th Regiment, established on a high part of a range of hills that extended in the shape of a horseshoe to the Waikato River, saw the Maori two miles away, digging rifle pits. The British commander, Colonel Austen, sent for reinforcements and for the General.

It was eleven o'clock in the morning when the buglers sounded the advance. As the second battalion of the 14th went forward the Maori retreated to their entrenchments. New to war, the battalion had never been under fire. The destruction of the grenadier company of the 40th Regiment in the Taranaki swamps was fresh in their minds.

Advancing in line, two hundred yards from the rifle pits they faltered as the Maori poured a fusillade into them. General Cameron, the man who had led the Black Watch up the blood-stained heights of Alma nine years before, saw them hesitate. Waving his cap in the air, he called on them to stand firm. Their officers rushed forward, swords in hand and led the way. At bayonet point they advanced. Without time to reload and against heavy odds, the Maori retreated. They made a stand on every hill to face successive bayonet attacks. For about five miles they were pursued relentlessly. Routed and pressed by the 14th, 12th and 70th supports they fled into the swamps as the troops poured heavy fire on them from above.

The next day, Saturday, as Jeremy prepared to return to town, the battlefield, miles away, was quiet. A white flag was fluttering below. The Maori were asking to collect their wounded.

'Tell them,' said Cameron, 'our surgeons will attend to them.'

The Maori refused. Their treatment of wounds was very simple. They plugged up the holes made by the balls with clay to exclude the air and let the patient take his chance. Jeremy had seen

170

some remarkable cures effected that way. The dock root was also used extensively for wounds and sores.

Depressed at the grim recognition that war had come to the district in earnest, Jeremy saddled his horse and set out for home. He joined the escort and followed them northwards. The road was empty except for one or two despatch riders galloping in the opposite direction. Fifteen miles from town he left the escort and rode ahead.

17

Standing on his own verandah the next morning, it was hard for Jeremy to realize that the town was at war. The church bells were tolling, the sea was patched with colour, green where the water lay over the mudflats close to the beach road, blue where a small piece of sky was reflected in the deep water in the channel and the remainder a cold forbidding grey merging into the distance. It was very much winter time, with cold showers sweeping across the bay, but leaf buds were forming on the rambling roses and the only English tree in the garden, the horse chestnut, was pointing its brown sticky buds upwards. Another month and spring would be with them.

Jeremy heard Jonathon's footsteps and without turning held out a hand. He felt the boy nestling into him. Absent-mindedly he let his hand wander down to the boy's head, ruffling his hair, stroking his cheek.

Jonathon snuggled in closer. 'When will Jos be back?' he asked.

Jeremy looked down at the patch of straw coloured hair.

'Do you miss him?'

'I can't ride George anymore.'

'Yes you can.'

'There is no-one to saddle him and take me to the domain.'

Jeremy felt his heart go out to his son. 'I will take you tomorrow. We could have a picnic at the pond.'

'Can we?'

'Yes, with cakes and trifle.'

'And mother?'

'Of course. Go and ask her.'

A crestfallen Jonathon returned leading a reluctant Paula.

'What is this nonsense' she asked, 'about a picnic in this weather?'

'I thought it would be a treat for the three of us.'

'Haven't you anything better to do?'

'There is always something, but I thought it would be one of those times to pause and pick the flowers.' He looked up at the sky. 'There's a wind change. It could be fine tomorrow.'

'Shouldn't you be working? I thought you were bankrupt.'

Jeremy smiled to himself. She was always trying to needle him but it no longer affected him. For a moment he let his mind go free. Pushed out any thoughts. Felt relaxed inside. Poor Paula, she was the one missing out. Why couldn't she give Jonathon more of her time? Forget about herself for a while. His voice hid his feelings. 'Are you coming or not?'

'I can't possibly. I have a fitting for a new dress.'

'Then you'll need Sergeant.'

'No. Caroline is picking me up.'

Paula left next morning before Jeremy and Jonathon had saddled the horses. The excuse of the dress fitting was correct enough but it could have been postponed. The truth of the matter was that she and Caroline had been invited to dinner at the officer's mess in the barracks to farewell a detachment which was leaving to man a post on the Razor Back Hills. They were to complete a chain of forts to keep the road open and maintain communications with the front.

'Thank goodness you've managed to keep the carriage,' she said to Caroline as she stepped up into the dogcart.

Caroline gave the reins a flick and the horse started down the hill. 'Actually I don't notice any difference with Wyndham gone. Only a blessed relief. I used to do all the household budgeting, give the maid her orders, even clean the carriage. The only difference is the expenses are down. No more monstrous bills from the liquor store.'

They took refreshment at the dressmakers, leaving barely enough time to drive to the barracks. It was a lively affair although the mess was sadly depleted.

'All the most handsome seem to have gone to the front,' remarked Paula.

After the toast to the Queen the champagne corks popped like corn. Newhaven was there, naturally. Caroline watched him out of the corner of her eye flirting with Paula.

'You're lucky,' he said. 'We had to get permission from the colonel to have you here. War and all that. But when he knew it was you, he capitulated. Don't blame him.' He raised his glass. 'Here's to the most beautiful pair in town.'

Caroline said nothing. She was not sure whether she was included in the toast.

'Damned awful weather,' Newhaven said, 'but at least it means we can keep the bubbly cold.' He insisted on refilling their glasses.

Caroline watched Paula. There were two pink spots glowing on her cheeks, a sure sign she was taking too much. When Newhaven turned to the steward she whispered, 'Paula darling, don't you think you should be a little careful?'

Paula looked down and straightened her bodice. 'Me? I am all right.'

It was mid afternoon before they could prevail on Newhaven to let them go. He took Paula's glass and put it down. 'I'll drive you home.'

Paula shot a glance at Caroline. 'Thank you, but no.' When she felt the cold air outside the mess she held on to Caroline to steady herself. 'Dear me, perhaps you were right. I believe I have

174

had a little too much to drink.' She took a deep breath. 'I think I'll walk home.'

'No you won't, I'll drive you.'

'No, no. I insist. I daren't let Jeremy see me like this.'

Reluctantly Caroline watched Paula walk along Princes Street and turn down towards the gully.

There was a seat half way down the hill. Paula rested there for five minutes and, feeling better, took a short cut down to the stream, which she knew was spanned by a narrow plank. The path was slippery. The rain had stopped and now and again the sun came from behind a cloud but it was damp underfoot, particularly under the ferns. She was about to step across the stream when she heard a voice.

'Paula!'

She looked up the slope. A soldier was coming down the track. She could see the tight military trousers but the upper part of the body was screened by a fern.

'Paula.' the voice had a thin wheedling sound to it. She recognized Newhaven as he ducked under the frond.

'Hullo.' She tried to hide her surprise.

'I say, I'm awfully sorry if I startled you but I was worried that you might have an accident going home. Fall in the stream or something,' He gave a laugh.

'I'm perfectly all right.' Thank God it is Newhaven, she thought. It could have been one of those horrible bushmen.

'I say, don't go home yet. Let's talk.'

She cast her eyes around. 'There's hardly anywhere to sit. I must go.'

'No, no. Stay.'

He pointed to a log a few yards up the hill. 'There. I'll put my jacket down and we can sit and have a chat.' He took off his coat and threw it over the log.

She took a few steps and sat down.

Newhaven smiled. 'Mind if I join you?' Without waiting for a reply he sat beside her.

Paula swallowed. 'Is this wise? If somebody saw us I might be compromised.'

Newhaven looked contrite. 'I wouldn't want that, but no-one ever comes down here in the winter. Far too wet.'

'What do you want to talk about?'

'You.'

'Oh.'

'You are so charming. So beautiful. So . . . ,' he hesitated, 'so delectable.'

'Captain, you flatter me.'

'Dear lady, no flattery could do you justice.' For a minute he remained silent. 'You know you are wasted on your husband. He doesn't appreciate you. Believe me, I know. With your wit, your looks, your brains, you could have the whole world.'

Paula coloured. She looked down at the moss underfoot. An ugly brown insect was crawling over a stick. As she watched, it tumbled on its back and lay upside down, legs waving frantically in the air. 'How ludicrous,' she thought.

'I say, did you hear me?'

She looked up. Newhaven's eyes were boring into hers. A tiny message of panic flashed into her brain and was gone.

'Don't be ridiculous, Sir.'

'I mean it. I have something to confess. I love you.'

Paula burst into hysterical laughter. 'You don't mean it.'

'I do.'

'Don't be ridiculous,' she said again.

He put an arm around her. She drew back and attempted to smile, afraid to move too far in case he was violent. She could smell rum on his breath.

'Come. Don't be silly. We must go.' Patting his hand she tried to stand up.

Immediately his manner changed. It was as though someone had opened an oven door and there behind it was a furnace. Flames. A roaring sound in her head.

'Let me go!'

Both his arms were around her, crushing her.

'My God,' he cried. 'If you won't, I'll take you.'

She felt herself being lifted into the air, carried for twenty yards and then as she struggled he stumbled and fell, knocking the breath out of her. She felt his hands fumbling at her clothes. There was the sound of his trousers tearing. A red mist came down over her eyes. Seconds later she awoke. She could smell him: a combination of excitement and sweat. She gave a pitiful cry of hopeless-

176

ness and fainted again.

When Paula regained consciousness she was alone. For a moment she wondered where she was and then the horror, the enormity of it all flooded back. She gave a low moan and turning over on her side lay motionless trying to convince herself that it had not happened, that it was a bad dream and she would wake up soon, safe in her bed. But the drops of water were real and she could feel the dampness of the moss through her bodice. She staggered to her feet and continued down the path. There were streaks of mud on her clothes and one of her shoes had lost its heel. Limping up the path, she pulled herself up the steep slope, clutching at the ferns and the overhanging branches. 'Merciful God,' she whispered, 'let no-one see me.'

The road was deserted as she crossed at the point where her children had gone so long ago. It seemed an age since that terrible day. Hurrying around the back of the house she saw that the horses were still out. 'Thank God, Jeremy is not home.' She fell in the back door and started to go up the stairs but as a wave of unconsciousness came over her, she staggered into the parlour and slumped into a chair. The maid, upstairs, heard the noise and came running down. Her eyes were like saucers. 'Ma'am,' she cried, 'what happened?'

'I fell over at the stream.'

The girl looked at the sodden clothes, the mud and the green stains as Paula stood up.

'I must have fainted.'

'Oh ma'am!' Sarah ran over and untied the bow at Paula's neck. 'How long were you there?'

'I don't know. Be a good girl. Fill me a bath. Put the tub in my room and don't breathe a word of this to Mr St Clair.' From somewhere Paula called up all the reserves of her mind and body. 'Hurry.'

As she undressed, fumbling with the buttons, feeling the damp clothes clinging to her, she shuddered. 'Take these and put them under the stairs.'

'Yes, ma'am. Shall I scrub your back?'

Paula shut her eyes and shook her head. 'No. No. Leave me.'

When the girl had closed the door Paula stood in front of the mirror and looked at herself. She gave an involuntary sob and then made herself stop. She could smell Newhaven on her. She felt soiled, unclean. Going to the washstand she picked up the lavender water bottle and poured the liquid over her thighs and abdomen, rubbing it into her skin. She collapsed onto the edge of the bed, feeling faint. Forcing herself to get into the bath she closed her eyes and lay against the high back. She tried to thrust away the memory of it as the full implications crowded in on her. No-one must ever know.

The hot water acted like a balm. She took the honey soap and lathered herself again. The shame, the humiliation would never go away. She dried herself and let the towel fall. Sarah had already turned back the bed cover. She put on her old flannel nightdress and fell into bed. Only then did she give way to the pain. Sarah paused outside the door. She could hear her mistress sobbing as she crept away. It continued for a long while and then at last Paula fell asleep.

When Jeremy came in after brushing down the horses, Sarah was preparing Jonathon's supper.

'Is the mistress home?' he asked.

'Yes sir. She is not very well. She has gone to her room and is asleep.'

The next morning Paula woke early and lay there dreading each moment that Jeremy might come into the bedroom to enquire after her. As soon as she could, she dressed and went downstairs to the fire in the front room. She was there when the Reverend Jones called.

He waited for her to offer him a chair. 'So sorry you have not been well but it appears you have recovered.'

He gave her the special smile he reserved for the sick.

'I'm much better thank you.' She surprised herself by being pleased to see him.

'We haven't seen you at communion lately.'

'No.'

'Why not?'

Paula was silent.

'Is there something worrying you?' He gave a nervous laugh. 'Surely my sermons aren't so bad. Are they?'

Paula wriggled uncomfortably.

The vicar smiled oozing charm. 'If there is something worry-

178

ing you why don't you come and pray, and ask your Father for forgiveness.'

She flushed and looked quickly up at him.

'Which father?'

'Either one, if you like, although I was referring to your heavenly one.'

'My father is dead. I hardly knew him.'

'That is so sad, tell me about him.'

'Certainly vicar.' Paula's face was flushed. She leaned forward on the edge of her chair. If he had known her well he would have recognized the signs of anger. 'My mother died in childbirth. When I was born. My father rejected me. Do you know what that means? It means that while he was tomcatting around the neighbourhood my brother and I were left to ourselves searching for the love we never received. We were brought up in a vacuum surrounded by servants, brick walls and farm fences. All the material things. Do you understand? And no love.' Paula fell back into her chair.

'Poor child. Poor child. I did not realize that such was your situation. You need help. I suppose you are aware of that fine lady who has a school for Maori children?'

Paula froze. 'I am.'

'I'm sure she could help you. I could arrange an introduction.'

'I already know her.'

'That is better still. She is a marvellous woman.' He beamed his special benevolent smile. 'I know you have been seen at a large number of social functions without your husband. People will talk you know. My dear, I know there is nothing in it, I am only trying to help. If you could use her as an example.'

'Yes vicar.'

'She is the model of perfection. So cool, so self possessed.'

Paula could contain herself no longer. She leapt to her feet, took three or four paces and swung around to face him. 'It is easy to pass judgement. Does she feel the loneliness and the pain that I feel? Does she feel the burning want that I do? Did your God give her coldness and me warmth. The kind of warmth that I can give to only one person. And then, did he say, "Thou shalt not commit adultery?" Is that fair? Are we to be judged equally? And men. Men. Can they do what they like? Make a game of it in the eyes of other men? Take what they want? Defile us? Rape us?'

Paula stopped as suddenly as she had begun. She fell to the floor, weeping.

The vicar stared in disbelief. 'Oh dear. Oh dear. Sarah!' he called. 'Sarah! Help me.'

The doctor ordered Paula complete rest for five days. 'And after that,' he gruffed, looking over his spectacles in his usual manner, 'avoid excitement, study and late meals. You are too highly strung my dear. When you feel better you could exercise in the open air, particularly on horseback.' He mixed her Battley's solution of opium, and a camphor mixture, one and a half ounces, in a draught for bedtime.

'Dammit,' said Jeremy when he heard. 'She looks as though she needs twenty days rest and none of his wretched drugs.' He took the stairs two at a time and burst into her room without knocking. 'Thank God it's nothing serious. It's stifling in here with that fire. I'll open the windows.' Going over to the cabinet he picked up the medicine glass and smelt it. 'Camphor! What good will that do?'

Paula looked at him with a blank expression on her face. He must never know, she thought. She closed her eyes forcing herself to put away the horror of it all, but it would not go away.

He saw her hands were shaking. 'You are cold. Sorry about the window. It seemed so warm in here.' He slammed it shut. 'Do you read my paper?'

'I can't be bothered.'

'But you like to keep up with news.'

'Yes.'

'Then I will read it to you each day. You will enjoy that.'

Paula was in no mood to argue.

Jeremy arranged for Sarah to bring trays to the bedroom for the evening meal. Jeremy settled back in the easy chair and picked up the newspaper. 'Where shall we start?'

'I suggest page one,' said Paula.

'There's Cameron's despatches to the Governor on the Koheroa clash.'

'That's not on page one.'

Jeremy made a show of a grimace. 'Do you want the advertisements?'

'I sometimes read them. They are more interesting than the despatches.'

'In that case, here they are. They want a first rate shoer at Peter Birley's forge. Mrs Adeane begs to inform the public that she has opened an eating house in High Street. There's a nine horse stable to let at the United Service Hotel. Colonel Hamilton, 1st Battalion Militia, gives notice that after Thursday he will deal summarily with all men who absent themselves without leave from parade. Private apartments may be had at Captain Pearson's Naval Hotel on the corner of Pitt Street and the Misses Thick beg to inform their friends and customers that they have replaced their establishment with an entire new stock of millinery, etcetera, etcetera.'

'Pax, pax,' said Paula. 'Perhaps you should go to page three.'

Jeremy turned the page over. 'Here's Cameron's latest report. He says "There must have been three hundred Maori on the Koheroas." I suppose those are reasonable odds. There were about five hundred British troops. Here's a return of killed and wounded. Twelve all together. And down here is a list of articles taken from old Isaacs. They had him in the compound when I was there on Saturday. They say he was lying on a whole stack of arms when they first saw him; he was pretending to be ill. The Albion Company crushed ten pounds of gold from twenty three pounds of stone on the goldfields and they've had a meeting at the Windsor Castle Hotel to organize a night patrol to replace the militia. Bishop Selwyn was there. The Superintendent, Graham, has issued a warning to boatmen. 'The last mail says that smallpox is raging in London and they must take special precautions.'

'Jeremy.'

'Yes?'

'Perhaps it would be better if I read it myself. Just tell me what is happening in town.'

'All the rumours?'

'Not all of them. Just a few.'

'They are talking about raising a company to scour the bush and to act as scouts. Beat the Maori at his own game.

'That's the thing you would like to do. I can't imagine you taking orders from some of these young ensigns that haven't been in action.'

Jeremy tossed the thought around in his mind. 'No, I don't suppose I would, but I don't intend to enlist in spite of what Newhaven says.'

Paula turned quickly away.

He looked over to her. 'Have you had enough?'

'Leave the lamp alight,' she said.

On the following Saturday, Jeremy was trying to decide whether to close the new warehouse he was renting or to stay open on the off chance that a customer might come along when the outer door swung open and the bell in his office jangled. Tonguer Brown advanced slowly through the maze of machinery and produce, looking up at the ceiling and at the walls hung with tools. He examined a patent plough that had just arrived from Sydney.

'Tonguer!'

The old whaler jumped.

Jeremy walked over to the counter and leaned on it.

'What can I sell you? What's the latest news from the island?'

Tonguer yawned. 'The usual. Everybody is jittery. I thought I'd get out of it for a while and come to town. The young bloods are talking of going bush.'

'Armed parties?'

'Yes.'

'Where will they get their guns?'

'It is not that hard to buy them. The captain of the *'Orpheus'* came in yesterday. Said he saw a queer-looking craft off the Three Kings Islands, a 'Jackass Brig.' It wasn't a whaler. He challenged her and after a bit of a fuss she hoisted the British colours. He thinks she might have been supplying Maori with guns and ammunition. I would not be surprised. Probably characters from Australia wanting to earn some easy money.'

Jeremy looked Tonguer up and down. He was wet and was shivering. 'Where are you staying?'

'I dossed out under a bridge last night.'

'In the rain?'

'Yes.'

182

'Do you want some work?'

'Not particularly.'

'A place to sleep?'

'I could do with that.'

'I'll tell you what we will do. I need help with Matt and Jos away.'

'Where have they gone?'

'They have been called up in the militia.'

'Oh well. Perhaps a few odd jobs. For tucker and a bed.'

'Done. You can lay a mattress under the counter.' Jeremy walked over to the wall, took a key from a hook and gave it to Tonguer.

He took it, turning it over in the palm of his hand. 'It's a long time since I've had one of these,' he said. He went over to the door and tested the lock.

A day or two later, Jeremy was re-stacking the sacks of grass seed when Tonguer appeared again. 'Have you heard the latest?' he asked.

Jeremy jumped down from the pile of bags. "No.'

'There have been two more murders.'

'I know about Hunt. They got him when he was sawing timber.'

'Not Hunt. Two more. Young Calvert and a settler, Charlie Cooper. At different places. The Calverts were having breakfast. They saw about thirty Maori outside the house. The father closed the doors and opened the windows to fire his gun but the Maori got into the kitchen. The Calverts ran into the bedroom and the young'un fell wounded and slowly died. His father went at them with a revolver and a sword but the Maori took to their heels.'

'What happened to Cooper?'

'He went out to fetch his cows for milking and they were waiting for him. A ball went right through his head. They set fire to his clothing and half roasted him.'

Jeremy looked from Tonguer to the bags of seed.

'Calvert is a good customer of mine.'

Tonguer had taken a knife from his belt and was balancing the tip on his fingers. 'I don't know why the settlers don't come into town.'

'It's like everybody else. They think it can't happen to them. They prefer to run the risk rather than to leave the house and have it ransacked. It isn't necessarily the Maori that do it. There are always a few in every body of troops who consider that anything that they can lay their hands on is fair game.'

'Well, I can tell you the Maori is well in command of the forest to the east and until General Cameron winkles them out of the hills he will have to stay on the defensive,' said Tonguer.

'There's talk of a flying column and a troop of volunteers to do just that.'

'About time,' said Tonguer.

Jeremy was surprised at his vehemence. 'Whose side are you on, Tonguer?'

Tonguer stabbed his knife into the wall. 'Blood is thicker than water,' he said.

18

On the morning of the 6th August 1863, His Excellency, the Governor, Sir George Grey, was in his office at Government House when Mr William Jackson was announced. There was a fire burning in the grate making the room warm and cosy compared with the wind and rain outside. His Excellency was in good humour. He rose quickly and walked across the carpet to shake hands. 'Mr Jackson,' he said. 'Congratulations.'

Jackson stood at ease. 'Your Excellency.' He was a few inches taller than the Governor. As men, they were quite different. Grey was polished, affable. Jackson was more formal, quiet, reserved.

'You have been chosen to raise a corps of sixty men to follow the Maori into the bush and scour the ranges. Will you have it on? You will be fairly independent and have an ensign under you. It will be dangerous work but the pay is good. Eight shillings a day for the men and find your own rations. Your pay as lieutenant is fifteen shillings and allowances.'

'I'll accept on certain conditions, sir.'

The Governor stepped back. 'And they are?'

'That each man gets a grant of land as well as myself.'

The Governor stroked his chin. 'Hmm. Fair enough.'

Jackson looked him in the eye. 'You are well aware, sir, that by following the natives I run a great risk of being killed. I don't want to show any disrespect, Sir, if I speak rather plain. A fair understanding now could save a great deal of unpleasantness later.'

'No, no. Carry on.'

'You say you will give me land. I may therefore tell you that it is not for pay I would do this. Neither am I anxious to get a name, but if I get through I shall expect a good lump of land.'

'You realize, Mr Jackson, we don't want to bind ourselves too tightly but I'll give you not only a good lump of land but a large slice in the choicest part of Waikato. I will settle you down in Rangiaowhia.'

'Thank you sir. In that case I have great pleasure in accepting the honour.'

'Good. Your commission will commence as soon as practicable. In the meantime you can have a forage allowance for your horse as from today. You can select whom you want. Any man in the Colonial Corps may leave it and join you.'

'Thank you, sir.'

'Oh! By the way. In addition to the ordinary one, we will make a special grant of land to any man who distinguishes himself and this also applies to the widow of any man who is killed in action.'

'Thank you, sir.'

'Well, there you are, go to it. You need only swear the men in for three months, the show will be over by then.'

Jeremy St Clair climbed wearily into the dogcart at noon. The last six weeks had been hectic because of the contracts combined with the difficulties of getting supplies and the consequent increase in prices. He was about to start Sergeant into motion when two forms leapt on to the seat beside him. The cart rocked from side to side.

A voice cried out; 'Not so fast, Sergeant.'

Jeremy pulled on the reins. Matt and Jos sat laughing at him. 'We are on leave,' said Matt.

Jos was sitting on the other side of the dogcart. He leaned over to look at Jeremy. His eyes were crinkled with laughter. Jeremy noticed there was an indefinable change in him. He looked stronger, had filled out and he had an air of confidence that was lacking before.

'We have joined the Forest Rangers. Eight shillings a day.'

186

Bouncing up and down on the seat Jos let out a call he had learnt in Australia, 'Coooo-ee!'

The startled Sergeant plunged in the shafts. 'Steady boy. Whoa!' Matt took the reins from Jeremy.

'You two clowns had better come home for a meal,' said Jeremy.

Paula had recovered sufficiently enough to have resumed her normal routine but had not left the house since her ordeal. She was pleased to see Matt and Jos. Apart from Caroline there had been few callers and as she had always discouraged visitors, not many people took the trouble to climb the hill to visit her. She had been cooped up in the house for almost two months so anyone was welcome. They sat around the table eating a leisurely meal.

'What made you join the Rangers?' she asked.

'The pay,' said Matt.

'The grant of land,' replied Jos.

'What are the rations like?'

'Good. Especially the rum ration,' said Matt.

Jeremy looked down at the empty holster on Matt's belt.

'How about equipment? There's a shortage I believe.'

'Not for us. Not the way we are loaded up, although we travel fairly lightly compared with the Imperials. Our swag is a blanket, a great coat, twenty rounds of ammunition, all wrapped up in a so-called waterproof, and a haversack with three days rations. Meat, biscuit and half a bottle of rum. Then there's a revolver, cartridge box and carbine. Some have sword-bayonets, others tomahawks. All hanging from our bodies. We look like donkeys.'

Jeremy interrupted. 'What carbines do you carry?'

'Various at the moment. Last week we did a patrol. Came across a camp and had a bit of a skirmish. It only lasted half an hour. I had a long rifle and a revolver. The rifle kept catching on the supple-jack vines on the track. A damned nuisance. At the moment we've only twenty-three of the shorter carbines for the whole troop, but we've been re-issued with revolvers, all fifty four gauge instead of the mixture of calibres we had before. I have a Trunter's Patent and Jos has an Adams.'

Matt took out his pipe and turned to Paula. 'Mind if I smoke?' He took a taper from the mantelpiece and lit it on the stove. 'How is business?'

Jeremy watched him puff the pipe alight. 'Fair. Remember Tonguer?'

'The whaler.'

'He is working for me now. When he's there.'

'And Rosalind?'

'We haven't seen much of her.' Jeremy glanced at Jos. He was looking at the floor pretending to be disinterested. There had been no word of Rata. She would be somewhere deep in the King Country. 'Are you two staying the night?'

They both shook their heads. 'No,' said Matt. 'Thank you. We are at the "Thistle". We only have two days leave. Can't waste valuable drinking time.' He stood up.

Jeremy drove them to town. Refusing an invitation to go inside the hotel he turned off the side of the hill to the school. As he tethered the horse he could hear the children singing. Their clear, unspoilt voices floated out of the window as he walked quietly along the verandah to the French doors. Peering through the curtains he could see Rosalind's back and the shiny faces as they concentrated on watching her baton. Dropping into a cane chair he sat and listened.

When the singing ended he felt relaxed. He stretched himself full length in the chair. The sky was overcast and the edge of the verandah wet with the rain that had fallen in the morning but he was in a little cul-de-sac where the wind could not reach him. His head was level with the verandah rail and when he looked down he could see the brick path with its pie-crust edging and the herbaceous border that Rosalind had planted. He fell asleep and did not hear her footsteps until she was almost level with him. She was carrying a basket and secateurs and was searching for spring flowers. The snowdrops had long since finished. Because of the mild climate they surprised everybody by appearing in mid-winter but now, in September, the last of the daffodils were flowering, competing for space with the perennials that Rosalind had planted in every spare patch of soil. Bear's breeches, not yet in flower, crowded out the columbines, the paeonies, the bergamot and the pinks.

Jeremy watched Rosalind pick some lavender and hyacinths and dogs-tooth violets. She was humming a tune as she pulled out some weeds. Quietly he stood up and leaned over the rail.

'There is one you missed,' he said, 'by the marigolds.'

188

He expected her to look up startled but she continued weeding, keeping her eyes on the ground.

'And how long have you been there, Jeremy St Clair?' she asked.

'Long enough to have heard some delightful singing.'

She did not reply immediately. She snipped another few violets. 'I expect you've come for tea and tipsy cake.'

'Now you've mentioned it.'

She straightened up, tidied the flowers in the basket and came slowly up the steps on to the verandah. 'It is nice to see you again. I thought you'd forgotten me.'

He shook his head. 'No. I've been very busy. Matt and Jos have enlisted.'

'I know. Come this way.' She opened the front door.

'They are in the Forest Rangers.'

She stopped on the doorstep. 'Oh! Jos too?'

'Yes. Remember Tonguer Brown?'

'From the island?'

'He is helping me in the warehouse.'

Jeremy followed her into the kitchen. 'It's good to have someone to talk to, especially someone like Tonguer. Behind that facade he is very articulate and well educated.'

Rosalind busied herself at the bench. 'We have many like him out here, pushed to the colonies with an allowance, an embarrassment to their families at home.'

'I don't think Tonguer is a remittance man. He hasn't a bean. Most of them have enough to live on, though probably not as much as they have been accustomed to. Tonguer has his own philosophy of life.'

'Which stands him in good stead. The trouble is most remittance men don't expect to work. Certainly none have a trade. They are what are called "gentlemen" on the ship's papers. This land needs workers; men who are prepared to roll up their sleeves and hoe in.' Rosalind put a cloth on the table.

'There are plenty of those,' said Jeremy. 'Look what has been achieved here in twenty odd years. From an empty harbour with perhaps one building and a tent to a town of ten thousand. At this rate imagine what it will be like in a hundred and fifty years.'

Jeremy watched her pour the tea. 'All the ingredients are here.

We get the adventurous and the down to earth. A good number of soldiers will settle after the war is over. That is, if the Governor confiscates all the land as he has promised. What an amalgam there will be. Soldiers, farmers, tradesmen, Maori.'

Rosalind's eyes darted at Jeremy as he mentioned confiscation. 'Do you think your great great grandchildren will be a golden colour in the years to come?' she asked.

'Goodness knows. But we shall go ahead in leaps and bounds. You can't stop progress.'

'Jeremy! You sound like a politician. Is there any news from the front?'

'Only what is in the papers.'

'Such as shooting defenceless Maori!'

'What do you mean?'

'Soldiers boasting about it.' Rosalind picked up a newspaper. 'Listen. This is in today's *New Zealander*. A letter dated the 17th of September. I quote, "On coming to where the first Maori was seen to fall they found the fellow — a fine big man — rolling his head. One gave him another shot and settled him." There! I am the child of a man who fought at the Nile when Nelson sent boats to pick up the drowning enemy. Does the public sanction such acts? Shooting a helpless man in the field?'

'War brings out the best and worst in people. Look at the Russian lancers in the Crimea, killing British wounded. Right now the Americans are killing each other in the North-South war. Look at the Maori tomahawking the Meredith boy. Killing a child is something I can't forgive.'

For a while they sat in silence. Rosalind put her hands in her lap. 'How is Jonathon?'

'Very well. He plays at being a doctor. Pretends he is in an ambulance wagon bringing up the rear of a convoy.'

'Poor dear. And your business?'

'Good. All military of course. The enormous increase in prices has meant I haven't been able to reduce the bank loan, but they don't seem to worry. You can't hire a man. They are all in the army.' Jeremy glanced at the Ansonia clock above the fireplace. 'Trust is coming this afternoon.'

'With the boys?'

'No. He is driving some cattle to the yards at Newmarket. He brings a few in every month.' Jeremy moved to stand up. 'He could be there now. Thank you for the talk and the tea.'

'Anytime,' smiled Rosalind.

Jeremy saw Trust riding down the hill towards the warehouse. He was moving slowly, resting his horse after the long trek into town. Jeremy quickened Sergeant's pace to catch up with him. Trust, hearing the noise of the dog-cart turned in the saddle and waited.

'Did you get your price at the auction?' asked Jeremy.

'I did.'

'Good. Everything has skyrocketed.'

'I'm glad we make our own butter. I see it is three shillings a pound in town.'

'It's bread and dripping for most of us. Come inside.'

They passed through to the office. The smell of leather and dried beans and cheese mingled with the wood burning on the stove.

'Your order is ready,' said Jeremy. 'How are you getting it home?'

'I don't know.' Trust scratched his nose. 'I wondered if you could help.'

'I've a cartload of supplies for No. 3 Company at Howick. Tonguer can deliver yours at the same time.'

'Good. The trouble is going to be next month. I'll need the same.'

'That's all right. We'll do the same again. Will you have more cattle?'

'Twice as many.'

'Then call in when you are ready.'

Towards the end of October Trust was back again. Jeremy helped load the cart early in the morning and watched as he started off with Tonguer. 'Give my regards to the boys.' Jeremy called as they turned the corner.

It had been dark for some time when Jeremy at last heard Tonguer returning. He had expected him to be earlier and, when he did not arrive, decided to stay and write up the books. He opened the big double doors at the back and watched as Tonguer drove in. The lamps on each side of the cart were burning a bright yellow. He watched Tonguer climb down slowly and walk inside without speaking.

'How odd,' thought Jeremy and followed him in.

Tonguer went through to the office as Jeremy closed the doors. 'No problems?' he asked.

'There are problems,' said Tonguer. 'Or there were.'

'What happened?'

'We were almost there when someone rode up and told Trust he was wanted urgently at home, so he rode off ahead of me.' Tonguer lapsed into silence again.

'Hurry up man,' Jeremy was annoyed. He had waited long enough for Tonguer as it was.

'When I arrived, Trust was inside lying on the bed. He'd shot himself getting off the horse in a hurry.'

'Is he all right?'

'Yes. Only slightly wounded.'

'Then what is all the fuss?'

'The boys. Richard and Nicholas. They are dead.'

'Dead?'

'Massacred by a bunch of Maori.'

'God!' Jeremy felt a wave of heat surge through him. He clenched his fists until the veins in his arms stood out like knots.

'What happened to Ambrose?'

'He got away. Shot in the arm.'

'Go on.'

'At about seven this morning they heard firing. There were five in the house. Trust's men, Lord and Courtney and the three boys. The next minute the windows were smashed in. There was a lot of screaming from the Maori including some women. They ran across the paddock towards the falls.'

'Who did?'

'Courtney, Ambrose, Richard and Nicholas.'

'Where was Lord?'

'No-one knows where he went. The Maori shot at them. Courtney was hit twice. Once in the thigh and once in the heel. Nicholas and Richard fell and Ambrose and Courtney crossed the

192

creek into the bush. They got Ambrose in the left arm. There were footprints down by the river. One of them had a deformed foot with two toes missing. If anyone ever comes across him he has signed his own death warrant.'

'Captain Antrobus's company was there from Howick when I arrived. A settler found Richard across the creek in a small gully by the falls. He'd been shot in the stomach and then tomahawked in the head and face. William Courtney found Nicholas. He was lying dead in a pool of blood, horribly chopped about on both sides of his head and face. He had a big hole in his left cheek and a piece of ear missing as though someone had shot him close up.' Tonguer stared listlessly at the floor. 'How old were they?'

'Richard was nine and Nicholas eleven years old.'

Jeremy pushed himself out of the chair and began pacing the floor. 'Is Ambrose badly hurt?'

'No. Not badly.'

Jeremy left Tonguer pulling out the mattress from under the counter. He walked home, turning the events of the day over in his mind. A slow, burning resentment welled up inside. These Maori, travelling in bands, making cowardly attacks on civilians. They called themselves Christians. Had been baptized. They condemned the soldiers for breaking the Sabbath and then turned and justified the slaughter of children by declaring it was a Maori thing. He pushed open the front door. There was a candle burning in Paula's room. He climbed the stairs, turned the knob and went into her bedroom. She was awake. He looked down at the pale face on the pillow. The straight black hair. Looking like the girl he used to know.

'I am joining the Forest Rangers,' he said.

19

General Cameron was forcing his way southward. At Meremere, the Maori had abandoned their fortifications. The expedition by-passed the Maori positions and steamed up the river to where the Maori had finally retreated.

The next stand was Rangiriri, where the entrenchments extended down to the river. The British went in with bayonets. A storming party scrambled through the ti-tree as a heavy fire poured down on the defenders. The soldiers burst into the frontline of the rifle-pits and set up scaling ladders as the Maori warriors fell back to defend their second line. They fought desperately and the British troops retired.

Cameron issued an order. 'Captain Mercer with thirty-six artillery men to make an assault.'

'Bloody murder,' said a soldier of the 65th as six hundred British infantry lying under cover watched the attack. The small band rushed forward, each armed with a sword and a revolver, to meet the fire from the defenders. A sergeant-major reached the top of the parapet, discharged his revolver into the mass of Maori below and reeled back with his right arm shattered. Captain Mercer fell, struck by a ball in the mouth which splintered his jaw and ripped away his tongue. Badly mauled, those still alive retired to their own lines.

Then the naval brigade attacked. Midshipman Watkins reached the top and was shot dead. They retreated.

At sunrise on the following day, short of ammunition, the Maori hoisted a white flag. They parleyed and asked for a supply of ammunition to continue the fight. This was refused and they surrendered.

The capture of the Maori King's capital followed in early December. The village had been abandoned and the advancing forces occupied the trenches and rifle-pits nearby to hoist the British colours on Tapane, the King's flagstaff. Now Cameron prepared to go deeper into the King Country. 'But first,' he said to an aide, 'I want to know what is there. I need a scouting expedition.'

The aide looked up from studying a map. 'The Forest Rangers.'

'I suppose so.'

'They will be a bit conspicuous.'

Cameron thought for a moment. 'You think one man, travelling lightly, holing up somewhere, might be more useful?'

'I do.'

'Then send a despatch to Jackson and ask for a man he can trust. I believe St Clair is with him now. He was a captain until the damned fool sold his commission. He will do.'

The big river glided silently along, snaking across the flats in its relentless journey to the sea. There was silence as Jeremy watched the ripples and eddies sweeping past. He adjusted the weight of the rifle on his shoulder and moved further along the bank to a gap in the foliage where some silver sand made a convenient spot for him to refill his water bottle. The sun was glinting on the water and the black-green of the water grass below the surface contrasted vividly with the white patches of fine sand.

The Waikato had its beginnings high up in snow country. A small, tumbling stream bounded over the volcanic rocks and pushed through the valleys to gather up the spring thaw and the run-off from the heartland until it became a massive volume of water that plunged into the great Taupo lake. It found a way out at the northern end and continued its two-hundred-and-twenty-mile journey to the sea.

For the Maori the river was their life. The eel traps were always full, wild ducks fed on its banks and swam in the swamps nearby. The whitebait collected near its mouth made a succulent change of diet and the leaves of the flax bushes around its edges supplied the fibre for clothing, mats, baskets and plates. It was an inland waterway. Canoes plied up and down transporting produce and carrying war parties. In the old days the Waikato Maori had returned down it after successful raids on enemy tribes, carrying back slaves and baskets of flesh.

Jeremy watched from behind the flax bushes and noted the number of canoes, the sizes of the villages, the fighting men they contained and the crops growing on the outskirts. A party of warriors filed past as he sat barely concealed among the leaves of a totara tree. Their dog sniffed at the trunk but no-one looked up and they continued in single file along the track. When they had passed, he slithered down and took a tomahawk from his belt to smash holes in the three canoes pulled up on the bank. He waited until darkness fell and made his way back to headquarters.

General Cameron was in his tent with a candle for a light, writing a report. 'Exactly what I wanted,' he said when Jeremy had finished. 'Would you like to stay on at brigade headquarters?'

Jeremy considered for a moment. It would be an easy job, and would probably mean a commission. 'I would prefer to go back to my unit, sir.'

Cameron raised his eyebrows. 'Then I won't hold you. Thank you, and good luck.'

Jeremy did not enjoy a brief stay at headquarters. The distrust that the professional soldier held for the amateur militiaman percolated down the ranks to the lowest private. The Forest Rangers in particular came in for a great deal of criticism. They were too free of discipline, there was not enough spit and polish and they were a law unto themselves. Until recently they had been paid more than the regular soldier but such was the outcry that all that had changed. Jackson's troops had been disbanded in November and re-enlisted on the same terms as the Colonial Defence Force, being attached to the 2nd Waikato Militia with a drop in pay.

Such was the morale of the men that many re-applied to join the two newly formed troops, one under Jackson and the other under Count Von Tempsky, who had become a naturalized British citizen in order to qualify for a commission. The Von, as his men called him, had gone off in a huff and written to the Colonial Defence Office complaining of being passed over when the first Forest Rangers were sworn in. But now he had his own troop, equipped with the bowie knife, a weapon he had used to great effect in the jungles of Spanish America.

On the other hand, Jackson had been roundly criticized for the lack of action in a sortie into the bush. After waiting for a supply of biscuit to arrive they had set out on an expedition into the ranges to the east. They passed the spot where Mr Cooper had been shot and where a Mr William's hut was burnt to the ground by the marauding Maori. Sergeant Cole, Henry Southee and little Rowland climbed some big trees and spied out the land to the south-east. It was hilly, open country heavy with ferns. Trekking single file through the forest they heard the distant bark of a dog followed by the sound of an owl in broad daylight.

'Po-ah, Po-ah, Po-ah.'

The rangers froze. They heard the chant of a war dance. The troop threw themselves down on either side of the track. Jackson retired to a position further back on high ground. There, it was decided that, because the enemy strength was unknown, they should turn back. The opinion around the Imperial camp-fires was that the Rangers were cowards and should have continued.

Jeremy had wasted no time in returning to his troop. Every day there were convoys of carts travelling along the Great South Road to the redoubts. He found a ride with a sergeant of the 14th Regiment who had been with the First Battalion in the Crimea, serving through the siege of Sebastapol and at the Redan. When the Second Battalion was raised the sergeant had transferred and had arrived in New Zealand in 1859.

'Fighting the Russians was a different kettle of fish,' the sergeant said, as they trundled along. 'These Maori are brave but are fighting for a cause which is doomed to failure. The women fight like men. And in the heat of the battle it is difficult to tell which is which and even against our superior manpower and weapons they rarely surrender. The women are as determined as the men.'

They talked of the old campaigns of India, China and of Afghanistan where the British troops had been routed on the retreat from Khabul.

Fifteen miles from town, where Jackson's troop was stationed, Jeremy said good-bye and jumped down from the wagon. He walked over to his tent and bent down to tighten a loose guy rope. Matt was standing by the centre pole with a blanket in his hand. He threw it on top of a waterproof spread on the ground. 'Where the hell have you been?' he asked. 'We are moving out, you will have to hurry.'

Jeremy stretched his cramped limbs. Good old Matt. One could always tell when he was pleased to see someone. 'Where are we going?' he asked.

'I don't know.' Matt jerked his head in the direction of the hills. 'Somewhere out there.' He threw some ammunition onto the pile.

Jeremy took a short cut through the lines to the orderly tent. Westrupp was checking a list of men. Sergeant-Major Bertram was talking to a soldier and Jeremy recognized little Henry Rowland. He walked over to Westrupp, who was second in command. 'What is up?' he asked.

The lieutenant stopped writing. 'The colonel has ordered us to reconnoitre towards the Wairoa River and the Hunua Ranges.'

'Why?'

'Tis not to reason why. Actually they suspect the murderers of the Trust children are in the area. We parade at 1pm in full kit.'

The hair on the back of Jeremy's neck prickled. 'Can I come?'

'Have you been marched in?'

'I will be before you leave.'

Westrupp looked quickly at Jeremy. He saw the set line on Jeremy's mouth.

'All right, go and draw your rations.'

Jeremy stepped out into the light as Alexander Hill, the guide, entered the tent. Jeremy strode over to the store and picked up his rations, three days supply of hard biscuit and pickled pork. It took up most of the space in his haversack.

Captain Jackson was already on the parade ground when they formed up for inspection. Their commander walked slowly along the two lines of men, picking out every detail. 'Ward, tighten those straps!' Jeremy helped the man re-arrange his equipment and re-place his cartridge box. At 1:15 they set off towards the hills.

Despite the criticism, Jackson's Forest Rangers were the pick of the forces. Volunteers, they came from all walks of life. The comparative freedom from the discipline of camp life, the promise of land, the fact that they chose to challenge the Maori in his own habitat although they were always far from help, meant that they were a special breed of men. George Ward, marching next to Jeremy, was from South Carolina. No-one had asked him what circumstances found him in the Rangers in this wild land in the South Pacific. Jeremy guessed that he had probably deserted from an American whaler. Little Henry Rowland, another sailor, had already proved his worth on previous expeditions by climbing the high kauri trees as though he was skimming up a mast.

As they swung along, Jackson gave an order. 'March at ease.'

Stephen Mahoney began to sing and the rest of the men joined in.

'We'll let the bottle pass,
And we'll have another glass
For the men of merry, merry England.'

The going was easy for the first few miles until they reached the foothills. At the beginning of the forest, where the road ended, Jackson halted his men. 'From now on,' he ordered, 'we move in single file. No talking. Keep the man in front in sight the whole time. Carry carbines at the ready.'

The path was narrow and steep, running up to the first ridge. As they climbed higher the vegetation became thicker and more luxuriant. Black vines of the supple jack, as thick as Jeremy's finger, tangled from above. Tree ferns spread their fronds to hide the sky and underfoot the track was muddy from the rains that had recently fallen. Jeremy could feel the stillness pressing down on him. He fixed his eyes on the man in front, his cap, his haversack. He thought of the Trust children. If it had not been for them he would still be in town adding up figures in the warehouse. He hitched up his holster. A bird flashed across the track. The Rangers marched on in blue-shirted single file.

At the end of each hour they rested and changed positions. Jeremy found himself behind Matt. Rain began to fall as they crossed an opening. Jackson ordered a halt. They threw off their packs and sprawled on the roots of an old tree while Matt took a long drink from his bottle. Setting off again they stumbled over logs and waded waist deep, through streams. Tired and ill-tempered they stopped at 6:30 pm.

'No fires,' ordered Jackson.

They made shelters under logs and beneath the dense foliage. Jeremy searched and found a hollow where a wild pig had slept the night before. He and Matt ate their meat and biscuit and washed it down with rum. Picquets were posted and Matt was detailed for duty at 2am. Jeremy fell asleep, comparatively dry in the pig's lair, unaware of the occasional sounds of the sentries and the continuous noise of a stream close by.

Next morning Matt woke him. 'Four o'clock,' he announced. 'We move at four thirty.'

Jeremy sat up. The sky was hidden by the trees and there was that eerie grey light heralding the start of another day. The time when nature stands still, gathering her strength. Matt thrust a water bottle into his hand. Jeremy took a cautious sip. As he suspected, it was liberally laced with rum. 'To keep out the cold,' explained Matt.

For two hours they climbed upwards. Jeremy was the first to hear the roar of a waterfall. They turned at a bend in the track and saw a wide column of water plunging ninety feet into a pool at its base. Bertram disappeared and returned. He had found a crossing lower down. They cut large bundles of fern from a clearing and tied them together with plaited strips of flax. Jeremy helped Bertram place bundles of fern under his chest and shins and pulled him across the stream. Another hour of marching and their clothes were dry once more.

'Breakfast!'

They halted at a ford strewn with boulders and ate biscuits and cold pork by the edge of the stream. Matt threw a piece of meat into the water and watched an eel slide out from under a bank and glide over to the bait. They followed it upstream as it wriggled over the stones and splashed against the current.

Suddenly, Matt stiffened. 'Look!' He was pointing to the edge of the stream. Jeremy saw a dozen footprints in the mud. Matt crouched down alongside them. 'This one,' his voice was vibrant with excitement. 'It has two toes missing.'

Jeremy leapt down the bank. Matt was pointing to a set of prints, a few feet from the others. Jeremy remembered what Tonguer had said the day that the Trust children had been murdered. 'Two toes missing. If anyone finds him he has signed his own death warrant.'

Jeremy spoke quickly. 'Get Jackson. I will wait here.'

Jackson and two or three rangers quickly arrived. 'I have seen those before,' said one of them.

'Where?' asked Jackson.

'Where Job Hamlin was killed.'

'And the Trust children,' added Jeremy.

It was 6:30am. Jackson turned to Jeremy. 'These are what we are looking for. Stay here. I will bring up the men.'

Bertram marshalled the troop together in line. 'It looks as though we have found what we wanted,' announced Jackson. 'We will follow this track. I want no noise, no talking, absolute quiet.' He looked across at one of the men. 'Mahoney! Uncock your gun. I don't want any caps going off by accident this time. Lieutenant, you take the rear. Sergeant-Major, come up in front with me.'

Lieutenant Westrupp moved down the line. Matt dropped in behind Jeremy in the centre as the column moved off. The rain had stopped but large drops gathered on the leaves above and splashed down spasmodically as they began the ascent again. A bush in front of them sprang back showering Jeremy with spray as the soldier in front brushed it aside. The route continued upwards for an hour then descended into another valley.

After a brief halt they changed positions in file with Westrupp leading. The footprints still showed up clearly on the track. The pace quickened and Jeremy began to feel the effects of the march. They had been tramping since 4:30 in the morning with only a few breaks. Once Matt fell against the black trunk of a king fern and stifled a curse. Jeremy helped him up and wiped the mud from his revolver. They caught up with the column. It was moving slowly into an opening beside another stream which flowed over a shallow bed of stones.

Suddenly, there was the sound of a branch snapping. They flung themselves down. Captain Jackson hid behind a tree and drew his revolver as the others remained motionless. Jeremy watched the clearing, quietly drawing his carbine up alongside him. There was a movement from a small clump of bush. A goat with a rope attached to its neck walked into the opening. They laughed as they detached themselves one by one from the trees and bushes. A ranger raised his carbine.

'Don't shoot,' called Jackson. The man lowered his rifle. 'You will have all Maoridom here, you fool.'

They started again, clambering up the other side of the valley. Jeremy was now in the rear group just ahead of Jackson who used his compass continually to check the direction that Lieutenant Westrupp was taking. The men began to spread out and lost sight of each other in the tangle of the undergrowth.

'Pass the word to slow down,' Jackson ordered.

The pace in front steadied. At the top of the ridge where the watery sunlight filtered down on to a troop of weary men they stopped. Jackson called for little Rowland.

'Can you get up there?' he asked, pointing to a tall tree.

Rowland nodded. He rolled down his sleeves and started to climb. The men threw themselves down on the ground.

Jeremy sat on the trunk of a fallen tree and watched the sailor disappear into the branches. The parasite plants on the log made a canopy that sheltered him from the rain and wads of rock-hard fungi bulged out like tumours from the crumbling bark. He pressed his boot down on a bare patch of clay. It left a perfect print on the ground. Footprints. Jeremy shuddered. If he found the bastard there would be no quarter. His mouth set in a hard line. He pulled out his revolver and took the bullets out one by one, wiping them on his shirt he replaced them slowly and deliberately. He sighted down the barrel and pushed the gun back hard in its holster.

There was a scrambling sound and a thud. Jeremy looked up as Rowland dropped down from the tree and addressed Jackson.

'There's a camp in a clearing due south, sir.'

'Any natives?'

'I couldn't see any.'

'Paths?'

'Only the one we are on.'

Jackson turned to Westrupp. 'We will have a look at it.'

The captain started downhill, taking the lead. Jeremy and Matt scrambled down the slope and slogged up the other side of the valley keeping the column in view with difficulty until somebody up front stopped. Jackson came down the line whispering to each man in turn. He paused in front of Jeremy. 'There's a hut thirty yards away. The door is facing this way. We are spreading out for covering fire. Two men will go in first. Corporal Johns is one. He wants you for the other.'

Jeremy did not hesitate. 'Yes, sir.'

The troop spread quickly around the perimeter of the clearing leaving two sides open to avoid crossfire. While they positioned themselves Corporal Johns and Jeremy mapped out their strategy. They waited until a raised hand from Westrupp told them that the left flank was in position.

'Go!' whispered Jackson.

Corporal Johns dashed to the rear of the hut with Jeremy close behind. They paused for two seconds then ran along the side to the door at the front. Corporal Johns stood off with his carbine at the ready as Jeremy hurled himself through the door and leapt to one side. With his back to the wall he crouched for a moment as his eyes became accustomed to the interior then he moved quickly to another position further along the wall. His eyes swept the length of the hut. He called out to Bill Johns.

'Empty.'

The corporal relaxed when he heard Jeremy and standing at full height waved his free hand in the air. He walked the few paces to the door. The bushes and ferns around the edge of the forest swayed and quivered as the circle of men came out of hiding and stood in the centre. Satisfied that the hut was uninhabited Jeremy and Corporal Johns came out into the clearing and reported, 'Nothing there, sir.'

Sergeant Bertram went in and came out with a pair of soldiers' trousers and a Maori shoulder mat. He rolled them up and put them in his shirt. While the men ate some biscuit and pork and had a tot of rum, Lieutenant Westrupp wandered around the encampment. Jeremy had finished his meal when he heard Westrupp call out to Jackson. 'This fire is still hot,' he said, kicking at the ashes of a Maori oven on the edge of the clearing. He peered into the pit. 'Someone was here yesterday.'

Jeremy walked over. The oven was large enough for thirty or forty people to have camped there. He looked at Matt. 'At least it will be an even fight,' he said.

'If we find them. Come on.' Matt helped him shoulder his pack.

At the end of each hour they changed places in line. Captain Jackson scanned the countryside with his glasses. All that he could see was ridge after ridge of verdant forest. He called for Rowland once again. There was an old rata tree leaning out over the valley. Rowland shinned up the trunk pausing in the crotch of a branch. He saw a hive of wild bees in the hollow and gingerly worked his way past them to be rewarded with a magnificent view of the surrounding countryside. A track wound down the hill and disappeared towards a small opening in the forest but there was no sign of the enemy. He slid down quickly. 'Nobody in sight, sir. There is an opening ahead,' he said.

They started off again, tangling with the vines and holding onto the low branches to slow themselves down. There was a small stream at the bottom where they filled their water bottles. Bertram appeared. 'Hurry up, you two.'

When Matt and Jeremy caught up to the column it was halted in a clearing. There was a group of old huts in the middle and a grove of peach trees laden with fruit. Matt picked a peach and took a bite. Rowland was up a tree throwing fruit down to the men below while Jackson stood on a mill wheel that was lying outside the door of a hut. 'We can't stay here,' he said. 'We would be sitting ducks for anyone. Let's go.'

'On your feet,' said Bertram.

Westrupp had been exploring the opposite side of the camp. 'Here is the track,' he called.

They were now in open country. The ground was covered in bracken except for a narrow path that disappeared in an easterly direction. An hour later they came to the edge of a swamp. The track had disappeared.

Bertram went up to Jackson and spoke to him quietly. 'The men are tired, sir.'

Jackson nodded. 'We will camp here.'

'Can we light fires?' somebody asked.

Jackson hesitated. 'I suppose so, but wait until an hour after dark.'

A small camp was soon established. Each man heaped up dry fern on the ground to make a comfortable bed with a waterproof laid down to keep out the rising damp. Jeremy and Matt collected some dry wood and twigs and set a fire ready to be lit when the order was given. Matt unwrapped a small cloth bundle and took out his clay pipe while Jeremy cut a pole from a small stand of scrub and made a tent with his blanket. Matt filled his pipe and lit it, taking a long puff and exhaling the smoke to watch it spiral upwards drifting slowly towards the hills they had just left.

The sergeant came up to them with a roster for night watch. 'You two are on at midnight. You wake George Cole and Henry. Find out where they are sleeping, before it is dark.'

An hour later the word 'Fire' was passed from group to group and one after another, small sparks of flame gradually fanned into life, lighting up the small area until a myriad of shadows danced and disappeared into the night. Matt and Jeremy halved their meat and biscuits keeping some for the next day. They sat with a pile of fern at their backs, sipping neat rum.

'Have you heard from Ireland lately, Matt?' asked Jeremy.

'Yes, only last week, from my sister to tell me my father is sick. It is the first letter I have had from her.'

'Will you go back one day?'

'I will have to, I suppose.'

'How big is the farm?'

'Just twenty acres. Pigs and horses. Mostly horses. Oh, and potatoes, of course.'

Matt stirred the pan that was heating on the fire and put out half the contents for Jeremy.

'Matt, do you think you will marry one day?'

'No. As soon as they talk about being hitched the magic goes.'

Jeremy laughed. 'I think you are a born bachelor. Have you regretted coming here?'

'Never. It means there is one less mouth to feed at home.'

'But if you had remained at sea you could have gone back sometimes.'

He looked up at Jeremy. 'Might as well be miles away as not,' said Matt. 'Would you go back to England?'

'Sometimes I think it would be better for Paula, but people would have thought I was giving in and I never give in.'

Matt was surprised that Jeremy had mentioned Paula. He thought very carefully. 'Some people,' he said, 'need constant companionship. Deep down it is because they are insecure. They make the most noise and appear the most confident.'

Jeremy felt a twinge of conscience. 'Perhaps I should not have joined up.'

'It wouldn't have made any difference,' said Matt. 'She worries about you but won't admit it.'

Jeremy was amused. 'How do you know?'

'I have seen her watching you. Eyes following you wherever you go, even when she's flirting with someone else.'

Matt could have kicked himself when he realized what he had said. He looked embarrassed.

'I mean,' he started to say and then stopped.

Jeremy smiled quietly. 'I don't assert myself enough. Perhaps I should. But I always feel sorry for her.'

'You are too much of a gentleman, Jeremy. People take advantage.'

'I can't change. I feel uncomfortable if I try to be someone else. According to the rules I should win in the end.'

'You lean over too far to help people. Be like everybody else. Grab what you can.'

Jeremy smiled. 'Sometimes I wish I could.'

They turned in after supper, finishing with a good tot of rum, and were soon asleep.

Picquet duty was uneventful and they were packing up at 5 o'clock next morning, ready for any eventuality. At 5:30 they turned back to re-examine the path. It was not until they had trekked back to the peach grove that a cunningly concealed track was discovered diverging to the left. Keeping in single file, appearing and disappearing amongst the undergrowth they climbed to another ridge. Men were posted to look for smoke. It was almost eight o'clock, the time when the Maori open their ovens for the morning meal. Rowland and three others went to their lookouts. Two of the men saw smoke simultaneously. There were five puffs of white steam rising in the air down where the steep gorge fell into a valley in line with the track they were following.

Captain Jackson called his troop together. The men gathered around their leader. Westrupp was on his right. Jeremy and Matt were next to him. 'The enemy is less than half an hour away,' said Jackson. 'Judging by the steam from the ovens there could be seventy or eighty in the group. The chances are it is the same war party that committed the Wairoa murders. We will be outnumbered. We are deep in their territory and even if we are successful there are sure to be others who will hear the fighting and we will be lucky to get out. I want you to decide. Do we attack?'

There was silence. The men stirred. Harry Jackson scratched his beard. Henry Hendry spoke up.

'We'll leave it to you officers, Sir,' he said.

'Then we fight.'

Jeremy and Matt looked at each other. Matt shrugged his shoulders. 'Come on,' he said, 'what are you waiting for?'

Within five minutes the men were on their way to battle. 'Keep close. I want absolute silence,' was the order. Jackson set off down the track. After fifteen minutes march they stopped again. Jeremy and Matt were directly behind Westrupp.

'Charley,' said Jackson, you take the first eight men and go ahead. We will follow a hundred yards behind to avoid ambush. Everybody strip to shirts, trousers, boots and weapons.'

They piled their gear under a tree and covered it with fern leaves. Jackson addressed them again. 'In case we don't get out of here, someone should go back to headquarters and report what is happening. Any volunteers?' No-one moved. 'Right,' he nodded to Westrupp.

Westrupp gathered eight men together. He sent a man to scout out front then after an interval, set off. Jeremy and Matt were directly behind Charles Westrupp while Sergeant Bertram brought up the rear. Ward, the big man from South Carolina was behind Matt. They moved slowly and silently along the path.

Jeremy felt cold inside. He could not forget the Trust children. Mercy and compassion had gone out the door. There was only a deep animosity for anyone who killed innocent children, no matter how just they felt their cause might be. This was why he had joined the Rangers. He admired the Maori people for their intelligence and for their courage. He understood how they had turned to Christianity to replace the bloody customs where men ate men and the rule was an eye for an eye and a tooth for a tooth. Blood for blood. Payment. 'Utu' they called it. He thought of the Jewish religion. Jeremy had seen Maori who, dressed in robes, would have been unnoticed on any Mediterranean shore and he wondered where the Maori ancestral home had been. He knew their legends, how they had sailed in great canoes across the ocean to this land of plenty. Had a wandering ship found its way here from the other side of the world and intermingled with the natives? Was New Zealand a land of plenty for the Maori? Why, in this beautiful climate, in seas that teamed with fish and shellfish, in forests full of fat birds and edible berries, with a soil so rich that the vegetation pushed itself upwards almost sensually, was the Maori population so small? Why did they consider the lives of their slaves of so little value? Were they the noble savage that the people back home in their secure middle class homes liked to imagine? Jeremy would have liked to have known the answers.

He was brought out of his thoughts when Matt stopped. 'If there is a shindy we will cover each other,' he said.

Jeremy nodded and put his revolver in its holster. 'Don't we always?'

It was true enough. Survival meant relying on the other man, and from the beginning they had made a pact to always share rations and duties and to act as a team. Teamwork moved mountains, loners were losers.

A few minutes later they came to a halt. Jeremy could see Westrupp talking to the scout.

'Something is up,' whispered Matt.

Westrupp beckoned the men forward and at the same time put a finger to his lips to signify caution. When they were all together Charlie Westrupp spoke quietly, his voice just audible above the sound of the stream. 'Their camp is across the river and about fifty yards down stream. There is a log across the ravine with a sentry on it. If you come up here you will see him.'

They shifted ten yards up the track and peered downstream

through the foliage. The sentry was washing himself on a log which spanned a small ravine. The noise of the water drowned any sound as it surged through the narrow opening and boiled across to the opposite bank. They could see the thatched roofs of some huts a little way from the river bank.

Westrupp turned to the last man in the group. 'Nip back to Captain Jackson and tell him we have found them,' he said.

Without a word the man disappeared along the track. Sergeant Bertram studied the Maori sentry carefully.

'He is a big bastard,' he said, 'how are we going to get him without raising the whole camp?'

Jeremy had an idea. 'The mat,' he said. Bertram was still carrying the mat in his shirt. 'Dress up George Ward, he looks enough like one of them and could get away with it.'

All eyes were on Ward. If he could get close enough without being discovered there was a chance. The man's eyes flashed. He handed his carbine to Matt and took off his boots and socks. The sergeant adjusted the mat over Ward's shoulder while he hid a long knife in its folds. 'Keep your head down,' he said. 'Don't let him see your face.'

They watched like men mesmerized as George Ward walked slowly down towards the river. Westrupp raised his carbine and drew a bead on the Maori's heart. Ward stopped on the end of the log and waited until the sentry saw him. He raised his arm in a salute. The Maori waved in reply. So far so good. Matt's eyes were glued to the spot where he knew Ward was holding the knife. The rangers were tense as they watched, in contrast to George who swaggered across the log with a sailor's gait as though on a morning stroll. It was all over in seconds. Matt caught the flash of steel as George Ward drove the knife upwards into the man's underbelly. He saw the look of surprise on the Maori's face as the body pitched into the torrent.

'Come on.' Westrupp led the way down and across the log.

'Good work, George.'

They reached the other side.

'Spread out at ten yard intervals along the bank. Where the hell is Bill Jackson?'

He had no sooner spoken when Jackson and his men appeared across the bridge. They had seen the tail end of the action and were quick to give support. 'Steve' Coghlan was one of the last to cross. He looked down at the warrior wedged between the rocks. The man's belly was split open and the stream was making a plaything of the entrails as they waved and twisted in the current. 'Steve' turned white, then green and was sick as he reached the other side. He hung on to a branch as the nausea swept over him. It was the first dead man he had seen. A soldier brushed against him knocking him off the path.

'Get out of the bloody way,' the man whispered fiercely, 'and for God's sake, shut up.'

Captain Jackson slid alongside Westrupp. 'Well done, Charlie,' he said.

Jackson crept up a bank on the other side and looked over the edge. The first hut was only fifteen yards away and beyond that was a group of Maori, cleaning their guns and talking in a circle. Some women were standing around a fire, plaiting baskets from the blade-like leaves of the kie-kie plant. He beckoned the men up to him. 'We will attack with carbines. After that use your revolvers. There are women there. Anyone firing on them will be flogged.' He paused, 'Are you ready?'

Jeremy felt the surge of excitement that he knew so well from the Crimean days. He had thought he had left all that behind. In his mind he saw the Trust children playing with their dog at the door of their cabin. He took aim.

'Fire!'

There was a roar of guns and a pause followed by the irregular crack of weapons seeking out their victims. The forty or more Maori who were scattered over the camp leapt up and ran to their guns. Some children appeared from a hut and disappeared into the forest. Two women dropped their baskets and ran to a warrior who had fallen at the first volley. Picking him up they dragged him into the bushes.

Jeremy and Matt leapt down the bank and drew their revolvers. As Jeremy took aim at a brown figure slipping away on the edge of the camp he saw a Maori out of the corner of his eye, with axe raised, rushing at Matt. Matt raised his revolver and pulled the trigger. There was an ominous click. It had misfired. Jeremy swivelled around. He had no time to aim. Simultaneously tightening his grip and squeezing the trigger he fired. The native hurtled into the air, his body arched backwards. He was suspended for a moment between the sky and the deep green of a myriad of leaves then crumpled downwards. The axe fell from his hand and hit Matt a glancing blow on the shoulder.

Jeremy turned again and ran to the front of a hut. John Smith was engaged in hand to hand combat about twenty yards away. It was impossible to get in a shot without endangering him. Jeremy threw himself at the Maori's head as Smith plunged a knife into the man's side. They fell in a heap. Jeremy picked himself up while Smith stood there shakily staring down at the twisted figure quivering on the ground.

Some women dragged more dead and wounded into the protection of the forest. The Rangers let them go. A native running between the huts turned and fired at Jeremy. The shot went wide, but the man had disappeared before Jeremy had time to take aim. Matt appeared alongside him. They were now at the perimeter of the camp. It would have been foolish to follow the enemy into the bush.

The Rangers spread out at intervals around the edge of the compound while two or three men entered each hut in turn. The firing had stopped as quickly as it had begun. The smell of gunpowder filled the air as the blue smoke from the carbines drifted away. The action had only lasted four or five minutes.

Captain Jackson walked from man to man enquiring about injuries. There were none except for Matt's bruising. He placed sentries around the whole camp, expecting a counter attack.

Suddenly, a woman came out of the bush. She ran swiftly to a Maori lying on the ground and knelt beside him, calling his name. 'Te Pai-tui.' She wept loudly, tears rolling down her cheeks as she rocked to and fro repeating her husband's name over and over again. He lifted his hand and she grasped it as she poured her feelings out in a long unintelligible chant.

A ranger gave Captain Jackson a questioning look.

'Leave her,' he said.

Somebody uncorked his rum bottle and handed it to her.

'Wai?' she asked. 'Is it water?'

'No. Wai piro. Fire water.' She gave him a withering look and swept the bottle away with her arm.

Matt handed her a gourd that was standing nearby. She smelt

its contents and then, propping up her husband's head slowly poured a little down his throat.

Captain Jackson turned to Corporal Johns. 'Have a look at him Corporal,' he ordered.

As Johns knelt down beside the Maori the woman threw him a wild look, but when he brought out a bandage from his pack she moved aside while he bound the wound. Johns looked up at Captain Jackson and shook his head, then moved to another Maori lying motionless. He was dead.

Captain Jackson squatted down and spoke in the Maori language to the woman's husband. 'What tribe are you?' he asked.

'Ngatipaoa.'

'How many here?'

'Twenty eight,' the Maori replied.

The captain knew there were more of the tribe than that in a camp of this size.

'How many?' he asked again.

'Twenty eight double,' was the answer. The Maori held up two fingers.

'What is your name?'

The man was silent. Captain Jackson did not press the point. He pointed a finger at the body alongside them. He noticed the heavy tattoo on the dead man's face.

'Who is that? Is he a chief?'

The man nodded.

'Who is he?'

'Matariki.'

Jackson turned to Sergeant Bertram. 'Get him some food and water. We can't do anything else for him, we will have to leave him here.' He jerked his head at the woman. 'She will have to look after him, poor devil.'

They walked over to examine the cooking area more closely. There was a good deal of tea and sugar lying around stacked in a pile together with a large bag of flour. A quantity of fern root was heaped up by the ovens. The women had been pounding it with some stones to extract the fibre when the attack had interrupted them. Large cuts of wild pork were hanging on a tree and three or four iron pots filled with meat were sitting by the fire.

Sergeant Bertram came over to Jeremy and Matt.

212

'Come on you two,' he said, 'help clean out the huts.'

The picquets were changing as Matt and Jeremy went into a hut. They started searching. There were no windows and the only light came from the opening that was used as a door. There were some scarlet window hangings lying on the floor, some fancy window blinds and a small box. Matt opened it. Inside were some papers addressed to Mr Richardson of Wairoa. There was a coat with Mr Johnson's name in it, from the same place.

'This settles it,' said Jeremy. 'This is the crew we have been looking for.' Angrily he picked up a small box of bullets that he found in a corner and hurled them out the door.

'Steady on it,' said Matt.

They carried the various pieces of loot outside and put them by the cooking pots. Already there were a number of articles gathered from the other huts. A double-barrelled gun, a large horse pistol, three or four cartridge boxes, a smaller pistol and some ladies' workboxes. They put several packages and tins of gunpowder into a heap away from the fire.

Lieutenant Westrupp looked down at the collection. 'We will get rid of the gunpowder and the bullets for a start,' he remarked.

Two or three rangers gathered them up and threw them in the stream. A ranger came from a hut holding up two small packets of European hair, evidently relics. 'You can hold on to those,' he said. 'Somebody may claim them.'

Suddenly a cry rang out from a picquet. There was the sound of a shot. Captain Jackson raced around the side of a hut followed by Jeremy and Matt. They saw a figure disappearing into the bush. A sentry ran up and fired into the foliage then turned to see his Captain standing there.

'He came out of a hut with something, sir,' he explained. 'I hit him in the arm. He dropped a box.'

The walked over to a small tin box lying on the ground. 'Open it,' ordered Captain Jackson.

The soldier knelt down and undid the clasp. They were curious to know why the Maori had risked his life for the contents. The lid lifted back with a creaking sound. They bent over, peering inside. In the box were three flags. The soldier lifted them out. The first was a large red one on which was embroidered a white cross and star and the word 'Aotearoa' in white letters. It was made of silk and very neat and handsome. Another was a large red pendant with a white cross while the other was handkerchief size, patterned with the Union Jack.

'They must be Kingites,' thought Jeremy. 'To think he risked his life for these.' It summed up the bravery and the altruism that the Maori felt for his land and people, and yet this very same group had killed young children in cold blood. He walked over to Matt.

'How is the shoulder?' he asked.

'Bloody sore.'

'Let me have a look.'

The bruise was beginning to show. A dark purple and yellow discolouration that extended from the shoulder downwards. 'You will live,' said Jeremy. He jerked his head in the direction where Matt's opponent lay. They walked over to the body and looked down at the lifeless heap. There were two toes missing on his right foot.

'The killer!' Matt cried.

Jeremy remained staring at the foot. 'Revenge,' he whispered, 'Utu . . . , Utu . . . .'

20

The evening meal was over and the fires low when Jackson's Rangers walked back into camp. The Von saw the trail of weary men drift down the road and waited at the guardhouse for Jackson. 'Where was the action?' He kept in step with them as they entered the camp.

'I can't tell you the exact position. A few miles from Paparata. Somewhere between there and the coast.'

'I saw footprints myself in that area but they were small. Women's.'

There was a look of disappointment in the Von's eyes. He had spent days tracking through the forest hunting the murderers of the Trust children and Jackson had beaten him to it. 'Are you sure you found the tribe we were looking for?'

'Yes.' Jackson's answer was definite. 'There were several articles from MacDonald's house lying about and other bits and pieces. Fancy window blinds. A coat belonging to Johnson. A bill of exchange for £1000. A watch.'

Jackson paused as he watched his troop disappearing towards the cookhouse. 'You will have to excuse me. I want to see that my men are fed. We used the last of the rations at breakfast.'

When he returned the Von kept up a barrage of questions. Jackson was tired but gave him a brief description of the action.

'The Maori were cleaning their guns when we attacked. Some were washing at a stream. We heard a cowbell ringing, probably one that had been stolen when they shot some cattle. We threw away their ammunition. Couldn't bring everything back.'

'Were there any casualties?'

'Not on our side. I saw three dead Maori carried away and they left four dead on the field. The men scorned to fire on the women although they assisted to take off the wounded. I saw them supporting one man and pushing him into the undergrowth and two of the Maori took to us, one with a bowie knife and the other with a carving knife. They were hove to with a shot. I would have surrounded the lot and taken them prisoners if I had had more men.'

The Von picked up a sketch pad. 'Can you draw what the position looks like so I'll know it if I see it?'

Jackson smiled. 'I can't draw as you can. Perhaps later.'

'How many women were there?'

'Quite a number. I told the men not to fire on them and I'm happy to say they didn't. One woman was hit in the leg, with a stray bullet but she got away.'

'How did your men perform?'

'Very well. Westrupp was right in the thick of it. John Smith had a hand to hand go with a native. He dropped his carbine and closed with him.'

'Do you think they are still there?'

'They wouldn't get far with the wounded.'

'Shall we go after them again?'

'I'll need a day's rest.'

'Right.' The Von rolled off the camp bed he was lying on and moved outside. Night had crept down and the line of tents was a ghostly blur against the evening sky.

'Wednesday,' he said and disappeared into the darkness.

Two days later the two troops set out together. They struggled over streams, clambered up the steep slopes and marched silently along the tracks that crisscrossed the forest.

They separated and met again in the evening. The Von sat with Jackson sharing some roast pig that two of the men had cornered and despatched with a bayonet. He poured out a tot of rum and handed it to Jackson. 'You British are strange animals,' he re-

216

marked, 'did you know they are criticizing you for that attack on Sunday?'

Jackson looked up from cleaning his revolver. 'No. Why?'

'One of the Imperials called it a shameful massacre.'

'The Imperials? What do they want me to do? Take a bugler with me to sound through the bush to let them know I am coming?'

'The regulars don't like us.'

'Because we are more effective. The last time they criticized me for not attacking and now when I do, they say it's murder. Have they thought of the Trust children or Job Hamlin?' The Von had taken out his bowie knife and was turning it over in his hand. The blade gleamed in the firelight. Jackson threw a piece of brush on to the flames. 'What is the flying column for if it isn't to scour the bush and take them by surprise when we find them?'

The Von grunted. 'Where shall we search tomorrow? I think we should look down the river.'

It rained and thundered all day Friday. The streams were swollen and the men wet and tired. They called off the search at midday and started back to camp. There was a message for Jeremy to report to headquarters. He marched in without bothering to change his clothes and saluted the Colonel.

'St Clair.'

'Sir.'

'I'm picking men for Christmas leave. You have done more than your share this month. The General was pleased with the report you gave him. You can have leave if you want it.'

Jeremy thought, 'Want it? Home for Christmas. Clean clothes. A good bath.'

'Thank you, sir.'

'Report for a pass on Wednesday.'

The town was surprisingly quiet when Jeremy dismounted from the commissariat wagon. There were a few Christmas decorations in the shop windows and a green arch of tree fern over the wharf entrance. Some naval ships lay in the harbour. The 'Curaçao', 'Miranda' and 'Esk' were anchored in the stream and liberty boats were plying between them and the shore. The weather was humid.

217

As he walked over the plank at the bottom of the hill he saw a large patch of water on the bowling green, still lying there after a storm the night before. Jeremy had sent word on ahead to Paula and he knew she would be expecting him.

He was surprised when he saw her dressed in her Sunday best. She had made a special effort to look attractive. Her grey silk dress, nipped in at the waist, shimmered with a touch of green thread woven through it and her hair shone with a hundred brush strokes just as it did when Emily had been there. In spite of their situation, in spite of being separate and yet living in the same house, whenever he saw her after being away for any length of time there was that magic moment of wonder and delight, as though he was seeing her for the first time and was falling in love again. He had learnt to accept the feeling and had become adept at hiding his reactions.

'Merry Christmas.' He saw she was wearing the ruby ring again. The one he had bought in London so long ago.

'Where is Jonathon?'

'With Rosalind.'

'Oh!'

'He asked if he could go and see her,' said Paula. 'There are only half a dozen children there now, from the Ngapuhi and Arawa. The others have been taken away.' She came towards him and stood a foot away. 'Jeremy, let's be friends. It's Christmas.'

He saw her round white breasts swelling under her bodice. Her eyes were downcast and hidden under long black lashes. 'Of course,' he said.

She held out her hands. He took them and they stood there, apart, and yet together. Looking up at him she poured her black eyes into his. 'Would you like to get Jonathon? He does not know you are coming. The dogcart is ready at the back.'

Sergeant recognized Jeremy and showed his pleasure by nuzzling him. There were a few carrots in a bucket by the back door and Jeremy fed them to the horse as he checked the harness.

When Jonathon saw Jeremy, the child stood stock still like a small wild animal, uncertain, unbelieving, then with a cry he ran at his father, and flung himself into his arms. Jeremy felt a surge of sad-

218

ness and a lump rose in his throat as he held the boy tightly. Rosalind watched the two of them sharing in the joy they felt.

'It is too hot inside,' she said. 'You two go out to the verandah. I will make tea.'

When she came with the tray Jonathon was riding on Jeremy's knee. 'This is the way the gentlemen ride, trit, trot,' he cried, jumping up and down. 'Over the fence we go.' They collapsed in a heap on the floor.

Rosalind spread a cloth on the cane table. 'Your favourites, bath buns and Betsy cake and Boston cream for Jonathon,' she said. She looked quizzically at Jeremy. 'Were you in the Paerata affair?'

He took a sip of tea. 'Yes.'

'You must be proud of yourself.'

'Why?'

'Murdering innocent Maori.'

He coloured. 'They were the group that killed the Trust children.'

'How can you be sure?'

'Footprints matched up. There was a coat of Johnson's there. Stuff from the house.'

She stirred her tea longer than she needed and put the spoon on the saucer without looking up. 'You said you would not fight.'

'Circumstances changed.'

'How?'

'The Trust children.'

'Captain Newhaven told me you attacked on a Sunday while they were having a church service. They were ringing a bell.'

'Newhaven is a liar.'

'Was it a Sunday?'

'Yes. I repeat. They were the group that murdered Richard and Nicholas Trust. Newhaven knows that.'

'I don't know what you have against Newhaven. He is a gentleman and most understanding.'

'When he wants to be.'

'What do you mean by that?'

'He is a cad.'

'Jeremy!'

'He is heartily disliked in the mess. Boasts about his conquests I am told.'

'What conquests?'

'The sort of talk hardly fit for a lady's ears.'

'Perhaps I'm not a lady.'

'Only last week he was fined for mentioning a woman's name in the mess.'

'I don't believe it. I find him most generous. He has donated money to the new stone church and has bought Maori prayer books for the school.'

'I would believe that. He is magnanimous when it suits him. He thinks he can buy friendship. His so-called friends talk about him behind his back.'

'As you are doing now.'

'I don't profess to be his friend. Rosalind can't you see the man's a bounder. He is a rack renter and gets his money from property in the East End of London. He has a rent collector that extracts the last penny out of his tenants and lets out his capital at twenty-five percent and more. He is only considerate to people if he thinks they can be useful to him.'

'You are jealous, Jeremy St Clair. He is simply a good business man.'

'And a rotten soldier.'

'He is a very generous and thoughtful man.'

'Generous? How?'

'He bought the children new choir cassocks and new Maori dictionaries.'

'European paraphernalia. He would do better to study Maori lore. Learn what they are thinking. It is the only time I have known him to give money away. And why? Because he wants to impress you. Show you how kind he is. He is after you. He refused to donate a penny when the 'Orpheus' went down. Called them bloody stupid sailors. I tell you Rosalind he is evil. Everything he touches turns to stone. He is only interested in his own self-aggrandizement and he wants you for his collection.'

As Jeremy stopped speaking a cloud crossed in front of the sun. A shadow spread across the lawn. He looked sadly at Rosalind who had risen from her chair and was standing in front of him.

She spoke quietly, hardly above a whisper. 'You can go now Jeremy. This killing, this war has changed you. Don't ever come back again.' She walked over to Jonathon, picked him up and kissed him, holding him briefly to her. 'Take Jonathon.'

Jeremy picked up the boy and walked away. Rosalind put up a hand to stifle a cry, looked around wildly and ran inside. Throwing herself on to the bed she wept.

It was a hollow time for Jeremy. On Christmas Eve he and Paula went to church at midnight and took the sacrament. Afterwards they filled Jonathon's stocking under the tree, leaving gifts for each other, but for Jeremy there was a feeling of emptiness. He was glad when his leave expired, although Paula had made every effort to please him. It was with a mixture of sadness and relief that he found himself once more on the Great South Road on his way back to camp.

After the fall of the King's capital the war had stood still. The townspeople hoped that it would fade away, that the Maori people would lick their wounds and then gradually return and forget. But that solution was too simple. There was the confiscation line, stretching to the middle of the Waikato district and then turning towards the coast, making a huge box of thousands of acres. This would have to be occupied and cut up to satisfy the soldiers who had been promised land for their services. The King and his people had retired deeper into Maori territory.

Cameron gradually extended his hold southwards with the Forest Rangers acting as scouts at headquarters. As the British advanced both troops of Forest Rangers scoured the country ahead.

Jeremy was under the cover of an old earthworks, driving away a band of Maori who attacked a bathing party, when Von Tempsky's men arrived. The Maori scattered into the high fern and scrub. There was a pop, pop of revolvers as the men engaged in hand to hand struggles until the firing slackened.

The shots flew around Captain Heaphy as he attended to the wounded soldiers. His clothes were riddled with bullets. With five balls piercing his jacket and slightly wounded in three places he continued to give aid until night fell. When he took off his jacket Jeremy saw where a ball had struck a buckle and seared around his waist leaving a red slash as though a whip had half-encircled his body. Later, Jeremy was to hear that Captain Heaphy had been awarded the Victoria cross.

On the wider front, the battle for supremacy continued. As the long hot summer came to an end the stage was set for the final struggle in the Waikato.

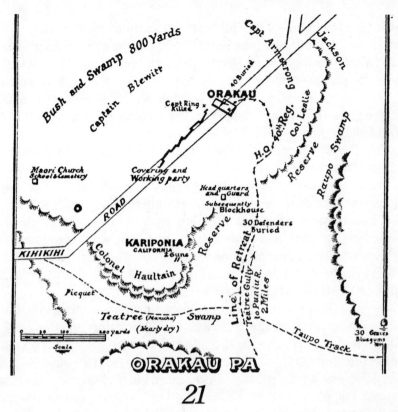

Bush and Swamp 800 Yards

Capt Armstrong

Jackson

Captain Blewitt

40 Buried

ORAKAU

Capt Ring Killed x

H.Q. 40th Reg.

Col. Leslie

Reserve

Raupo Swamp

Maori Church
School & Cemetery

Covering and
Working party

Headquarters
and Guard

Subsequently
Blockhouse

ROAD

KARIPONIA
CALIFORNIA
2 Guns

30 Defenders
Buried

KIHIKIHI

Colonel

Haultain

Reserve

Line of Retreat

Teatree Gully
to Puniu R.
2 Miles

Picquet

Teatree (Manuka) Swamp
(Nearly dry)

100 yards

Taupo Track

30 Graves
Bluegums

Scale

ORAKAU PA

21

Orakau
March 1864

Moihi, Maori warrior, raised his calabash and drank deeply. The
cool water splashed over his face and across his chest soaking the
flax kilt at his waist. Sunlight filtered through the king ferns dap-
pling his face and the mud on the edge of the stream oozed between his toes. It was autumn and the nights were cold but warm
days had forced the vines and crops into ripeness as they intermingled and climbed over the huts, bowing towards the rich brown
earth. But there was no one to gather the crops. The Waikato and
their sub-tribes were preparing for battle.

    'Let us stand here, let us make our challenge now,' said the
chiefs. 'We have our guns, let us use them.'

    They gathered fern leaves for an offering to their gods and

war chants shattered the quiet groves as their priests intoned the rites over powder cask, axe and rifle. There were two feverish days and a restless night of digging, spades stabbing into the clay, shaping the parapets, hollowing out the trenches and putting up the breastworks. They cut fern and laid it down, piling the earth on top, more fern, then more earth, making a barricade that would defy the British guns.

'Dig for your gods, Maori, dig for your women and children, dig for your land.'

Moihi walked to the spring where Moana was waiting. Anxiously she wiped the smudges of dirt from his body and poured the cold clear water over him. Washing away the dust and grime she smelt his strength and gave him her love. She wanted to pray, but should she turn to the old gods or to those of the missionary? Whose mana might be stronger? Can a God of love be a God of battle? Can this be the time to turn the other cheek?

There was another night of sleeplessness, as chants lifted on the night air, echoing down the valleys. The warriors and the women deepened the trenches and made the parapets higher. Tupotahi directed the work, an art learnt on the Australian gold fields. 'A trench here, another layer of fern, more earth. Make the burrows small. Dig for your lives Maori. The land is yours and no one can take it away. Who is he without the land? Like the white heron without its mate, like the mountain without its mantle of cloud, like the mighty giant tree of the forest, the totara, without its roots, dying, dying.'

At last daylight came and there was a rest from the night's work. The ovens were uncovered and as the steam rose to mingle with the mist, they ate their pieces of pork, green thistle and sweet potato served in baskets made by the women from woven flax. The women, hot from the smoking ovens, were weary with the sweat of fetch and carry, but still proud and purposeful and defiant.

After the meal there was a Christian prayer, with Wi Karamoa leading. 'Lord have mercy upon us, protect us from the enemy, give us strength to guard our land against the whites who devour our tribes as their bullocks destroy the leaves of the forest. Grant us victory so we may carry our hearts freely among our people.' Heads were bowed. 'Our father, which art in heaven.'

Te Waro, high priest of the Maori gods watched quietly from

the edge of the gathering. He had no faith in missionary prayer. Missionaries had tricked the Maori into selling the land and had brought nothing but disease and distrust and hate and war. It was a bad omen when the warriors had returned from the village of Rangiaowhia without the fern leaves that the prophetess had demanded in order to placate the old Maori gods. He sent up his own prayer to the god who shows himself in the evening sky, a war god glimmering with fire and dancing flame. 'When battle comes, make us strong.'

There was a shout from the lookout guarding the approaches. 'A war party! A war party!'

A long second of understanding. A rush for the fence. Muskets glinting in file along a winding track. Red coats patching the deep green of the forest.

'Every man to his place.'

'Defend the outer trench.'

'Load the guns.'

'Women and children into your holes.'

'Rewi, you are commander in chief, go inside the parapet.'

'Check the powder. Our testing time has come.'

The morning sun glinted on the rifles and bayonets of a long line of British infantry snaking along the track. They stopped, spread out, and slowly advanced in open order moving like set pieces in a choreography of war. There was no movement from the fort. The soldiers could see only a low mound of freshly turned earth, yellow against the dark green of the fern and a post and rail fence. The silence was deeper than the forests. Von Tempsky's troop of Forest Rangers were on the left and the Royal Irish on the right as they advanced slowly across the uneven ground with bayonets fixed.

In the fort, Maori warriors manned the outer trench while the women and children found shelter in the inner ditches and burrows. Rewi, their chief, was in the centre, to be protected at all cost.

A bugle sounded. 'Charge.'

The soldiers broke into a run with bayonets at the ready. Rewi's order was firm. 'Hold your fire, Maori. Let them come.'

The warriors could see the straps crossed on the soldiers tunics and white faces distinct and recognizable under pill box hats. One hundred yards. Fifty yards. Rewi shouted to the outer trenches. 'Puhia! Fire!'

Two hundred guns crashed out, flashing their hate in a wall of lead and flame, mowing down bushes, grass, fern and men. Scarlet coats plucked at random crumpled to the ground and were still. Captain Ring lay dead. A bugle sounded. 'Retire.'

The soldiers fell back and reformed with another company of the 40th Regiment. Again they attacked. Again the defenders waited as the troops advanced.

Rewi ordered a volley. 'Puhia e wako.' The outer line of defence fired cutting down more men.

'Puhia e roto.' The inner line fired.

Soldiers faltered, paused, then retreated. Captain Baker of the 18th Irish galloped up. He dismounted, rallied the men and called for another charge.

'Closer, Maori, closer. Now fire, reload, fire! Make your bullets tell.'

The rangers reached the trenches and were faced with a wall of brown faces, bloodshot eyes, matted black hair, axes, guns, fierce hatred and contempt.

'Come on, Jack. See how the fern and clay turn your bullets.'

'Come on, Jack. Three hundred Maori ready to fight for their land.'

'Come on, Jack. We will never give in.'

The mauled British forces fell back.

Captain Von Tempsky walked over to headquarters. There were blank faces and looks of dismay. Captain Fisher was severely injured and eight men either killed or wounded. There was a conference. Ideas were tossed back and forth and the Armstrong guns brought up.

Six pounder shells crashed into the fort but Tupotahi had done his work well. The shells tore into the mounds of fern and clay but caused little damage. Bullets clipped the flax bushes and thudded into the earth as soldiers dug in with their bayonets. Shouts and volleys continued to fly from the Maori defenders. Soldiers began digging a sap towards the outer trenches of the stronghold and soldiers were detailed to cut bundles of brushwood for gabions to protect the diggers.

There was the distant sound of wailing as Maori reinforcements lined the hills to the north. The high pitched chant carried across the swamp. The garrison began a war dance, stamping out a

226

wild chorus, and were answered with cries from their allies. Gun fire punctuated their song. All through the long afternoon a sentinel kept up a chant, urging the garrison to be alert and to be ready to fight.

Jackson's No. 1 Company of Forest Rangers moved up to Orakau, in file, scouts out front, their dark blue uniforms brushing the fern aside as they listened to the distant crackle of muskets overscoring the crash of the cannon. There was a mixture of fear and excitement in the bellies of the men.

'Come on, Coghlan. Has mother's boy brought something to puke into this time?'

'You are a bastard, Edwards.'

Coghlan threw the words out in anger. He was white and taut, signs of strain and anxiety showing on his young face as he snapped a reply to his companion in line. Ever since that day in the Hunua when he had seen the disembowelled body wedged between rocks Coghlan had taken more than his fair share of chaff from the company. After all, as the Von had said, many a man has turned green at the sight of a corpse in battle. But Edwards was persistent and vicious, taking delight in twisting the shame that Coghlan was feeling, giving him no chance to forget. A sergeant moved up.

'Pipe down you two. You will get all the fighting you want, soon enough.'

They halted in a clearing. Major Jackson moved forward for orders. Jeremy and Matt listened to the rifle fire as Jos flung himself down on the side of the track. He took off his pack, inspected his carbine and went over the gleaming parts with a rag. It was early evening. The smoke from the battle hung in the air. Jos closed his eyes. Where was Rata now? She could be anywhere in the Waikato. He dreamt of those far away days, her cool brown skin against his, her blue black hair, her warm brown eyes and those long hours in the sun. His thoughts went back to their last few weeks together. He remembered that day when Rata, his brown goddess, was snatched in daylight and there was no one with the courage to help her. Soldiers, sailors, settlers, afraid of provoking the Maori, afraid of the tribes descending from the hills and swallowing up the settlers in one gigantic sweep.

What had Britain's indecision achieved? Only disrespect from the Maori, the opportunity missed to govern wisely and strongly. It had caused the King movement to become a rallying point for dissatisfied tribes and made war inevitable. Maori accepted Christianity with its rules and turned their backs on the old religion, but the white man did not obey his own commandments. What are the use of laws if they are not enforced? The white man took away the old religion and left a gap he could not fill. It was filled now with death and hate and cannon, with bravery and fear, with charity and lust, with calculated murder and noble mercy, in fact with all the ingredients of war in a hotch potch of move and counter move, and all for land.

'Prepare to move.' The order came down the line as a mumbled transfer from soldier to soldier. The men grumbled.

'Forward.'

No. 1 Company of Forest Rangers moved into battle.

Friday morning, 1st April 1864, dawned with a thick fog that closed the battlefield. There was little movement and an eerie silence that pressed down upon them all. A conference of chiefs was held in the fort. They were low in ammunition, there was no water and the garrison ate raw potatoes to relieve their thirst. Should they escape while the fog lay so heavily on the ground?

There was a conference, Rewi spoke. 'Listen to me, chiefs of the council and all the tribes. It is we who sought this battle, wherefore, then, should we retreat? Let us abide by the fortune of war, if we are to die let us die in battle; if we are to live, let us survive on the field of battle.'

The mist swirled in pockets warmed by the late morning sun, lifting the curtain on another day of tearing sound and hopeless bravery. The firing commenced. It was sporadic at first, then gained momentum as targets became visible. The mist was replaced with the haze of gunsmoke and the smell of powder. A war dance set ablaze the courage of the Maori braves.

'Oh when will your manhood rage?
Oh when will your courage blaze?

When the ocean tide murmurs.
When the ocean tide roars . . .

They jumped over the earthworks and down the slope as the troops retreated in the face of the charge.

Who will stop us now?
Who will avenge the dead.
Charge them. Kill! Kill!

Guns were loaded on the run as they threw themselves down. Fire. Reload. Forward. Another barrel. Reload. Sound seemed to float remotely above them and every action suspended in slow motion. Each shot was isolated with fierce clarity. Every step appeared to have been mapped out before and this was the consummation of a play that had been rehearsed many times.

'Charge.'

'Fire.'

'Reload.'

The Maori advanced two hundred yards. Far enough from the fence. They fought their way back, hot, breathless, but with spirits high. The redcoats had felt their sting. Let them come.

Twenty Forest Rangers from No. 1 Company sweated inside the flying sap approaching the fort. Jeremy, Jos and Matt, dressed in blue shirts and heavy navy blue trousers, took their turns with rifles and with spades. Gabions, large wicker baskets woven with manuka tree sticks, had been brought forward the previous day and were now filled with earth from the trench. These were lifted up into position giving cover on either side. In front a sap roller, four or five feet thick, and consisting of green manuka stakes tied together was rolled ahead as the trench advanced. A traverse was dug and then a parallel for the riflemen to give covering fire for the diggers.

It was a hot day and the clay was hard after a long summer but they had volunteered for the duty and attacked the work with a will. They took turns to stand in the parallel and cover the diggers, getting in a shot now and again as the defenders showed their heads over the parapet. A bullet splintered the gabion and fell into Jos's pannikan which was lying on the bottom of the trench. He picked it up, looked at the dented round ball of lead thoughtfully and put it in his pocket.

They made another traverse to avoid a flax bush and lifted a gabion into position. Half a dozen angry heads appeared at the top of the fort and poured a volley on them. The whole battle field burst into action. Shots flew in all directions some passing over the fort and landing dangerously close to the Von's men who were dug in on the other side. A ball struck one of the rangers in the head as he attempted to duck behind a gabion. He sat propped up on the floor of the sap with his back to the wall while Jeremy tore a piece from his flannel shirt to stop the flow of blood from the man's temple. Matt and Jos helped carry him to the rear.

Twice the Maori rushed the head of the sap but were turned back each time by the steady aim of the sappers and by the fire from the troops now surrounding the fort. Fifteen hundred soldiers against three hundred Maori. The Von and his men were down in a hollow, waiting for action, dodging the lead from their own side's Enfield rifles and occasionally from the balls fired from the fort. Captain Herford from the 3rd Waikato Regiment walked over to the Von.

'I've had two close ones,' he said. 'A ball has bruised my chest and another creased my hip. I am glad my wife will not hear of all this, until it is over.'

The Maori decided to run out a counter sap and the firing from both sides became rapid and incessant. For Jeremy the afternoon wore on in the heat and sweat of digging and firing. Matt and Jos went back to the end of the trench for a rest and Coghlan accompanied them. Reaching for his flask, Matt, took a long pull and handed it on as they sat with their backs to the sides of the sap.

'Not for me,' said Jos.

Coghlan reached out and took the flask and holding it high drained it.

Jos glanced at him. 'I don't know why you worry about Edwards. He's a bastard. Ignore him.'

The strain of battle was beginning to tell on Coghlan. He was flushed and there was a nervous tick in his left eye. 'That's all very well. You don't have to listen to it day after day.'

'Men pick on others to hide their own shortcomings. Edwards hasn't volunteered for this job.'

'And he won't, either. Have you ever seen him here, at the

sharp end?'

Jeremy crawled down to where they were talking. He looked at them clearly for the first time in two days. Their faces were covered in hard stubble and Matt's beard was daubed with dirt. 'The chief wants you back,' he told them. 'There's another gabion to go into position.'

Matt loaded his rifle while Jos and Coghlan worked at the clay face. The bullets kept thudding in, clipping the sap roller and sometimes dropping into the trench. 'As big as bloody potatoes,' remarked Matt.

Evening was approaching. There were two raids from the fort. At the head of the sap, Captain Jackson and Lieutenant Whitfield helped throw the attackers back. A new gabion was levered into position and Jos and Coghlan attempted to drag it upwards. It was badly constructed and difficult to handle. The two men struggled with it as it caught on some stakes. Jos took a quick look at the obstruction.

'We need to cut that out from the front,' he said, 'but bugger that.'

Coghlan stood up. 'I'll do it. We will see who is the coward.'

He leapt on to the parapet and heaved. There was a single shot from the fort and he fell back into the trench with a bullet in his head, a still, lifeless form.

Matt jumped down, saw the hole and shook his head.

'Poor bastard,' he whispered.

They carried Coghlan to the rear and returned to the attack with a furious intensity. Jos picked up a spade and shovelled while Jeremy stood at the parapet firing coolly and carefully at every head that showed itself above the palisade. The Armstrong guns pounded their shells into the fort, seeking out the shelters and blasting women and men indiscriminately.

Inside, Maori wounded needed water desperately. The dead were buried in shallow trenches while the chants and the war cries continued and the high pitched wails of Maori reinforcements in the hills who were unable to reach the fort, rolled across the battlefield. The volleys became fewer as ammunition became scarce. They cut apple wood for bullets.

'Save your ammunition, Maori. Keep the lead for daytime when every shot must count.'

The hot afternoon came to an end and there were more war dances from the garrison. A chief's voice was raised in a chant. The warriors shouted their replies and with their courage up, leapt into the night. Thirty natives dashed out of the fort onto the top of the gabions at the front of the sap. The Waikato Militia with Captain Herford fired a volley into them. The Maori retreated once again and a strange quietness came down broken only by the occasional sharp crack of a rifle and flashes of flame lighting the night.

'Should the Maori fight his way out under the cover of darkness?' Rewi deliberated. The chiefs were assembled. Paerata said no. The debate went on. The Urewera tribes said no. The first glimmer of a new day filtered through — the hour of doubt and worry. A decision was made to fight on.

Potatoes were roasted in the hollows of the parapet but Maori mouths were too dry to chew them. Rewi grunted and stood up. He strapped on his powder boxes. 'We must go.' The fog would hide the escape. The best men in front, women and children in the middle and warriors on the outsides.

But it was too late. While they were preparing, the sun had cleared the mist from the valleys and the hills, laying the battlefield bare and making escape impossible. The gods had decided.

'I bet you three beers at the Exchange they will have a white flag up,' said Matt.

'Taken,' replied Jos. They stared through the gabions as the morning mist lifted. The sap was only a few yards from the post and rail fence, close to the north west outlook. 'There is no flag,' said Jos and fired his rifle at a post, then corrected his range. Suddenly he stiffened, reloaded and fired again, calling out, 'They are attacking.'

Matt leapt up beside him on the banquette as twenty or thirty of the natives rushed at the sap roller. Aiming carefully he fired. A Maori spun around and dropped to the ground. Major Jackson, Captain Herford and the others were alongside in seconds.

'Aim! Fire!' Another attacker down. The Maori turned and fled back to the fort. Some of the militia scrambled over the gabions and followed them. One Waikato soldier was brought down in the open. There was a pause in the firing, then gradually the fighting resumed with the steady sound of guns and rifles increasing.

'Bring up the grenades.'

Sergeant Mackay appeared at the head of the sap with rolls of fuses and boxes of grenades, dragging them along the bottom of the trench. With his eye he measured the distance to the fort and cut the friction fuses to length. Jos and Matt watched from behind.

'Stand by.'

Mackay struck the fuse on the back of a spade.

'Throw.'

The grenade curved over in a high arc and landed in the fort, shattering into white hot steel fragments, and tearing into the bodies of the defenders. More grenades were prepared and thrown. Hoani, Maori warrior, leapt at one as it landed, picked it up and threw it back towards the sap.

'Shorten the fuses.'

There was another throw into the fort. Hoani darted forward and took the full force of the blast as the grenade exploded, leaving a crumpled mess of hair and quivering flesh on the ground.

Grenades kept lobbing over, while Captain Batty of the Royal Artillery supervised the placement of a six pounder in a gap between the gabions. Gunners rammed a missile home.

'Ready. Fire!'

The six pound ball crashed point blank into the palisade, splintering the timber, breaching the earth works and silencing the men behind.

'Fire.'

The guns caused havoc in the confined space. The firing went on. Jos and Matt no longer appeared to be individuals. They were a small part of a drama acted out on a stage set against a backdrop of earth and sky. Their nerves were sharpened to such an intensity that they were oblivious to everything except the movement from the fort. Death was too close and too easily recognizable to allow for any relaxation.

When the sound of the cease fire curved up the hill and into the sap the notes seemed muted and far away and only when the firing from the surrounding regiments stopped did Matt and Jos realize that a halt had been called. As they stepped down they saw interpreters approaching with a white flag. The party came to the head of the sap. The quiet continued as Maori after Maori appeared at the head of the fort. Soon the garrison was crowding the walls of the pa, a fearsome cluster of bloodshot eyes and wild black hair. They held their rifles at the ready.

The interpreters had their orders from the general. 'Tell them,' he had said, 'they have done enough to show that they are brave men. Their position is hopeless. If they surrender their lives will be spared.'

Ensign Mair stood on the banquette and looked upwards. 'Friends listen, this is the word of the general. Great is his admiration for your bravery. Your position is hopeless. Stop fighting. Surrender so that your lives may be saved.'

A messenger detached himself from the line of warriors and disappeared into the fort. Jeremy watched silently as a Maori stood pointing a rifle at Ensign Mair. A woman was beside him, sturdy and magnificent, proud and erect with defiance.

Matt whistled softly. 'Look at that one, I could put a bun in her oven.'

'She's more likely to put you in the oven,' whispered Jos. Rewi and the chiefs sat deliberating in the middle of the defences. Will they surrender? They were hopelessly outnumbered. Better to live to fight another day. Should they make a bargain that the British leave and the Maori evacuate?

The short arguments continued.

'Peace shall never be made. Never. Never.' The words came from the parapet.

Ensign Mair was not surprised. 'That is well for the men,' he replied, 'but it is not right that the women and children should die. Let them come out.'

'There was a short pause.'

'How did you know there were women here?'

'I heard the lamentations for the dead in the night.'

Heads were bent together. A woman's voice cried out. 'If our men die the women and children must die also.'

Ahumai and Te Paerata called out. 'We shall fight against you forever. Forever!'

The defenders took up the cry. 'Forever. Forever! E pai ana. The word is ended.'

234

Ensign Mair stepped quickly into the sap. A shot crashed out. A bullet cut into the ensign's shoulder strap and tore at his tunic. The parley was over.

The Waikato Militia with the Forest Rangers and regulars under the command of Captain Herford commenced firing. Grape shot from an Armstrong gun ripped into the stockade and Sergeant Mackay continued to lob his grenades into the centre of the fort. Lieutenant Whitfield reorganized the sapping party and the work went on. Soon they were only a short distance from the outer defences.

Suddenly a soldier threw his cap towards the fort and dashed after it followed by Herford and some of the men. They burst through the light outer palisading, rushed into the inner trench and commenced to scramble up the embankment.

A Maori appeared silhouetted on the parapet. He fired and Herford fell with a bullet hole in the forehead. Ensign Chater of the 65th was shot through the side. Privates Armstrong and Levitt were killed and several others wounded. The natives discharged their pieces and ran into another trench out of sight. The British party scrambled back to the sap with the dead and wounded.

Jos and Matt watched from the gabions. 'There's a militiaman out there, alive,' cried Matt.

'Where?'

'There,' Matt pointed.

They called to Lieutenant Whitfield.

'That man's alive, Sir,' said Jos. 'The militiaman about twenty yards from the pa.'

'You would last ten seconds out there,' said Matt.

'Wait,' said Whitfield.

He selected twenty tense and eager men, checked their weapons and detailed a carrying party. The remainder lined the traverses to give covering fire.

'Ready.'

'Go.'

There was a silent rush this time. The wounded man was carried back before a shot was fired.

The others continued the charge, taking themselves to the outworks before the Maori could act. Comparatively secure, the soldiers reorganized as a party with hand grenades and dashed into position alongside. Grenades, hurled over the palisade, burst among the garrison. The noise of battle, of guns and grenades, reached new heights.

The Maori were tired and thirsty and beyond care. The wounded and dying lay in the trenches without help and the dead were buried in layers in the hollows. The grenades blasted on, picking at the bravery of the garrison, wearing it down.

It was four o'clock on that heavy warm afternoon. The 40th Regiment were posted on the south side of the pa, under the brow of a hill, cutting gabions on the edge of the swamp. Three or four men were posted below a scarped bank made by the Maori to keep wild pigs from the cultivations. The line of sentries had been removed to enable an Armstrong gun to be directed on the enemy's works.

Suddenly, there was the steady sound of bare feet thudding on the ground. A solid body of Maori warriors with their women and children cut through the thin line of soldiers and plunged into the high tea-tree and scrub that lined the edge of the swamp close to the road.

Moihi was there with Moana, who was wounded in the thigh. Watching her closely, he helped her as she stumbled and ran.

'They are pulling out.' Jeremy heard the cry and seizing his rifle squeezed through a gap to leap up the embankment into the fort. Soldiers were already at the outer fence, disappearing through the splintered walls. The rattle of rifle fire increased as the garrison ran through the swamp and were picked off as they fled. Matt caught up to Jeremy and passed an old Maori standing in the middle of the fortifications with a white flag held up high, it was Wi Kamaroa, who had led the prayers.

The last of the Maori were leaving the pa as bayonets flashed. In. Out. A body dropped between the palisade and the earthworks. In. Out. They rushed up to the parapet on the far side. There was the crash of a carbine as another Maori dropped. Jeremy ran back to the middle of the defences. A wounded woman wailing with grief was scraping the earth from the dead body of her partly buried man. Ensign Mair carried her to a corner and went to attend a wounded man. An 18th Irish Regiment soldier was alongside. In. Out. There was the spurt of blood from the woman, a tangle of arms and legs and breasts and a chilling silence. Jeremy ran with his rifle reversed to club the soldier but the man jumped over the palisade and disappeared.

Rewi ran to the swamp, stumbled and fell. He said a prayer to his Christian God. 'O Lord, save me and visit not this sin upon me.' He rose, ran a short distance and fell again. He turned to his Maori gods.

'Remain there where you are.

I will fly on from here.

Fly like a bird.

Rising high in the heavens.'

Rewi did not move when his younger brother knelt beside him. 'All my friends who come to fight for me are dead,' he said, 'and I will not survive them.' Maori followers forced him up. He recovered himself and together they dodged between the flax bushes and finally reached the higher ground to disappear into the forest.

Moana limped slowly through the swamp with Moihi supporting her. They were behind the main party and soon separated from them. She had a cut in her thigh and they crouched and ran through the bushes, slipping past the cordon of soldiers. Moihi had no charges left. They saw a group of soldiers on the left. Moihi, his white shirt torn and stained with powder, turned and knelt aiming his gun at the pursuers. They scattered for shelter. 'Run for the river,' he said.

Moana limped on. Moihi followed, kneeling and aiming as he went. They lost themselves in the swamp, then the water became deeper, the flax bushes were larger and further apart. They knew they were close to the river. At last they came to the bank and half floated, half pushed each other across. They scrambled up the steep slope, hiding among the tall trees. Finding a dry patch of forest leaves they lay down, hidden and safe together.

Gradually the firing stopped, soldiers straggled back with the wounded and the afternoon wilted to a tired end. There was quiet and death and destruction in the air. As the shadows lengthened Jos and Matt made a shelter from their blankets, joined them together and threw them over a frame of small stakes. Pickets were

237

arranged for the night, chosen from units that had not been heavily involved in the fighting.

The two friends lay on their ground sheets with haversacks for pillows. Matt took out a plug of tobacco and unwrapped his clay pipe. 'It is as good as over, Jos. You will have your piece of dirt before you know where you are'

Jos remained silent, staring at the walls of the shelter.

Matt kicked at the fern root. 'Where do you think you will get your farm, Jos?'

'I don't know.'

'It might be at Rangiaowhia. Grand country. Good ploughable stuff.'

Jos sat up. 'They can keep their bloody land,' he said.

There was a scuffle outside. A ranger's head appeared.

'Jos. We have found Rata down by the Puniu. She is wounded. Jeremy is looking after her.'

Jos dived through the opening and ran towards the river. 'Rata is alive. Rata is alive.' Passing the fort he raced headlong down the slope.

The ranger shouted. 'To the right. On the left bank.'

Jos struck the river and turned down stream. He saw Jeremy, kneeling over a form covered with a mat.

There she was. Jos's face was contorted with grief as the forces of stress and care burst. He stood still in time, then gently took her in his arms, his tears mingled with her tears as they clung together.

Sunday dawned a warm, clear day with a soft haze rising from the river. All was still, except for the clash of spades and picks and the thud of the hardness of late summer's clay. There was a pile of dead bodies near the pa and a larger one further away on the Maori's line of flight. They buried them on the edge of the swamp and on the spur above the Puniu. The dead in the pa were put in their own trenches — Piripi with his wife Mere, Reweti with his wife, Moroto. The last body went into a shallow hole as the men in the burial party straightened up. Standing silently, they gathered their tools together. The corporal took command.

'Form fours.'

They took up their positions slowly, waiting for an order. Slowly, in front of them, an arm rose above the shallow surface, thrusting through the soft earth, its clenched fist held stiffly upright.

A soldier muttered an oath, walked over and trampled it back into the dirt.

22

It was a grey day with the wind ruffling the surface of the sea. Beyond North Head Jeremy could see a cutter leaning sharply as a gust of wind caught her and heeled her over. Once there would have been a dozen canoes hauled up on the beach but on this day there were none. One old woman with a pipe in her mouth and with a tattooed chin squatted with her back to a wall as she stared into the distance. A dozen seagulls and a pied oyster catcher were exploring the mudflats. Jeremy loosened his collar and began to climb up the road to the house.

Paula was not expecting him. She knew, of course, that the Forest Rangers were being disbanded and many of the men were enlisting in the Armed Constabulary, but she was unaware that Jeremy and Matt and Jos had not volunteered for further service and were being discharged.

Opening the front gate Jeremy walked slowly to the front door, drinking in the luxury of being a civilian again. The clank of a bucket sounded from the stables. Looking through the top half of the door he saw Jonathon feeding Oliver. He watched as the boy talked to the pony. Jeremy measured his son against its height. Soon he would be able to mount without the aid of a box.

'Jonathon,' he called.

The boy's head turned sharply and Jeremy saw the delight in

his son's eyes. Jonathon ran and threw himself at Jeremy. Gently Jeremy carried him into the kitchen. The door swung back with a crash. 'Lordie!' A middle aged woman stood on the other side of the table. 'You'll be Mr St Clair,' she said. 'I am the new help. Mrs St Clair engaged me last week.'

'How do you do.'

'It was all on the spur of the moment. My engagement I mean.' She wiped her hands on her apron.

Jeremy picked up a card lying on the table. It was an invitation to a military ball and addressed to Mrs St Clair. He turned it over and read the inscription.

The woman patted the boy's head. 'I do general duties and look after Jonathon. Don't I little man? Mrs St Clair found that with all her social commitments she needed someone more permanent-like to look after him.'

'Commitments?'

'Well, your wife is very popular, isn't she. Receives so many invitations and has so many social functions to attend.' The woman cocked her head to one side. 'Suitably chaperoned by Lady Caroline, of course.'

'What is your name?'

'Oh dear, I am so sorry. Laura. Laura Beatson.'

Jeremy hung his jacket on the peg behind the door. 'Well, Laura, we may as well have tea, I suppose. What time do you expect the mistress home?'

'She did not say, sir.'

'Then I will have it right away. In the parlour.'

'Yes, Sir.'

Jeremy picked up the boy and slung him over his shoulder. 'Show me your favourite toy,' he said.

It was almost dark when Jeremy heard a cab pull up outside. He watched Paula dismount. Laura ran outside and he heard the click of a latch and footsteps in the hall. Paula stood for a moment at the open door. Hurrying over to Jeremy she pecked him on the cheek and stood back.

'Well, well, what a pleasant surprise.'

She is overacting, thought Jeremy.

'If I had known you were coming I would have been home earlier. What are you doing here?'

'You are talking to St Clair, civilian.'

She stood open-mouthed.

'I am no longer in the army, and neither is Matt, nor Jos.'

'Oh dear.'

'Oh dear?'

'I mean to say, Jeremy. Why didn't you let me know?'

'There was no time. We had the opportunity quite unexpectedly, talked about it, and here I am.'

'Where are the others?'

'They will be out in a week.'

'What are you going to do?'

'Take up where I left off. Hopefully double the turnover of the business.'

'You mean you are going to stay in trade?'

'Yes. Any objections?'

'I was hoping you would give it up.' She went to the window, turning her back to him. 'We will talk about it later.'

'And what have you been doing?'

'Oh. The usual.' Taking off her muff she let it hang from the chain that dangled just below her waist. 'I see quite a bit of Caroline. I hope you didn't mind me engaging Laura.'

'No. Not if you needed her.'

'The money has come through from the farm at last. Quite a tidy sum. Caroline feels I should live up to my station a little more.'

'Then Gerald has come up with the cash at last.'

'Jeremy, you are being vulgar again. I know none of the details. I have dealt only with the solicitors.'

'Where have you been?'

'At a whist afternoon.'

'Was Newhaven there?'

Paula's hand trembled. 'Not that I know of.'

'Surely you would know if he was there.'

'He wasn't. Why do you ask?'

'There is an invitation from him on the table. For a ball.'

'Oh that.' Paula changed the subject. 'Would you tell Laura I will have tea with you.'

Jonathon tugged at Jeremy's hand. 'Come and play with me.'

'After tea,' said Jeremy. The boy was reluctant to go. Only a promise by Jeremy to ride with him in the morning settled him down. Jeremy went back to the parlour where a log fire was burning. He sat opposite Paula at the other side of the fireplace. She was crocheting. 'What's that?' he asked.

'A comforter. In Berlin wool.'

'Who is it for?'

'Caroline. Did you think it was for a man?'

'I had no idea what it was.'

She cast off a loop and made a chain. Putting the hook down she stared into the fire. 'Do you remember, Jeremy, before the war, talking in the carriage one night about ourselves. About my having freedom to go to dances and parties?'

'Yes.'

'Now you are back, I don't expect to have to alter my ways.'

'What ways?'

'Going to a few balls. Picnics.'

'I'm looking forward to them, after the last few months.'

'You don't quite understand. I mean without you.'

'But you can't. People will talk and it's not done. Paula what's got into you. What has happened?'

'Nothing.' She picked up her needle again. 'I've had my freedom while you have been away. I want to keep it.'

'And have everyone talking! I suppose they are gossiping already.'

'I don't care what they say.'

'How about me? My feelings?'

'Jeremy, we have been living a lie for years now. I am sick of it.'

'Is there someone else?'

'No. I don't want to talk about it tonight.'

'Very well, but I'm not going to let it rest there.'

Next morning, after taking Jonathon to the domain and exercising Oliver, Jeremy walked to town. On the other side of the hill there was the usual activity at the barracks. A line of carts was moving out with supplies to the camps and a picquet was marching down towards the main street.

Arriving at the front of the warehouse he knocked on the door.

There was a shuffling on the other side and it opened a few inches to reveal Tonguer's face. The hinges creaked as they swung back and Tonguer disappeared into the rear of the shop. Jeremy saw an empty rum bottle on the counter and another on its side on the floor. Rumours had filtered back that Tonguer was on the bottle. It was another problem that would have to be faced, but not today.

Jeremy did not go inside immediately. He stood at the door looking across the street. The wind had a winter sharpness to it, sweeping into the corners of the buildings, tossing pieces of paper into the crannies and whirling them away, heaping them outside the horse bazaar at the end of the cul-de-sac. There was a pile of horse droppings swept against one of the walls. He gazed at the front of the building. The sills and the windows needed painting. It was something Jos could do when he returned.

It was difficult to concentrate in the office. After the army life and the free and easy way of the Forest Rangers he felt confined. His new olive cloth jacket and cord drill trousers were too restrictive after the open-necked shirts he had been wearing.

The morning dragged on. At lunchtime he put on his hat and called at a land agent's office. Robert Wood had given him some good advice when they had arrived six years before.

'Robert,' said Jeremy, as the agent stood up, 'I'm interested in buying a farm reasonably close to town. I have a tidy sum in my London bank from the rent of the farm in Devon.'

Wood looked surprised. 'What. Run it with your business?'

'No. It's not for me. I'm thinking of putting Jos on it.'

'Mmm. You could do worse. He's a lucky lad. How will you work it?'

'I will buy it and give him a half split. He can pay me from his share of the profits.'

'That's very fair. There are one or two properties on the market. There'll probably be more as the troops move out and the demand for produce drops.'

'You think there'll be a downturn.'

'Nothing surer. The demands of the military account for most of the money spent in this town.'

'Then some people will be sorry to see them go.'

'Indubitably.' Wood went over to a cabinet and pulled out a file. 'Here's a property. Ideal for what you want.'

244

Jeremy and Jos rode out to look at the farm the following weekend. It was not far off the Great South Road and extended to the east towards the ranges, facing northwest. Half of it was flat and the remainder undulating towards the hills. There were thirty acres of virgin bush that would need to be cleared but the timber from it would pay for part of that. There was a deserted village on its south side.

Still hostile to the Europeans, many Maori had retreated deep into the centre of the island and the others, the peaceful ones, were returning only slowly to their old haunts. There was a dejected air about them, a feeling of loss, a lack of the drive they once had. Leaderless, they mourned for their warriors and for the chiefs that had died for a lost cause.

'What do you think of the property Jos?' asked Jeremy.

'It looks fine to me.'

'We could run a few cows to start with and build up a herd.'

'What breed?'

'I don't know. Ayrshires I suppose. They seem popular.'

'How about the bush?'

'We could start cutting it right away. Burn it off in the early summer.'

A month later Jeremy and Jos loaded a cart with saws and axes and food for a week and went back. The first essential was to identify the boundaries. They cut a line through the bush and put in a peg to mark a corner on top of a high ridge. Another line went diagonally across a valley to the northernmost point and returned to the road.

After a week of hard work they were able to see the main boundary from most parts of the property. They came in to the camp tired and hungry.

'I think we should have sawyers in to cut out the best timber and fire the rest,' said Jeremy.

'It will be the cheapest way,' replied Jos. 'Have a good burn and sow the seed afterward. The ashes will send the grass off like nobody's business.'

'Where do you want the house?'

'See that flat mound there, on top of that, facing north. It will be out of the damp and away from the mosquitoes. There's room enough for a shelter belt and half a dozen fruit trees.'

'How about water?'

'We'll have to use butts with a runoff from the roof.' Jos pointed down the valley. 'If there is a drought we will take water from that stream. The next door neighbour says he has never known it to dry up.' There was a pause. 'Sir?'

'Yes?'

'Can Rata come here? We want to be married.'

'That's up to you. I have no objection. You'll have to wait for a while. It will take a year or two to get the fencing done and the house up.'

They returned late in November. Jeremy had made arrangements with the neighbours to make one big burn-off in the area. The first three days were spent in mustering cattle which had strayed into the bush and then to sort them according to earmarks. The discarded trees cut by the sawyers were lying on the slopes in the tangled undergrowth. Many of the finest trees, the totara and the kauri had to be left lying to burn as they were inaccessible to the bullock teams that dragged the timber to the mill. Jos picked out two trees that would give him more than enough timber for a good-sized house.

The settlers discussed the situation at a dance held in a woolshed on a neighbouring property. The decision about when to make the burn was not made lightly. The degree of dryness of the logs and the undergrowth were of vital importance. If too damp it could result in only a partial burn. But if the country was too dry it could start an uncontrollable fire destroying possibly thousands of acres of grass and the fencing already established. As the fiddlers fiddled and a man with an accordion played, the settlers decided to make the burn the very next day.

Jeremy watched the shed hands dancing jigs with each other long into the night. The wife of the owner danced good-naturedly with each of the men in turn. There were only three women there, and they were in great demand. The men looked ludicrous dancing with each other. Everybody was up for the quadrilles except Jeremy. In the second figure, the L'ete, he watched the 'leading lady', a giant of a man with a beard and wearing a high-crowned hat with a floppy brim, advance and retire, chassé to the right and left and cross over to his partner with all the nimbleness of an ungainly bull. But the music was the thing.

Supper was set out on long tables in the shearing section. There was the usual array of wild pig that had been captured in the surrounding hills, pigeon pie and smoked eels.

Jeremy and Jos raced their horses back to camp in the moonlight and were up again before dawn ready for the day. A light northeasterly breeze ruffled the tops of the trees on the crest as Jeremy and his men spread out along the stream in the valley below. They fired the underbrush with torches cut from the manuka on the edge of the clearing and watched as the flames crackled upwards until they met the forest. Here the rate of progress slowed as the fire curled around the larger trees and the green undergrowth. As the vines dried out with the heat the flames leapt into the smaller trees until, with a roar of hot wind, the whole hillside was ablaze.

The men moved upstream, repeating their actions, gradually covering the perimeter on the eastern side. They came to a small creek that marked the boundary. It flowed down a narrow gully. While the men sat and watched, the smoke and the flames advanced steadily towards it. Above, the clouds were moving slowly, mere puffs of white against the sky. At the bottom of the valley the wind had dropped, but the draught from the hot air sent clouds of half burnt leaves and smoke high into the sky. Jeremy saw the tongues of flame go over the ridge and leap across the gully to the other side. The fire skirted a valley to leave a small green patch unburnt.

The leader of the group stood up. 'We'll have to get that later,' he said.

They cut a few sticks and boiled a billy for mugs of tea. Someone had brought a few loaves and a wedge of cheese. Before they had finished lunch the fire had run up to the next ridge.

'We'll go back and check the gullies.' said the leader. 'Who wants this one?'

'I'll take it,' Jeremy ran his eyes up along the crest.

'Fine. It is pretty big. Start at the top and fire every hundred yards 'till you get back here. Watch the wind.' The man peered up at the sky. The scuds were almost stationary. 'It's dropped. You should be safe.'

Jeremy climbed up the gully and waded through the shallow

stream. He skirted a pool, passing two or three small spurs that led into the main valley. Reaching the top he plunged his torch into the undergrowth. It flared up instantly. He fired every fifty yards from one side of the gully to the other. Engrossed in his work he did not see the clouds sailing in the opposite direction to the north west. It was only when a gust came over the crest and whirled sparks and smoke towards him that he realized the wind had changed. He heard a scuttling in a clump of fern and saw a kiwi running swiftly down the hill. A native rat jumped into the stream and swam across. Suddenly the smoke and the flames were upon him. Dropping his bag he crouched low and pushed through the ferns. A wild pig ran across his path knocking him over. It careered on.

Jeremy stopped to get his bearings. The tops of the trees ahead were already alight. There was a sledging sound and a large tree trunk that had been held on the slope by a binding of vines crashed past and stopped with a splash in the stream. He leapt over it, running through the shallow water, stumbled, fell, recovered himself and dashed for the safety of the river at the bottom of the gully. His way was barred by a wall of fire.

He remembered the pool. Gasping for breath, with his hair singed and clothes smouldering he dived into it. Inhaling deeply he plunged his head under the water until his lungs were bursting then rose to the surface. He was completely surrounded by fire. A dead bird with singed feathers floated past. The roaring stopped almost as quickly as it had begun leaving the crackling and the heat a constant torture. He immersed himself again. The water felt cool and comforting. There was an explosion of sound as a tree with its roots bordering the pool burst into an inferno. The water on the surface began to turn to steam. Forcing himself up Jeremy looked for an escape. Everywhere there was fire.

The sound came from the top of the ridge behind him. A long call that ended in a sharp, upward note. There it was again. 'Cooooooo-ee.'

He plunged his head in the water and then stood up as high as he dared.

'Cooooo-ee.'

Shading his eyes from the glare and the heat he saw a figure silhouetted against the sky. Jeremy remembered the call that Jos had learnt in the Blue Mountains in Australia.

248

Cupping his hands, he replied, 'Cooooo-ee.'

He saw Jos standing motionless. Again the call. As Jeremy answered the heat became unbearable. He sank back into the pool. It was impossible to get up to Jos. A barrier of fire lay on both sides of the hill. With his head out of the water Jeremy considered his options. He would have to remain where he was. Then two calls came from high up, downstream. They were close together. The same sound but further away where two spurs led into the gully. Perhaps there was an escape route. Jeremy listened again. A single call almost above him. A long wait and then two calls lower down.

'He wants me down there,' thought Jeremy.

He looked up at the tree burning directly above him. A branch crashed down a dozen yards away. 'Now or never,' he thought.

Dragging himself up in one quick movement he crouched low and followed the stream bed downwards. Within fifty yards his clothes were dry. He put up his hands to protect his face making a chink for his eyes with his fingers. Stumbling over burning stumps, pushing aside red hot sticks of flame without noticing the pain he staggered the last few yards to the side gully.

A shout came from Jos, somewhere above.

'Mr St Clair! In the gully on the right!'

Without answering Jeremy turned and clambered over the smouldering logs that lay across the entrance. He stopped and looked ahead. Where before there was only smoke and red heat a green-black oasis of calm lay hidden in a cleft and stretched upwards. The fronds of the king ferns on its edge were shrivelled and brown but further on they stood majestically untouched, unmoving. Jeremy tripped over a root and fell on to the cool, black, mouldering earth. He remained motionless but safe.

Jos climbed down the steep face. Leaning out from the bank he grasped a frond and looked down at Jeremy.

'Bloody hell, sir,' he said, 'you're a bloomin' mess.'

They walked out of the valley in the late afternoon, black with ash, muddied, exhausted. A search was already underway. The settlers had expected to find blackened heaps that may once have been human and were overjoyed to find they were alive. They drove back in the bullock cart to a farmhouse and were bathed and put to bed. The next day, Saturday, they returned home.

Laura Beatson bandaged Jeremy's burns. 'You should have

wrapped them in fine wool or cotton yesterday. It guards against the irritation of the atmosphere.' She spread some linen thickly with chalk ointment and applied it to Jeremy's hands.

'Where would I have found chalk ointment out there?' asked Jeremy.

'You could have used treacle and flour.'

'I don't suppose you'll want to come to church tomorrow,' said Paula.

'Why not?' said Jeremy. He climbed to his room and, tired and in pain, he lay on the bed and tried to sleep.

It was the first Sunday in Advent and the church was almost full when they took their regular seat near the front. Jeremy half listened to the first lesson. The words gradually penetrated his mind.

'Why should ye be stricken any more? Ye will revolt more and more. The whole head is sick, and the whole heart faint. From the sole of the foot even unto the head there is no soundness in it, but wounds, and bruises and putrefying sores, they have not been closed, neither bound up neither mollified with ointment. Your country is desolate, your cities are burned with fire; your land, strangers devour it in your presence and it is desolate, as overthrown by strangers.'

Jeremy glanced across to Rata and Rosalind in the choir seats close to the altar. He saw Rosalind look away quickly. He had not spoken to her since that day when she had asked him not to call again. He wondered what she thought of it all now. Of the defeat of the Maori. Of the confiscation of their lands.

'Your land, strangers devour it in your presence and it is desolate.'

His eyes strayed to Rosalind again. She was reciting a prayer. Rata was her usual composed self. Serene. Patrician-like. A goddess.

They rose for the last hymn. Jeremy listened to the pure tones of the children as the clear notes soared to the roof. He didn't hear the benediction. Paula nudged him to move out of the pew. He blinked as they filed into the sunlight.

There were the usual familiar faces standing on the path. Only

250

Caroline was absent. The vicar made polite comments regarding Jeremy's bandages, and there were the usual nods and smiles. A woman who was a stranger to Jeremy came up to them, all bonnet and long trails of lace.

'My, my,' she said, 'Mr St Clair, what have you been doing?'

Paula smiled weakly. 'He's been in the wars again Mrs Newton. I don't think you have met my husband. Jeremy, let me present Mrs Newton.'

'How do you do,' Jeremy made a supreme effort to be polite.

'So nice to see you back in the fold as it were. The little man is growing up.' She patted Jonathon's head and glanced at Paula. 'And so splendid to see you have another little one on the way. You are lucky. My poor husband always said that large families were essential for the well-being of the nation.'

Jeremy looked startled.

'Come, come, Mr St Clair.' The woman waggled her finger under Jeremy's nose. 'Don't act so coyly. Everyone knows and is talking about it. You can't hide these things forever, you know.' She sailed down the path like a flagship with bunting streaming behind.

Jeremy followed Paula to the carriage. Neither spoke. Even Jonathon was quiet, sensing the tension between his parents. They drove in silence to the house. Jeremy put the carriage away, gave Sergeant a quick grooming and went straight up to Paula's room. She was sitting in front of the mirror at the dressing table, holding her bonnet and staring at the mirror. He could see her reflection. There was no way of telling what she was thinking, she was wearing that mask again. Her retreat from reality. The white forehead again. The black eyes.

He had to admit that she was beautiful, but her beauty was like a work of art that had been created with a dedicated disregard for inner feelings. It was a cold beauty as mountains and lakes are cold but beautiful. It was more than that — glacial, so that when one looks at them the mind leaps in wonder at their beauty, and the heart stands still at the despair of knowing that they are inaccessible.

'Paula! What is this all about?'

She continued staring at herself in the mirror.

'Paula! Answer me.'

Turning she faced him. 'Jeremy, I have nothing to say.'

His eyes bored into hers. 'You will have to explain. Is it true?'

She stood up. 'Look at me. What do you think?'

He looked down at her stomach. It was quite swollen. He hadn't noticed before. He breathed in sharply, 'I'll go to the warehouse. When I come back I want an explanation.'

It was late evening when he returned. Laura was on her own in the kitchen, bending over the stove. 'Where is the mistress?' he asked.

The oven door shut with a clang. 'She went out, Sir, after lunch. Said she would be late.'

'Where did she go?'

'She did not say, Sir.'

'Did she take Jonathon?'

'No Sir. He is in bed.'

Jeremy went into the parlour.

'Do you want supper, Sir?'

'No thank you, Laura.'

A few minutes before midnight Jeremy went to bed. He lay awake wondering where Paula could be. Should he go and look for her? Where would he start?

A noise on the stairs made him turn and listen. The door opened and Paula was silhouetted against the light from the hall. He sat up.

'Jeremy.'

It was a small room and she was close to the bed.

'Yes?'

'I want to talk to you.'

'Sit down.'

'No, I would rather stand.' There was a long pause. 'Jeremy, I am not pregnant.' She began to cry. Quietly at first and then uncontrollably. She collapsed, lying half across the bed.

All the pent-up love that he had felt for her came flooding back. He slipped out of the covers and sat beside her, his long nightshirt trailing on the floor. As he put his arms around her she leaned against him and the sobbing increased. At last she stopped.

'Tell me about it,' he said.

'I am frightened.'

'Why?'

'There is a lump down there, I don't know what to do.'

252

'When did you first know it was there?'

'I don't remember. Perhaps a year. Perhaps six months. I forget.'

'Why didn't you tell me?'

'I hoped it would go away. I tried to tell you once. I am frightened, Jeremy.'

'I'll take you to Doctor Moore first thing in the morning.'

'No, no. I don't want to know.'

'You must. You can't go on like this.'

She burst out crying again.

'Get into bed.'

'I can't, I am still dressed,'

'Never mind. I'll loosen your stays. Turn around.'

He undid her bodice. 'Damn.'

'What's wrong?'

'I pricked my finger.'

She started laughing hysterically and began to sob again.

'Get into bed.' He held back the sheets.

'Hold me, Jeremy. Hold me tightly.'

She went to sleep in his arms. The sobbing stopped.

He lay awake, not daring to move lest he should wake her. At daybreak, when Jeremy slipped out of bed and dressed, she slept on.

Doctor Moore had a grave look on his face when he came out of the surgery. Jeremy knew the worst before he began to talk.

'I am afraid it is very serious. It has been going on for too long but even if we had known sooner there is little we could have done.'

Jeremy waited for Paula to come out. She looked directly at him. 'It is the end, isn't it?' she asked.

He did not answer directly. 'Come home, dearest,' he whispered.

They walked the few yards down the hill to the house. He led her to where the late morning sun slanted across the verandah and sat her on the chaise lounge tucked in the corner.

'Are you comfortable?'

She nodded. He looked down. The dew was still on the lawn.

His eyes returned to Paula. She was so very composed. There were no tears, they had all been shed the night before.

'I will get you some tea.'

'Don't go.'

He stood gazing out to sea, past the town, past the northern shore to the islands beyond, grey shapes low on the horizon.

'I want to talk. For the first time I want to talk about us. You. Me.' She turned her head toward him. He saw the shadows under her eyes. 'Jeremy!'

'Yes?'

'There hasn't been anyone else. Only Gerald.'

'I believe you.'

'You say that as though you are not certain.'

'No. I believe you.'

'I have never wanted anyone else so much as Gerald. Not even you, really.'

His heart sank. 'Go on.'

'But now I feel changed. Cleansed. As though I am paying for my sin and I feel better.'

'Paula!'

'Let me go on please.'

He glanced at her. She looked ethereal. Elated somehow.

'Please, Jeremy. You see while you have been away I have had time to consider. I know you think I have been to a lot of balls and parties, but I haven't. Not really. Ask Caroline. I've tried to be bad but I can't. I've needed to have people about me, I've been frightened to be alone. I have dreaded the thought of going out by myself.'

'Why?'

She did not answer.

'How long have you been like this?'

'Six months. Perhaps a year.'

'Since this...,' his voice trailed off.

'No. Before that.'

'Did something happen?'

She shuddered. 'Promise me you will never ask.'

'But Paula!'

'Promise me. For my sake.'

He felt that sinking feeling again. Waves of despair.

254

'I promise. What did Dr Moore have to say?'

'I must rest as much as possible. Stay in bed.' For the first time there was a tremor in her voice. 'To prolong things. I don't want to stay in bed, there is too much to do to make up for the time we have lost.'

'You must rest if the doctor says so.'

'No, I'm going to be a good wife and mother.' Her voice sank to a whisper. 'Please give me the chance, Jeremy. Remember our dream home, "The Wilderness", that we planned on the moors? I'll pretend we are living in it now.'

In spite of himself, Jeremy smiled. 'Where is the independent, "I'm not your slave" girl?' he asked.

'Here.' Jeremy watched the fire return to her eyes for a moment. 'You've missed the point again,' said Paula, 'I can be a good wife and mother and still be independent.'

He picked her up gently and walked carefully down the steps. She was as light as a child.

'Jeremy, let me down.' Laughing she tried to beat him with her fists.

Crossing to the gazebo he lowered her to the floor. 'We'll build "The Wilderness". My God, Paula, I know the perfect place. We'll make a lake and have your swans. We will grow your wild roses.'

The next day Jeremy bought a piece of waste land not far from the town, towards the western hills where he had found the timber for his cutter. There was a spring that would supply enough water for the house and would fill a small lake. Someone, years before, had planted weeping willow staves that were already mature trees so that they and the cabbage palms formed a nucleus for a formal garden. When Jos and Matt arrived he explained the details.

'I'd rather the house was in brick and stone,' he said, 'as English mansions are, but we will have to settle for wood. There's blue stone on the property but stonemasons are rare and wood will cost much less. The house will have two storeys with upstairs and downstairs verandahs facing east, north and west. There'll be a ballroom and a decent sized stable and married quarters for you and Jos until the house is built on the farm.'

'It suits me,' said Matt, 'provided there's an inn handy.'

The house was completed by midsummer. Lawns were laid

out. The spring was diverted and soon filled the lake. Jeremy imported black swans from Australia and bought a pair of white muscovies that were soon joined by wild ducks and widgeons as the food supply in the lake built up.

Paula had to be helped from the carriage when they arrived to take possession. She took Jeremy's arm and walked around the banks of roses to the herb garden with its sun dial. It was a soft summer day with a light breeze rippling the surface of the lake. A pair of swans swimming along the edge with a cygnet following gave a welcome call as Paula stretched a hand towards them.

'Jonathon and I will be able to feed them each morning,' she said.

Jeremy saw the high colour in her cheeks. 'Come,' he said, 'don't tire yourself. I'll carry you over the threshold.'

He cradled her in his arms and walked slowly up the new path to the steps onto the verandah. She shut her eyes, absorbing his strength.

'Are you all right?'

'It is wonderful, Jeremy. So wonderful. I want to cry.'

'Then cry if you wish.'

The tears glistened on her cheeks as he took her inside and laid her on the couch. A silent declaration of their happiness. The end of pretending. The beginning of a new life.

All too short.

The warm weather ended. Autumn came haphazardly, as it does in that part of the land. The native trees stayed green, the leaves on the weeping willow gradually turned a pale yellow and then, one day, a north-east wind came and blew them away, tumbling them into the lake where they floated for a day and vanished. Winter had come.

On one particularly cold Saturday evening, Jeremy put Sergeant away and went to the back door to the boot-jack. A pair of old slippers were lying at the entrance and he put them on before going inside. They had been busy at the warehouse. Matt had remained behind to close the doors and Jos was out at the farm which would soon be in production. Jeremy could hear the clatter of pots in the kitchen as Laura prepared supper. Paula was in the study, the room off the hall at the bottom of the stairs with French doors that looked out to the lake.

256

'Come over here by me,' she said.

He sat on the stool by the couch. She was propped up on pillows with her legs covered with a crocheted rug. He could see how thin her limbs were.

'Have you been busy?' she asked.

'Yes, surprisingly so considering the time of the year and the way trade is at the moment. In another year I will be able to pay off the bank loan.'

Her eyes widened in approbation. 'Clever man, and then what?'

'Nothing. It is time to consolidate.'

'Jeremy, I've been thinking.'

'Mmmmm?'

'When I go, I want you to re-marry.'

'Don't be silly. What's for supper?'

'Don't change the subject. I've matured in the last few months. I can talk about it now. I want you to marry Rosalind.'

'Please, Paula, you are being ridiculous. Besides, Rosalind and I haven't spoken for months, she despises me.'

'I have often wondered what happened between you.'

'She objected to me fighting the Maori. I had no more stomach for it than she had. But murder is different.'

'Murder?

'The Trust children.'

'Of course, I had forgotten.'

'Rosalind argued that it was the Maori way. Their custom was to fight without reserve and therefore they should be forgiven.'

'And I. Am I forgiven?'

'Forgiveness comes from within ourselves and you know in your heart that you are forgiven. Besides, I love you and that is all.

'Promise me you will marry Rosalind.'

'I am sorry, Paula dear, I won't promise.'

'I want to leave some money for her school.'

'Let's talk about it another time.'

'Promise me you'll give her some of my money for the children?'

'I promise.'

'Good.' She fumbled in her gown and bought out a packet. 'Here is a present, wrapped and sealed. Not to be opened for a week.'

He laughed and tossing it in the air, caught it and put it in his waistcoat pocket. 'That is better, my love. I'll fetch the supper.'

As usual Jeremy was the first to go down on Sunday morning and according to his custom he washed and shaved in the room by the back door. Laura had the water boiling on the stove and the breakfast was under way. He took a cup of tea up to Paula. As he opened the curtains the noise of the rings sliding along the rod woke her.

'How strange,' she said, 'everything is green. We haven't green curtains, have we?'

Jeremy handed her the tea.

'And a green cup. Everything is green.'

'Green?'

'My eyes must be funny. Everything has a green tinge to it. It happened last week for a minute or two and then went away.'

'You didn't tell me.'

She closed her eyes and opened them again. 'It is still there.'

'Do you feel well?'

'Yes. But very tired as though I haven't had any sleep.'

She pushed back the eiderdown.

'Don't get up. I'll send Matt for Doctor Moore.'

It seemed a long time before the doctor arrived. He questioned Paula carefully. Outside on the verandah he folded his spectacles and put them away very deliberately.

'It has gone to the brain Jeremy. The end is close.'

Back in Paula's room Jeremy hid his feelings. 'The doctor is prescribing some pills,' he said, making a pretence of tidying the fireplace.

'Why pills?'

'He didn't say.' Jeremy was relieved when she did not pursue the question. It was not like her. Usually she would worry it out.

'Is it fine outside?'

He undid the catches on the French doors and looked across the lake to the low hill behind and the sky. 'Yes, remarkably so.'

'I would like to go on to the verandah.'

'It's not that warm.'

'I can wrap myself up.'

'I don't think you should.'

'Please Jeremy, the green has gone. I feel better.'

'Then I'll get Matt to help bring out a settee. You'll need to cover up.'

'I promise I will.'

She walked out on Jeremy's arm and grasping the rail looked down on the garden below. 'Those edges need cutting,' she said.

He nodded without absorbing what she was saying. She looked frail, misshapen, hollow-cheeked. Only her eyes had not changed and they were bigger than ever, dominating her face. He arranged the pillows against the settee and she lay back, half-sitting, half-lying so that she could see the lake. A wild duck rose leaving a long trail of disturbed water as it flapped upwards.

'Would you like me to fetch Caroline?' he asked.

'Not today. I would rather that you were here. By yourself. Need you go to town?'

'No.'

'Then will you stay?'

'Yes.'

'Good. It's back again.'

'What is?'

'The green.'

She felt his concern. 'Don't worry, it came and went last week. You don't need to stay if you don't want to.'

'I want to stay.'

'I'd rather not see anyone else today. I don't want sympathy. Why are people so ready to give it to you when you are down? I prefer them to be sympathetic when I am ordinarily well and they are happy for the real me. That is the test of a true friend.' She smiled across at him. 'It has been a wonderful year, Jeremy. The happiest of my life.' There was a moment of silence. 'It's changed.'

'What has?'

'The colour. It is yellow now. A soft sunshine colour.'

He quickly sprang the two paces to her side.'

'Don't look so worried,' she said. 'It is beautiful. I'm ready to go, Jeremy. Any time. Please. Hold my hand.'

'I'll get Dr Moore.'

'No. Stay here and leave Jonathon to play. I want him to re-member me feeding the swans. Not like this.'

She closed her eyes. He sat on the chair with his hand gently clasping hers. She seemed to be asleep. Half an hour went by. He tried to slip his hand away. She spoke without opening her eyes,

'What time is it?'

'I don't know.'

'There's the green again. Now it's blue . . . Yellow . . . Green . . . Oh Jeremy, it is really beautiful. I feel so peaceful. I am so happy. Good-bye, dear Jeremy, good-bye.'

Matt and Caroline found him still holding Paula's hand. She appeared to be asleep and he was slumped beside her with his head on the pillow.

Matt put a hand on his shoulder. 'Are you awake, Jerry boy?'

Out on the lake a swan called.

23

July 1865

The last of the mourners had gone and Jeremy was alone again. Turning towards the library he saw that the door of Paula's room was open. Inside, it was exactly as she had left it, the dressing table set, her silver-backed brush, the bottle of lavender water, a miniature mahogany stand was piled with rings that were stacked haphazardly, one on top of the other. He picked up a brooch and examined the silver mount set with an emerald, her birthday stone. Pulling back the wardrobe curtain he looked at the neat row of shoes on the floor and at her clothes hanging in careful order. The room seemed cold and impersonal. He swung the door shut and locked it.

Pushing out the French doors at the end of the hall he walked on to the verandah where Paula had often rested. The lake had taken on its evening colours, a splash of red reflected the sunset while a blanket of mist was rising slowly to hide it from the night. Absent-mindedly he slipped the key into his waistcoat pocket and felt the hardness of something there. The memory came back. Paula's gift. Carefully unwrapping it he opened the box. The ring he had given her in England years before, lay in the palm of his hand. The amethyst glistened in the rays of the setting sun. He looked across at the lake. Her swans were gathered in the small bay where she had always fed them. 'Promise me you will marry

261

Rosalind,' she had said.

The sound of footsteps on the gravel path roused him and looking down he saw Caroline climbing the steps to the front door. Before he could put away the ring she was on the stairs.

'I saw you on the verandah,' she called. 'Jeremy, what are you going to do with Jonathon?'

He climbed down to her. 'I haven't thought about it.'

She was suddenly brusque and to the point. 'I think you should send him to Rosalind. He could come back here at weekends.'

'Isn't that a bit soon? I need time to think.'

'You should do it at once, before he has time to miss Paula. He will be kept busy there. He loves Rosalind and she loves him.'

'He hasn't seen her for a year.'

'So? He will need someone. It will be better than a succession of inept governesses.'

'I suppose you are right, Caroline, you usually are, but you know that Rosalind and I are not on very good terms. I haven't seen her for a long time.'

'She was at the funeral.'

'Was she?'

'I saw her slip away after the service.'

'Oh!' Jeremy turned this intelligence over in his mind. 'I'll give it some thought.'

'Don't think about it. Act! You men are all the same, so smart at everything except that which really matters. At the moment, all you must think about is Jonathon's welfare.'

'She may not want him.'

Caroline picked up the purse she had put on the hall table and closed it with a snap. 'She will.'

Jeremy watched her drive out the gates in a carriage and pair. He went into the empty kitchen. Matt had taken Jonathon for a drive in the dogcart with Laura. He sat in front of the fire awaiting their return.

When they arrived Jonathon jumped down from the cart and ran towards him. Jeremy took him up. 'How would you like to stay with Rosalind?' he asked.

'Oh could I, Father? And with Rata?' The boy's eyes shone. 'Yes!'

'Oh good.' Jonathon's face clouded over. 'But Father, won't

you be lonely?'

'You will come home Saturdays and Sundays.' Jonathon let himself down and ran up the stairs. 'Where are you going?'

'To get my clothes.'

'You are not going tonight. Perhaps Sunday. We will need to ask Rosalind.'

The child called down from the top of the stairs. 'You'll look after Oliver for me, won't you?'

When Jeremy rode down to the farm he was surprised at the amount of grass still in the fields. The rain from the hills had maintained pasture growth well into the winter but at last the cold weather had come. Cold, that is, in relation to summer. It did not snow in that part of the country and there was still some growth. The cattle remained outside the whole year round with supplements of hay fed out each day.

Jos remained on the farm during the winter months, eating and sleeping in an abandoned whare built by Maori. Once a week he rode to town for provisions and reported to Jeremy, spending the evening with Rata and setting out again for the farm at first light the following day.

Meanwhile, to compensate for his loneliness, Jeremy had become completely involved in the newspaper. Each Saturday morning he picked up Jonathon from the school and returned him the following evening.

It was on one of these Sunday evenings that Rosalind invited him to supper. They took it in the sitting room. There was a fire burning in the grate with a small table set for two. Seeing the coal scuttle he picked the shovel and opened the lid.

'May I?' Jeremy asked.

'Certainly.'

Scooping up some coal he stoked the fire.

'There is wood in the box if you prefer it,' she said. 'How is business?'

'Only fair.' Sitting opposite her, he sunk into a leather chair. The room was warm and cosy, the padded curtains on the windows were drawn, Jeremy felt a comfortable drowsiness spreading over him. 'We don't sell as much equipment as we did. The Maori do not plough any more.' He glanced at the clock on the mantelpiece and then at Rosalind. 'Do you ever feel lonely, here by yourself?'

'Never. I have the children.'

He nodded. 'I can sense an aura in this room. A "lived in" feeling. A few churches have it, so do some houses. "The Wilderness" is different.'

'That is because it is new.'

'No. It needs a presence. Someone living in it all the time. Someone caring.'

There was silence. Rosalind looked across at Jeremy. 'The trouble is you are not often there. You don't give yourself a chance. You work too hard. Try and be more sociable.'

'It is awkward on ones own. At least I am financially sound again, thanks to the bank being so helpful.'

'Financial security doesn't guarantee happiness.'

'It helps. It seems to count here. Ever since the war finished, everybody is grabbing land and chasing the almighty sovereign.'

'And the Maori, where is he? Jeremy, we are back where we began. We left our homes for a new world and what has happened? We are once more in a society that equates manhood solely with his ability to make money. Nothing has changed. Until we realize that hard work is necessary to produce the goods that give us the quality of life we demand, we are undone. All this buying and selling without creating is counterfeit.'

'With new-fangled machines coming in and the military moving out, times are bad.'

Rosalind's eyes showed her concern. 'What will happen to the Maori?'

'He will become extinct. A short while ago there were sixty thousand of them. Now there are only fifty thousand. He is demoralized. Once, he was the centre of his family. He worked beside his wife and children and had a close relationship with them. He was a protector, a husband, a father. Above all he was a man.'

'I don't believe he will become extinct but if he goes his separate way we will have two nations instead of one. There will be dissension. Trouble in the years to come.'

'I concede that we will have to work together for our mutual advantage, but the Maori has lost faith in both the Pakeha and his own leaders. Now he feels that he is nothing.'

Rosalind turned her head away. 'I disagree.'

'Why?'

'His past is the key to the present.'

'What do you mean by that?'

'Through the family and his arts he will re-discover his identity. His dignity.'

Jeremy took a deep breath. 'Not only the Maori needs dignity. All people, black, brown, and white need that. I need it.'

'Jeremy, don't belittle yourself. Because you are honest and true to your word you have more dignity than anyone I know.'

'Do you really mean that?'

'Yes.'

He struggled for the right words. 'Rosalind, could we see more of each other? A sort of companionship?'

She felt her heart beat faster and there was a shaking inside. Jeremy sought her eyes. On the outside she was cool and in command.

'Let us be practical, Jeremy. You and I are both very independent people, I am not one to walk in anyone's shadow. You need a mother. You must get about more and find someone to spoil you.'

Jeremy smiled with a look of wistful innocence.

She jumped from her chair. 'Don't try that with me, Jeremy St Clair. I know there is a glint of steel behind those eyes.'

They both laughed.

'Play something,' he said.

She went to the piano and struck up the 'March Militaire'.

When Jeremy returned to "The Wilderness" the house was empty. Laura had gone for the afternoon and Matt could have been anywhere. He went into the study and, after lighting a candle-lamp, took the warehouse books from the shelf. He felt unsettled and unable to concentrate. Was Rosalind right? Should he get out more? Sometimes he felt he needed a change. It was a long time since he had used the cutter. A sail up the coast, part holiday, part business might help to get rid of that prickly feeling in his scalp. He walked over to the cabinet and poured himself a cognac, warming the glass with his hands. 'That's it, dammit,' he thought. 'Get out and around.'

* * *

Jeremy strolled around the grounds at Government House admiring the lawns, as fine as any in England. He made his way to a table by the band. The usual crowd was there: politicians, clergy, a few of the local Maori chiefs. The women were dressed in their best with bonnets and parasols, the men were in black, balancing their tall hats on stilted heads. He began to study the crowd. A voice from behind startled him.

'Mr St Clair, this is a surprise. It is a long time since we have seen you here.'

He tried to place her but couldn't. Who the devil is she? he thought. Jeremy searched back in his mind. 'How do you do?' he said.

'The garden parties aren't what they used to be, are they, with the military moving away?'

'There are still a few regiments about.' Jeremy looked around for an escape.

'But somehow it is not the same. It used to be such a lively capital.'

'The war has altered that.'

The woman made a face. 'I expect you are right. Oh dear.' She began searching the grounds with her eyes. 'There she is.' She waved to a figure, dressed in green satin, walking toward them. 'Mr St Clair, may I present Mrs Auriol King.' Jeremy saw a woman of about twenty-five years of age picking her way through the crowd. She curtsied. The other woman's voice flowed on, 'My dear, Mr St Clair lives in that wonderful house, "The Wilderness". You know it, out by the springs.'

Mrs Auriol King smiled. 'Everybody knows of Mr St Clair.'

Jeremy looked surprised. I'll be damned, he thought, she is a beauty. He bowed.

Her eyes were a tawny green, matching her dress. 'I pass your residence on the way to 'Alberton', she said.

Jeremy threw an appraising look at her. 'You ride often?'

'Whenever I can.'

There was a silence. The band began to play another tune. Jeremy cast around for an escape. He saw the vicar in the distance. 'Oh, excuse me,' he said, 'I have a message for the Reverend Jones. Delighted to meet you.'

Relieved, Jeremy buttonholed the vicar. Grasping his arm he

led him toward the gate. 'You have saved me,' he said.

The vicar laughed. 'I saw you snared there.'

'Who are they?'

'Mrs Martin and her protégé Auriol King. Mrs King lost her husband at the Rangariri battle.'

'She seems most presentable.'

The vicar's voice wavered, 'Ye-es.'

Jeremy left Government House before the refreshments were served. He had had enough of society for one day. Mounting Sergeant he returned to "The Wilderness". Matt was standing on the path by the rose garden when he rode through the gates. The clip of Sergeant's shoes on the path made him look up, and Jeremy saw the serious expression on his face. Dismounting at the stables he hitched the horse to a post and walked to the front of the house.

'I have bad news,' said Matt. 'My dad has died.'

'Oh. I am sorry. When?'

'Four months ago.' Matt waved a letter in front of him. 'This was sent by the overland mail to the Cape and then by fast ship.'

'I am sorry, I don't suppose there is anything I can do.'

'No thank you, Jeremy. It had to happen sooner or later. They want me at home so I will have to go. I'll tidy things up before I leave.'

'I will miss you, Matt.'

'And I, you,' said Matt.

'What was the levee like?'

'Boring. I met a Mrs Auriol King.'

'Jesus!' said Matt.

'Why do you say that? She looked rather smashing.'

Matt opened his mouth and closed it again. 'She lost her husband at Rangiriri.'

'I know.'

'They took up a collection for her passage back home but she didn't go.'

'Why not?'

'I don't know. She would have spent most of the money by now.'

'Oh well.' Jeremy dismissed the subject. 'Come inside and have a nobbler.' They lit the fire in the study and talked of home, of the farm back there that now belonged to Matt, and of Ireland. It was after midnight before they retired.

'I'll shoe Sergeant tomorrow,' said Matt. 'Probably for the last time.'

Next morning Jeremy watched Matt at the forge in the stables, working the bellows, heating the iron shoes in the fire and hammering them into shape before plunging them in a bucket of water at his side. The water hissed and bubbled as he held them down with long tongs. Bending over Sergeant's hind legs he lifted a hoof and began paring away the horny bone. They were both engrossed in the work when a voice called from outside.

'Ooh-hoo, Mr St Clair.'

'Jesus,' said Matt. 'It's her.'

An apparition appeared at the door. Mrs Auriol King was wearing a pale grey riding dress and a matching pill box hat with a blue veil. In her hand she carried a leather crop. She had an ease and gracefulness about her that surprised Jeremy. 'My apologies for calling so early,' she said, 'and without a card. I am on my way to the Kerr Taylors and simply had to call after hearing about your establishment from Mrs Martin. What a glorious position.'

Matt cast his eyes up to the roof and crouched lower over Sergeant's hoof. Mrs King examined Sergeant carefully and walked slowly around him. 'He needs more exercise,' she said.

Jeremy nodded. 'I'm afraid I haven't the time to ride him.'

'How does he go over fences?'

'He hasn't been schooled for jumping, but he is quite versatile. As much at home in the shafts as he is a useful hack.'

'I could exercise him for you.'

Matt dropped the hammer on to the floor with a clatter. Jeremy looked delighted. 'That would be tremendous. When could you start?'

'Tomorrow.'

'Splendid. I say, have you time for tea?'

'Of course,' she said, with a confident glance at Matt. "You must show me the house.'

While Laura made the tea they went upstairs. 'What a splendid view,' said Auriol. Jeremy followed her as she went from room to room, fingering the drapes, pausing to admire a portrait of Jonathon. 'Such a dear boy,' she said. Picking up a vase from the table at the head of the stairs, she placed it on a crocheted centrepiece. 'You should have red roses in it,' she said.

'I am afraid Laura's talents extend only as far as the kitchen.'

Jeremy led her down the stairs. 'Shall we have tea?'

'Thank you. Perfect housekeepers are few and far between, I'm afraid. You poor man.'

'We are very much a bachelor establishment now. How can I make it more like home?'

'Flowers in a vase, no dust in the corners.' She looked at him with her green and gold eyes, half hidden under lowered lids, 'and a woman's touch.'

Jeremy saw Laura frowning at the kitchen door. 'I have put the tea things in the small dining room under the stairs,' she said.

Auriol smiled. 'Thank you Laura, you are so kind.' She glanced at Jeremy. 'Shall I pour?'

When Auriol had gone, after promising to return to exercise Sergeant, Jeremy went back to the stables. 'What do you think of her, Matt?' he asked.

Matt took time to hang his apron on the nail by the forge. 'She is no different from the rest,' he said.

Auriol was back at ten o'clock the next day, but Jeremy was in town. Matt helped her saddle Sergeant. His easy familiarity soon established an understanding between them. When she returned from the ride the horse was lathered in foam. A bit hard on him the first day, thought Matt.

Together they rubbed Sergeant down.

'How long have you known Mr St Clair?' she asked.

'Seven years.'

'Is he a good employer?'

'He is more of a friend than a master.'

She took a blanket from the bench and threw it over the horse. 'Do you intend staying with him?'

'I'm going back to Ireland at the end of the month.'

'Oh!'

He could see her turning the thought over in her mind.

'That's a pity,' she said. 'We could have got on very well together.'

Matt led Sergeant into a stall. Auriol seemed reluctant to leave.

'Laura will have a pot of tea ready,' he said.

'That would be most acceptable. Do you think Mr St Clair would mind if I walked around the grounds?'

'No. Help yourself.'

He watched her cross the yard and go down the grass slope to the lake. He turned to the horse. 'Well, Sergeant, pity help your master if she gets her claws into him.'

Auriol King came every day. Sometimes Jeremy was at home, other times at the warehouse. Soon she was going in and out of the house at will. She brought flowers and spent hours arranging them in vases, and one day when Jeremy came back early she was at the top of the stairs putting the finishing touches to a bowl of rosebuds.

'Very elegant,' he said, standing back to admire them. 'Can you stay for supper?'

'I would be delighted,' she said.

He put an arm around her shoulders. 'Come.' He noticed another flower arrangement on the landing. 'There are flowers everywhere. I could never make them look like that.'

She looked up at him coyly. 'A woman's touch,' she said.

For the rest of the week Jeremy stayed home in the mornings and together they fed the swans, took tea on the verandah and talked until it was time for Auriol to ride Sergeant. One morning, a month after they had first met, Jeremy was waiting for her as she rode Sergeant to the stables and dismounted. He took the reins and led the horse to the trough. His voice had a catch in it when he spoke.

'Auriol. May I call you Auriol?'

She lowered her eyes. 'Of course.'

'I am going south for a week or two. Please feel free to come and go as you have been doing while I am away.'

'Thank you.'

'I will have something to say to you when I return.'

She felt a hot wave of excitement course through her. She looked away. She did not want him to see her triumph.

'Don't be away too long,' she said.

Matt woke early and looked at the watch on the bedside table. There were no sounds of activity and he guessed Jos and Laura were still asleep. He rolled out of bed and stared into the mirror.

'Look at you.' He spoke aloud. 'Is there any colleen in Ireland would want to wake up and see that alongside her?'

Smoothing out his beard with the brush hanging on the mirror he went into the kitchen. The stove was cold and the fire out. Raking the ashes into a pile he crumpled up a few pages of the *Daily Southern Cross* and stuffed them into the grate. He bundled in some kindling and blew on the coals. On the third attempt there was a flicker that finally set the paper alight, sending twists of orange flame up the chimney. As he adjusted the damper and put a kettle of water on the hot plate, there was a knock on the door. Before he had time to answer, it the handle turned and Auriol King walked in.

'Hullo Matt,' she said, 'are you sailing tonight?'

He saw her breasts cleaving in the neckline of her dress with what he thought was calculated intent. Her green and gold eyes stared boldly into his. 'I have to be on board by midnight to catch the early morning tide,' he said.

'Then you will have time to come and see me tonight before you leave. I might have a sort of going away present.' She looked at him sideways.

'Perhaps,' he replied. She was Jeremy's girl, for better or for worse; he did not want to be involved. He's a bloody fool, he thought.

She came over to him and kissed him on the cheek.

'Goodness! Trim your beard before you come.' She slipped out the door.

Matt turned and addressed the mantelpiece. 'Like hell I will.'

By the time Jos came in for breakfast Matt had bacon sizzling in the pan and the kettle singing merrily. 'Do you want porridge?' he asked.

'No thank you,' said Jos.

'You're having bloody porridge,' said Matt.

Jos laughed. They finished breakfast and piled the dishes into the sink, adding them to those already there from the night before. Matt made the tea and carried the cups onto the bottom verandah. He was still feeling the effects of the night before. He slipped some whiskey into the cups. 'We are going around the traps for the last time,' he said.

271

They started at the Rob Roy down in the bay by the timber yards then went to the Alexandra Tavern, before moving on to the Wynyard Arms, where a free counter lunch was served. A carter wearing an apron helped himself to a rissole made from yesterday's leftovers, and a smithy, black-faced and hot from the forge, tossed back a pint. Matt threw some coins on the counter. 'Two of the usual,' he said.

The barman fumbled for glasses under the bench and filled them from the pump. He pushed the money back to Matt. 'This one is on Dryballs.'

'Dryballs?' Matt looked astonished.

'Yep. Old Dryballs. He's hit the jackpot at last.'

'Holy hell.' Matt turned and lifted his glass in the direction of Dryballs who was in the corner where the bar met the wall. One hand clutched a pint pot and the other was around a barrel of Madeira that sat on the counter. Dryballs' eyes already had a glazed look about them.

'He can't believe it,' said Nick the barman, taking up a cloth and guiding some spilt beer into the trough behind the bar. 'They've been married twelve years.'

'Good on you, mate, you old bastard.' Matt shouted against the increasing noise. 'Here's to Peaches. When is she going to drop it?'

'In about six months,' said Nick.

Matt put his glass down and counted on his fingers.

'Hell,' he said, 'it must have been after the annual picnic. At least Peaches will be staying home a bit more.' He pushed a plate of hot potatoes towards Jos.

'Eat up and get a good foundation. You'll need it. I don't want you flaking out too soon.'

The room was almost full with men taking a break for a midday snack. The door swung open and three more came in. 'There's Liquid Len, me old drinking companion,' said Matt. 'Hey! Liquid.'

Liquid pushed his way to the bar. 'What's it going to be?' Matt dug into his pocket.

'Beer and a whisky chaser.'

They dragged some chairs to a table, making a spidery trail in the sawdust on the floor. Liquid shifted a spittoon to a more acceptable position. 'Well, this is it.' said Matt. 'My last day.'

'And a bloody good thing too.' Liquid tossed down his whisky. 'Is St Clair back?'

'No. He must have had some trouble. He promised to see me off.'

Matt looked at the reflection of his two friends in the mirror on the wall. It was going to be hard to leave them. They had been in wars, fights and frolics together and rarely separated. It only needed Jeremy to complete the party. He should have been back three days ago, but a swollen river and a high spring tide could easily wreck his timetable. Deep down Matt felt he was letting Jeremy down. Jeremy had saved his life twice. Once when they first met at sea and a second time at the headwaters of the Wairoa. They had talked about it only a year ago. 'You don't owe me anything,' Jeremy had said.

'I'll make up for it somehow,' Matt had replied and Jeremy had laughed and clipped him over the ear. Matt took another sip of beer. He felt a thump on his back.

'Come on dreamer boy. We are going to Seccombes brewery.'

The cab rank was not far away and they laughed when Liquid jumped up by the driver and took the reins. He whipped up the horse and started at a great pace up Queen Street and finally down Khyber Pass Road. The great Northern Brewery held old memories for Matt and it was fitting that they should go there. In their war days, marching back from the front they always halted outside the main door where a kilderkin of the best stood, cool and inviting, and what was more important, free to every soldier.

Mr Seccombe smiled widely when he saw Matt. He led them to a side room and left them with clean pewter tankards and a small keg, newly sprung.

'Silence.' Liquid rose to his feet weaving from side to side. 'Here is to your safe return, Matt.'

'Hear, hear,' said Jos.

'I am not coming back,' Matt looked at them owlishly. 'I might never see you two again.' He laughed. 'We will drink to that.' They refilled their tankards.

'St Clair should be here, the bastard,' said Liquid after a long silence.

'I presume you mean that in endearing terms, Liquid.' Matt stretched out his legs full length and yawned.

'I certainly do. There's none better. I hear he has cottoned on to that King woman. Why, I don't know.'

Matt sighed. 'Do I have to spell it out for you Liquid? He's been starved for years and hasn't realized it. Well, I hate to see him sucked in but it can happen to the best of us.'

'I had always thought with a name like Auriol, she would be a kind of gentlewoman.'

'That is what Jeremy probably thinks. There's a lot in a name. A Sally is always saucy, a Jane prim and proper, a Fiona, very elegant,' said Matt.

'Do you think a girl acts according to her name?'

Jos raised his head for an instant. 'You mean is it post hoc or propter hoc.'

Liquid looked astonished. 'Bloody hell,' he said, 'what does that mean?'

'I don't know, but my ensign said it once when we were talking about the same thing. He was very educated.'

Matt stood up. 'Stow it, Jos. We'll go to Flora's place.'

Flora opened the front door wide when she saw Matt. She wiped her hands on her apron and put her arms out.

'Matt, darling, I thought we might never see you again. Come in to the kitchen.' She bustled them down the hall.

'Girls, girls,' she called, holding onto the stair post and peering into the darkness of the top landing. 'Drat them,' she said, 'They've shut the top door again. They're up to no good. Probably still in bed and there are three ships in today.'

There was some scuffling and giggling behind the door. Three girls dressed in kimonos came down the narrow staircase, one behind the other.

'Where's Angela?' asked Matt.

'Having a holiday.' Flora cast a professional eye over the girls as they drifted into the kitchen.

Matt was disappointed. 'She was off this time last month.'

'That's the way it goes,' said Flora. 'She'll be sorry she missed you. I've made some scones, help yourselves.'

Liquid Len eyed the plate. 'To hell with the scones,' he said.

'No swearing, thank you,' said Flora. 'This is a respectable establishment. Matt, you will have one, won't you?'

'I'll take Penelope,' said Matt.

Penelope looked shyly at her slippered feet and raised her eyes, peering under the lids at Matt. Len grabbed at the other two girls and dragged them playfully toward the door.

'Slowly, slowly, never rush it,' said Flora as Matt and Liquid Len followed the girls out.

'Aren't you going up, lad?' asked Flora as Jos stood, bewildered, by the table. He eyed the scones. 'You'd rather have something to eat?' She took a dish from the safe and taking a knife spread the scones with generous helpings of butter. Jos took the plate. 'Sit down, boy. Tell me. Have you got a girl?'

Jos nodded. His mouth was full and a driblet of butter was coursing down his chin.

'What is her name?'

'Rata.'

'Uh, uh.' Flora took another batch from the oven.

'Is she from these parts?'

'No. She is Waikato.'

'A Ngati Maniopoto?'

'Yes.'

Flora glanced sharply at Jos. 'What is she doing here in town?'

'She is going to school.'

'How old is she?'

'Seventeen.'

'Let me give you some advice. Keep away from these places.'

'We are getting married soon,' said Jos. He took another scone. 'Do your girls get married?'

'Sometimes. But before you know it they are back again. It doesn't last.'

'Why not?'

'We have all sorts of men come here. You'd be surprised if I told you who my customers are, some very respected citizens. But mum's the word. They come to this house because they know we are discreet.' She opened the fire door and shovelled in some coal. 'It never lasts.'

'What doesn't?'

'A man gets a crush on a girl. Comes nearly every day. Then I guess he figures it would be cheaper to marry her and poof, they're away. A month or two later, she's back again. They've had a row. He's thrown it up at her and Bob's your uncle. What are you going

275

to do when you are married?'

'Mr St Clair has bought me a farm, a part of it rather. He's given me a share.'

'You're a lucky young man. Is that the Mr St Clair who owns that big house out west of here?'

'Yes.'

'He's a widower, isn't he?'

'Yes. He won't stay that way for long.' Jos put on a confidential tone. 'He's nearly hitched already.'

'Oh. Who is the lucky girl?'

'Auriol King.'

'Who?'

'Auriol King.'

'Holy catsmeat. Are you serious?'

'I swear it. Mr St Clair is away but due back any day. I wouldn't be surprised if he popped the question any time. Do you know her?'

Flora pursed her lips. 'Sort of,' she said. 'Sort of. These amateurs are no good for my business.' She looked at the clock. 'What are they doing up there? It is time they were down.'

'Do you like it here?' asked Jos.

'It's a living. I am lonely sometimes and I don't exactly get invited to all the socials. Anyway, what am I doing talking to you like this? Have another scone.'

'No thank you.'

Flora looked at the clock again. 'Come on,' she said, 'We'll get them down.'

Jos climbed the stairs behind Flora. She pushed at the door at the top of the stairs. Jos saw a long corridor with half a dozen doors on either side. There was a stained glass window at the end reflecting its colours on to the walls and floor.

'It looks like a church,' said Jos.

'Well,' said Flora, 'Some people have different ways of getting rid of their problems. Church is cheaper.' Flora opened the first door. The room was empty except for a bed and a small dressing table. Girls! Girls! Where are you?'

There was a scuffle behind the door at the far end. 'They are in the best room drat them.' She marched up the corridor and flung the door open. Jos looked over her shoulder and saw the largest bed he had ever seen. It was a full tester that reached up to the ceiling, all brass and black metal. The curtains hanging from the top had been pushed aside and the girls were lying on their stomachs with elbows on the bed and chins on their hands. Matt and Liquid Len were putting on their boots.

'What are you doing?' exclaimed Flora. 'This is a respectable house. I want none of your fancy tricks here.'

Penelope stood up and wrapped a kimono around herself.

'It's all right,' she said, 'we have just come in here. We've been talking.'

Flora snorted. 'Well, get downstairs. The rush will be starting soon and you won't be ready.'

'Don't be hard on the girls,' said Matt, pulling out his wallet. 'I was telling them as how I was leaving for good old Ireland tonight. Home sweet home.'

'Going home?' Flora turned to face Matt.

'Yes. Tonight. On the tide.'

'Glory be. We'll miss you, Matt.'

'And I'll miss Angela. Give her my love.' He put a sovereign on the table.

Flora picked it up. 'Take it, Matt. This one is on the house.'

The three men stopped at the Rob Roy, drank a nobbler of rum each, and climbed back over the hill to the cabstand. When they arrived at "The Wilderness" they saw that Jeremy had not returned.

'I hope he gets back before I leave,' said Matt, 'He is cutting it fine.'

'He'll be back.' Jos kicked open the back door. 'Unless of course he has gone to Mrs King.'

Len went to the cupboard and took down a bottle, topping up the whisky with water from the filter. 'Why the hell doesn't someone tell St Clair he is making a fool of himself. Half the 18th Irish have used her, she is the regimental joke.'

'Are you game to tell him? You know what he would do. He would be quiet, terribly polite, then show you the door. I hate to see it happen to a chap like him.' Matt flopped into a chair.

Liquid Len was angry. 'All right. A man has a sick wife for almost a year. Life was not that good for him before that. And then she dies. This piece turns up, full of charm and you know what. What do you expect? There is an old Chinese saying, something like wait a year before taking another wife. Anyway, Matt, are you going to marry when you get home?'

'I might or might not.'

'No one would have you. Besides she might make you work too hard.'

'That settles it.' Matt refilled his glass. 'Only fools and horses work.'

Liquid Len fetched another bottle to the table and poured more drinks. They finished it as the light began to fade and the cold night air crept in from under the door. When Liquid Len and Jos fell asleep at the table Matt stood up and looked out the window. He was surprised to see Jeremy leading a horse out of the stables. Len and Jos were both asleep. One of them had knocked a glass over and the amber liquid was spreading slowly over the table. What a home coming for Jeremy, he thought. 'I suppose he's going up to see Auriol King.'

The idea came to him suddenly, as though from heaven — or the devil. He looked at his two companions and walked quietly to the door. 'Good-bye and good luck, you sods,' he whispered. He led his horse out the back way, across the lawn so that Jeremy would not hear him. Fifty yards further on he mounted and spurred his horse up the hill to turn into toward Auriol King's house. The light was on in the parlour.

'Matt,' she exclaimed, 'What a surprise.'

'You asked me to come.'

'I know, but I didn't expect you.'

She steered him into the breakfast room. 'Madeira or brandy?'

'Brandy, thank you.'

She poured the drinks carefully. 'Here's to us.' Taking a long sip she looked at him over the glass. 'What can I do for you?'

'Get into bed and I'll show you.'

She walked over to the bedroom door, looking over her shoulder as she went.

'My God,' he thought, 'what will I do if he doesn't arrive?'

'Is there a glass somewhere?' he called out.

'In the cabinet.'

278

He filled it from the tap at the kitchen sink and drank the water slowly.

'Hurry up, Matt,' she called.

There was no sign of Jeremy.

'I won't be long,' he said.

Sitting on a chair he undid his boots then tied them up again. He looked out the window. In the dim light he saw Jeremy striding up the path. 'This is it,' he muttered.

He unfastened his belt and waited at the door.

The footsteps paused for a moment. As Jeremy put up his hand to knock, Matt threw open the door and began buckling up his belt.

A voice called from the bedroom. It was petulant, like a child's. 'Come on Matt, I am waiting.'

For a moment the world stood still. He looked straight into Jeremy's eyes. 'Your turn,' he said, and leaping on his horse spurred it over the ridge to the ship.

24

On a warm sunny January day in 1866, the officers who owned drags in the various regiments assembled at the domain. The chairman of the 'Four in Hand' club, Captain Creagh, parked on the path running alongside the reservoir on Domain Hill and waited. The captain was proud of his private coach. It was very smart, all French polish and bright brass, and he was even prouder of his team of horses. There were considerable differences of opinion as to the best heights of wheelers and leaders. Some liked them all exactly the same size, others preferred a big wheel-horse and a small leader but Captain Creagh preferred a low, thick wheel-horse and a taller but more thorough-bred looking leader. If it was a matter of taking the eye, the smaller, thick wheelers and the tall, light leaders of Captain Creagh's team were the pick of the barracks. Except, of course, for those of Captain Newhaven.

Newhaven's drag was built for racing, painted in bright colours and with a team of horses for which no expense had been spared. Three of them were matching 'duns', buff-coloured thoroughbreds, a little on the light side but fast. The fourth, the outside leader, was a magnificent grey. All were exactly the same height, all mettlesome and brilliantly turned out; it was the crack team of the town. His drag was the next to arrive. There were four passengers inside it, another four on the roof, two on the seat at the back and in the box seat was Auriol King. She sat next to Newhaven wearing a new hunting costume and a wide-brimmed black hat with a ribbon floating behind.

Another drag arrived. Before long there were seven coaches and fours lined up around the edge of the reservoir.

A voice came from the inside of Captain Creagh's drag. 'Where is St Clair?'

Jeremy and Captain Creagh were old friends. They had been to military college together, raced their drags together and had gone to the Crimea in the same troopship. There, they had gone to different regiments, but had always kept up some sort of correspondence. When Jim Creagh was posted to New Zealand Jeremy was one of the first persons he met there.

'We will give him another five minutes,' said Jim Creagh.

As he spoke, Jeremy came into sight through the trees, with Jos next to him. 'My apologies Jim,' he said. He looked back at the other coaches. 'Who is that next to Newhaven?'

'Auriol King.' Creagh shortened the reins of the off-wheeler. 'She made a pass at you, last year, didn't she?'

Jeremy did not reply. He buttoned up his coat, for there was a steady wind blowing from the south.

'She's acting as a chaperone for the debutantes in Newhaven's party,' continued Captain Creagh.

'What debutantes?'

'They are inside the cab. Four of them. What happened between you two, Jeremy?'

'Nothing.' Jeremy leaned forward. 'That near-side leader of yours has his tail caught.'

Captain Creagh let out the top left rein he was holding between his thumb and first finger and with his whip, touched the horse up lightly under the bar. The leader swished his tail free. 'Auriol King still has a disposition towards you. Says she can't understand why you suddenly became very cold to her.'

'I would rather not discuss it, Jim. Have you any winners for today?'

'Not really. Speak to the owners and ninety percent say they have a chance. Newhaven's pony, Topsy, should win the last, the jockey's race.'

'Is Newhaven riding it?'

'No. If it wins he is throwing a party.'

The drags looked a fine sight as they passed the saleyards at Newmarket. They turned into the entrance of the racecourse and wheeled in line to the outside fence. There were rows of coaches stretched out on each side of the grandstand.

'There,' said Jim Creagh, pulling up his horses beside the fence. 'A perfect view.' The other drags came up within a few yards of each other. The inside riders tumbled out, laughing and giggling.

'Who is for champagne?' asked Newhaven.

Auriol King clapped her hands. 'I am,' she said.

Newhaven went to the boot and pulled it down, forming a table. Inside were bottles of champagne and padded trays for glasses. Half a dozen corks popped. 'Here's to Topsy,' they chorused.

It was three-quarters of an hour after noon when the first race got away. Before the start they all climbed on to the top of the drags to get a good view, sitting three in a row on the outside seats. 'Native,' a bay gelding shot ahead at the finish to win. 'Time for lunch,' said Auriol when the excitement had died down. Canopies were set up over the roof seats and the boots opened to reveal the picnic baskets. There were cold collations and fruit tarts as well as lobster, cold boiled beef, veal pies, tongues and gallons of strawberries, cherries and cheese. The champagne flowed. Newhaven went to look at his pony.

A tall figure reeled past. Piccolo Charlie was a virtuoso on his instrument, his shock of grey hair quivered and weaved above the heads of the crowd as he played. He was wearing an old Crimean shirt unbuttoned at the waist, moleskin breeches fitted with an unruly front flap and on his feet were a pair of boots fastened with string and flax. Charlie was in town to blow the money he had earned felling trees in the bush. Jeremy was watching him take a bow after a particularly dexterous piece, when he heard a voice at his elbow.

'Jeremy, you have ignored me for six months. Why aren't we friends?' Auriol King was gazing up at him with wide-open eyes. She had a nymph-like quality about her that Jeremy found hard to define.

'Auriol,' he said, 'I would rather not talk about it.'

She shrugged her shoulders and, wrinkling her nose, walked away. Jeremy heard a cheer as a racegoer won a prize at the Aunt Sally booth.

Newhaven returned. 'I have put two to one on Topsy in the last race,' he said. 'Here are tickets for everybody.'

The girls squealed. Auriol threw him a smile and, pulling the ribbon decoration from her hat, pinned it on his breast pocket. 'For luck,' she said.

'Open more champagne.' Newhaven went to a box between the two roof seats and brought out three bottles. The ribbons streamed out as he climbed down from the drag. He then went over to walk his pony and give last minute instructions to the jockey.

They watched the race from the tops of the drags. It was quickly over. Topsy took the lead at half way and maintained it until the end.

Jim Creagh turned to Jeremy. 'By jove, he's done it.'

Newhaven appeared with his groom and jockey. 'We will break open the rest of the champagne,' he said.

'Hurrah!' cried Auriol.

They all turned to Newhaven. He was flushed and triumphant. 'We will celebrate tonight,' he said. 'At the Royal. Champagne for all.'

'I'm afraid I won't be able to come.' There was silence as the whole party turned to Jeremy.

'Did I hear you say you can't come, St Clair?' Newhaven put his glass down on the steps of the drag.

'I am afraid I won't be able to come,' Jeremy repeated.

'Oh, Jeremy, you must.' Auriol had walked over and was standing at the head of the grey.

Jeremy turned on his heels and climbed on to the seat of his drag.

Newhaven let out an oath and strode toward Jeremy. 'St Clair!' His face reddened. 'Mrs King spoke to you. I demand you give her an answer.'

Jeremy turned to Jim Creagh. 'I am driving back to town.'

'St Clair!' Newhaven pulled at Jeremy's arm. 'You cut Mrs King dead. No one does that to my friends.'

Jeremy broke free.

'I give you one more chance to apologize, St Clair.'

Jeremy turned to Jim Creagh. 'I am off,' he said.

'St Clair, I challenge you to a duel.'

'Don't be a fool, Newhaven.' Jim Creagh flung out the words.

'Nominate your seconds, St Clair. You have choice of weapons,' shouted Newhaven.

Jeremy looked down at Newhaven then flicked his head at Captain Creagh. 'Jim will be my second. You will hear from him.'

'Damn you both,' said Jim Creagh. He shook the reins. The horses tossed their heads and moved off. For a while the drag took all of Jim Creagh's attention as they weaved through the crowd. Back at the stables he spoke angrily to Jeremy. 'You are both bloody fools. How long has duelling been outlawed?'

Jeremy stared straight ahead. 'We can keep it a secret.'

'In this town? It will be common knowledge in no time. The high command will hear of it. Probably tonight if I know the way news travels. It is ridiculous.'

'Will you be my second?'

'I will have to be, I suppose. For the last time, will you change your mind?'

'Back down? To that man? He has never seen a shot fired in anger. Can I tell you something that will surprise you, Jim? I am looking forward to it.'

'Damn you and double damn you.' Jim Creagh whipped up the horses. 'You won't get away with it.'

Captain Creagh waited until noon the next day before making a move. He had been hoping the quarrel would simmer down, but Jeremy was adamant. 'It is my reputation, Jim,' said Jeremy.

Captain Creagh waited on Captain Newhaven at headquarters. The meeting was short and to the point. Returning to "The Wilderness", Creagh found Jeremy in his study.

'Well?' said Jeremy.

'I have seen him.' Jim Creagh slapped his side with his cane.

'What did he say?'

'The commandant has had wind of it, as I said he would.'

'Yes?'

'Newhaven has been ordered to abandon it.'

'And?'

He has challenged you to a drag race instead. To satisfy his honour. The loser to apologize.'

'What did you say?'

'I accepted on your behalf.'

Jeremy jumped to his feet and began pacing the floor. He

swung around and faced Jim Creagh. 'We have much work to do if I am to race that old bone-shaker of mine. we will start right away.'

They hitched Sergeant to the dogcart and drove to the stables. Jeremy walked twice around the drag assessing its good points and the bad. He looked at the pole. It was made of the toughest ash. The ironwork was in good condition, no chance of the end cracking. Crawling underneath he examined the springs hung on a wooden perch undercarriage. Getting out from underneath he went towards the horse-boxes. There were traces and reins hanging on the doors. 'We will have a look at these,' said Jeremy. 'I don't want them too long. They are better about three inches shorter than normal. If a horse stumbles when you have too much slack it is long odds against saving him from a fall.'

'I've watched Newhaven,' said Jim Creagh. 'He holds his reins a bit low. Almost three inches below his heart.'

Jeremy looked up from measuring one of the traces. 'If he has one.'

'Then he should hold them where his heart would normally be. Have you any gloves?'

'Only my ordinary ones.'

'You had better have mine. You need quite two sizes larger than your dress ones. How about shoes?'

'I have a good thick pair, just right for the footboard. Let me see the horses.'

Jeremy watched as Jim Creagh brought out the wheelers.

'We need maximum horse power. I like the strongest horse at the near-wheel. With the roads so high in the centre the near wheeler will have to pull like the devil. Let me see the near-leader. I want both near-siders to be tall.'

They poled up the wheelers, adjusting the traces so that the horses were far enough forward not to touch the footboard but less than a foot away from the drag.

'Otherwise we are wasting power,' said Jeremy. The other two horses were brought out and matched with the pole.'

'I'll take six inches off the end of the pole. That will make sure each horse does its share.' He lengthened the coupling reins and examined the bits. Jeremy ran his eye over one of the horses. 'That wheeler has a weak-looking neck. He is not a puller and he carries his head too high. We will change him.'

Jim Creagh went away and returned with another horse. 'I know Newhaven's drag like the back of my hand,' he said. 'His horses are always too far from their work.'

Jeremy backed the new wheeler into position. 'You can play around as much as you like with fancy ideas, but in the long run it is the horsepower that counts,' he said.

'What are you going to do? Get into top speed and go?'

'I don't know. I would like to tool along for a while. Maybe wait until he makes a mistake. Check those pole chains, Jim.'

'How much play do you want in them?'

'Enough or the horses will get sore withers. That wheeler you brought out has her head down. She looks as though she has come out of a brewer's cart.'

'Don't worry. Wait until she feels a touch of the whip. Just a flick and she will change into the most beautiful piece of racing horseflesh you have ever seen.'

'Incredible.' Jeremy stood back and studied her critically. 'As long as she does her share.'

'I had a good look at Newhaven's drag at the races. It is very light and looks first-class.'

'To hell with looks. We will strip all the rubbish off this one now. First the lights, then the boot and boxes.'

'And the seats.'

'All the seats, inside and out.'

'Hell, there will be nothing left.'

The following day they dismantled the springs and the axles and put them back again, piece by piece, greasing them with mutton fat. They checked and adjusted the driving seat, the brake and the bits, neither too high or too low in the horse's mouth. One horse was working on one trace more than the other. Jeremy took one side up a notch. 'I'll drive the drag as much as I can in the next two weeks,' he said.

The next day they went out and rode slowly over the course. It was a track little used, just wide enough for two drags to pass each other with something to spare and had been made for bullock wagons to haul timber to the mill. From the starting point which was marked by a long pole the course went straight along a gradual decline for a quarter of a mile before making a left hand turn up a small hill, coming down the other side into another straight piece

286

of road. At the end of this was another short hill, bearing left, steeper than the other.

'There is only room for one of us here,' remarked Jeremy.

The road went into an 'S' shaped bend at the top. There was a rough track cut straight over the hill that joined the road again some distance ahead. Jeremy could see that some single horsemen had used it to avoid the bend. They went through a cutting with high banks on either side and around a corner, where a finishing post could be seen seventy-five yards ahead. Jeremy studied the camber of the road as it hit the straight and he filled in a pothole with some small stones. He called out to Jim Creagh who was back up the track. 'What distance do you think it is Jim?'

'About a mile and three-quarter.'

Jeremy nodded. 'It will be a fair test of nerve, going into that last curve.'

'It depends how fast you are prepared to take it.'

'Now I've seen the track I think I will shorten the wheelers' reins a bit more for going downhill. It is a matter of picking the right gear for the right situation.'

When the sun rose on the day of the race Jim Creagh was already in the stables, polishing the drag. It was shining in the yellow lamplight. A groom was strapping the horses. They were in perfect condition after working continuously every three days and being rested every fourth day. Jim Creagh poled them up and Jeremy followed him around, checking every strap and piece of equipment. Newhaven's drag was by the starting pole with half a dozen people standing around it when Jeremy arrived. He saw Auriol King on a low mound not far away.

'Draw straws for pole position,' said Jim Creagh.

Jeremy drew the largest and took the inside. Both seconds marshalled the drags into line. The starter was a few yards down the track with a blue and white scarf held high. 'Are you ready?' Jim Creagh felt the tension as complete silence fell. A chain clinked against a pole as a horse shook its head. Down came the flag.

Jeremy was first away. His wheelers took up the load as Newhaven's horses, unsettled by the whip, plunged forward. There was a mix-up. One of Newhaven's leaders grazed the side of Jeremy's off-wheeler. Moments later, Jeremy was a coach-length in front as both found top speed and pounded down the straight. At the first turn, Jeremy was still in front. Newhaven's horses had picked up the rhythm and with a lighter drag were only a neck away. The next bend came up. Jeremy went into it at full speed, drawing on the two left reins. At the beginning of the straight they were still in the same position but the speed and lightness of Newhaven's team began to tell. Another quarter of a mile and they were locked together side by side. Gradually Newhaven forged ahead.

Jeremy made a quick decision. He would tool along and conserve his horses' strength for the last dash. He put his off-leader as close as possible to Newhaven's offside rear wheel and hung on. At the end of the straight he was still there. They rounded another bend and began the climb up the hill. Jeremy glanced at Newhaven's horses. The leaders, built for speed, were making hard work of the hill. As they came out of the next bend, Jeremy flicked his whip above his horse's heads. They responded magnificently, pulling as though they sensed the urgency of the race and were giving all they had.

Suddenly Newhaven swerved across the track, taking up a position in the middle. There was no room for Jeremy to pass. One false move and the horses could be badly injured. He dropped back. They came to the brow of the hill. Newhaven slowed to go into the 'S' bend before entering the cutting. In the split second that followed, Jeremy decided to miss the bend and go over the top, down the bridle track in one straight, wild, sliding line. There was no room to spare. Checking the horses slightly he plunged downward not daring to use the brake. The leaders had to gallop fast enough to keep ahead of the drag. Over and down they went. The drag rocked from side to side as it hit the bottom road with a crash. Miraculously the springs held. Jeremy saw Newhaven bearing down on him. At the last moment Newhaven's nerve failed him and he used his brake, but only for a second. Jeremy was in front. They thundered towards the cutting with the finishing post beyond as Jeremy went wide to give the horses room. It was a straight run to the finish. Newhaven began to gain once more. The clay of the bank rose on each side of them. Jeremy heard the crack of a whip as Newhaven cut inside on the left. There was no room to move as his opponent put Jeremy up against the wall. Newhaven deliberately swerved and caught Jeremy's back wheel, ramming him into a spin. Gathering in his horses Jeremy heard the back axle snap as he slewed across the finishing line. Out of the corner of his eye he saw one of Newhaven's horses somersaulting through the air behind him. There was a crash, a blinding flash and Jeremy was catapulted to the ground, unconscious, unheedful of the sound of running feet and cries of terrified horses.

It was four days before Jim Creagh was allowed to visit Jeremy. The hospital in the domain was a two storeyed, wooden building in the waste land on the hill. Jim went quietly into the ward to find Jeremy propped up on pillows with his arm in a sling.

'Jim!' cried Jeremy. There was a bond between the two friends that only a lifetime of comradeship and adventure could have forged.

Jim sat down. 'How is your leg?'

'Not bad. Are the horses all right?'

'Yours? A few bruises, that is all.'

'How about Newhaven's?'

'They have been destroyed.'

There was a pause.

'And Newhaven?'

'In disgrace for coming in on you. The drag landed across his lower body. They have amputated a leg at the hip, and the other one will be useless. They say he will be in a chair for the rest of his life.'

'Oh. I am sorry about that.'

'Don't feel sorry for Newhaven.'

There was another long pause.

'I have been thinking about the business. What is happening, Jim?' said Jeremy.

'Jos has come into town and a neighbour is keeping an eye on the farm. Tonguer has pulled up his socks and hasn't touched a drop since your accident. I look in each day and do the banking.'

'Thank you Jim. Does Jonathon know I am here?'

'Yes, and so does Rosalind of course. Jonathon is fine. She looks after him as though he was her son. Jeremy, why don't you do something about it. Rosalind I mean. What you need is a good woman.'

'What I need at the moment is a pair of crutches.'

'You need a woman and a pair of crutches.'

'I haven't been too good at picking them, have I?'

'No. Or have they been picking you? Why don't you leave it to me. I'll arrange it. Remember the dances when we were training? The girls on one side of the hall and we on the other. The chaperones kept an eagle eye on us and we wondered how we could get them outside for a few minutes. You weren't much good at picking them even then. The good ones or the bad ones.'

'I remember you once said that there were no bad girls. The trouble was I thought they were a different species from us. Paula was the only girl I really knew. I didn't think much about them at all except when we were on leave, otherwise women were there to bear children, keep the home fires burning and all that. I didn't think of them having minds of their own.'

'Like Rosalind?'

'Yes, I suppose so.'

Jim looked out the window. 'Speaking of different species,' he said. He walked to the door.

'I've brought some soup.' Rosalind went to the bedside locker and put down a bowl. 'Jonathon sends his love. They tell me you are over the worst.'

Jeremy felt her presence as soon as she walked in the door.

'Do you feel better?' she asked.

'I do now.' Watching her sit down he sought her eyes under the shadow of her bonnet. 'I am sorry.'

'Sorry. Why?'

'All that business with your friend Newhaven. I didn't mean it to end like this.'

'He isn't a friend in the manner you seem to think, Jeremy. I try to help anyone who needs it. At least I listen to them when I can. Let us change the subject. Is there anything I can do?'

'No thank you.'

'The business?'

'Jos is running it. Jim has been a tower of strength. I am thinking of winding it up.'

'Really?'

'I don't need it. I thought I might take a rest. Live on the farm and keep a house in town, something smaller than "The Wilderness".'

'That is a good idea.'

'The rents from the farm in England have been building up. Each year I have put them into British consols at two and a half percent. There is a goodly sum there now and the rents are still coming in. In fact, as soon as I am out of here I am going to tidy it all up. Tonguer can be odd-job on the farm if he wishes.'

'And you will be a man of leisure.'

'Not quite. I could never be idle for long.'

Afterwards Rosalind walked down the hill and up to the school. Jonathon was playing with his soldiers. 'Did you see father?' he asked.

'Yes.' She picked him up. He struggled to go back to his game. 'How is he?'

She kissed the boy on the cheek. 'Wonderful,' she said.

25

There was a new bank manager at the desk when Jeremy made his call, but everything else was the same. The high stools, the money counter, the big heavy doors around the banking chamber. The manager was young as managers go. Probably about fifty-five years old, thought Jeremy. Aloud he said, 'I would like a statement of my accounts if I could have them.'

'Certainly Mr St Clair. I hope everything is in order. You are not thinking of transferring your funds?'

'No, no.'

'They are all in credit of course. Is there anything I can do?'

'Not really. I am going to wind up the business. Perhaps sell it if I can find a buyer. What is the balance of the main account?'

'I shall not be able to tell you until later, the clerks write them up after we close. I could keep someone back to bring them up to date.'

'There is no need for that.'

'I will find your file.' The manager returned and sitting down leafed through the papers. 'We won't require this anymore.'

Jeremy frowned. 'What is it?'

'The guarantee from Mrs Earle.'

'From whom?'

'From Mrs Rosalind Earle.'

'Rosalind has not guaranteed my account. Nobody has. My assets in London covered that.'

The manager smiled again. 'You have probably forgotten. It was before the wars.' He passed the document to Jeremy.

Jeremy stared at the bold copper-plate handwriting. There it was. Her signature. Rosalind Earle. Guarantor.

Jeremy reached for his hat. 'I will be back,' he said.

A bewildered banker let him out the door. Jeremy found a cab by the jail in Victoria Street and ordered it to take him to Rosalind's school. 'And hurry,' he said.

Rosalind was in the parlour. Brushing past Rata, he went in without knocking. He thrust the guarantee at her. 'What's the meaning of this?' he asked angrily.

She looked at him and sat down. 'Calm yourself, Jeremy,' she said. 'When you have stopped being irrational I will explain.'

'Did you sign this?'

'Yes.'

'That is all I want to know. You had no right to do this for me.'

'I was helping you.'

'When I want help I will ask for it. Thank you. Good day.' He turned sharply and left the room.

The following morning Jeremy finished breakfast early and waited for Laura to clear the dishes away. She looked down at the half-empty plate.

'Was everything all right, sir?'

He folded his napkin into three and put it down. 'The toast was cold and the coffee like dishwater,' said Jeremy.

Laura's mouth dropped open. 'Sorry, sir.' Her eyes went up to the ceiling and down again. In the kitchen she put the plates in a basin and addressed the cat. 'What's wrong with 'im? Never seen 'im like this before.' The cat stared at her, closed its eyes and opened them. 'I see,' said Laura, 'you think he is in love. Again. Pity 'elp the poor girl. She can 'ave 'im with knobs on, I say.'

Feeling restless Jeremy went outside and onto the lawn. He walked slowly to the lake, pausing at the rosebed and at the herb garden. Absent-mindedly he plucked a sprig of rosemary. Its pungent smell overlaid the perfume of the roses. There was no wind. Young cygnets were following their mother in line like little ships, pulling busily at the lake weed on the surface. He stooped down to pick up a pebble and threw it into the lake. The cygnets darted to their mother as the widening rings of water spread outwards.

The guarantee. He had never for one moment thought it existed. It accounted for the ease with which he was able to borrow in those times after the fires. How could it have been done without his knowledge? Was it legal? The damage was done now. Poor Rosalind. She had always given him support with Paula and with Jonathon, but he had not realized she was backing him financially as well. There were all those times when he had gone there feeling depressed and had been lifted up again. And, of course, there was Jonathon. 'She is like a mother to him,' Jim had said. Jeremy sat on the seat where the swans came to be fed. Paula had asked him to promise to marry Rosalind and he would not. They all liked her. He did too, but she had all that money and a bee in her bonnet about independence.

He pulled out his watch. Ten o'clock. Better go to the warehouse. Another three months and it would be closed down so that he could concentrate on the farm.

Jeremy ignored the turning into High Street when he rode into town. Instead, he kept on up the hill and found himself tethering the horse to the iron ring at Rosalind's gate. He knocked on the front door. It seemed a long time before Rata opened it. Later he could not remember exactly what he said.

'She is not here? Where is she?'

'I don't know.'

'In town?'

'She has been away for two days.'

'When is she coming back?'

'She did not say.'

'Where is she?'

'I don't know.'

Jeremy rode straight to Caroline's house.

'Do you know where Rosalind is?'

'I may do.' Caroline was standing on the top step looking down at him with her arms folded over her chest. 'You have made a mess of it, haven't you.'

294

'I suppose so.'

'Come in.' She threw open the door and followed him inside. 'Why have you come here?'

'I thought you would know where Rosalind is.'

'I do.'

'Where is she?'

'She asked me not to tell you.'

'Oh.' He looked down at his feet.

'You men. You don't know what you want, half the time. Here is a good woman, in fact too good for you, and what do you do? Chase her away. Jeremy St Clair you should have done something about it a long time ago.'

'We have discussed our position before.'

'Discussed your position! You infuriate me. What a woman wants is to be swept off her feet. To be loved. Have you ever taken her to a ball? To a garden party?' Caroline mimicked Jeremy. 'I wonder, Mrs Earle, if we could discuss our position. Position my foot, Jeremy St Clair.'

'But she is so independent. And there is all that money.'

'Money, money, money. It is your pride, Jeremy. False pride. We are what we are. If she is handsome, God made her so. If she is learned, someone instructed her. If she is rich, God, or her father gave her what she owns. There can be no comfort in two people in love feeling that one is better than the other. Go and get her and forget everything else. Only respect her, and always be honest with her and yourself.'

'I don't know where she is.'

'She has gone to Whangaparaoa, the Bay of Whales, to a cottage there belonging to Captain Carter.'

'I know it.'

Caroline went out of the room and returned with a packet. 'This came for her yesterday in the English mail. It is marked urgent and confidential. Take it to her. And if she never talks to me again I will kill you, Jeremy St Clair.'

Ceta the whale and her calf had been separated from their family and were moving up the coast looking for the pod.

Two years before, in the autumn, in the same bay, Ceta had mated with the leader, Odo. That season the old bull had fought with more than his usual strength to keep his harem together and to remain in control of the herd. When Ceta came into season there were many prepared to court her, but the old man kept them all at bay. In their love play she deliberately brushed past his fins causing his penis to slip out from the genital slit like a thin hard rope. Gliding past, they stroked each other with their bodies and their flippers, and the big bull nibbled at her flukes as she rolled gently over. They gambolled all morning. He butted her gently with his nose and they came together in a whirl of surging foam. Finally, in a burst of exhilaration they rose through the water vertically, mating as they swam upwards. As Ceta fell back into the water she uttered a succession of excited piping sounds. Bubbles escaped from her blowhole. Three times they rose through the water, belly to belly and three times fell back with a gigantic splash into the rim of the sea. At last, as the evening sky darkened, they separated and Ceta swam lazily back to her place in the herd.

Three months later the foetus had become well established in Ceta's womb and most of its organs were formed. For another six months she swam and fed with the herd in their migration and she began to feel the movements inside. As her weight increased and her belly swelled she became slower in her movements and kept more to herself.

Soon after she had become pregnant the herd moved away from the Bay to follow their food supply. Unlike the baleens which sift thousands of tonnes of krill through their jaws and have no teeth, the pilot whales chase and live on fish by encircling the schools, herding them together and attacking them in large groups.

A year after Ceta had conceived she was back in Whangaparaoa with the herd and the birth of her baby was imminent.

The first labour pains had come on suddenly and lasted for over half an hour. Ceta instinctively began swimming very slowly until she felt the muscles of her abdomen contract violently and the tail of her baby appeared. The other cows kept close to her as she laboured, making sure she was not left behind or attacked. One in particular showed greater interest in her than the others. It was the 'auntie' who stood by her throughout the birth and when, finally, the snout of the baby appeared and the cord was broken, it was she who took control and pushed her new charge up to the surface. The atmosphere acted as a stimulus as the new-born calf took in the first of its life-giving air before sinking back under the surface. It returned every few minutes, helped by its 'auntie', opening and closing its blowhole instinctively. Ceta felt weak and tired, but together they shepherded the calf to the herd.

The baby almost immediately began swimming strongly and half an hour later was looking to be suckled. Ceta did not have protruding udders as most mammals. Her nipples were recessed in openings on each side of her genital slit and the baby, swimming from behind, found the emerging nipples as Ceta rolled over on her side. Seizing one between its tongue and palate the calf took his first drink. For the first few weeks he was fed every half-hour, day and night. Ceta spouted the milk into her calf's mouth. To an old whaling man who had captured a cow and tasted the creamy white milk it had a fishy smell and was like a combination of fish oil, liver and milk of magnesia, but to Ceta's baby it was nectar.

By the time he was six months old he was having only seven feeds a day and was chasing fish although he never seemed to catch one. Ceta kept him under control by her calls and when she slept, he slept under her tail fin. Once the herd was attacked by killer whales and the calf was in great danger, but Ceta did not abandon her baby; instead she put herself between him and the killers.

As time went on he had become more independent. Now, on his first birthday, he was back in his birthplace again. She watched while he ate his first fish, which he brought up immediately. Worried, she gently massaged his belly with her nose and pushed him towards the shore where it was warmer.

It was late in the day when Jeremy changed course to keep outside some wash-rocks showing ahead. He eased the mainsheet and pushed the tiller over. The *'Echo'* pointed reluctantly outward. Peering under the boom he saw the cow and the calf again, moving along parallel to the *'Echo'*. It seemed that they had become separated from the pod. He watched as Ceta dived out of sight.

Captain Carter's cottage was on the far side of the peninsular jutting into the sea to the north. Realizing he would not reach his destination that night he changed course and found shelter in an inlet protected from the sea. Early the next morning he set off to find Rosalind.

The sea was a glassy calm, with a low mist rising gently in the air and a lazy swell crashed at long intervals onto the sweeping sand. A soft haze extended only a few feet above the water, transforming the sea into a grey plain that met the blue of the sky at the horizon. Toward the shore, the rocks and the coves were hidden by the same amorphous band, making the cliffs rise as though from nowhere, hiding a thousand nooks and crannies and secret entrances.

Jeremy sat in the stern of the cutter with the sails limp and the boom rolling from side to side as the swell picked the 'Echo' up and put her down again. As the sun rose higher and the sea breeze began to flow onto the land the sails filled enough to enable Jeremy to change course and head for a small sheltered inlet under the cliffs. A quiet stream spilled onto the sand where a jetty leaned outward. He manoeuvred alongside and tied up. Walking slowly toward a cottage nestling in a tiny valley he climbed the few yards from the beach to a lawn. There were stocks and hollyhocks growing on each side of the shell path and an English honeysuckle stitched its way upwards, its creamy blooms wild with scent intermingling with the grey-green leaves of a pohutukawa tree. The gentle folds of the earth, the sweep of the grass and a jagged shelf of rock that protruded into the sea reminded him of Devon.

Rounding the corner of the house he saw her. She was tending a rose bush. A pale blue dress fell from a gathered bodice to her ankles and the ends of a yellow sash dangled from her waist. A wide-brimmed straw hat was pushed to the back of her head and as he watched she brushed a lock of hair from her eyes. Jeremy stood transfixed with this picture of old-world charm painted with such delicate strokes under the harsh sub-tropical light of this new world. All his doubts, all his ambitions were of no consequence. He walked over to her, and as she saw him a soft blush spread over her cheeks. They stood there together, surrounded by the hills and the sea and the warmth of the sun.

298

'What are you doing here?' she asked, showing her surprise.

The words brought him back to reality. 'I have a letter for you from England. It is marked urgent.'

'Come inside.'

He followed her around the side verandah to a door leading into a sitting room.

She frowned at the packet. 'It looks ominous to me. I suppose I should open it.' Cutting the string with the scissors from her work-basket she let the seal fall on to the table. Jeremy watched while she read the letter. When she had finished she folded it neatly and put it back in the envelope. Her eyes went to the floor and stayed there. 'My father,' she said, 'has passed away.'

He saw the tears forming. Rising quickly from the chair she walked over to the window and looked out to sea. 'His last letter should have warned me. It was full of advice and memories. I will have to go home to settle the estate.'

'Rosalind.' He took a step toward her. 'I am sorry.'

She brushed away a tear. 'Thank you. I will have to find a ship.'

'The *'Liverpool'* leaves for Callao at the end of the month,' he said. 'You could get a passage on her. It will be quicker that way.'

She nodded. He could see she was distressed, holding back her grief.

'Would you like me to leave you for a while?'

'No. I would rather you talked to me.'

'I saw two whales on the way up. A cow and a calf.'

'On their own?'

'Yes. Pilot whales. It is unusual to see them away from the pod.'

'Perhaps the calf was sick.'

'It could be so.'

She took a deep breath and then looked out to sea. Her eyes had a far away look in them. 'If I am to go I may as well pack my trunk now. Can you take me back?'

'Of course. We could start this afternoon.'

As they left the bay Jeremy looked to seaward and watched the clouds. Their shape had changed since the morning. Whereas before, they had been soft and white, piling upwards, they were now moving quickly across the sky and were tinged with grey.

'There is quite a breeze,' he said.

Half a mile out from land he pointed the *'Echo'* to the south. Again he looked at the sky. He glanced at Rosalind who was sitting in the cutter on the windward side. 'The trouble with these nor-easters are that they usually last a couple of days and can cut up rough,' he said. There is a full moon, we will keep sailing and hope we get there in one go.'

'The sooner the better,' she said. 'I won't have much time to pack everything.'

'Jos and I can help you.'

'Where is Jos?'

'In town. Probably with Rata. They make a fine couple. I will be signing a farm agreement with him when I get back.'

'You don't think there will be any more fighting around those hills?'

'No. The Maori have been soundly beaten.'

'Not beaten, Jeremy. Out-manoeuvred by numbers.'

'You are right, but they are demoralized.'

'And bewildered. The old people can't make the change to civilization and the young have lost their sense of values.'

'That is not new. It happened in England after the war. Napoleon's war, I mean. The youth of the nation were standing on street corners unemployed while the politicians talked.'

'It is happening here now with the Maori race.'

A gull wheeled in on the wind with wings motionless.

'You know,' said Jeremy. 'when I talk to a man, face to face, I never think of his colour. I look at his eyes and he is another human being to me. The eyes tell you all. In the Crimea, there was no difference between men, ally or enemy. They were only doing what they were told to do for their country. I saw a lot of prisoners. They had letters from home, families, mothers, just as we did but they had no real knowledge of why they were fighting.'

'The Maori knew what he was fighting for,' said Rosalind.

'His land?'

'Yes.'

'But Britain thinks she is doing the right thing by declaring the land belongs to the Maori and buying it from them.'

'And how do you explain the confiscations?' asked Rosalind.

'As Tipene did in 1861 when referring to the cattle they stole. The name for that is spoils of war.'

'Watch out!' Jeremy pushed the tiller over and released the mainsheet. A wave crashed on to the boat, pouring into the cockpit. He straightened the *'Echo'* up and held fast to the sheet. 'It's getting really dirty. There is a bucket in the locker.'

Rosalind began bailing. Jeremy held the *'Echo'* to her new course. The wind had increased to gale force and the waves were mounting rapidly.

'I'll take her in. There will be some sort of shelter at Lookout Point.' He gripped the tiller lightly as the *'Echo'* ran down a wave.

They flew before the wind into the bay, rounding Lookout Point and narrowly missing some rocks that were breaking the surface. They went about as a gust of wind struck. The gaff swung round and a rope holding it to the mast snapped. Jeremy tried to steer the *'Echo'* with the tiller but they were at the mercy of the waves. She drifted to the beach. As she grounded he leapt out. 'Hold on to me.' He dragged Rosalind over the side and staggered ashore as the waves rolled over them. She collapsed on the sand.

Jeremy looked back at the boat. It had come ashore and was lying on its side in the sea. Running back he undid the anchor and went up the beach to bury it in the sand. When he returned Rosalind was lying face down with her head cradled in her arms. Her dress was clinging to her body and she had lost her shoe. Jeremy took off his jacket and put it over her. The sea was crashing on to the beach a few yards below and the boom was clattering from side to side as it rolled heavily in the surf.

While Rosalind rested, Jeremy waded through the water and brought her trunk ashore. He recovered all the loose gear and when the tide had receded took down the sails and dried them. 'We will make a shelter over there,' he said, pointing to a patch of grass. Wrapping the sail around themselves they tried to sleep.

After dawn, the wind picked up slightly. They climbed to Lookout Point. A curtain of rain came down, hiding the distant islands and flattening the sea with a swathe of grey.

'We won't get away today,' he said. 'Back home, when I was a child I often went up on the cliffs and leant against the wind.' He leaned over and watched the waves breaking below. 'Like this.'

'Jeremy!'

He pulled back from the cliff edge.

'Jeremy!' Rosalind cried out again. 'You will fall.'

'Until now, I have not fallen.'

Rosalind looked into his eyes, then looked out to sea. 'Everything is so wild,' she said.

They stood together as the gale buffeted them.

He turned. 'Come down to the beach.'

She took one last look at the sea and swung around to gaze at the long strip of sand below. 'Jeremy!'

'What is it?'

'There is something in the water. It is a whale. There!'

He put his hands up to his eye, forming a telescope. 'There are two of them. They will be the cow and calf I told you about.'

They ran down the hill and along the beach where Ceta and her son lay. The shape of the bay had trapped them. She had been using her deep-water echo sounder and was deceived by the gradually sloping sand and its density. When Jeremy and Rosalind reached the whales, Ceta was making a series of high-pitched squeaks they could plainly hear. As they went up to her the sounds changed to chirps and then to a number of clicks. Jeremy sensed that Ceta was frightened. Her calf was a short distance away, barely covered with water, but Ceta was only half submerged.

Rosalind put a hand on the whale's flipper. 'She is warm,' she said.

'We need the bucket from the boat. Keep splashing water on them.' Jeremy ran back along the beach. Picking up the sails and the bucket he returned to Rosalind. The sun had come out. She had hitched up her skirt and, barelegged, was wading in the shallows. Jeremy joined her with the bucket, throwing water over Ceta and her son. Ceta's flukes and flippers were only half-covered by the sea and the tide had retreated to its lowest ebb. 'If we keep them wet we may save them,' said Jeremy. 'The sea should cover her in about three hours.'

Rosalind stood up and arched her back. 'She is peeling,' she cried. The black thick skin was beginning to blister. Jeremy unfolded the sails and dragged them along the sand to the water, wetting them thoroughly. As he covered Ceta, Rosalind went back to

302

the calf. 'I think they know we are trying to help,' she said. 'They are much calmer.' She wiped the sand from her cheek. 'I will dig a hole for his flippers and fill it with water.' Bending over the calf, with her legs straight, she shovelled at the sand. 'There,' she said, 'is that better?' The squeaks and clicks continued.

Jeremy looked down to the edge of the sea. The tide was returning, putting a thin mirror-like glaze on the sand. 'It will be some time before the beach is covered,' he said. 'I will dig a channel for the big one to float on.'

When he returned with the shovel, Rosalind was sitting on a log that had been cast up in the storm the day before. She was exhausted. He could see the lines around her eyes.

'Are you all right?' he asked.

'I am tired.' She rose from the log and strode back to Ceta. 'I'll keep the sail wet. You start the ditch. Can we save them?'

'I am going to give it a damn good try.'

She flashed him a look. A mixture of admiration, hope and concern. 'We must,' she said.

Jeremy commenced the trench a few yards above the water mark, digging a hole a little larger than the width of Ceta's body. The sand was soft and wet and he made good progress. When he reached Ceta, Rosalind was wetting the sail with buckets full of water. Gradually the tide crept inwards, the water flowed into the ditch only yards away from Jeremy as he advanced up the sand. He dug around Ceta until she was lying in a hollow of water. The signals she was making appeared to be weaker. At last the water almost covered her. They waited impatiently as the sea crept over the remainder of the beach and was level with her. The calf was now completely submerged but was making no attempt to leave.

'I will have to make a pool large enough for her to turn around,' said Jeremy. He attacked the sides with his spade.

When he had finished the water was up to his chest and Rosalind was having difficulty keeping on her feet. 'We will try and push her around.' He dragged the sail from Ceta's back and put it under her. Ceta did not move. Together they hauled on the sail underneath her.

'Don't pull on her flukes or fins,' called Jeremy, 'you may damage them.' A final desperate haul on the sail and Ceta faced the sea. The tide had reached high water mark.

'The calf!' cried Rosalind. 'It is moving.'

As they watched the calf swam a few feet parallel to the beach towards his mother.

'Damn!' said Jeremy. He waded out to the calf. 'If we can get it away perhaps she will follow.'

Splashing and shouting they advanced. The calf stopped. They pushed it around and headed it to sea. It began to swim slowly away. They saw Ceta lift upwards on a wave and suddenly and surely she followed her baby.

'We have done it!' Rosalind threw her arms around Jeremy. They stood clinging to each other and watched as the two shapes swam out of the bay. A high stream of spray shot into the air as the whales cleared their blowholes of sand as though signalling good-bye.

Hand in hand Jeremy and Rosalind waded ashore and climbing to the top of a sandhill looked out to the horizon. 'They have gone,' she said and facing Jeremy saw the triumphant look in his eyes. His arms encircled her. For a moment he pressed her to him and together they sank into a hollow in the warm dry sand.

The sun slipped below the hills behind. There was that feeling of eternity, an all-encompassing togetherness, a blinding flash of supreme happiness. They lay together in the warm, evening air. Picking up a handful of sand she let it fall in a stream on his bare chest. 'I think I like you after all, Jeremy St Clair,' she said.

They woke with the morning sun climbing out of the sea. At first Jeremy was bewildered by the strange surroundings, until the events of the previous day came flooding back. He turned his head slightly to see her face. Her eyes opened. He put his arm over her and she smiled her shy, quiet smile. He stroked her hair.

'Please, Jeremy,' she said, 'be still.'

He rolled over on to his back and looked up at the sky. 'Thank you for yesterday,' he said. 'When we get married we will come back here.'

'Married?'

'Of course.'

'But Jeremy, you have not proposed to me.'

He sat up. 'But it goes without saying.'

'I am not certain if I want to be married again.'

'Why not?'

'I don't want to make the same mistakes I made before.'

'But I love you.'

She nodded. 'I believe you do.'

'Then, I am proposing now. Will you marry me?'

She sighed and turning her back gathered up her clothes.

He began rolling up the sails. She noticed the set of his chin. 'I am going to marry you,' he said.

Around mid-morning the wind changed and blew steadily from the north-east. They were silent all the way back to town. Jos was waiting for them at the boatshed. 'I have been coming down twice a day,' he said. He grabbed at the line that Jeremy threw ashore. 'Mr St Clair, Rata and I are getting married soon.'

Jeremy glanced quickly at Rosalind.

'We have a licence,' said Jos. 'Rata is old enough. I am twenty-four now.

Yes, Jeremy thought, it is eight years since we landed in Auckland. 'Congratulations,' he said.

'Thank you. Rata has permission from her tribe.'

'Then there is nothing else you need. When are you going to do the deed?'

'Next week.'

Rosalind's pupils formed the choir for the wedding and Rata's people sat on one side of the church to give their blessing to Jos and his bride, putting behind them the conflicts of the last five years. Jeremy's eyes wandered around the church. He gasped. Emily was seated opposite. She saw him and half-smiled. The ceremony soon ended and Jeremy hurried outside to wait for her. She was dressed in the latest fashion in a velvet gown decorated with flat plaitings of the same material. She looked up and acknowledged him with an inclination of her head.

'What are you doing here?' he asked. 'Come with me.'

They stopped on a patch of grass at the back of the church. 'Oh, Sir,' she said. 'I am sorry I put you to so much inconvenience. I had to leave. I had no choice. How are the twins? They must be quite big boys now.'

Jeremy's mind was in a whirl. He looked deeply into Emily's

smiling eyes. Obviously she did not know the truth. 'Jonathon has a pony now,' he said.

'And Mrs St Clair?'

'I am afraid she has died. She nursed a large growth that became fatal.'

'Oh dear, I am sorry.' Emily looked away. 'I must apologize for running away, but I had no choice. Please forgive me. You see my sergeant found me a passage to Sydney when he was transferred and I could not face you to say good-bye. He is out of the army now and I prevailed upon him to set up a small business like yours. He has been very successful and we are quite well off. We have three children, a girl and two boys.'

'What are you doing here?' asked Jeremy.

'My husband had business in Wellington and we are on the way home by way of Auckland and leaving this afternoon. I heard of Jos's marriage in town.'

Jeremy thought quickly. Why burden her with the truth? She need never know. 'I am pleased with your good fortune, my dear,' he said, 'and let us hope you will always be as happy as you obviously are now.'

Her eyes shone. 'Thank you, Sir. I must get down to the ship at once. Good-bye.'

He watched her as she walked down the hill and turning towards the harbour waved farewell.

The singing and the celebrations went on into the night. Jeremy gave a speech which Jos translated into Maori. 'May this union show the way to love and peace between us, for always,' he said.

The following day the wedding party was at the wharf to farewell Rosalind when she left for England. Jeremy watched a poi dance and listened to the waiata of farewell. Captain McEwen brought out his watch and looked at the sky. 'Time to cast off,' he said.

Jeremy took Rosalind's hand. 'Good-bye.'

She smiled wistfully and turned to the captain. 'Do you make regular trips from Callao to Auckland?'

'All the time.'

'Then save me a cabin in about six months.' She looked up at

Jeremy. 'What was it you said to me on the beach at Lookout Point?'

'I said,' he stumbled for the words. 'I said, will you marry me?'

Her eyes twinkled. She curtsied. 'Then Mr St Clair, I have much pleasure in accepting your proposal and hope that our union will be a happy one and that you will not be disappointed in the trust you have put in me.'

'You minx!' He grasped her shoulder and folded her into his arms. 'I can wait a short while but not too long,' he said.

As the tug towed the ship into midstream Jeremy took a horse and rode along the foreshore to the bay opposite North Head. On his right, one of the Bishop's little churches stood on the slope overlooking the bay. The judge's house was behind him. The wind was dying as the *'Liverpool'* came into view. The tide took her down and he waited until she sailed out of sight. He closed his eyes and took a deep breath. At last the wind was still.